NEVERLANDERS

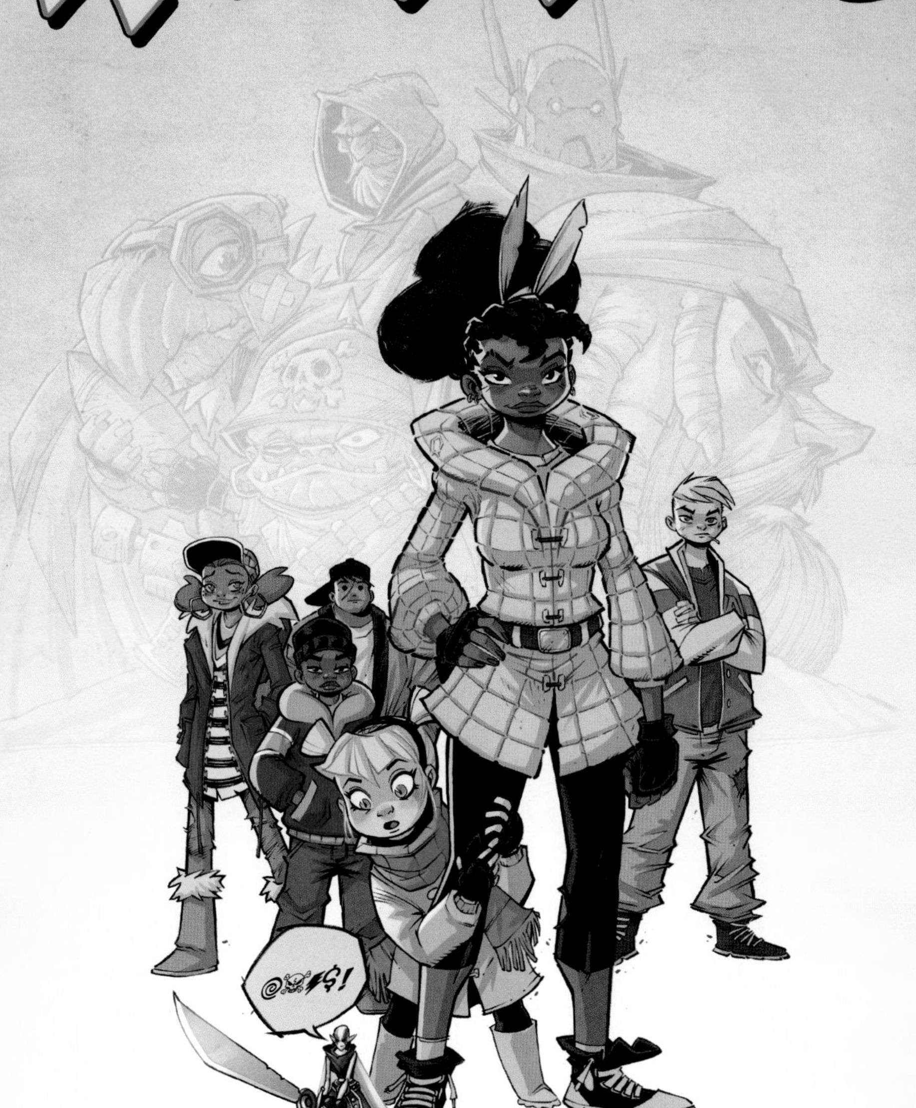

CREATED BY
TOM TAYLOR
AND
JON SOMMARIVA

RAZORBILL

WRITER
TOM TAYLOR

ARTIST
JON SOMMARIVA

COLORS
MSASSYK
(CHAPTERS 1-3)
VANEDA VIREAK
(CHAPTERS 4-6)
JEAN-FRANCOIS
BEAULIEU (EPILOGUE)

LETTERS
WOLFGANG BYLSMA

EDITOR
CHRISTOPHER
HERNANDEZ

RAZORBILL

An imprint of Penguin Random House LLC, New York

First published in the United States of America by Razorbill,
an imprint of Penguin Random House LLC, 2022

Razorbill & colophon are registered trademarks of Penguin Random House LLC.

Visit us online at penguinrandomhouse.com.

Library of Congress Cataloging-in-Publication Data is available.

ISBN 9780593351710 (hardcover)
ISBN 9780593351758 (paperback)

Manufactured in Canada

10 9 8 7 6 5 4 3 2 1

TC

TO MY SON, FELIX, MY HAPPY THOUGHT
NOW AND FOREVER.

—JON SOMMARIVA

FOR CONNOR, FOR FINN, AND FOR MEGAN.
WHEREVER WE'RE TOGETHER, THAT'S HOME.
I'D BE A LOST BOY WITHOUT YOU.

—TOM TAYLOR

CHAPTER
ONE

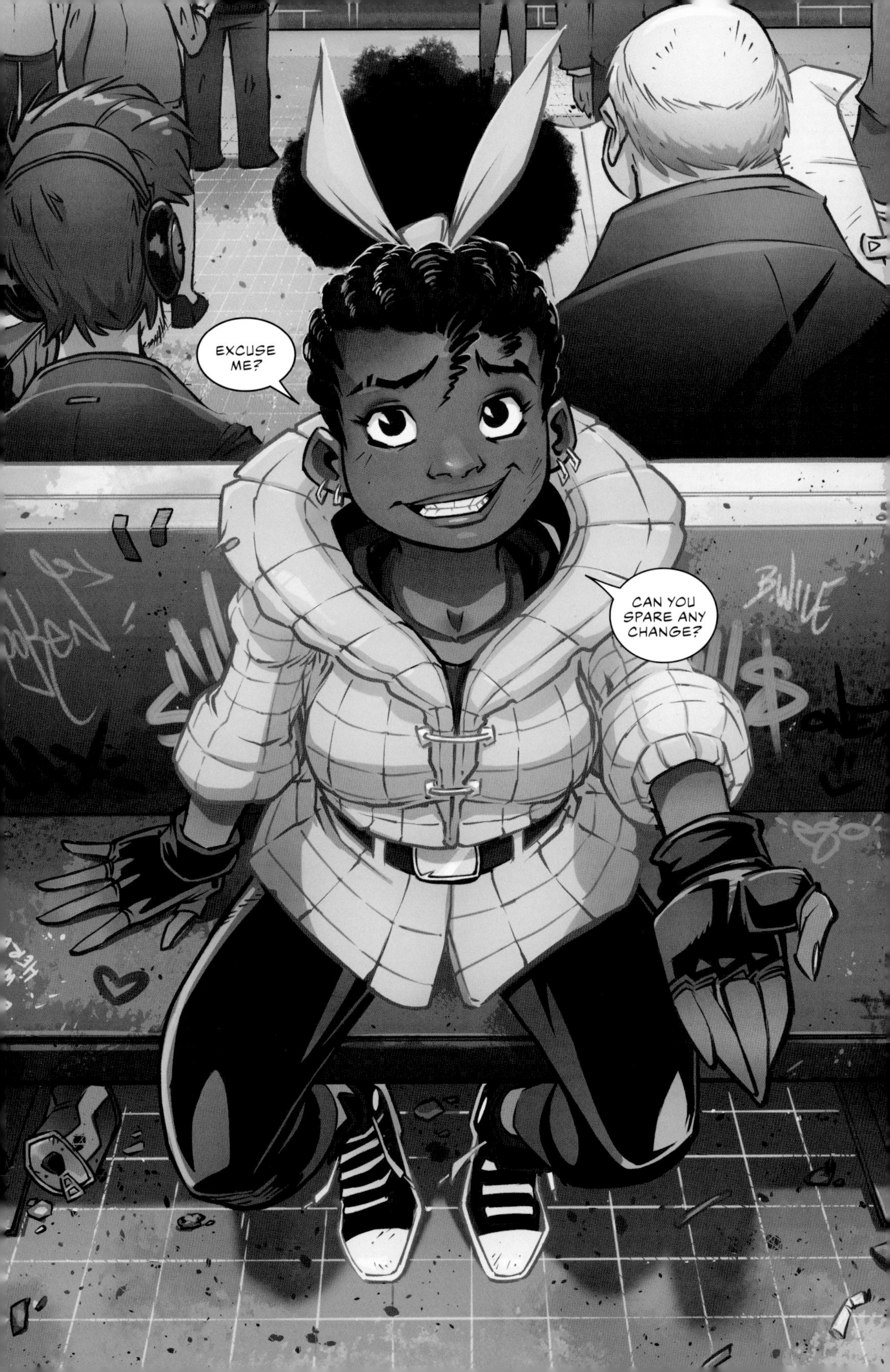
EXCUSE ME?
CAN YOU SPARE ANY CHANGE?

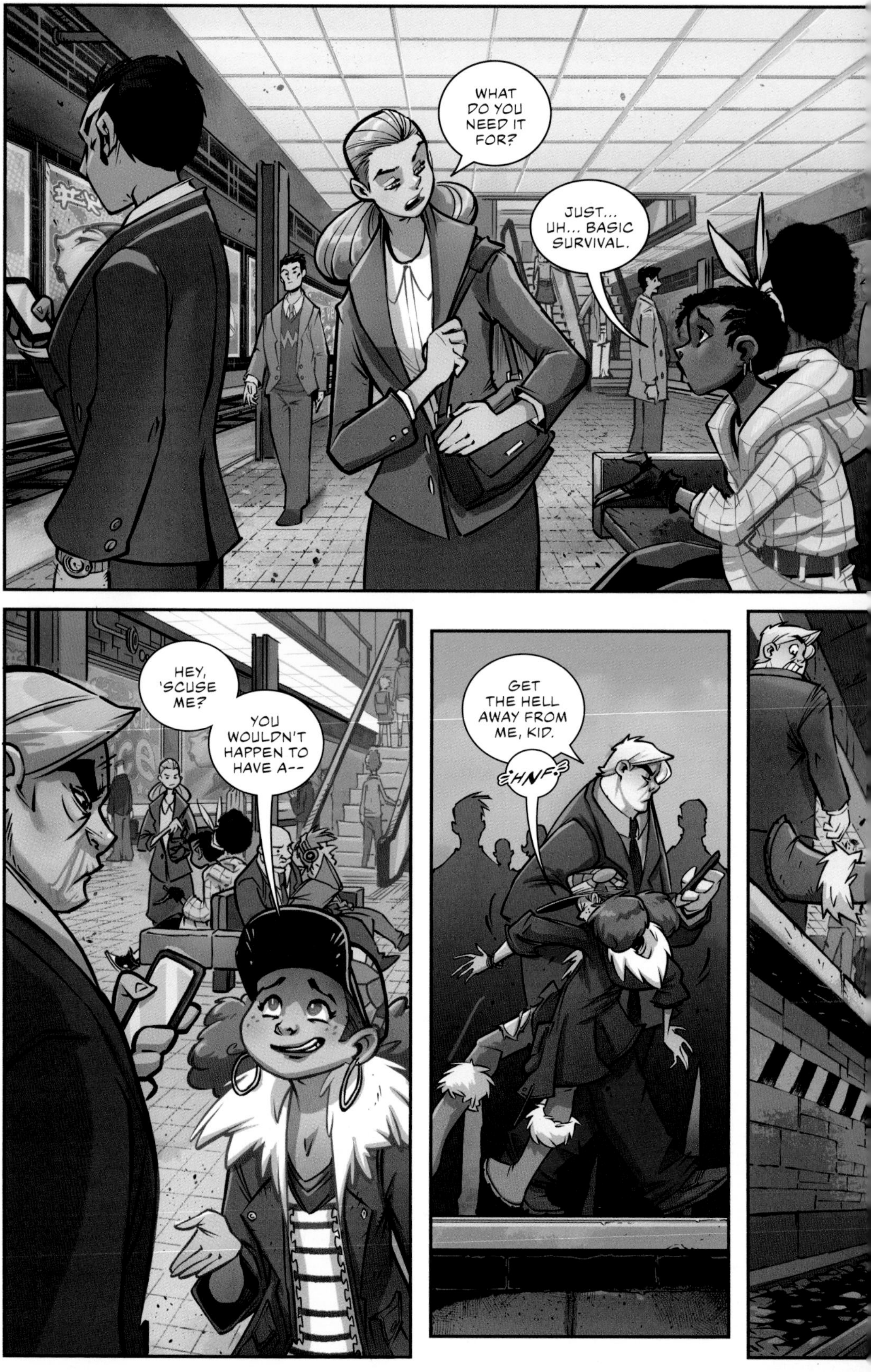
WHAT DO YOU NEED IT FOR?
JUST... UH... BASIC SURVIVAL.
HEY, 'SCUSE ME?
YOU WOULDN'T HAPPEN TO HAVE A--
GET THE HELL AWAY FROM ME, KID.
HNF

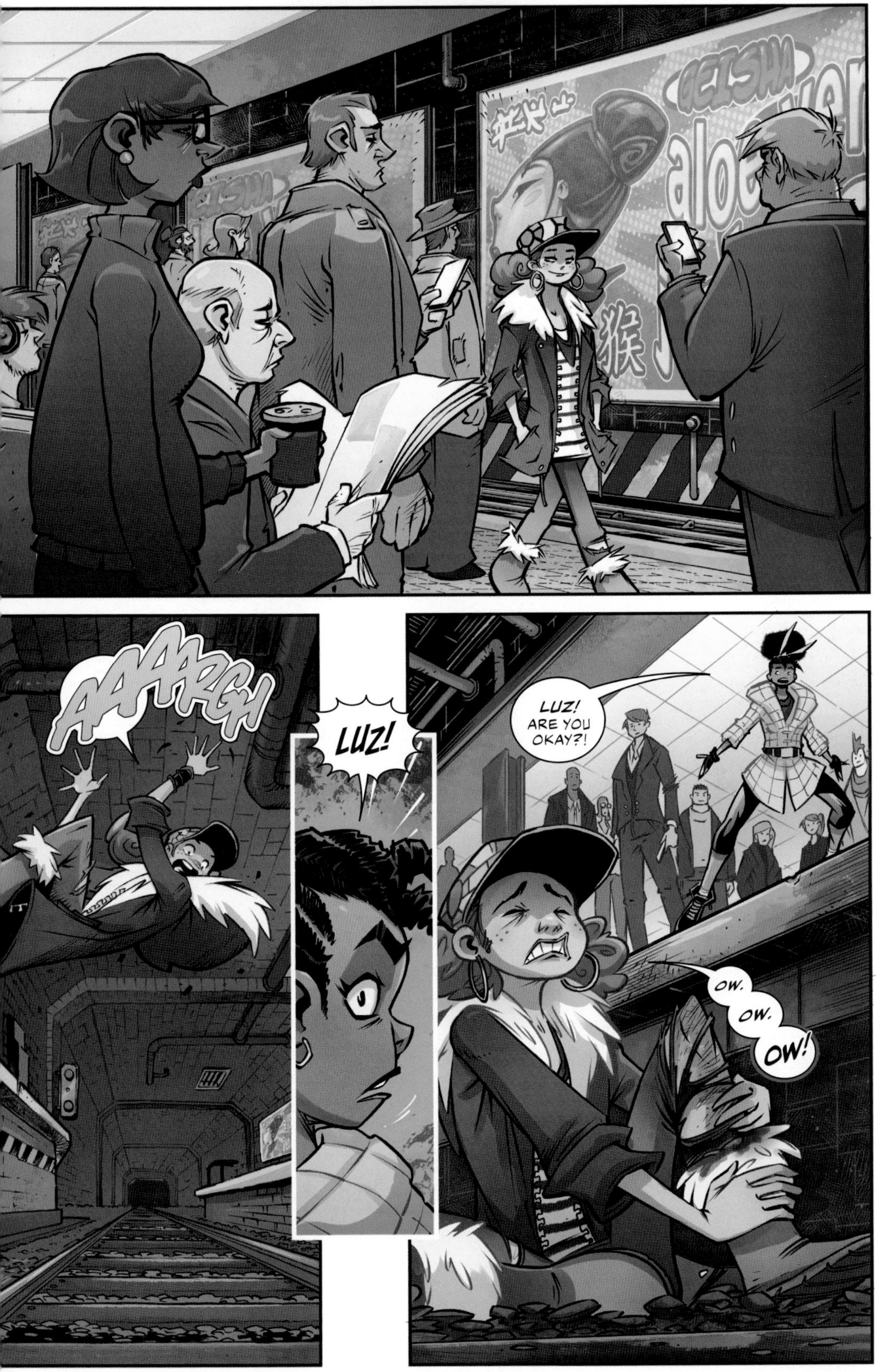
GEISHA
AAAARGH
LUZ!
LUZ! ARE YOU OKAY?!
OW.
OW.
OW!

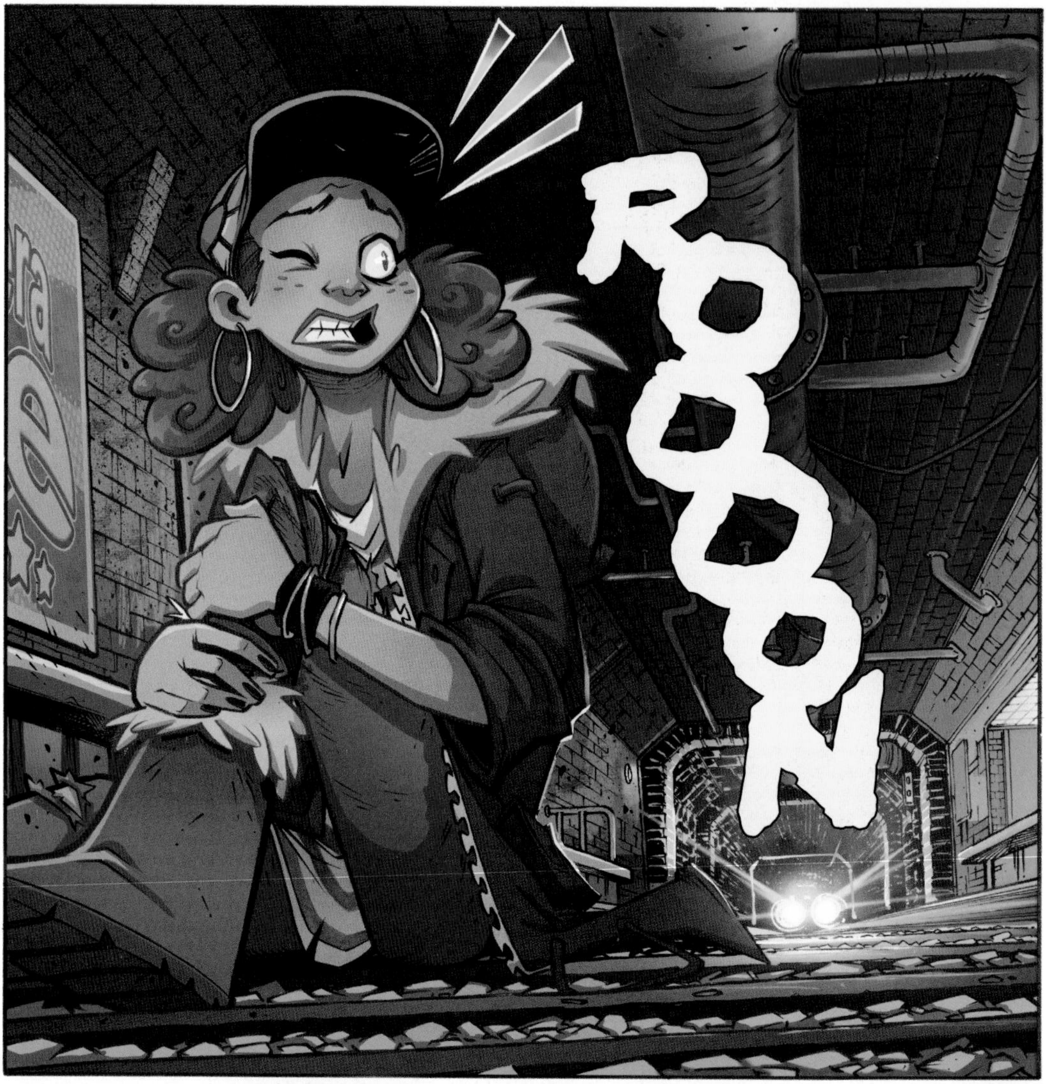
ROOOON

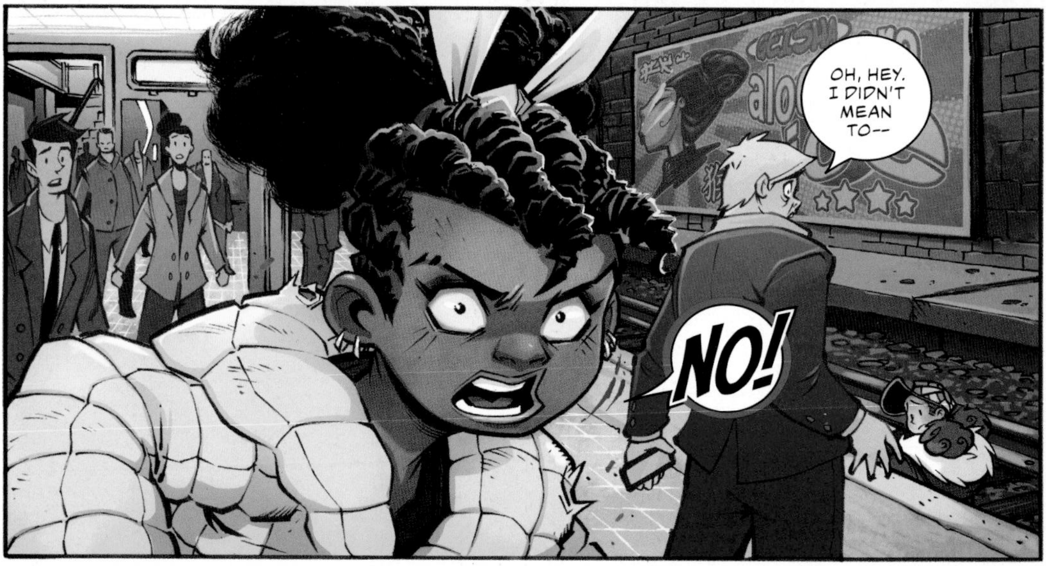
OH, HEY. I DIDN'T MEAN TO--
NO!

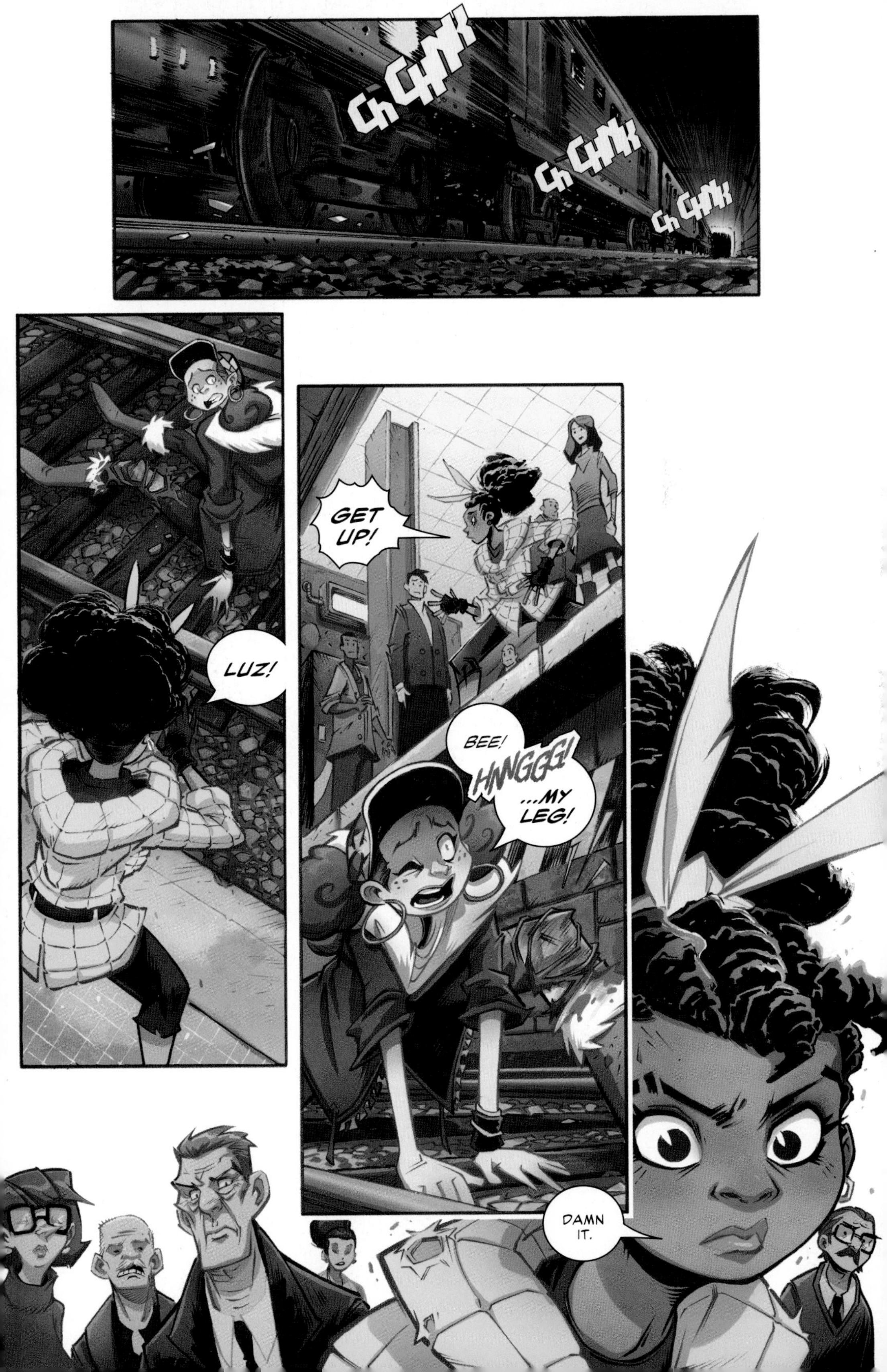
Ch CHNK
Ch CHNK
Ch CHNK
LUZ!
GET UP!
BEE!
HNNGGG!
...MY LEG!
DAMN IT.

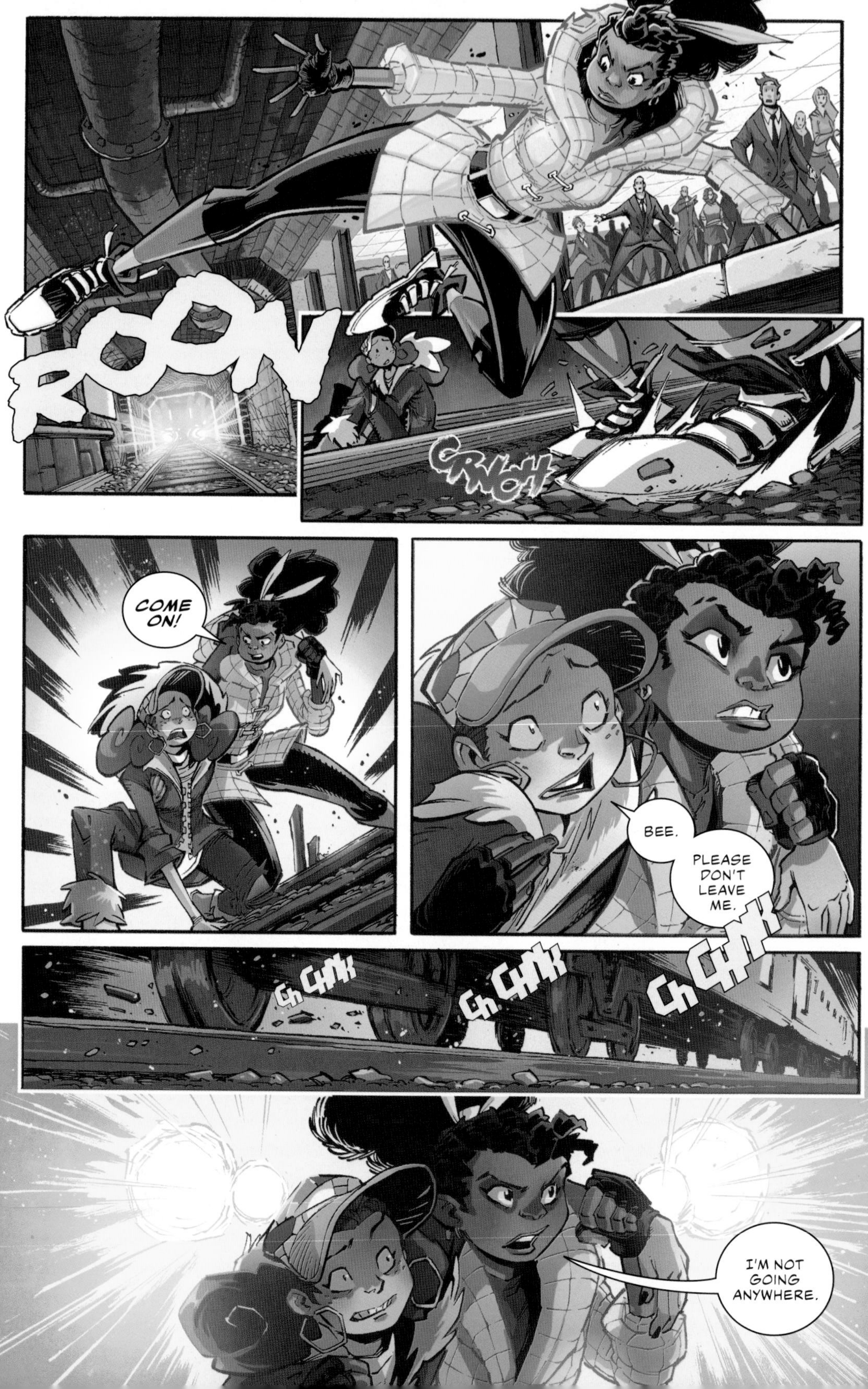
ROOON
CRUNCH
COME ON!
BEE.
PLEASE DON'T LEAVE ME.
Ch CHNK
Ch CHNK
Ch CHNK
I'M NOT GOING ANYWHERE.

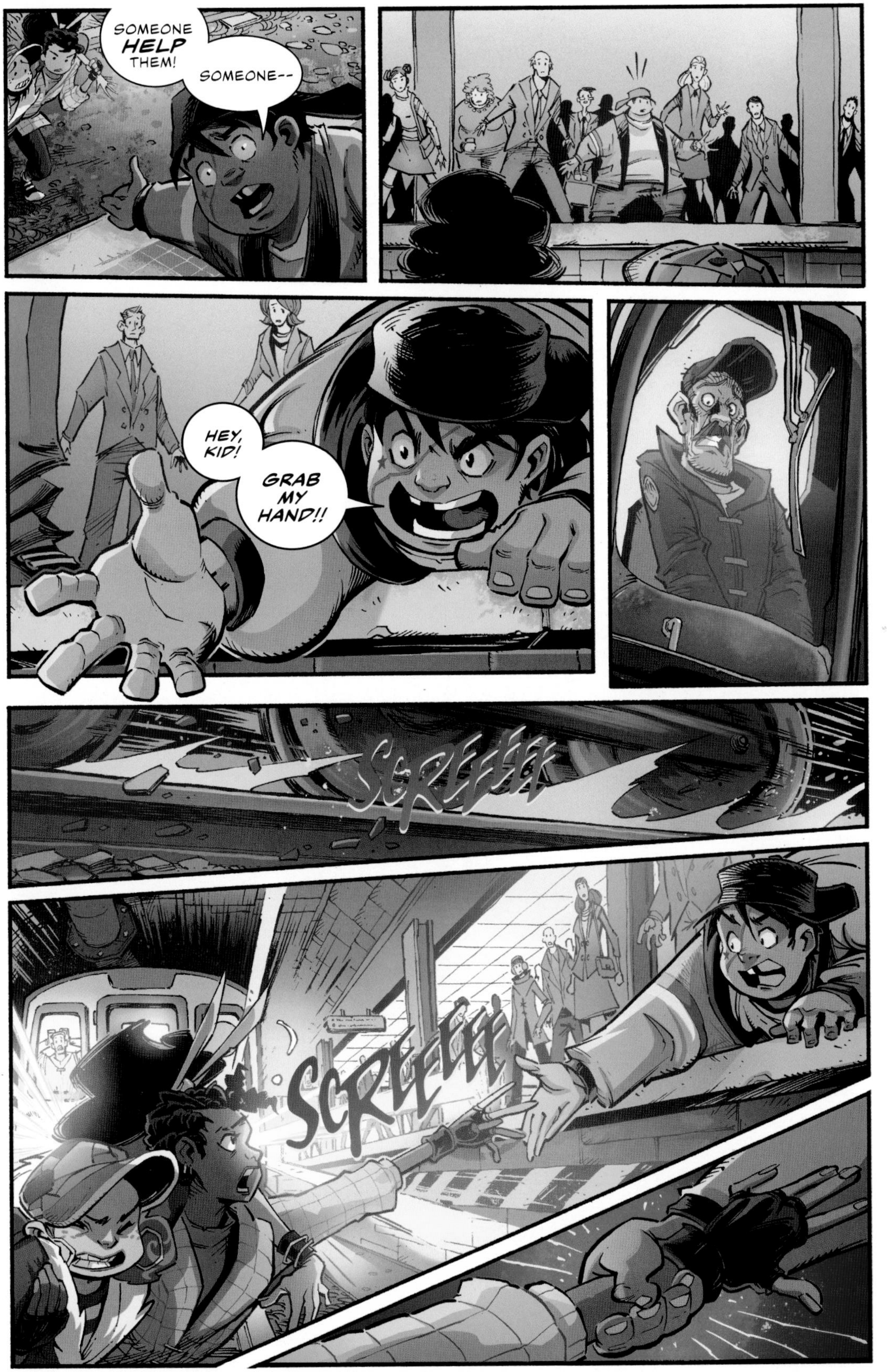
SOMEONE HELP THEM!
SOMEONE--
HEY, KID!
GRAB MY HAND!!
SCREEEEE
SCREEEEE

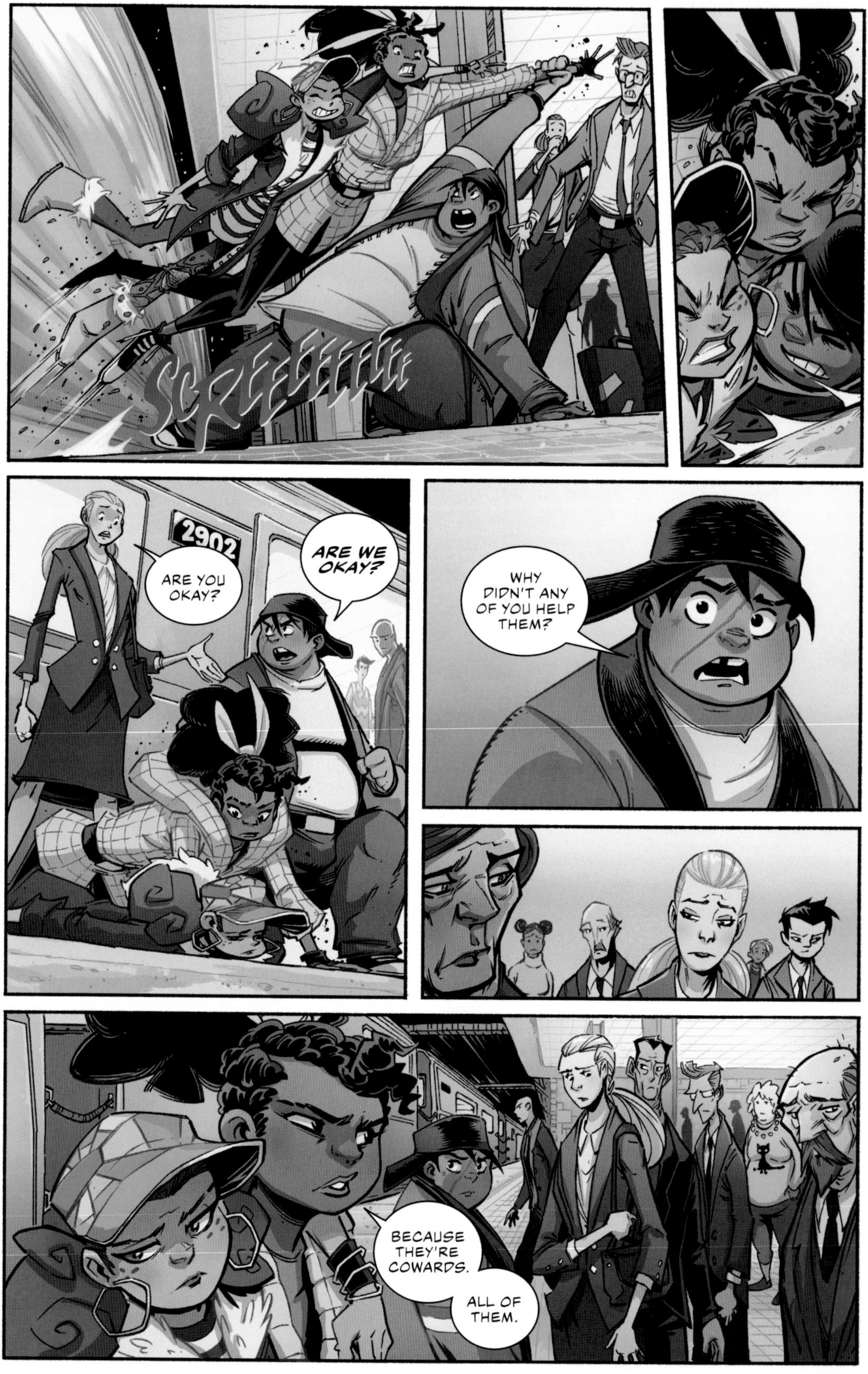
SCREEEEEEE
2902
ARE YOU OKAY?
ARE WE OKAY?
WHY DIDN'T ANY OF YOU HELP THEM?
BECAUSE THEY'RE COWARDS.
ALL OF THEM.

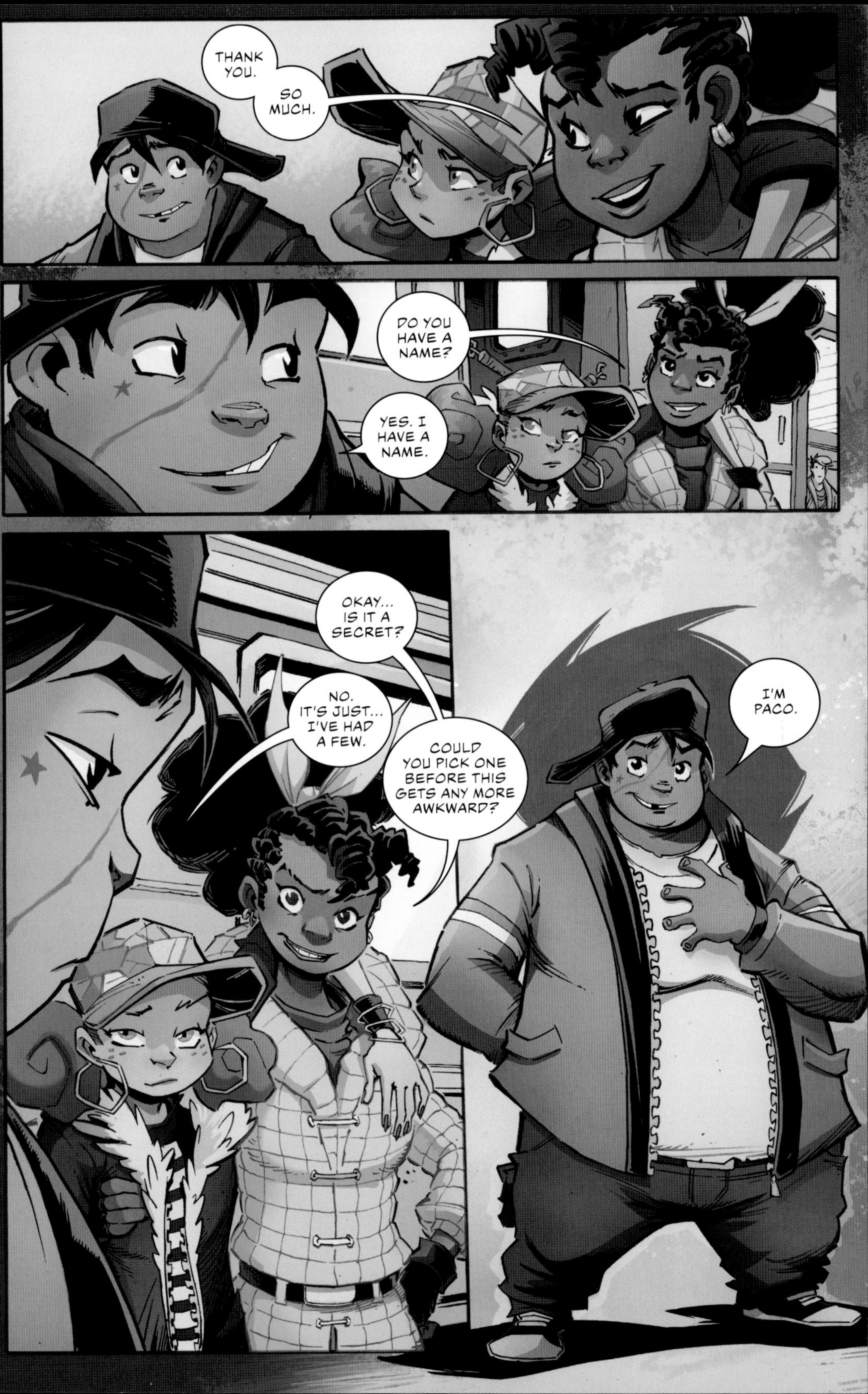
THANK YOU.
SO MUCH.
DO YOU HAVE A NAME?
YES. I HAVE A NAME.
OKAY... IS IT A SECRET?
NO. IT'S JUST... I'VE HAD A FEW.
COULD YOU PICK ONE BEFORE THIS GETS ANY MORE AWKWARD?
I'M PACO.

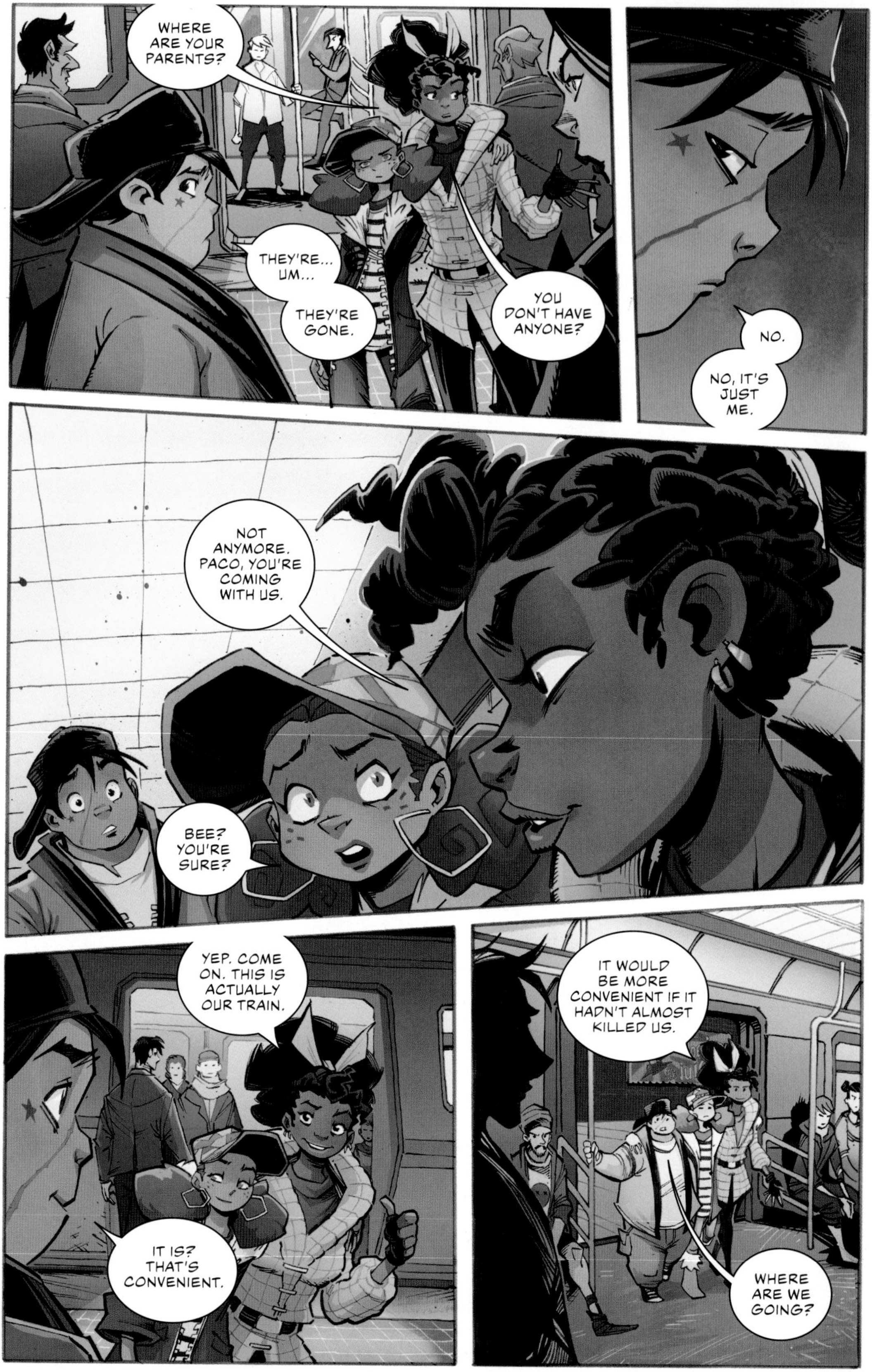
WHERE ARE YOUR PARENTS?
THEY'RE... UM...
THEY'RE GONE.
YOU DON'T HAVE ANYONE?
NO.
NO, IT'S JUST ME.
NOT ANYMORE. PACO, YOU'RE COMING WITH US.
BEE? YOU'RE SURE?
YEP. COME ON. THIS IS ACTUALLY OUR TRAIN.
IT IS? THAT'S CONVENIENT.
IT WOULD BE MORE CONVENIENT IF IT HADN'T ALMOST KILLED US.
WHERE ARE WE GOING?

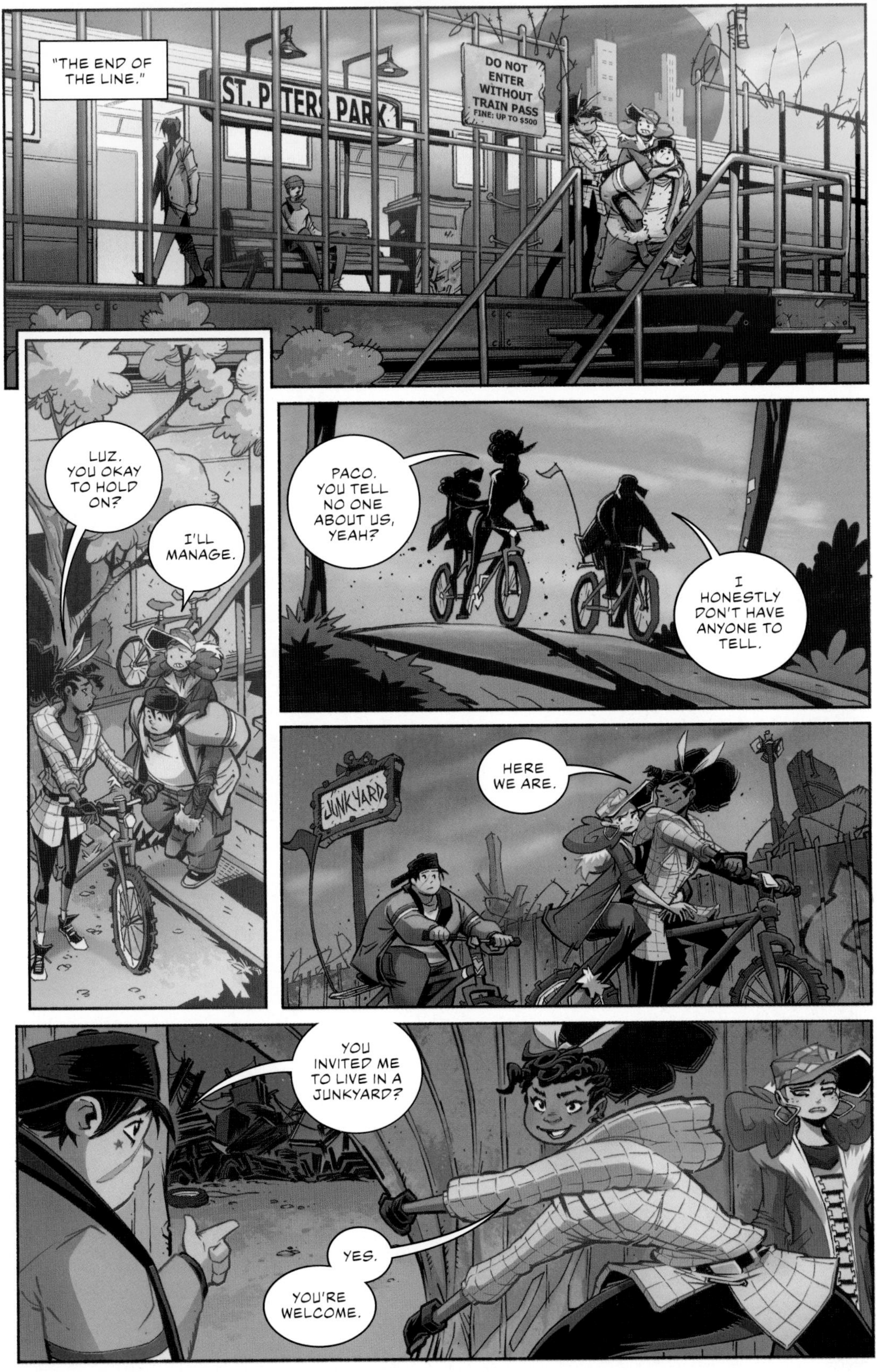
"THE END OF THE LINE."
ST. PETERS PARK
DO NOT ENTER WITHOUT TRAIN PASS
FINE: UP TO $500
LUZ. YOU OKAY TO HOLD ON?
I'LL MANAGE.
PACO. YOU TELL NO ONE ABOUT US, YEAH?
I HONESTLY DON'T HAVE ANYONE TO TELL.
JUNKYARD
HERE WE ARE.
YOU INVITED ME TO LIVE IN A JUNKYARD?
YES.
YOU'RE WELCOME.

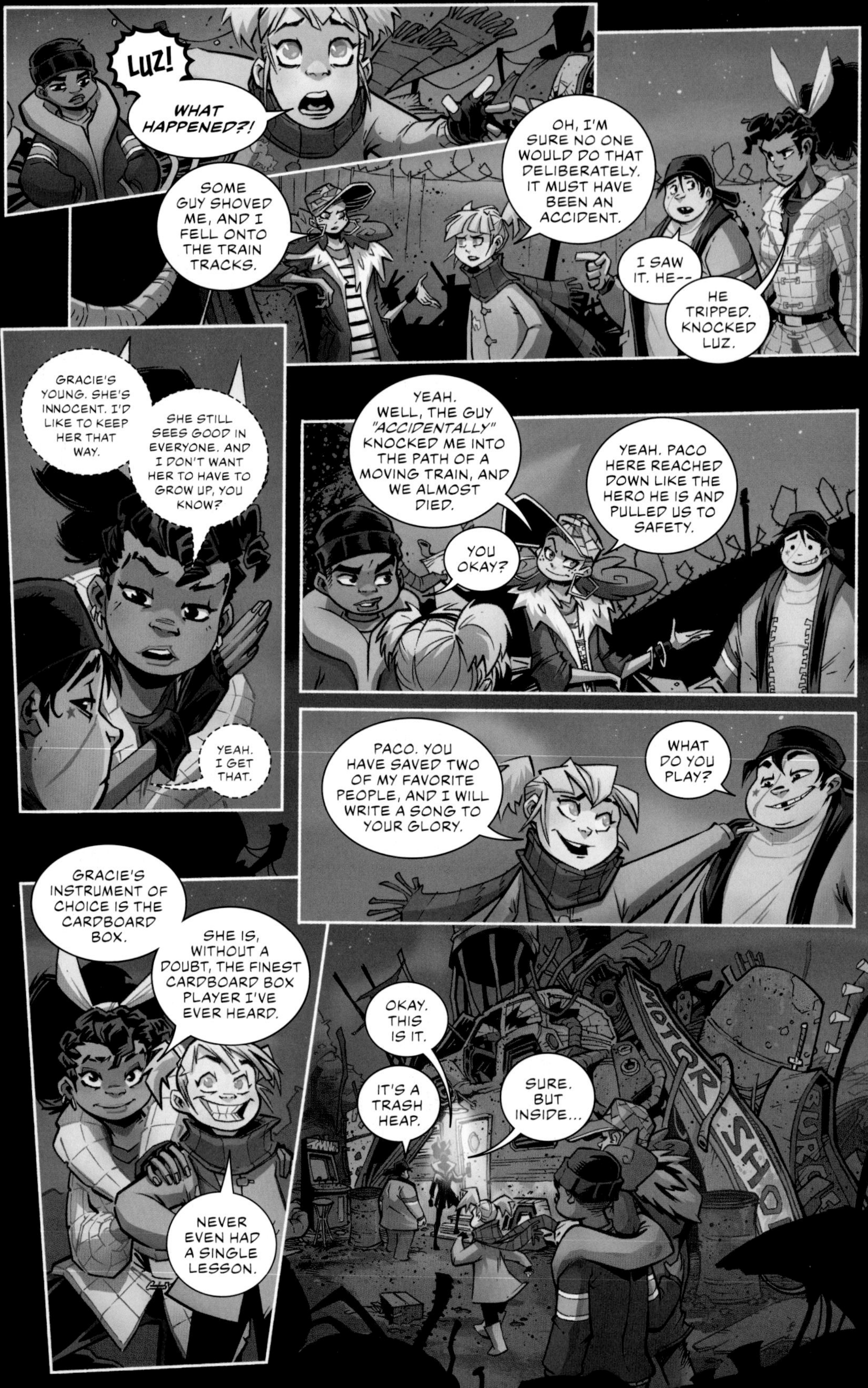
LUZ!
WHAT HAPPENED?!
SOME GUY SHOVED ME, AND I FELL ONTO THE TRAIN TRACKS.
OH, I'M SURE NO ONE WOULD DO THAT DELIBERATELY. IT MUST HAVE BEEN AN ACCIDENT.
I SAW IT. HE--
HE TRIPPED. KNOCKED LUZ.
GRACIE'S YOUNG. SHE'S INNOCENT. I'D LIKE TO KEEP HER THAT WAY.
SHE STILL SEES GOOD IN EVERYONE. AND I DON'T WANT HER TO HAVE TO GROW UP, YOU KNOW?
YEAH. I GET THAT.
YEAH. WELL, THE GUY "ACCIDENTALLY" KNOCKED ME INTO THE PATH OF A MOVING TRAIN, AND WE ALMOST DIED.
YEAH. PACO HERE REACHED DOWN LIKE THE HERO HE IS AND PULLED US TO SAFETY.
YOU OKAY?
PACO. YOU HAVE SAVED TWO OF MY FAVORITE PEOPLE, AND I WILL WRITE A SONG TO YOUR GLORY.
WHAT DO YOU PLAY?
GRACIE'S INSTRUMENT OF CHOICE IS THE CARDBOARD BOX.
SHE IS, WITHOUT A DOUBT, THE FINEST CARDBOARD BOX PLAYER I'VE EVER HEARD.
NEVER EVEN HAD A SINGLE LESSON.
OKAY. THIS IS IT.
IT'S A TRASH HEAP.
SURE. BUT INSIDE...
MOTOR SHO

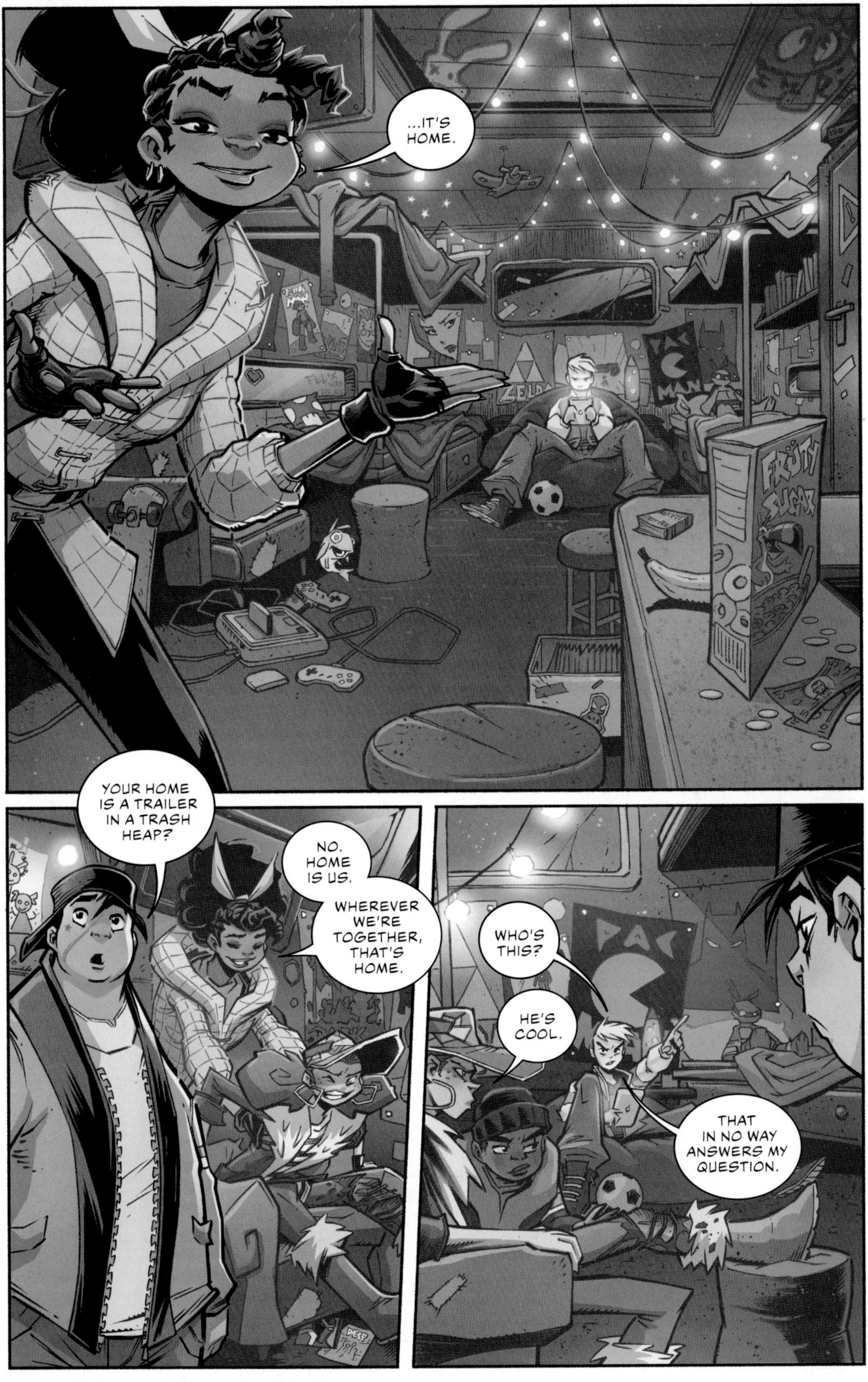
...IT'S HOME.
YOUR HOME IS A TRAILER IN A TRASH HEAP?
NO. HOME IS US.
WHEREVER WE'RE TOGETHER, THAT'S HOME.
WHO'S THIS?
HE'S COOL.
THAT IN NO WAY ANSWERS MY QUESTION.

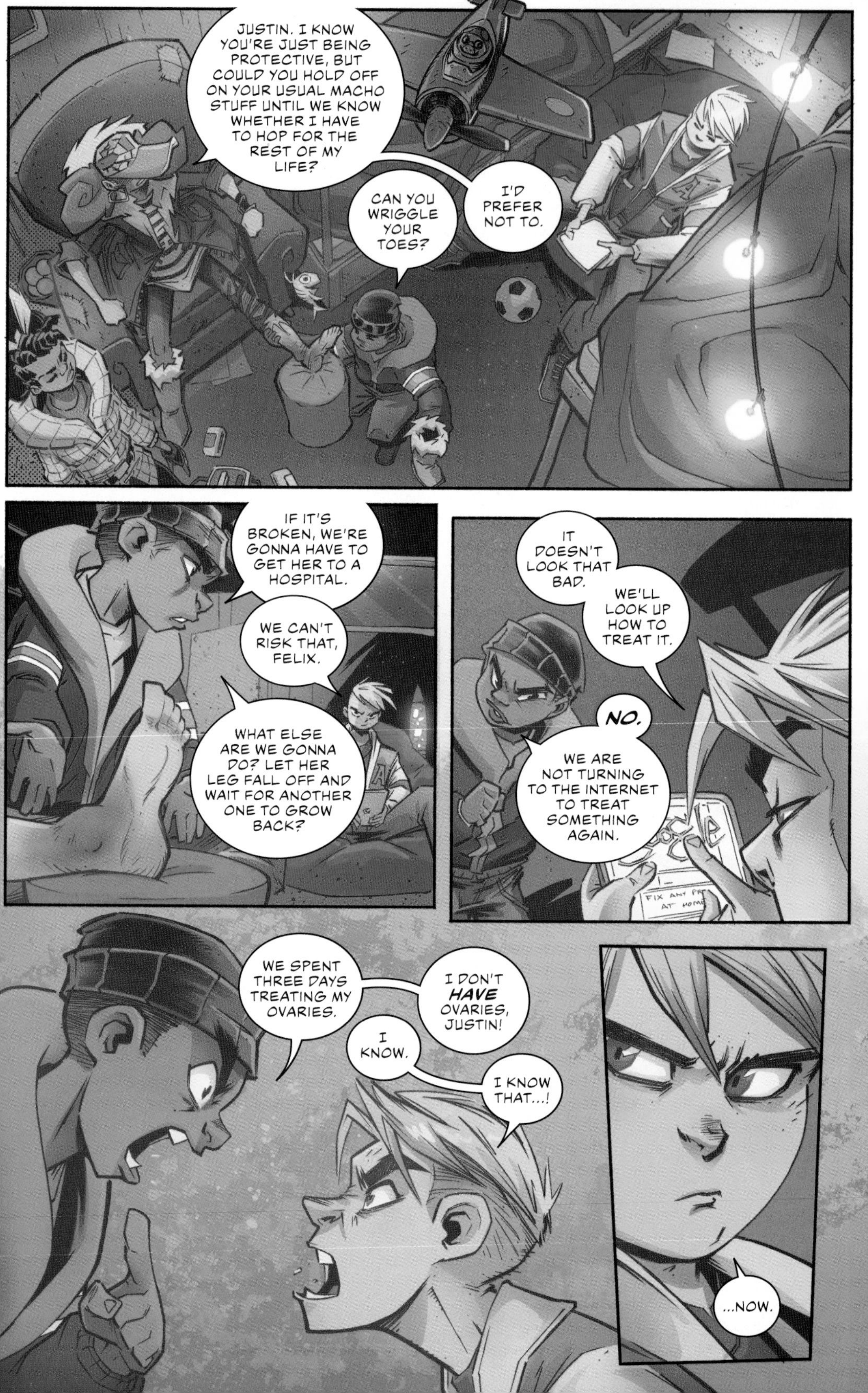
JUSTIN. I KNOW YOU'RE JUST BEING PROTECTIVE, BUT COULD YOU HOLD OFF ON YOUR USUAL MACHO STUFF UNTIL WE KNOW WHETHER I HAVE TO HOP FOR THE REST OF MY LIFE?
I'D PREFER NOT TO.
CAN YOU WRIGGLE YOUR TOES?
IF IT'S BROKEN, WE'RE GONNA HAVE TO GET HER TO A HOSPITAL.
WE CAN'T RISK THAT, FELIX.
WHAT ELSE ARE WE GONNA DO? LET HER LEG FALL OFF AND WAIT FOR ANOTHER ONE TO GROW BACK?
IT DOESN'T LOOK THAT BAD.
WE'LL LOOK UP HOW TO TREAT IT.
NO.
WE ARE NOT TURNING TO THE INTERNET TO TREAT SOMETHING AGAIN.
WE SPENT THREE DAYS TREATING MY OVARIES.
I DON'T HAVE OVARIES, JUSTIN!
I KNOW.
I KNOW THAT...!
...NOW.

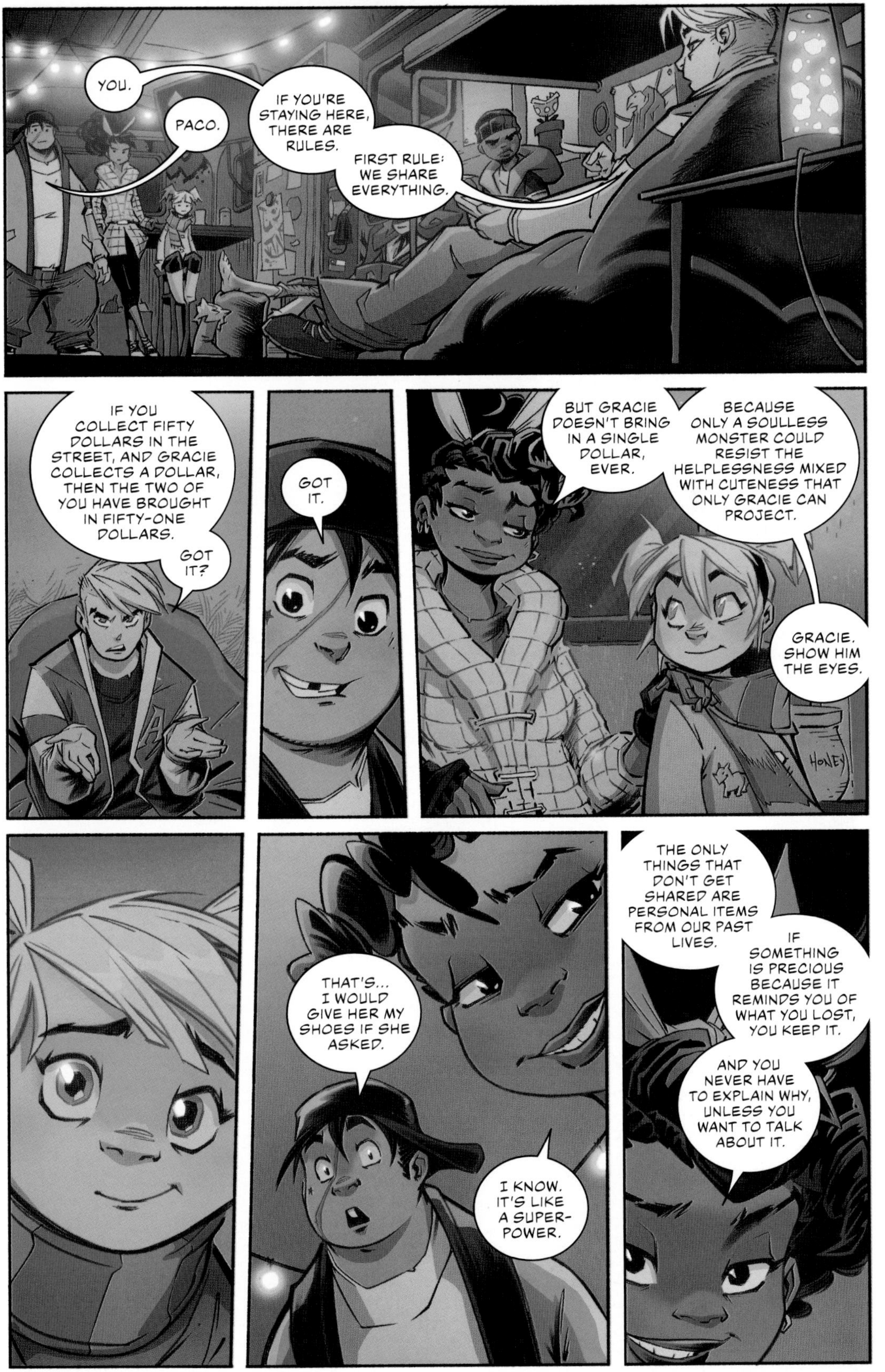
YOU.
PACO.
IF YOU'RE STAYING HERE, THERE ARE RULES.
FIRST RULE: WE SHARE EVERYTHING.
IF YOU COLLECT FIFTY DOLLARS IN THE STREET, AND GRACIE COLLECTS A DOLLAR, THEN THE TWO OF YOU HAVE BROUGHT IN FIFTY-ONE DOLLARS.
GOT IT?
GOT IT.
BUT GRACIE DOESN'T BRING IN A SINGLE DOLLAR, EVER.
BECAUSE ONLY A SOULLESS MONSTER COULD RESIST THE HELPLESSNESS MIXED WITH CUTENESS THAT ONLY GRACIE CAN PROJECT.
GRACIE. SHOW HIM THE EYES.
HONEY
THAT'S... I WOULD GIVE HER MY SHOES IF SHE ASKED.
I KNOW. IT'S LIKE A SUPER-POWER.
THE ONLY THINGS THAT DON'T GET SHARED ARE PERSONAL ITEMS FROM OUR PAST LIVES.
IF SOMETHING IS PRECIOUS BECAUSE IT REMINDS YOU OF WHAT YOU LOST, YOU KEEP IT.
AND YOU NEVER HAVE TO EXPLAIN WHY, UNLESS YOU WANT TO TALK ABOUT IT.

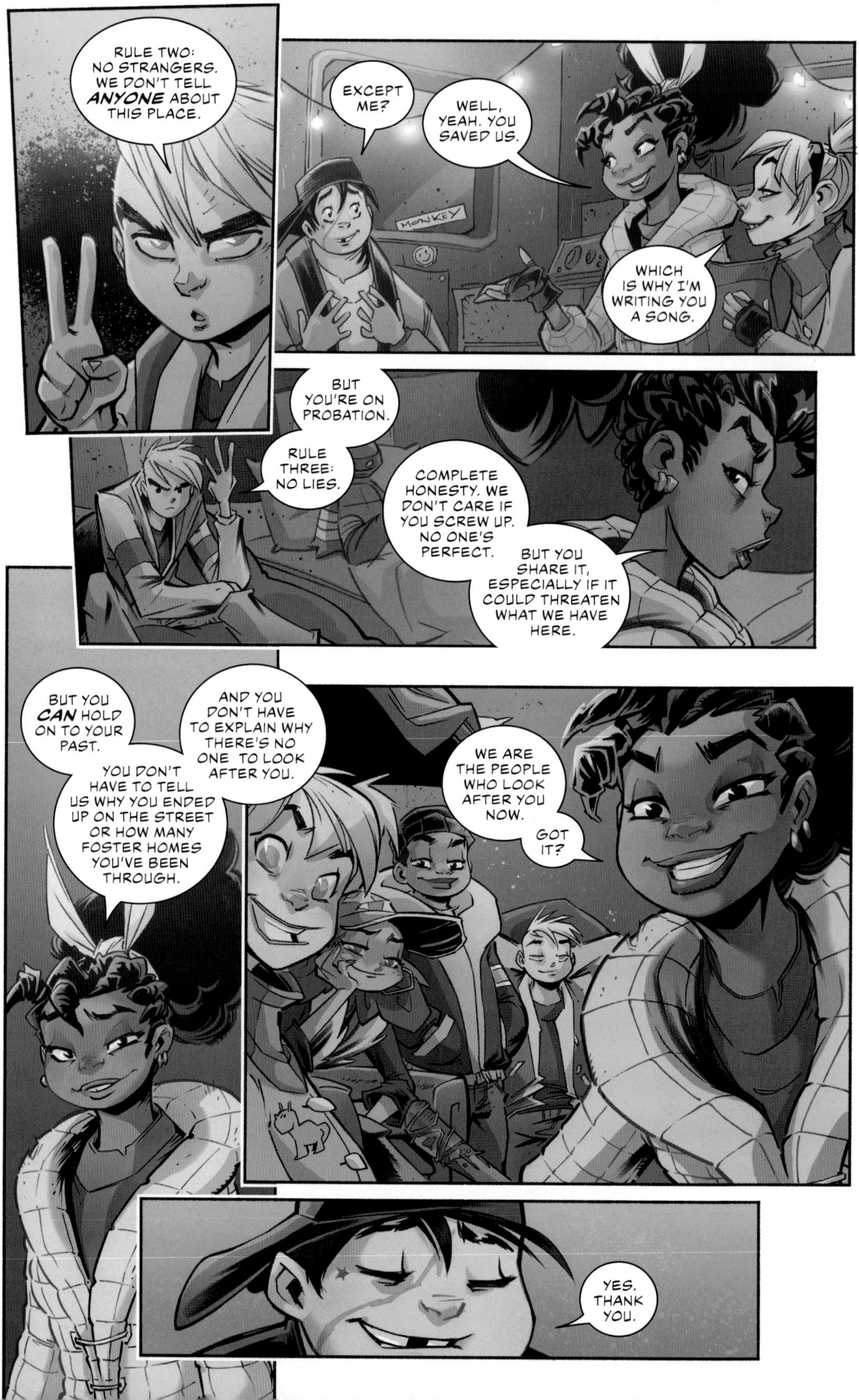
RULE TWO: NO STRANGERS. WE DON'T TELL ANYONE ABOUT THIS PLACE.
EXCEPT ME?
WELL, YEAH. YOU SAVED US.
WHICH IS WHY I'M WRITING YOU A SONG.
MONKEY
BUT YOU'RE ON PROBATION.
RULE THREE: NO LIES.
COMPLETE HONESTY. WE DON'T CARE IF YOU SCREW UP. NO ONE'S PERFECT.
BUT YOU SHARE IT, ESPECIALLY IF IT COULD THREATEN WHAT WE HAVE HERE.
BUT YOU CAN HOLD ON TO YOUR PAST.
YOU DON'T HAVE TO TELL US WHY YOU ENDED UP ON THE STREET OR HOW MANY FOSTER HOMES YOU'VE BEEN THROUGH.
AND YOU DON'T HAVE TO EXPLAIN WHY THERE'S NO ONE TO LOOK AFTER YOU.
WE ARE THE PEOPLE WHO LOOK AFTER YOU NOW.
GOT IT?
YES. THANK YOU.

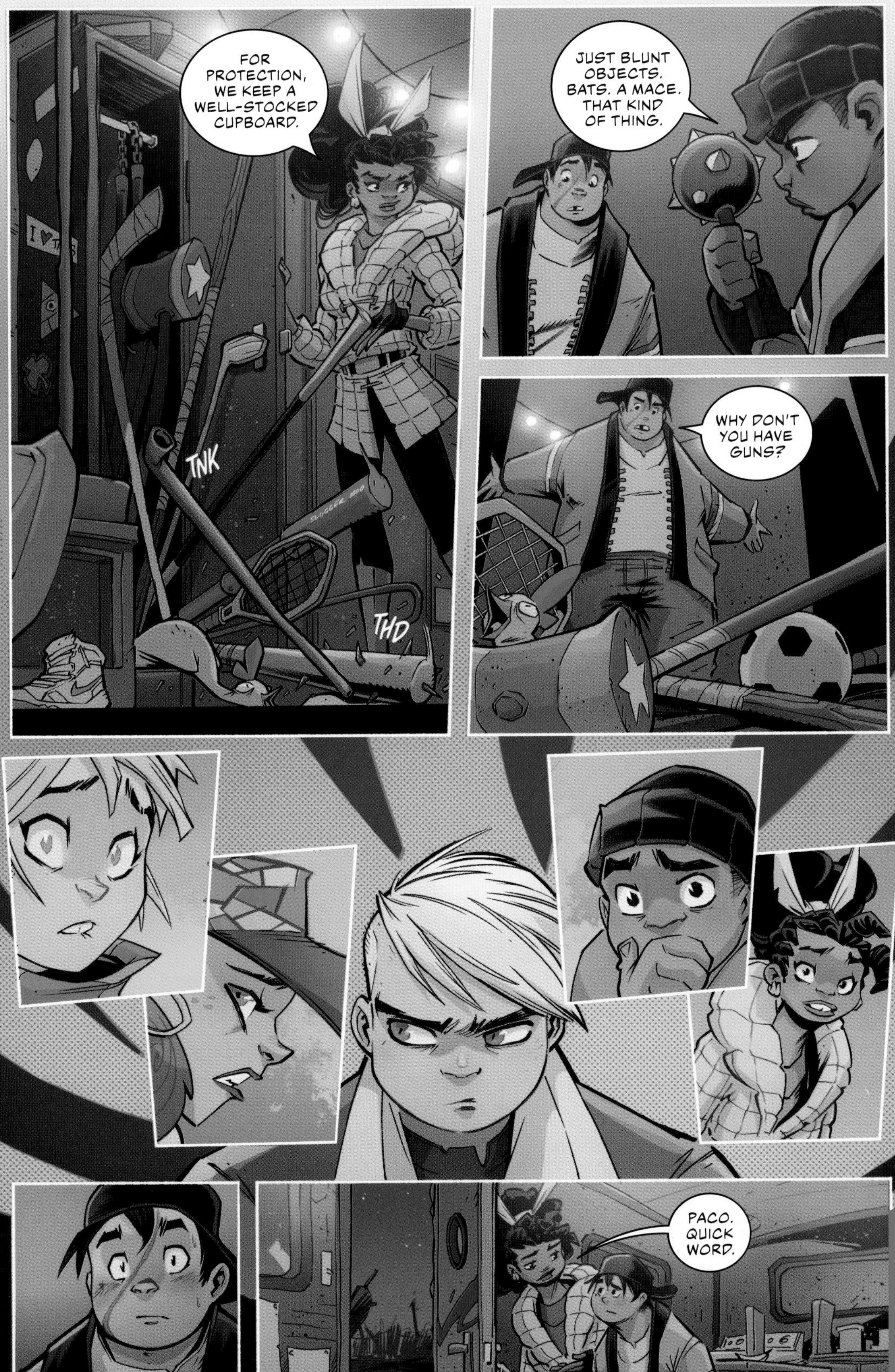
FOR PROTECTION, WE KEEP A WELL-STOCKED CUPBOARD.
TNK
THD
JUST BLUNT OBJECTS. BATS. A MACE. THAT KIND OF THING.
WHY DON'T YOU HAVE GUNS?
PACO. QUICK WORD.

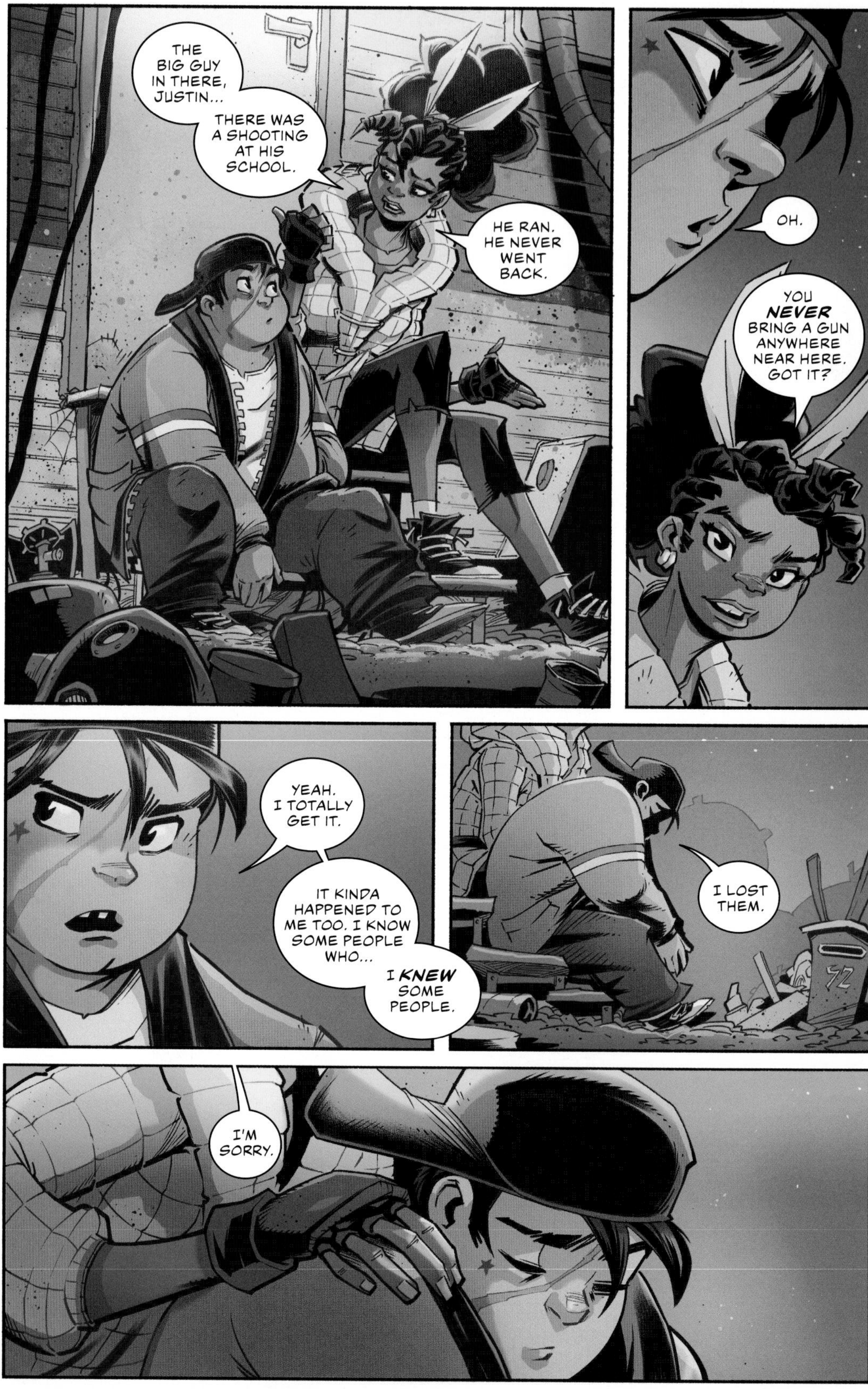
THE BIG GUY IN THERE, JUSTIN...
THERE WAS A SHOOTING AT HIS SCHOOL.
HE RAN. HE NEVER WENT BACK.
OH.
YOU **NEVER** BRING A GUN ANYWHERE NEAR HERE. GOT IT?
YEAH. I TOTALLY GET IT.
IT KINDA HAPPENED TO ME TOO. I KNOW SOME PEOPLE WHO...
I **KNEW** SOME PEOPLE.
I LOST THEM.
I'M SORRY.

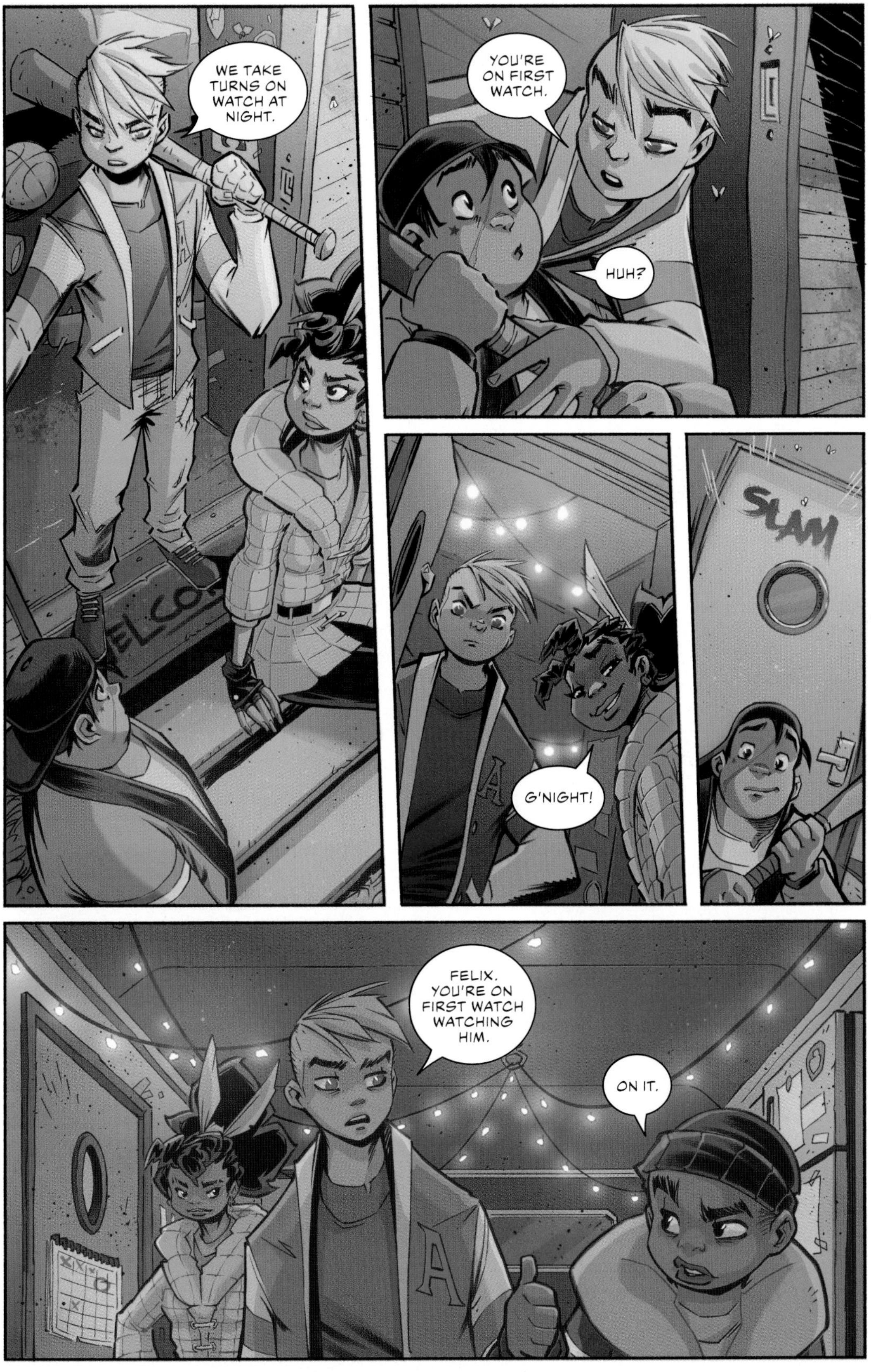
WE TAKE TURNS ON WATCH AT NIGHT.
YOU'RE ON FIRST WATCH.
HUH?
G'NIGHT!
SLAM
FELIX. YOU'RE ON FIRST WATCH WATCHING HIM.
ON IT.

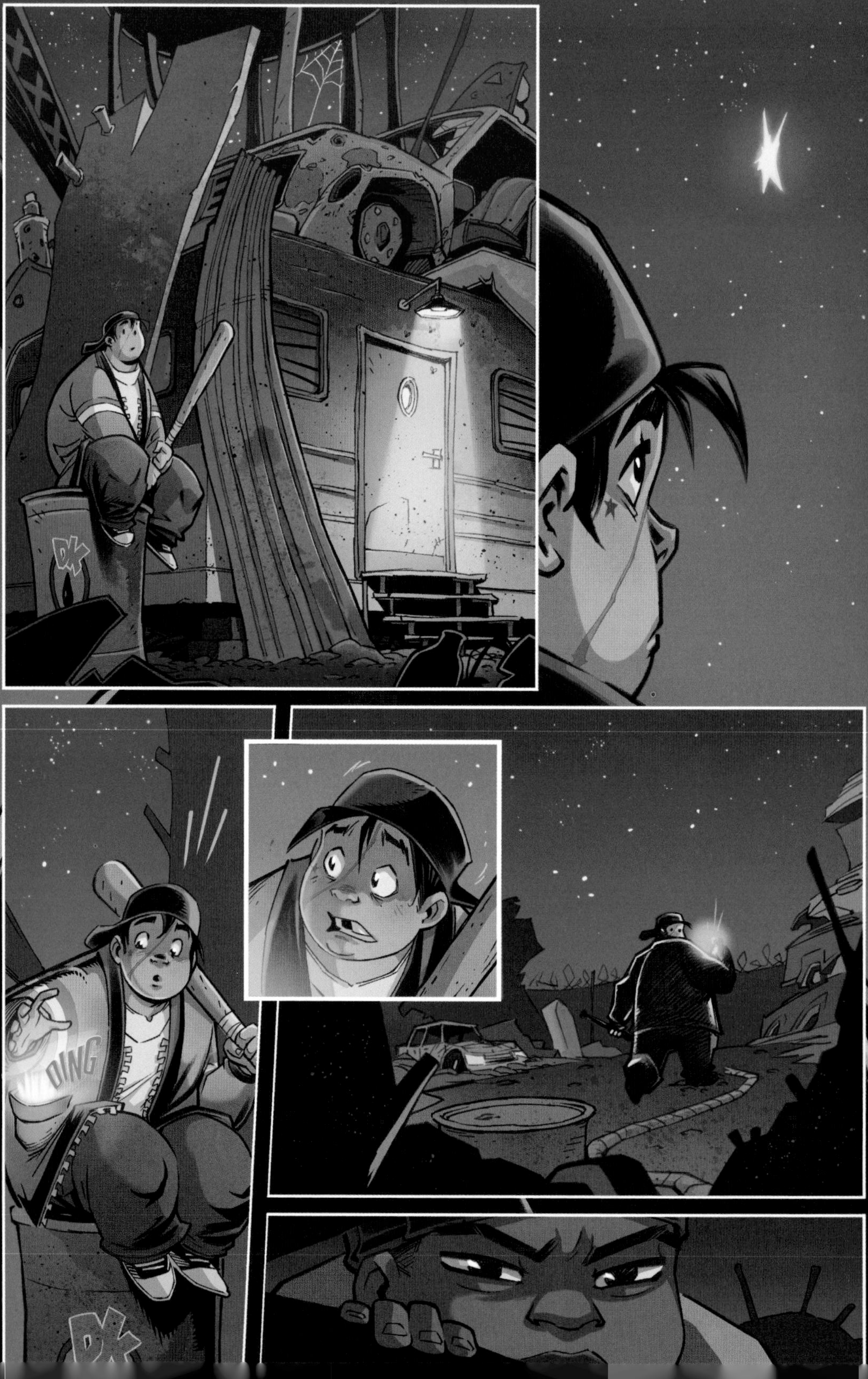
DK
DING
DK

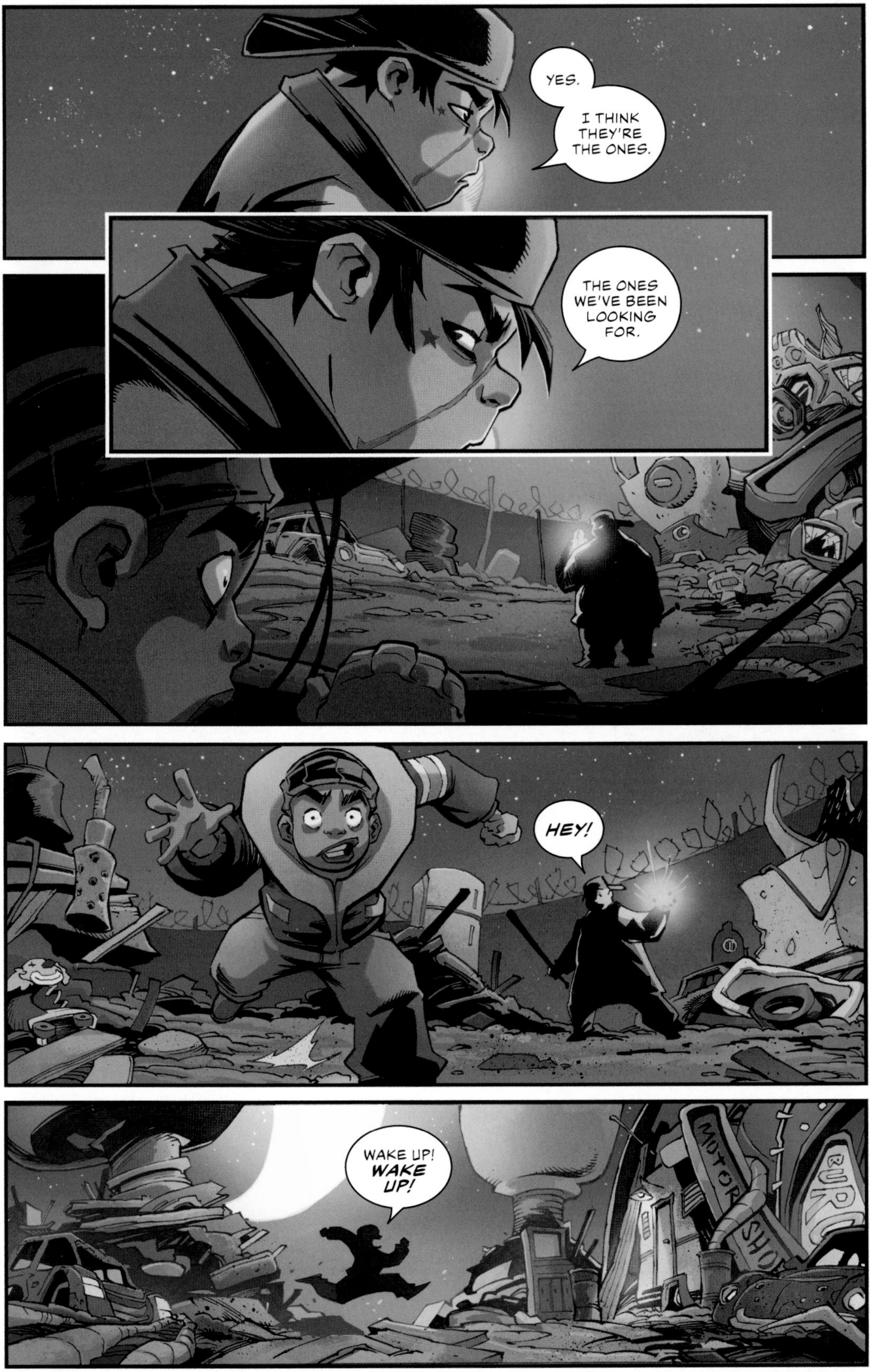
YES.
I THINK THEY'RE THE ONES.
THE ONES WE'VE BEEN LOOKING FOR.
HEY!
WAKE UP! **WAKE UP!**
MOTOR SHO
BUR

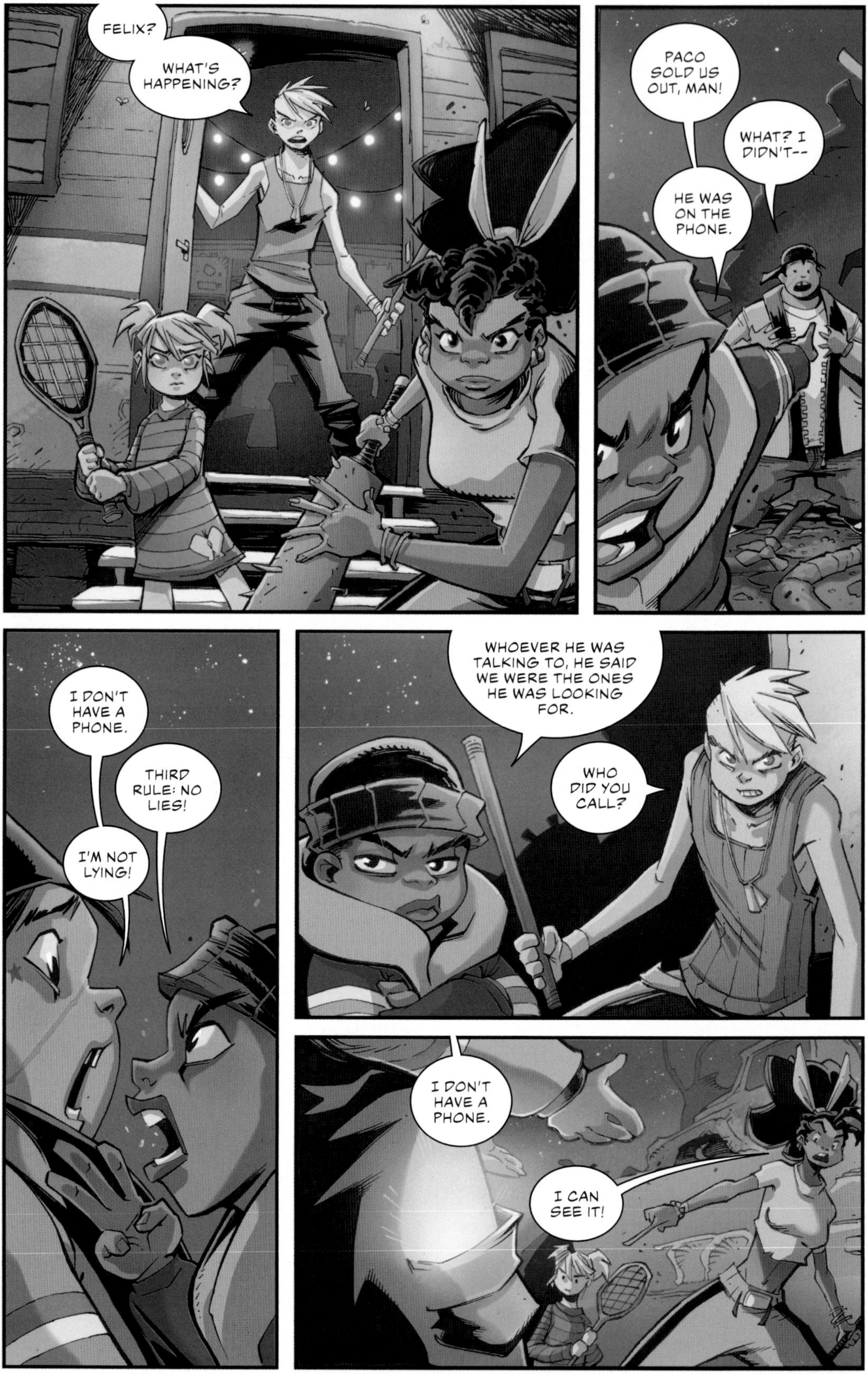
FELIX?
WHAT'S HAPPENING?
PACO SOLD US OUT, MAN!
WHAT? I DIDN'T--
HE WAS ON THE PHONE.
I DON'T HAVE A PHONE.
THIRD RULE: NO LIES!
I'M NOT LYING!
WHOEVER HE WAS TALKING TO, HE SAID WE WERE THE ONES HE WAS LOOKING FOR.
WHO DID YOU CALL?
I DON'T HAVE A PHONE.
I CAN SEE IT!

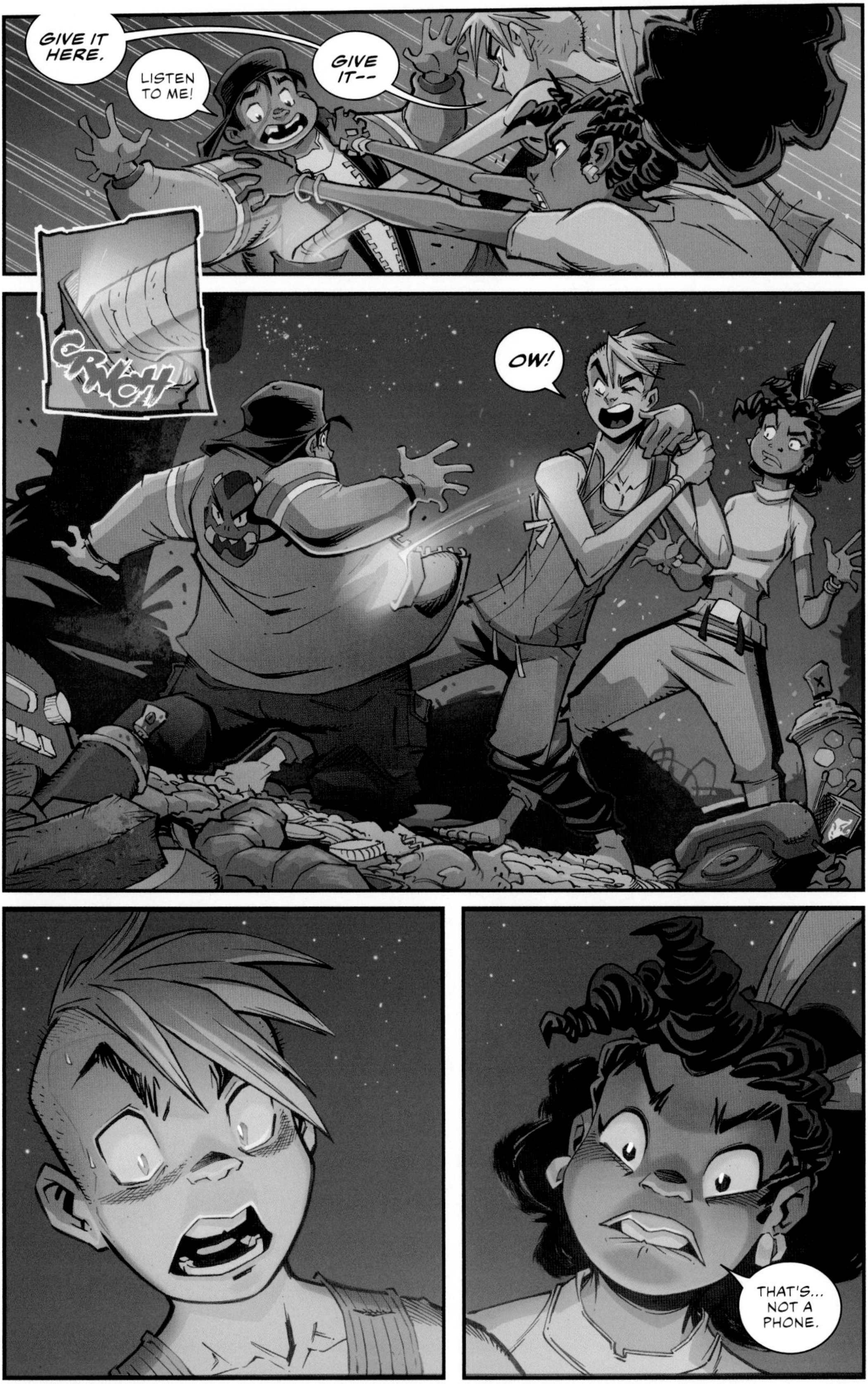
GIVE IT HERE.
LISTEN TO ME!
GIVE IT--
CRUNCH
OW!
THAT'S... NOT A PHONE.

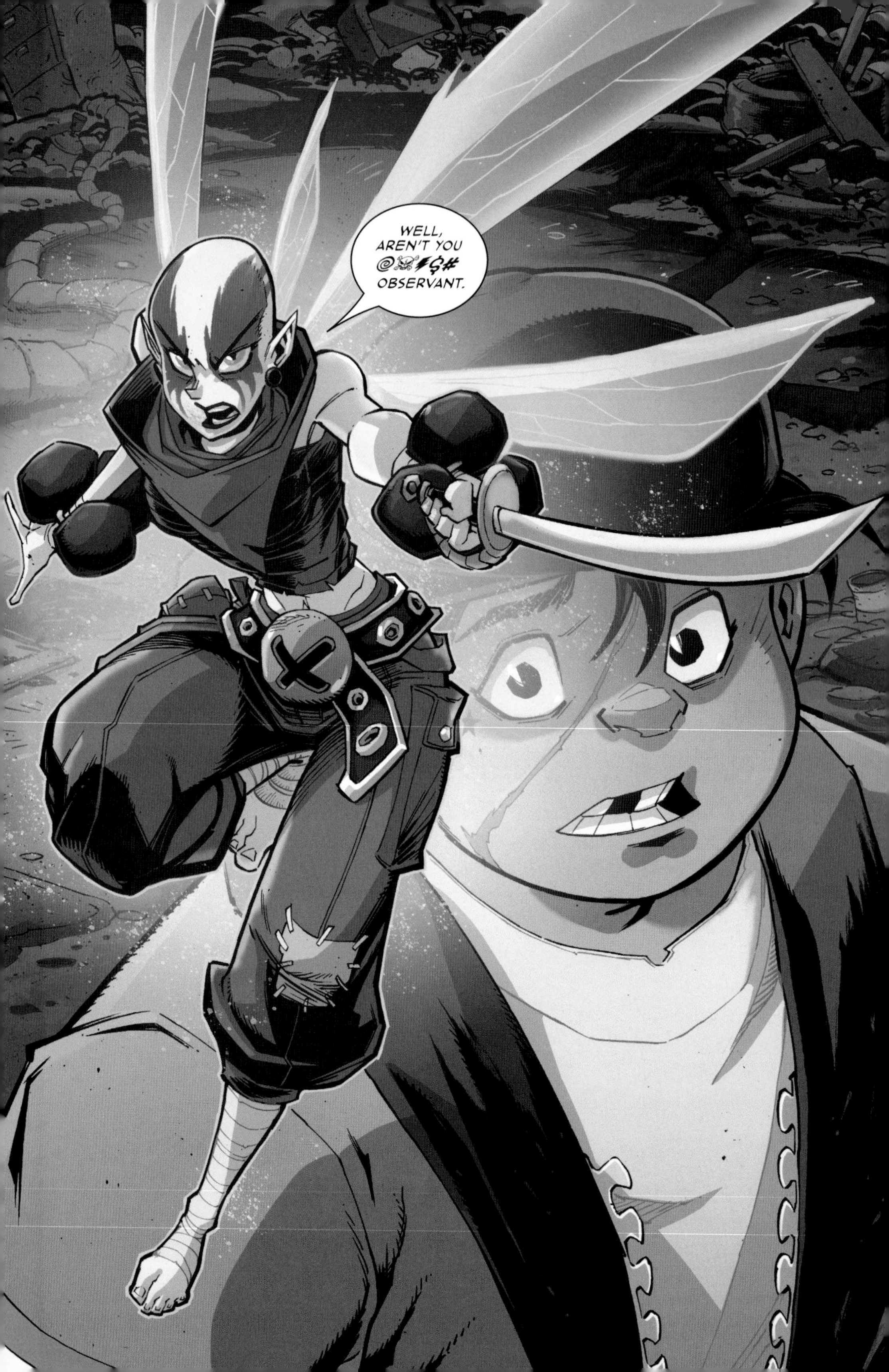
WELL, AREN'T YOU @☠⚡$# OBSERVANT.

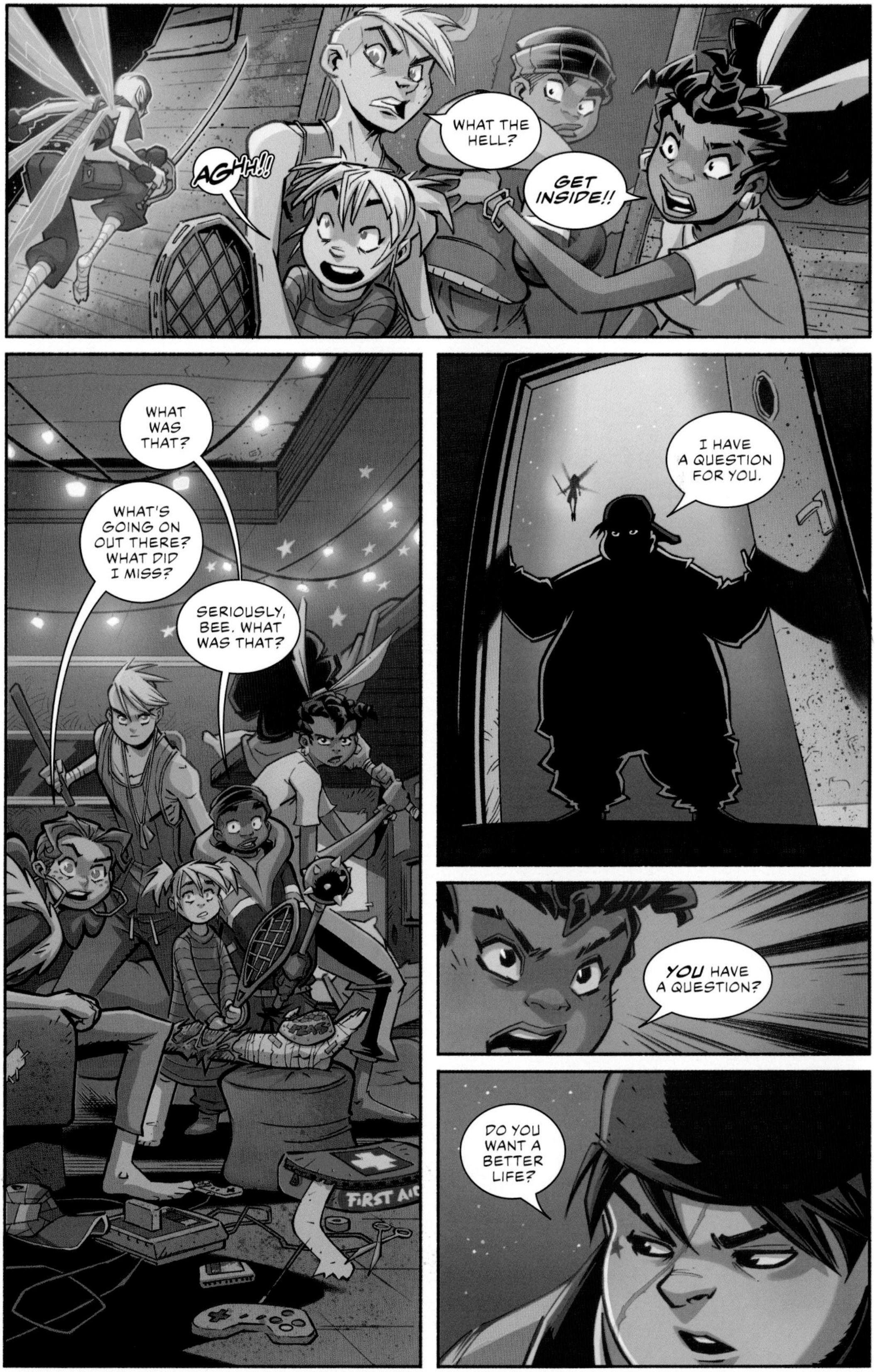
WHAT THE HELL?
AGHH!!
GET INSIDE!!
WHAT WAS THAT?
WHAT'S GOING ON OUT THERE? WHAT DID I MISS?
SERIOUSLY, BEE. WHAT WAS THAT?
FIRST AI
I HAVE A QUESTION FOR YOU.
YOU HAVE A QUESTION?
DO YOU WANT A BETTER LIFE?

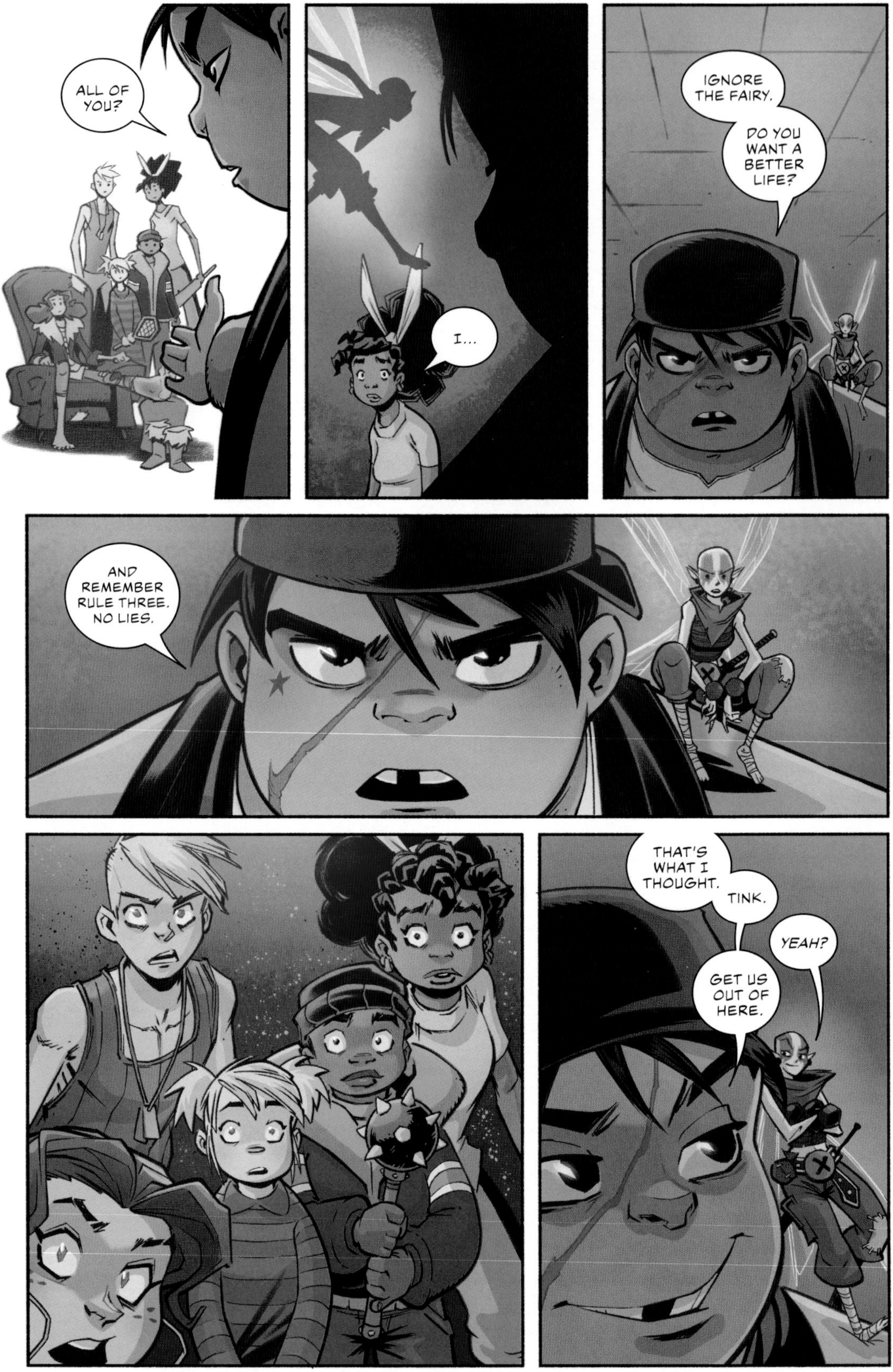
ALL OF YOU?
I...
IGNORE THE FAIRY.
DO YOU WANT A BETTER LIFE?
AND REMEMBER RULE THREE. NO LIES.
THAT'S WHAT I THOUGHT.
TINK.
YEAH?
GET US OUT OF HERE.

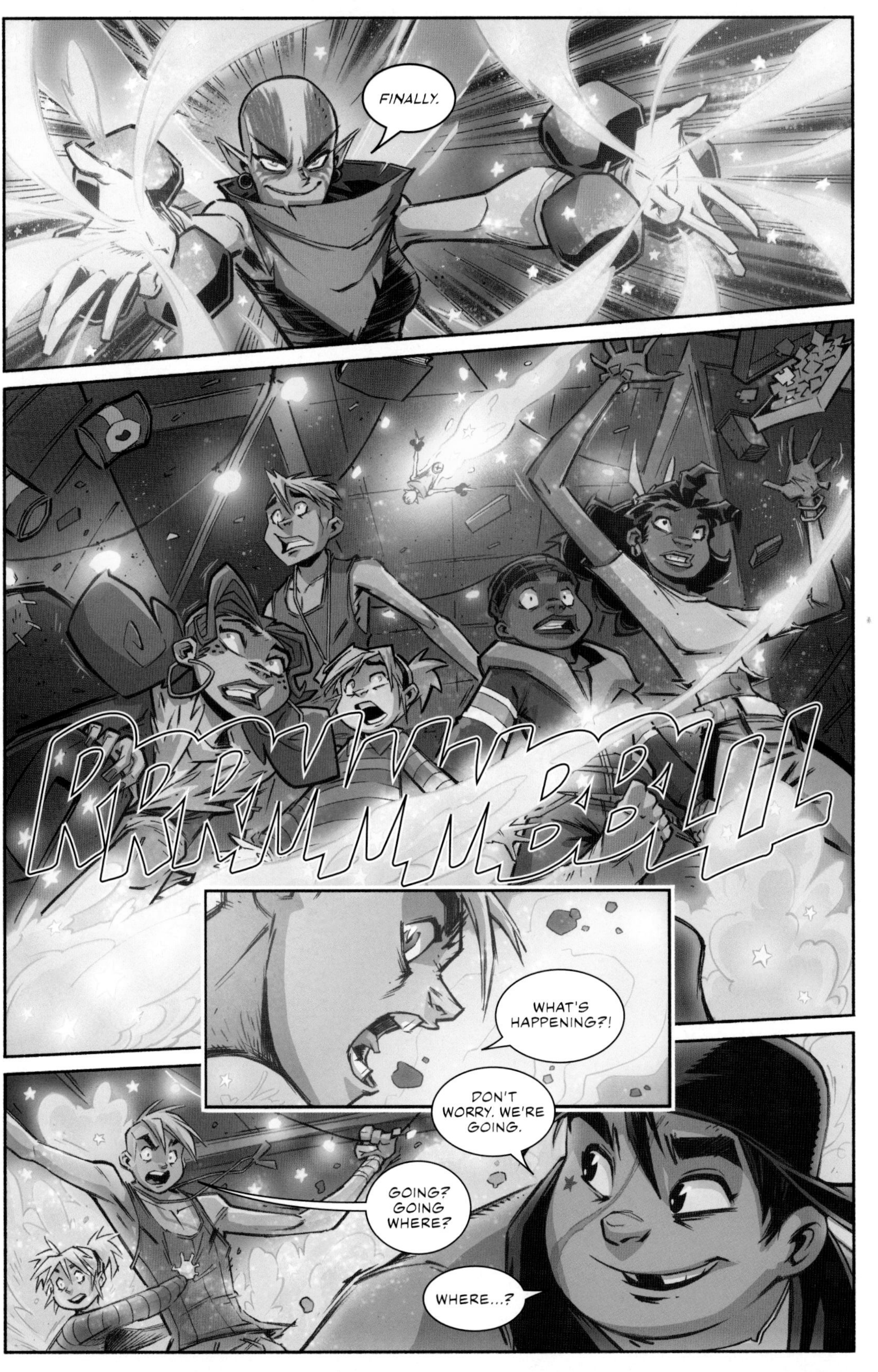
FINALLY.
WHAT'S HAPPENING?!
DON'T WORRY. WE'RE GOING.
GOING? GOING WHERE?
WHERE...?

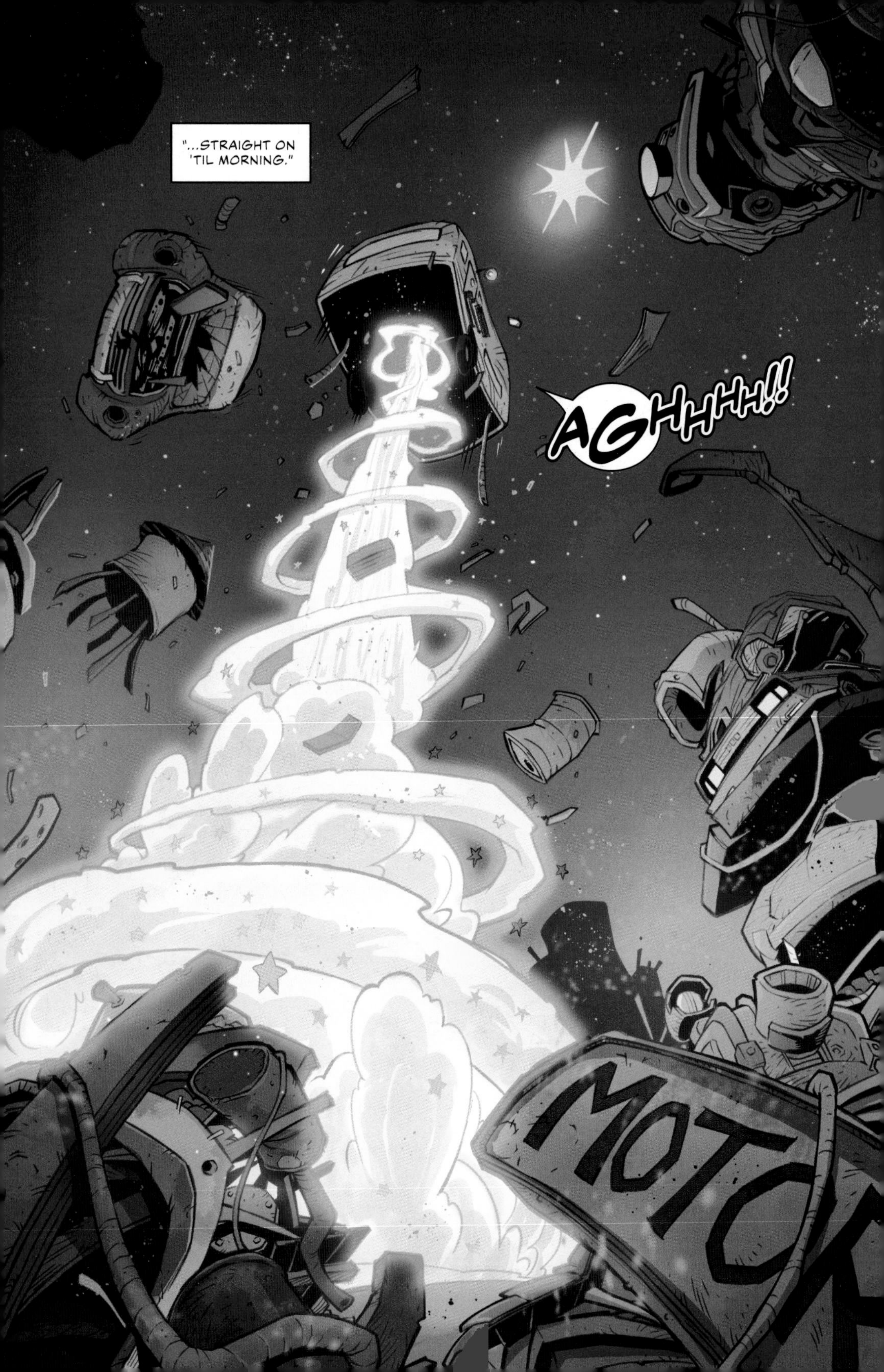
"...STRAIGHT ON 'TIL MORNING."
AGHHHH!!
MOTO

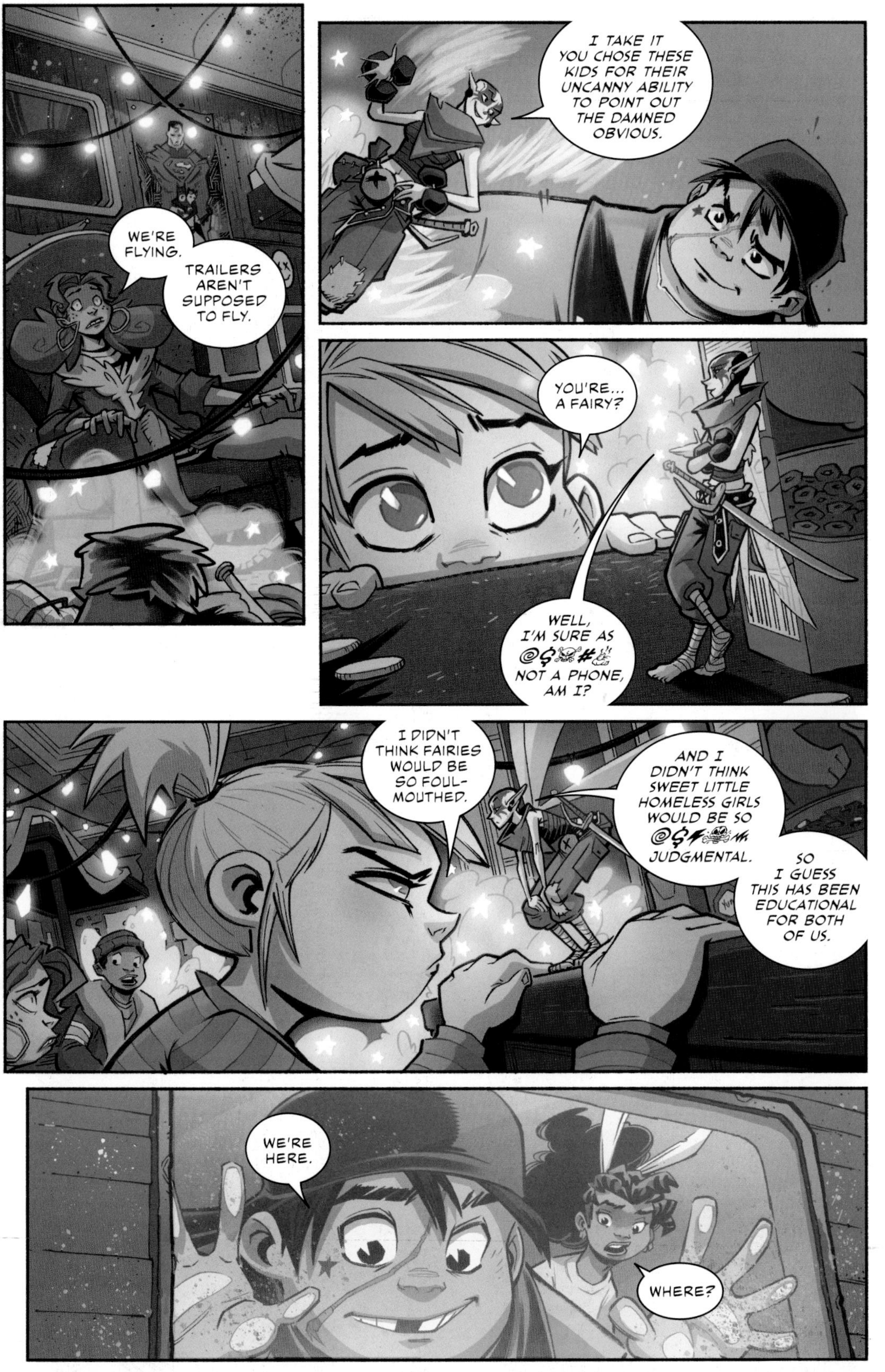

WE'RE FLYING.
TRAILERS AREN'T SUPPOSED TO FLY.
I TAKE IT YOU CHOSE THESE KIDS FOR THEIR UNCANNY ABILITY TO POINT OUT THE DAMNED OBVIOUS.
YOU'RE... A FAIRY?
WELL, I'M SURE AS @$☠#! NOT A PHONE, AM I?
I DIDN'T THINK FAIRIES WOULD BE SO FOUL-MOUTHED.
AND I DIDN'T THINK SWEET LITTLE HOMELESS GIRLS WOULD BE SO @$⚡☠ JUDGMENTAL.
SO I GUESS THIS HAS BEEN EDUCATIONAL FOR BOTH OF US.
WE'RE HERE.
WHERE?

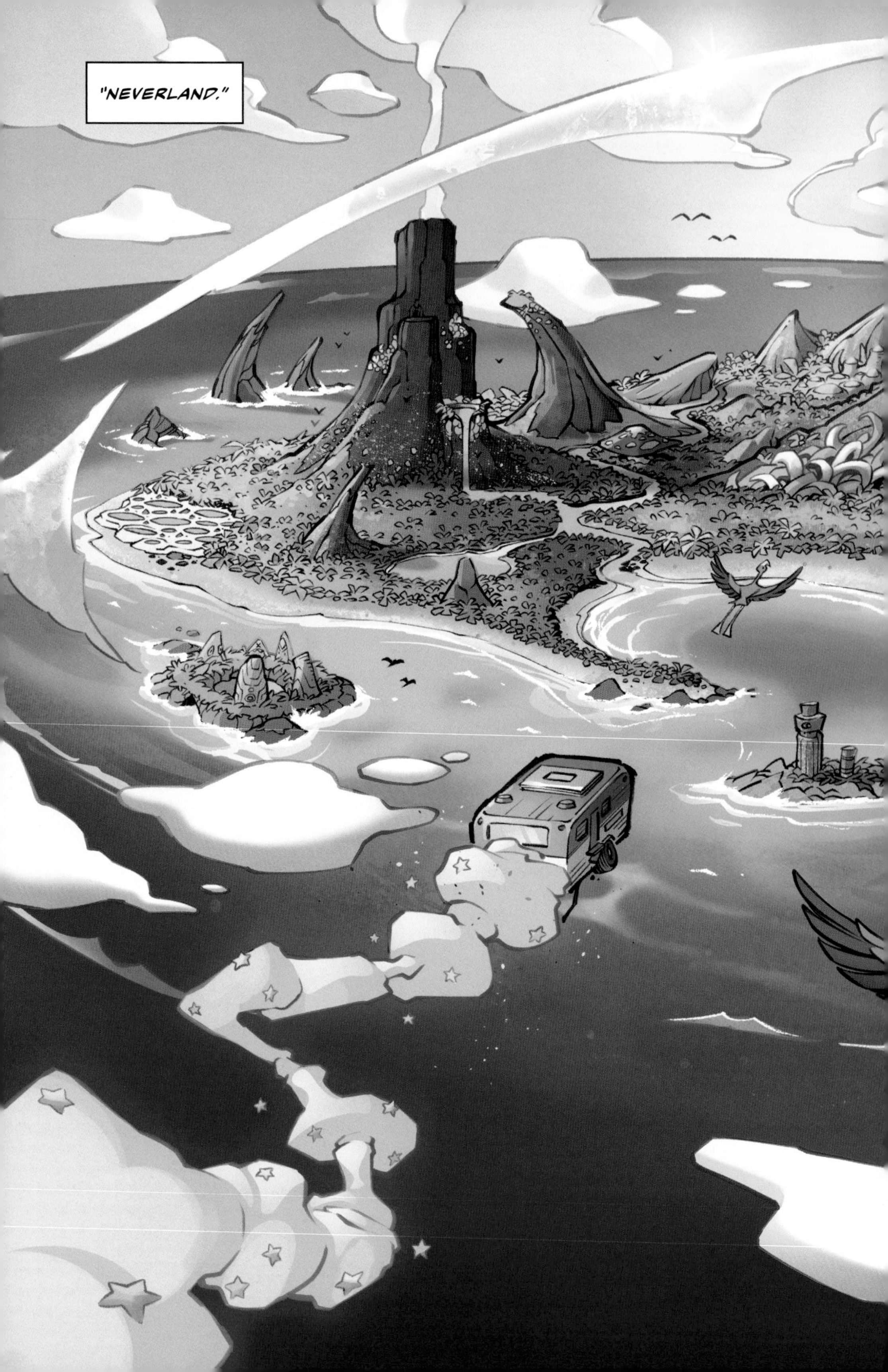
"NEVERLAND."

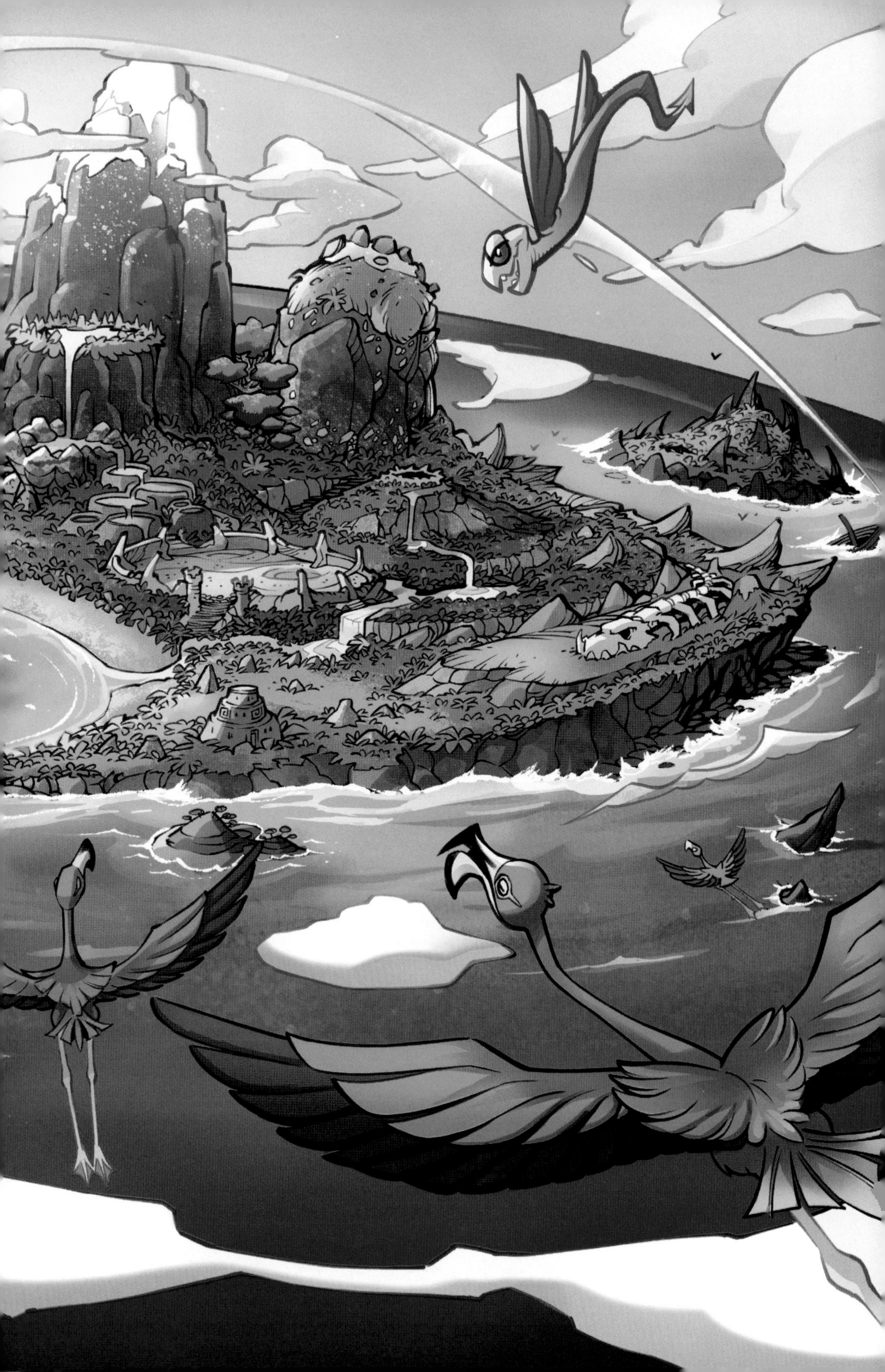

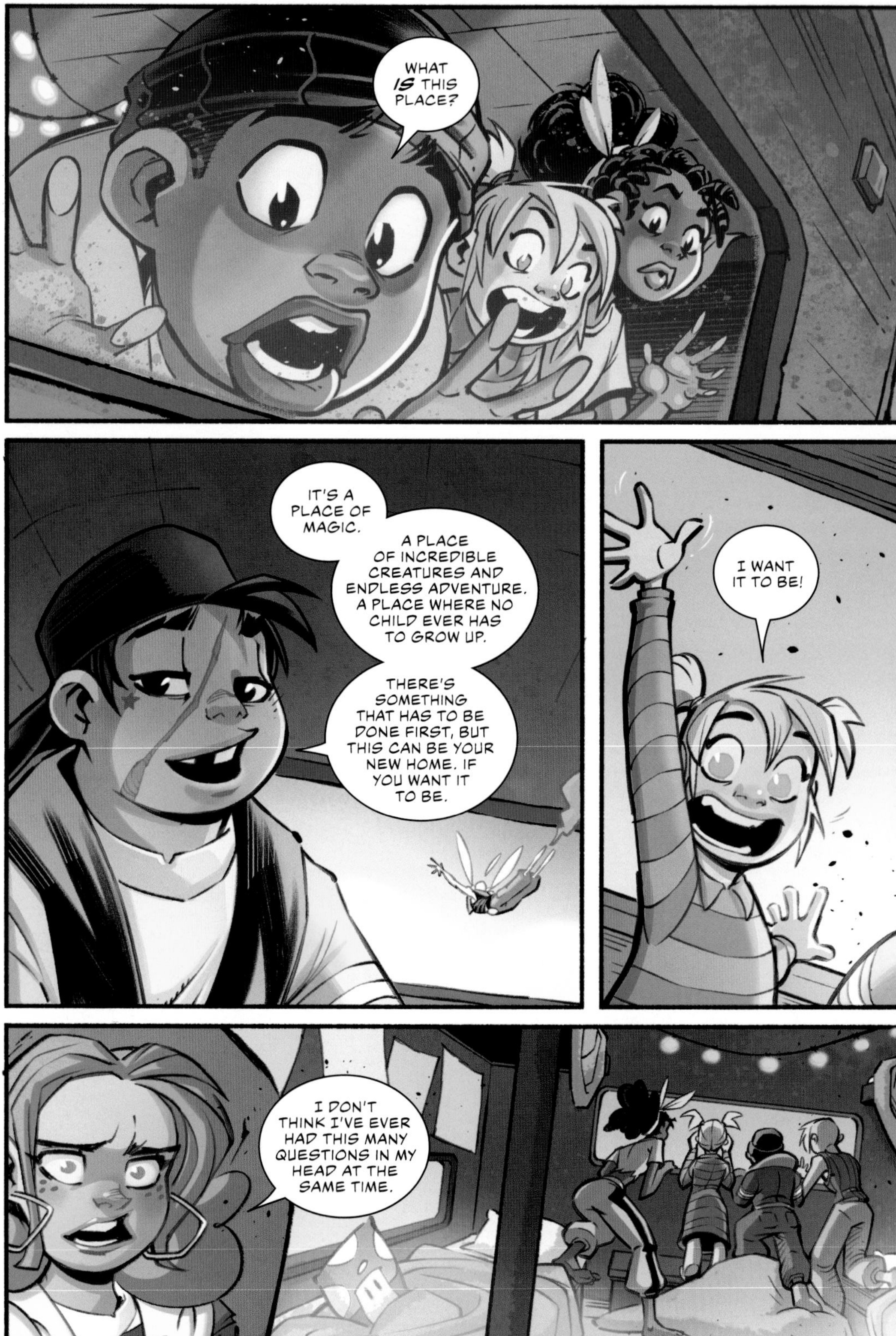
WHAT IS THIS PLACE?
IT'S A PLACE OF MAGIC.
A PLACE OF INCREDIBLE CREATURES AND ENDLESS ADVENTURE. A PLACE WHERE NO CHILD EVER HAS TO GROW UP.
THERE'S SOMETHING THAT HAS TO BE DONE FIRST, BUT THIS CAN BE YOUR NEW HOME. IF YOU WANT IT TO BE.
I WANT IT TO BE!
I DON'T THINK I'VE EVER HAD THIS MANY QUESTIONS IN MY HEAD AT THE SAME TIME.

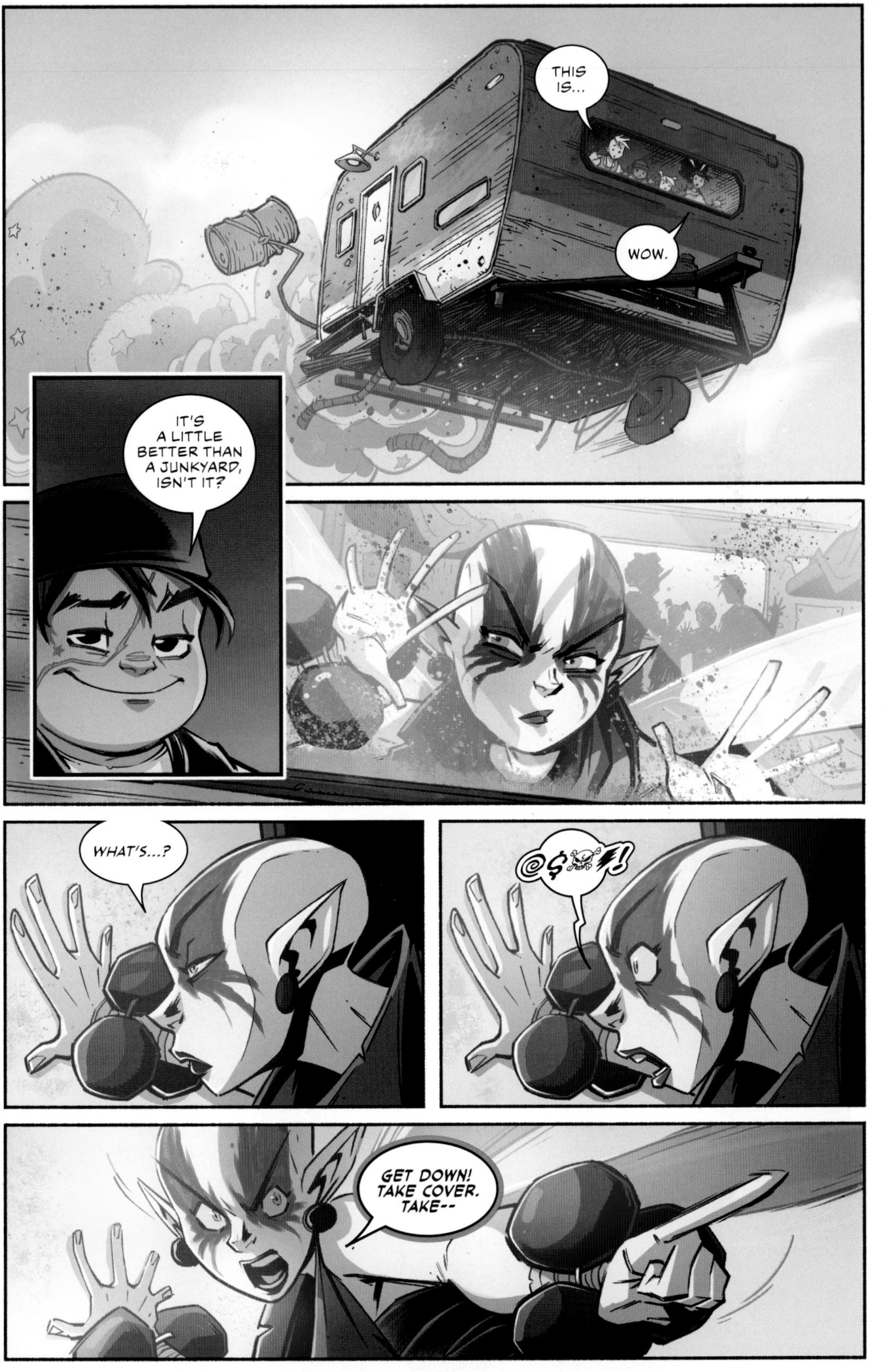
THIS IS...
WOW.
IT'S A LITTLE BETTER THAN A JUNKYARD, ISN'T IT?
WHAT'S...?
GET DOWN! TAKE COVER. TAKE--

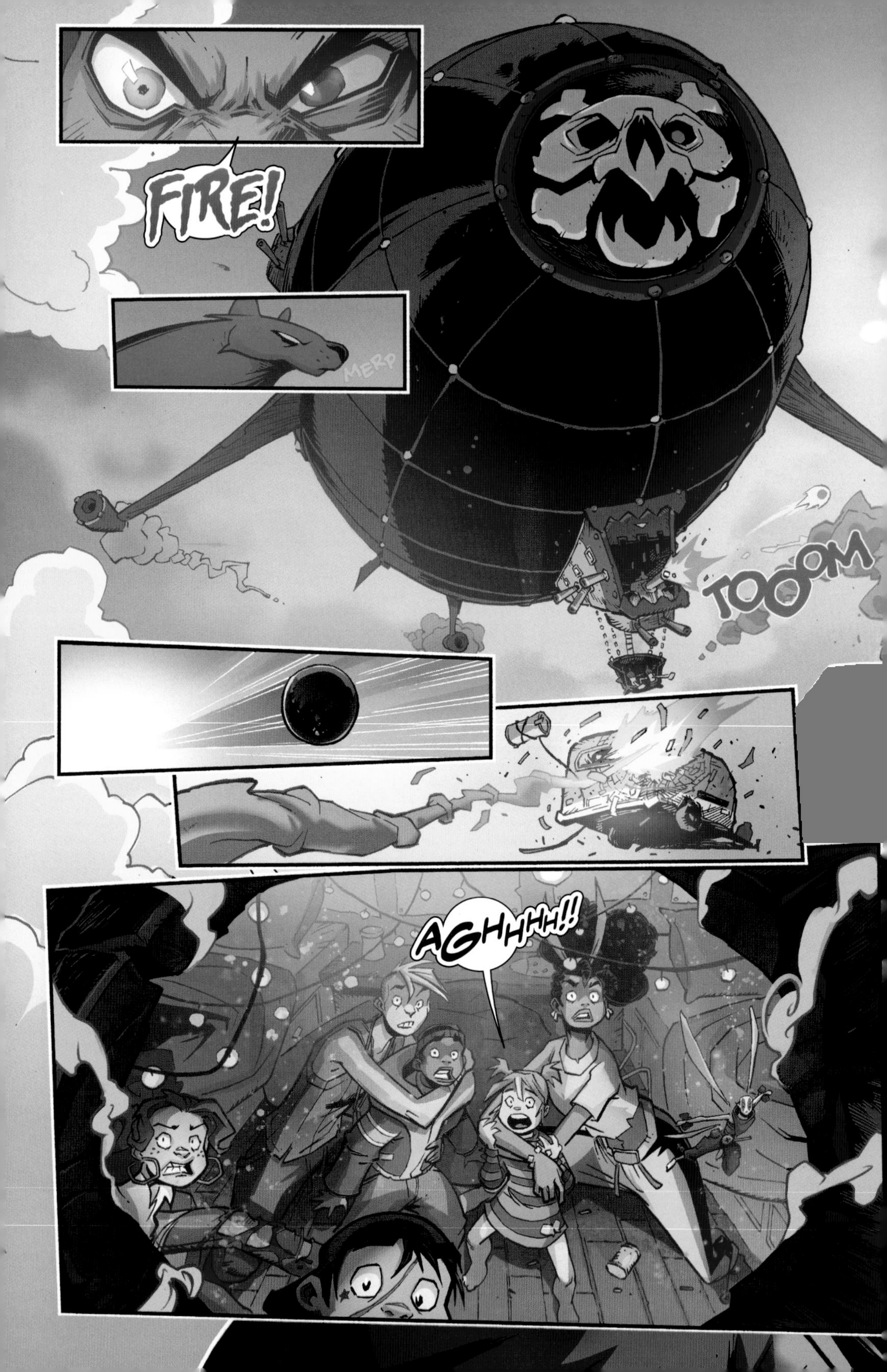
FIRE!
MERP
TOOOM
AGHHHH!!

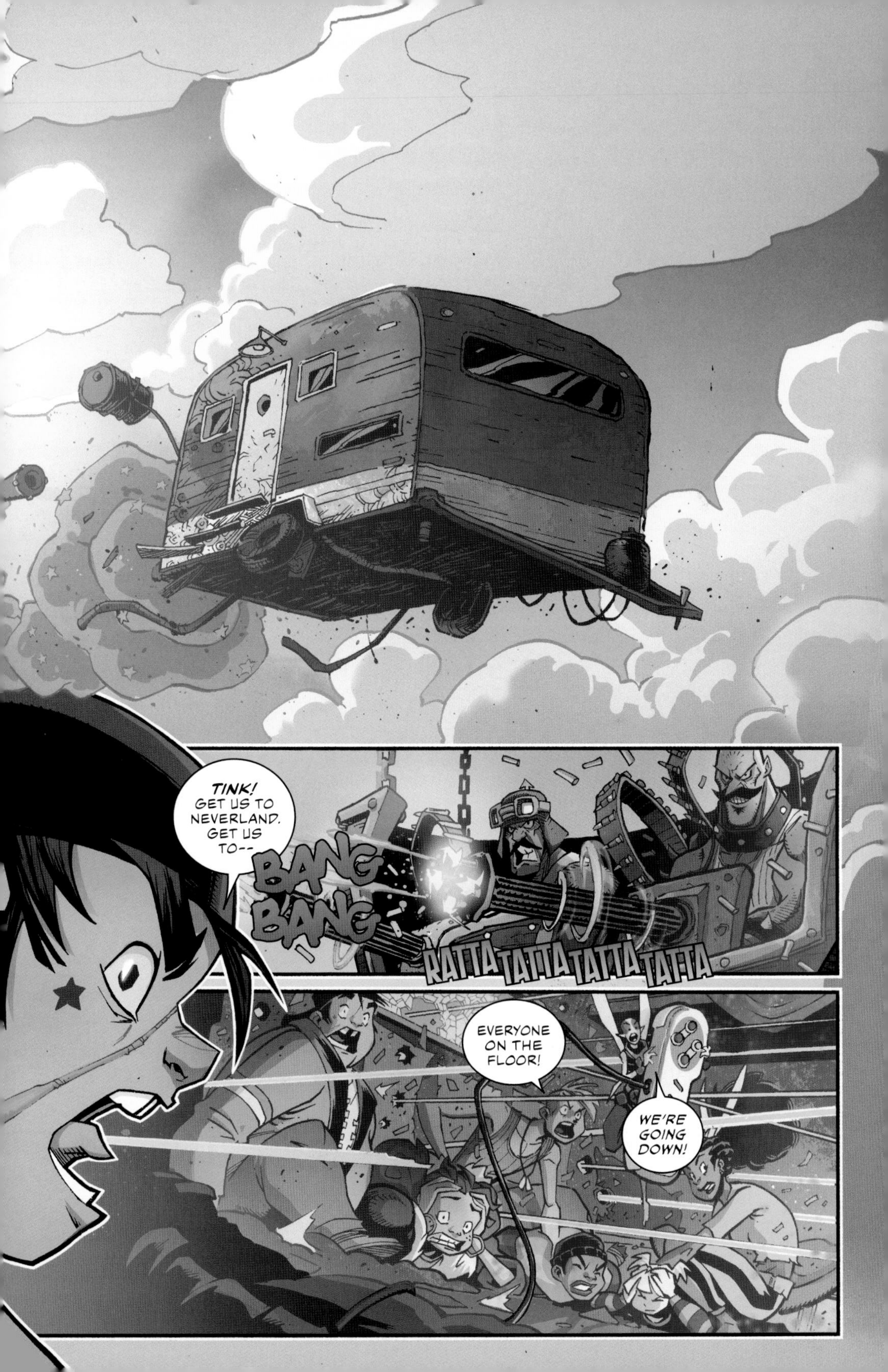
TINK! GET US TO NEVERLAND. GET US TO--
BANG BANG
RATTATATTATATTATATTA
EVERYONE ON THE FLOOR!
WE'RE GOING DOWN!

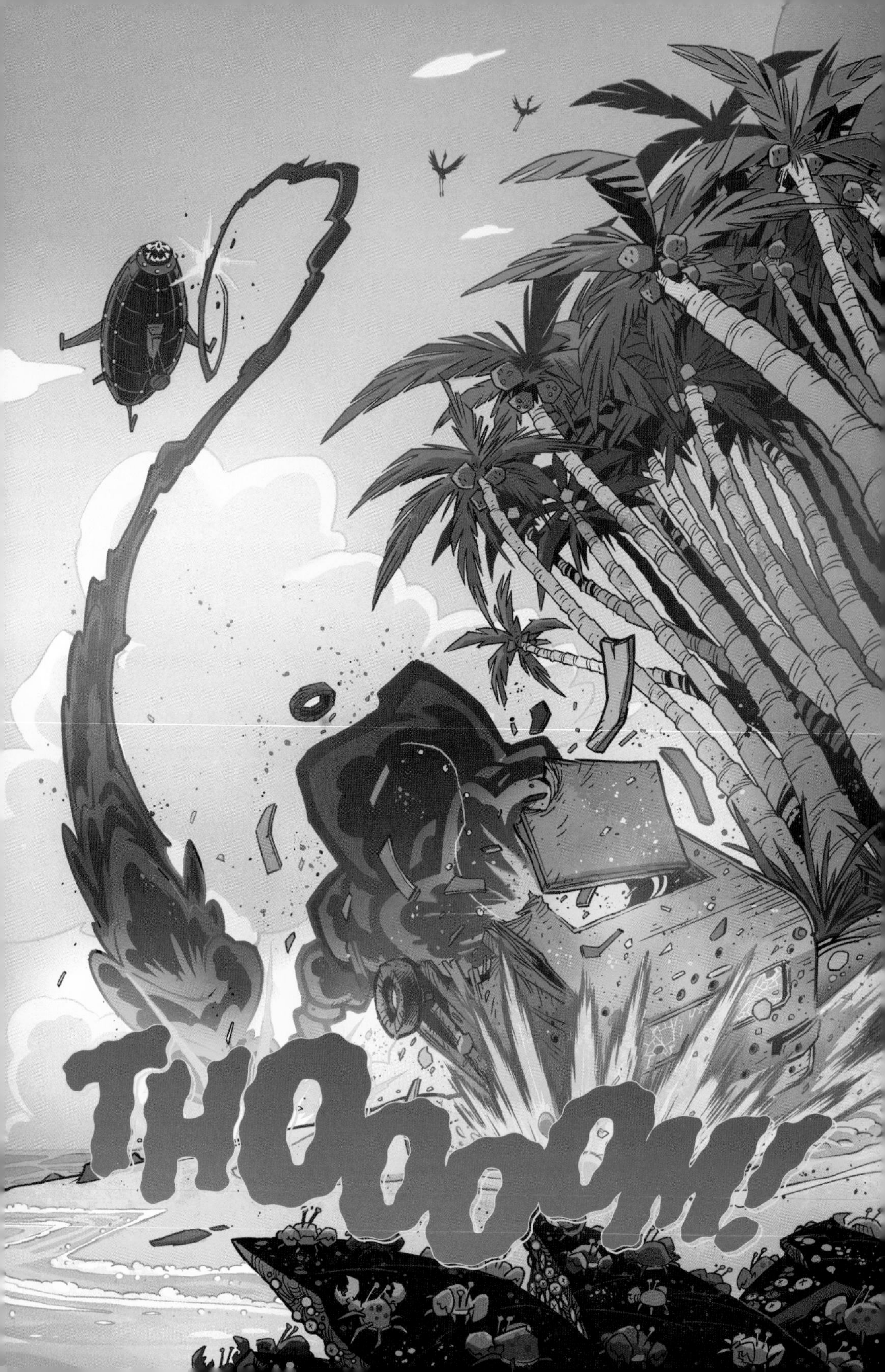
THOOOM!

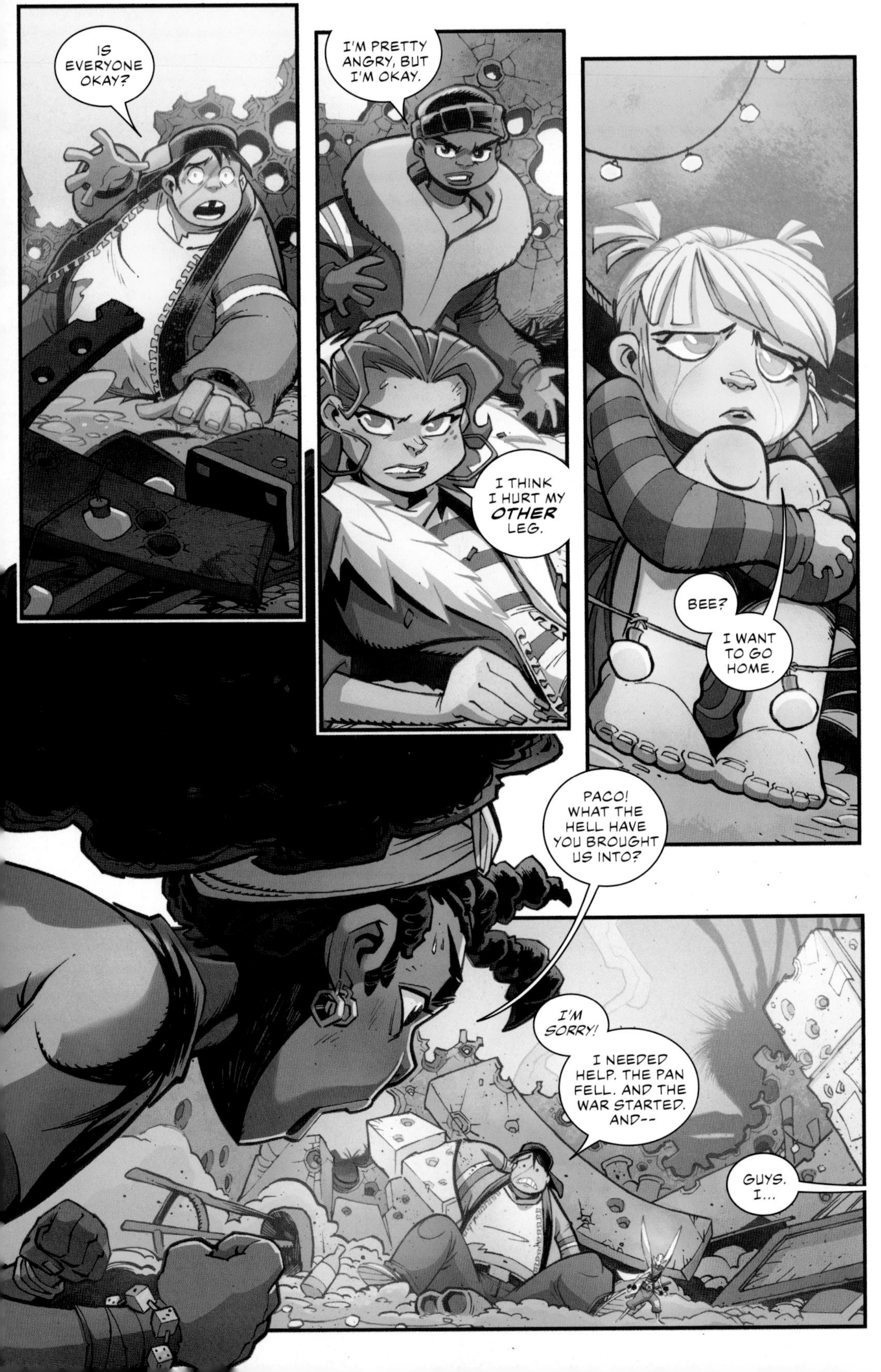
IS EVERYONE OKAY?
I'M PRETTY ANGRY, BUT I'M OKAY.
I THINK I HURT MY *OTHER* LEG.
BEE?
I WANT TO GO HOME.
PACO! WHAT THE HELL HAVE YOU BROUGHT US INTO?
I'M SORRY!
I NEEDED HELP. THE PAN FELL. AND THE WAR STARTED. AND--
GUYS. I...

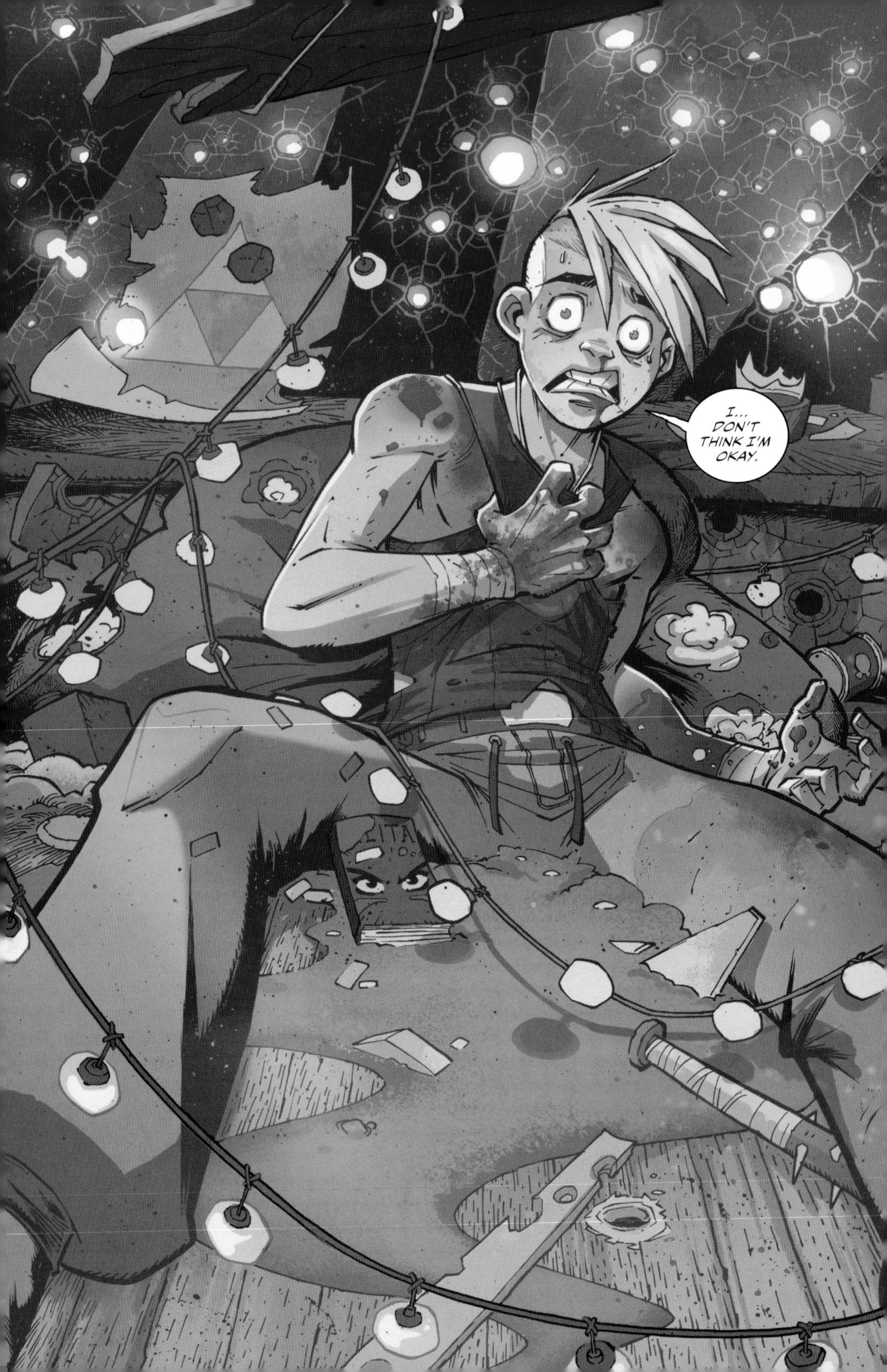
I... DON'T THINK I'M OKAY.

CHAPTER
TWO

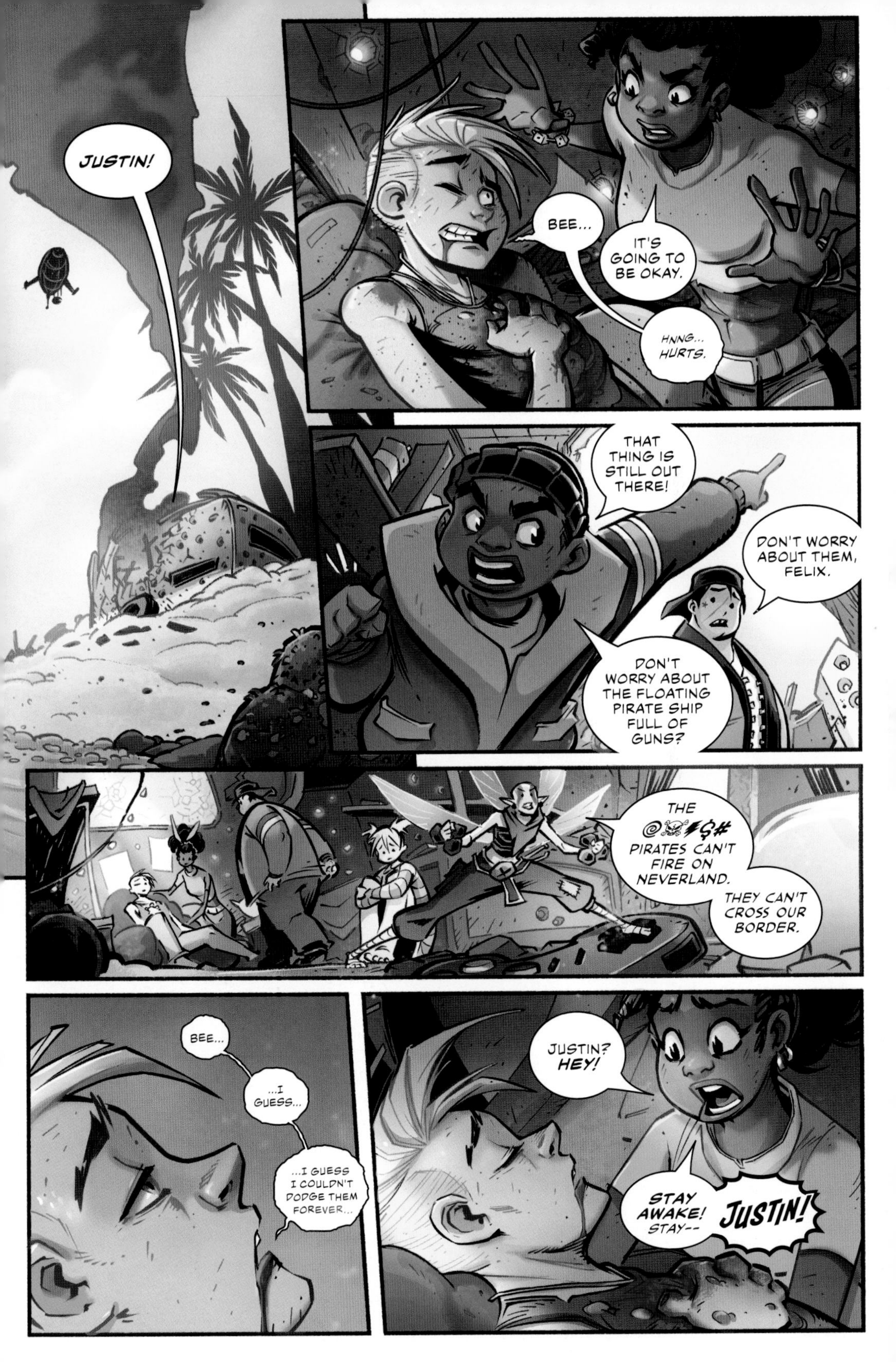
JUSTIN!
BEE...
IT'S GOING TO BE OKAY.
HNNG... HURTS.
THAT THING IS STILL OUT THERE!
DON'T WORRY ABOUT THEM, FELIX.
DON'T WORRY ABOUT THE FLOATING PIRATE SHIP FULL OF GUNS?
THE @☠⚡$# PIRATES CAN'T FIRE ON NEVERLAND.
THEY CAN'T CROSS OUR BORDER.
BEE...
...I GUESS...
...I GUESS I COULDN'T DODGE THEM FOREVER...
JUSTIN? HEY!
STAY AWAKE! STAY--
JUSTIN!

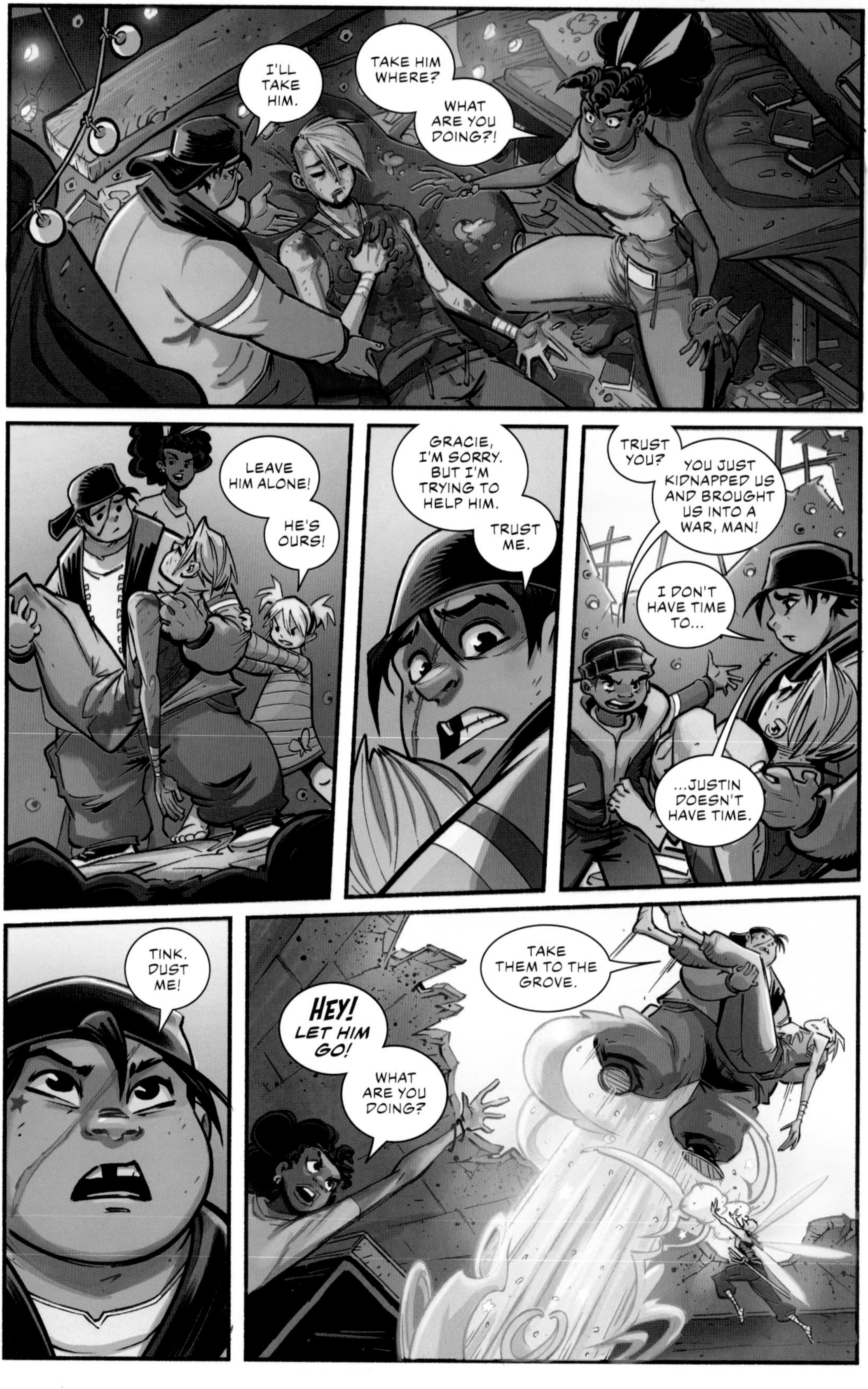
I'LL TAKE HIM.
TAKE HIM WHERE?
WHAT ARE YOU DOING?!
LEAVE HIM ALONE!
HE'S OURS!
GRACIE, I'M SORRY. BUT I'M TRYING TO HELP HIM.
TRUST ME.
TRUST YOU?
YOU JUST KIDNAPPED US AND BROUGHT US INTO A WAR, MAN!
I DON'T HAVE TIME TO...
...JUSTIN DOESN'T HAVE TIME.
TINK. DUST ME!
TAKE THEM TO THE GROVE.
HEY! LET HIM GO!
WHAT ARE YOU DOING?

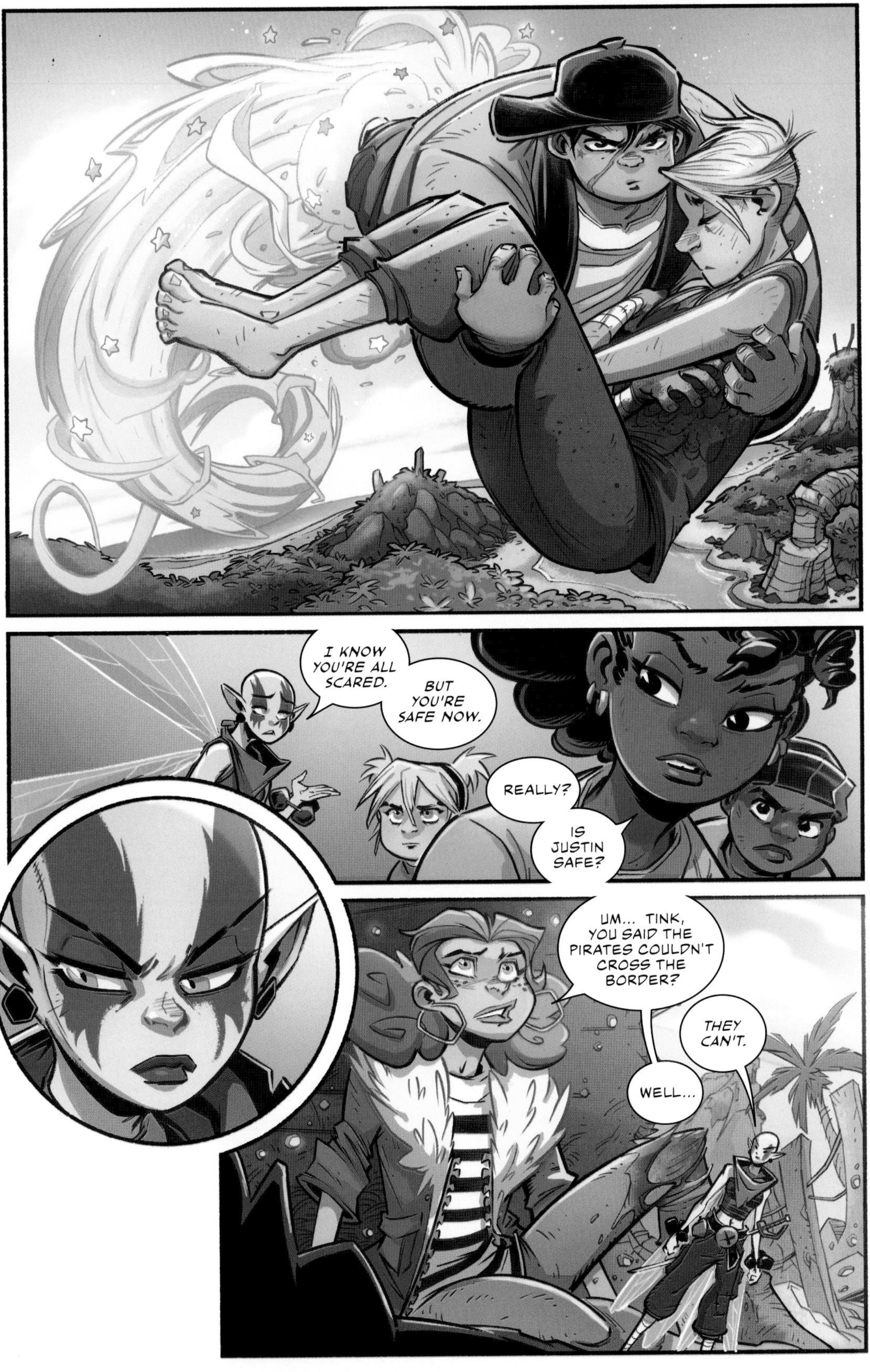

I KNOW YOU'RE ALL SCARED.
BUT YOU'RE SAFE NOW.
REALLY?
IS JUSTIN SAFE?
UM... TINK, YOU SAID THE PIRATES COULDN'T CROSS THE BORDER?
THEY CAN'T.
WELL...

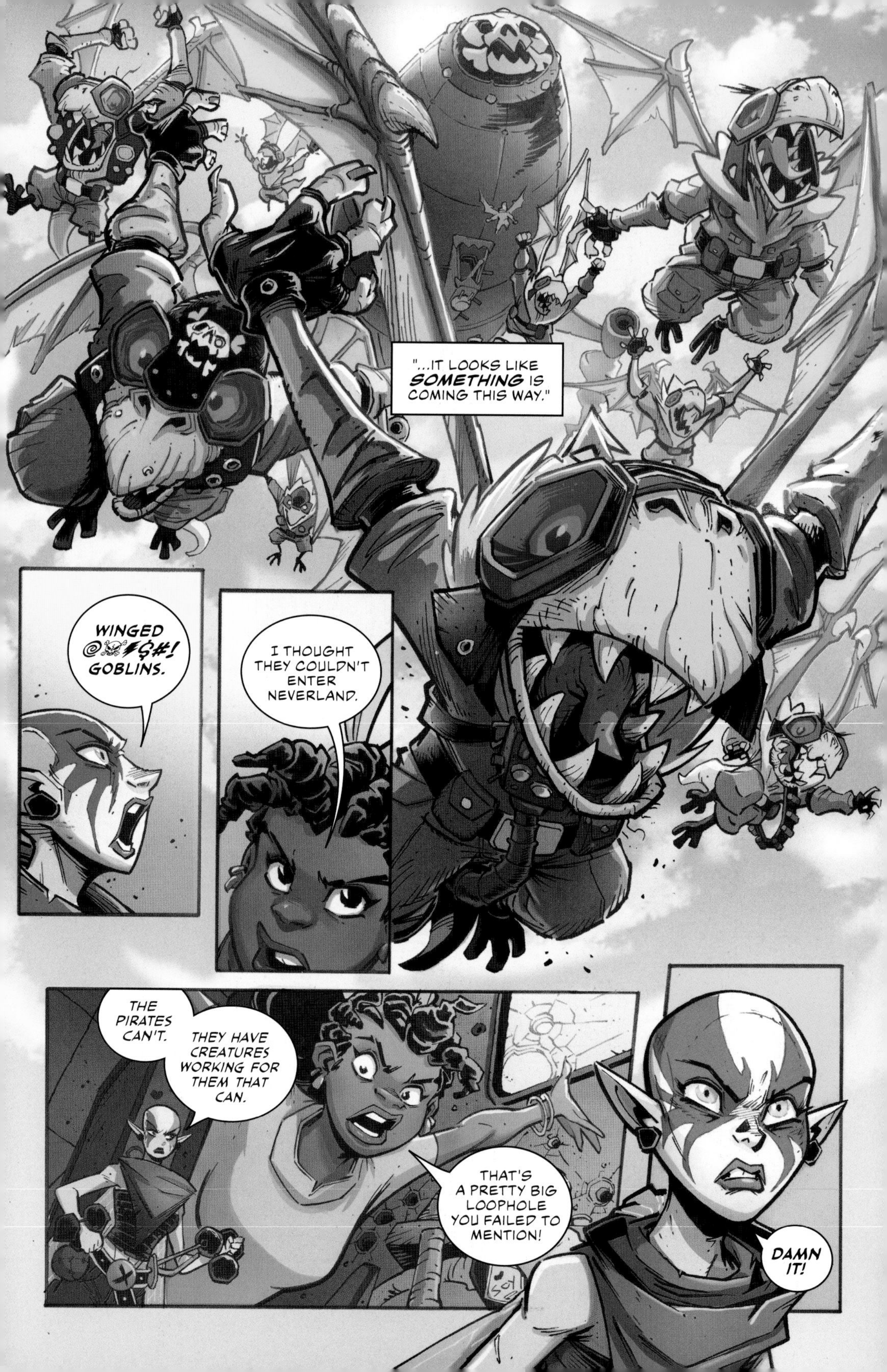
"...IT LOOKS LIKE *SOMETHING* IS COMING THIS WAY."
WINGED @☠⚡$#! GOBLINS.
I THOUGHT THEY COULDN'T ENTER NEVERLAND.
THE PIRATES CAN'T.
THEY HAVE CREATURES WORKING FOR THEM THAT CAN.
THAT'S A PRETTY BIG LOOPHOLE YOU FAILED TO MENTION!
DAMN IT!

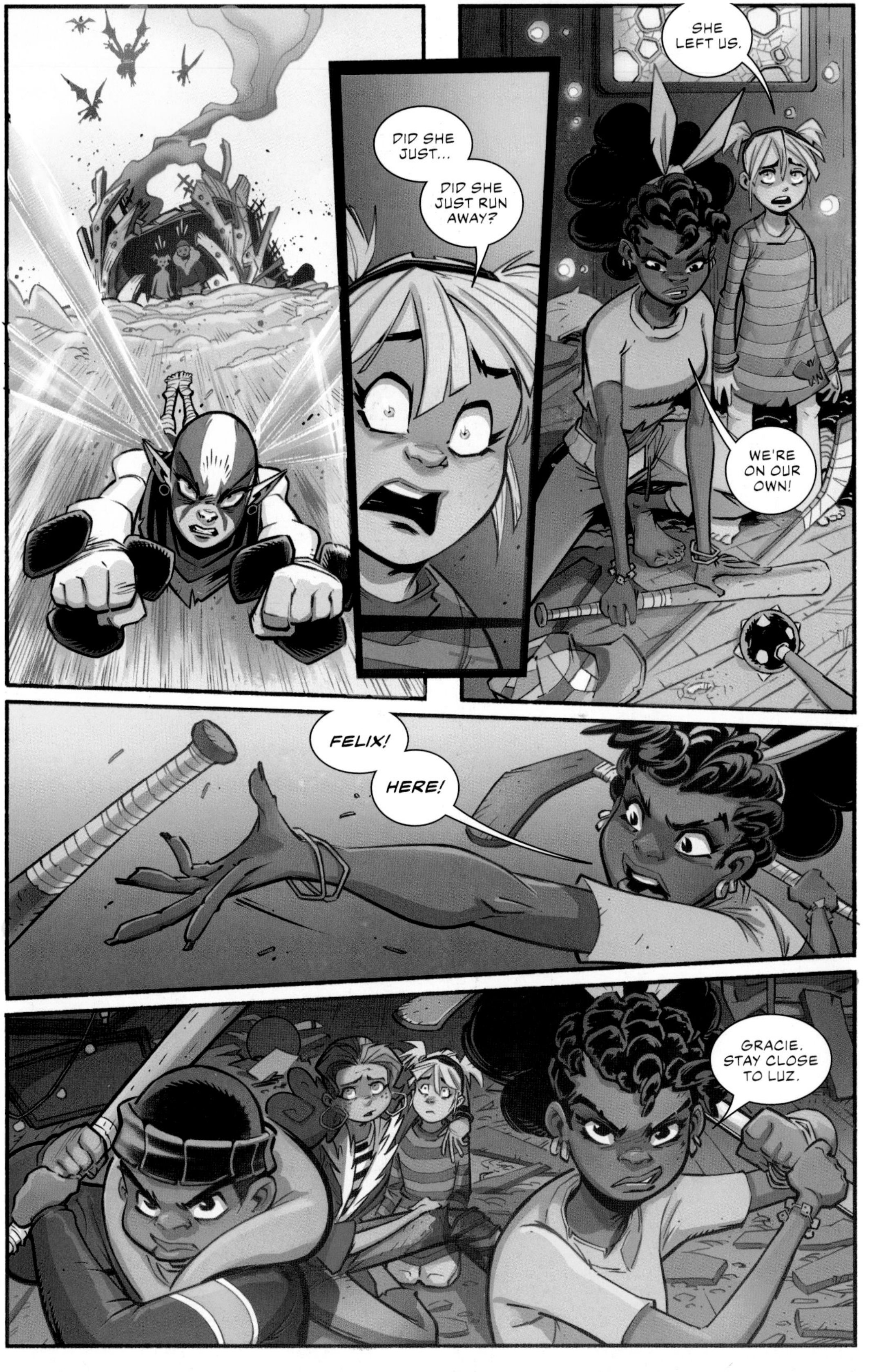
DID SHE JUST...
DID SHE JUST RUN AWAY?
SHE LEFT US.
WE'RE ON OUR OWN!
FELIX!
HERE!
GRACIE. STAY CLOSE TO LUZ.

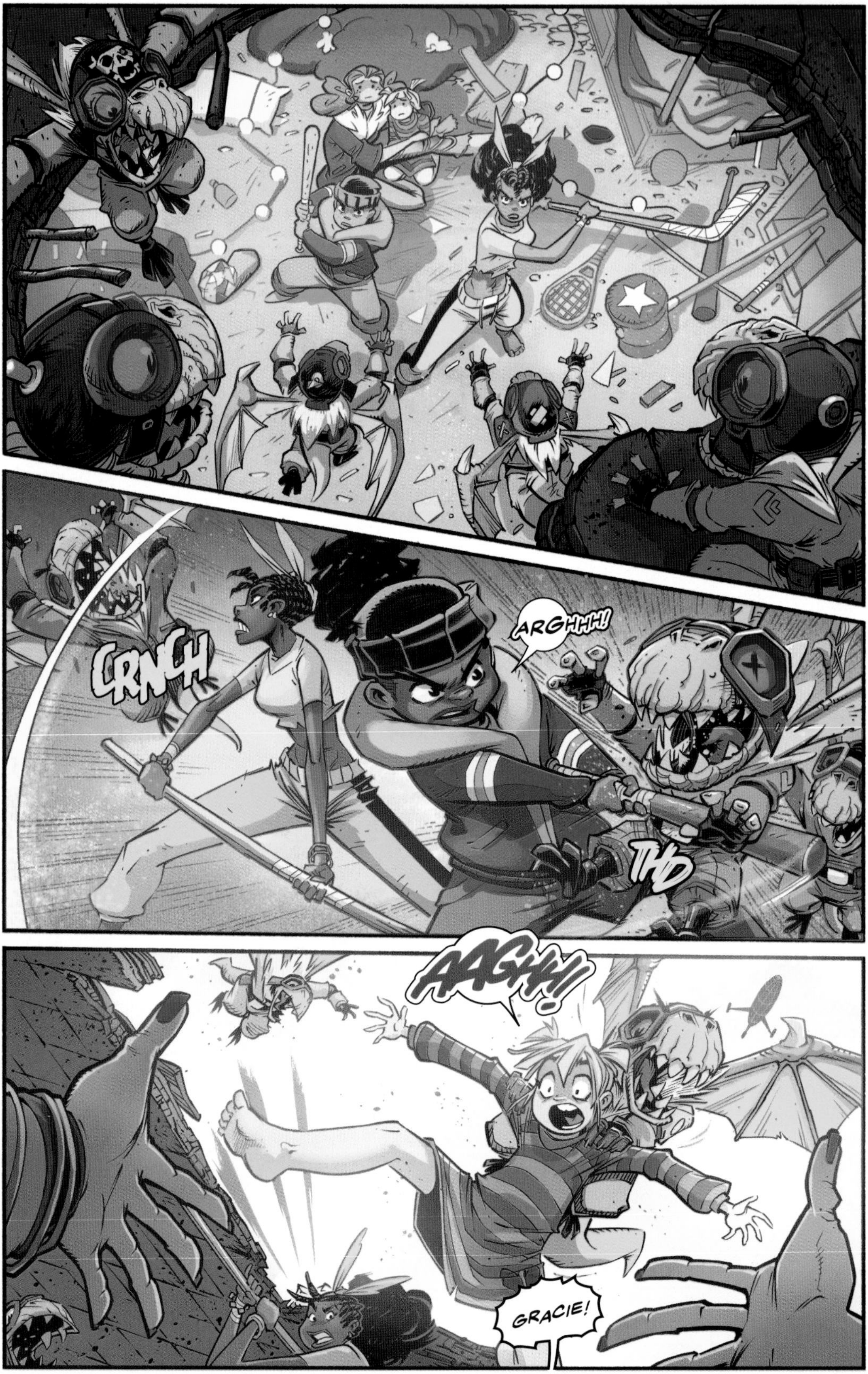
CRNCH
ARGHHH!
THD
AAGHH!
GRACIE!

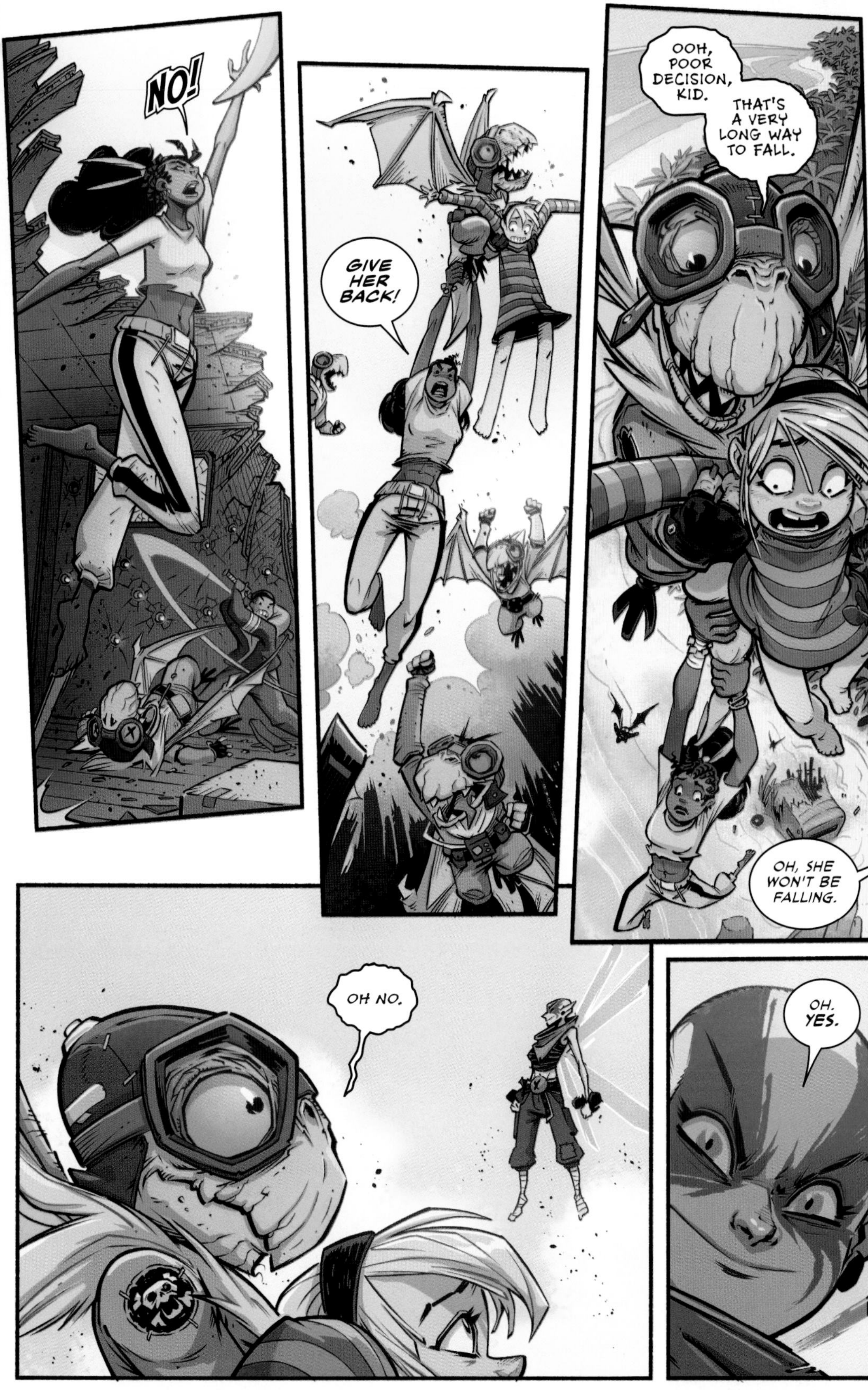
NO!
GIVE HER BACK!
OOH, POOR DECISION, KID.
THAT'S A VERY LONG WAY TO FALL.
OH, SHE WON'T BE FALLING.
OH NO.
OH. YES.

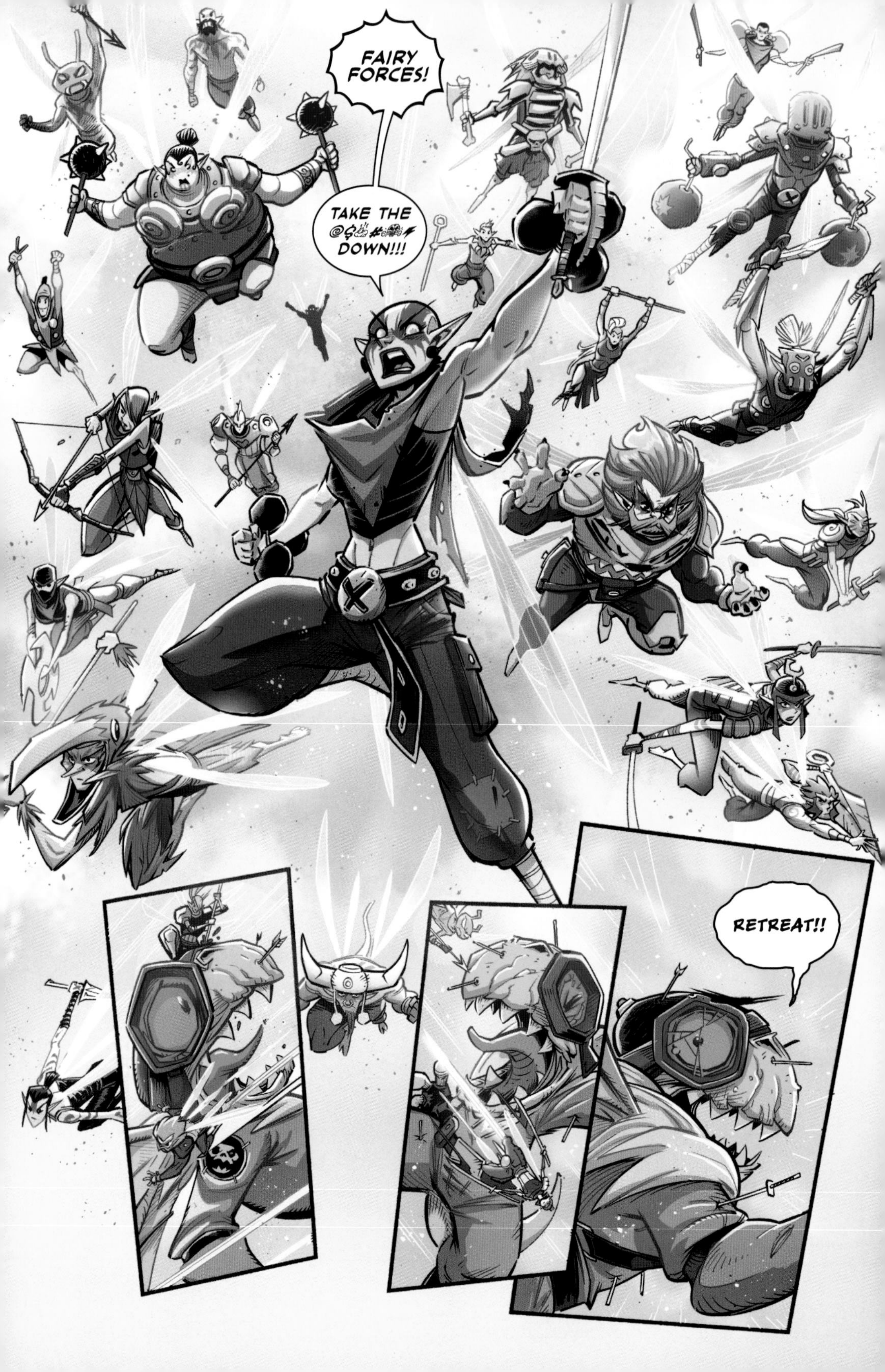
FAIRY FORCES!
TAKE THE @$#&#! DOWN!!!
RETREAT!!

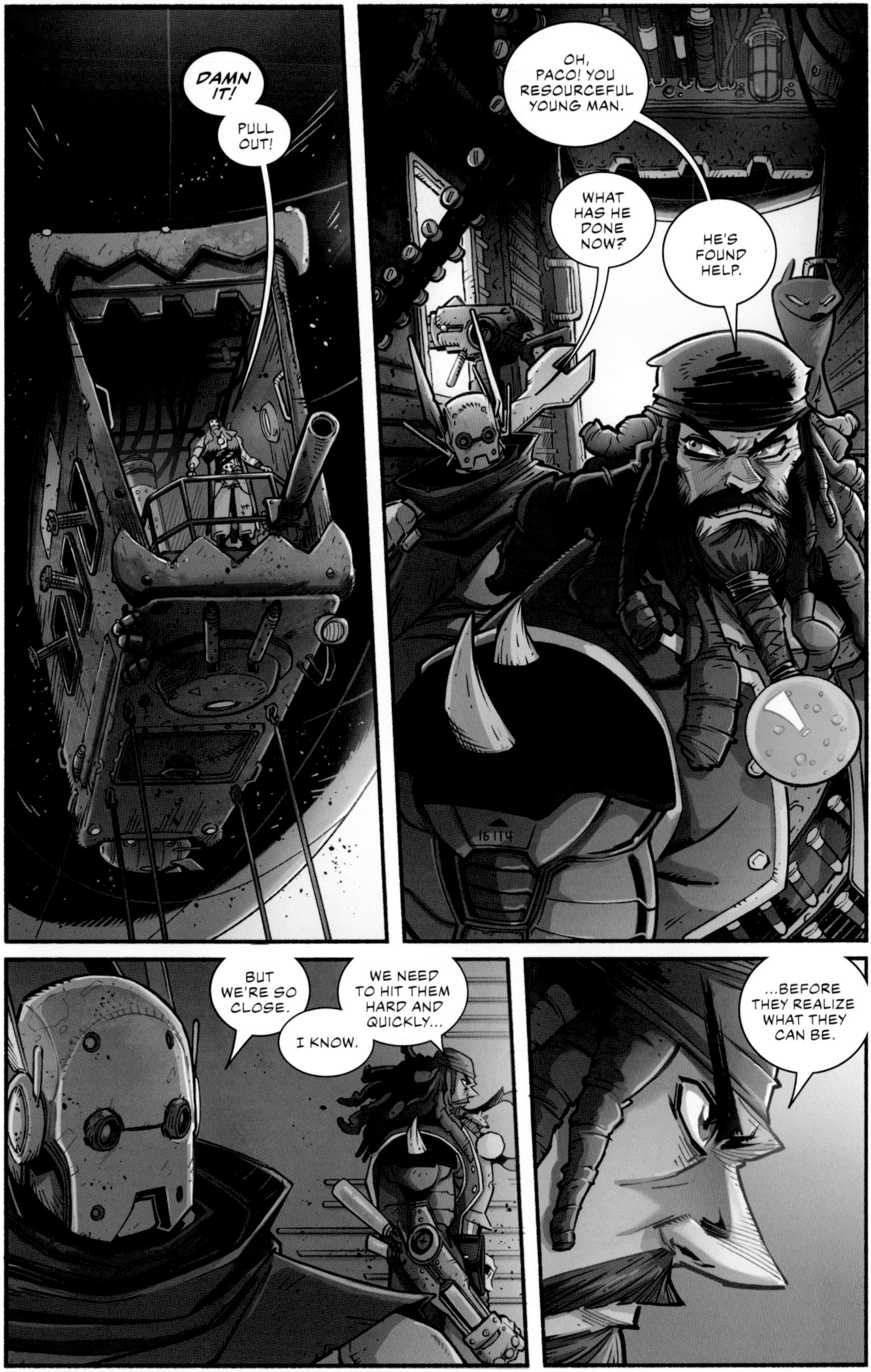
DAMN IT!
PULL OUT!
OH, PACO! YOU RESOURCEFUL YOUNG MAN.
WHAT HAS HE DONE NOW?
HE'S FOUND HELP.
16114
BUT WE'RE SO CLOSE.
I KNOW.
WE NEED TO HIT THEM HARD AND QUICKLY...
...BEFORE THEY REALIZE WHAT THEY CAN BE.

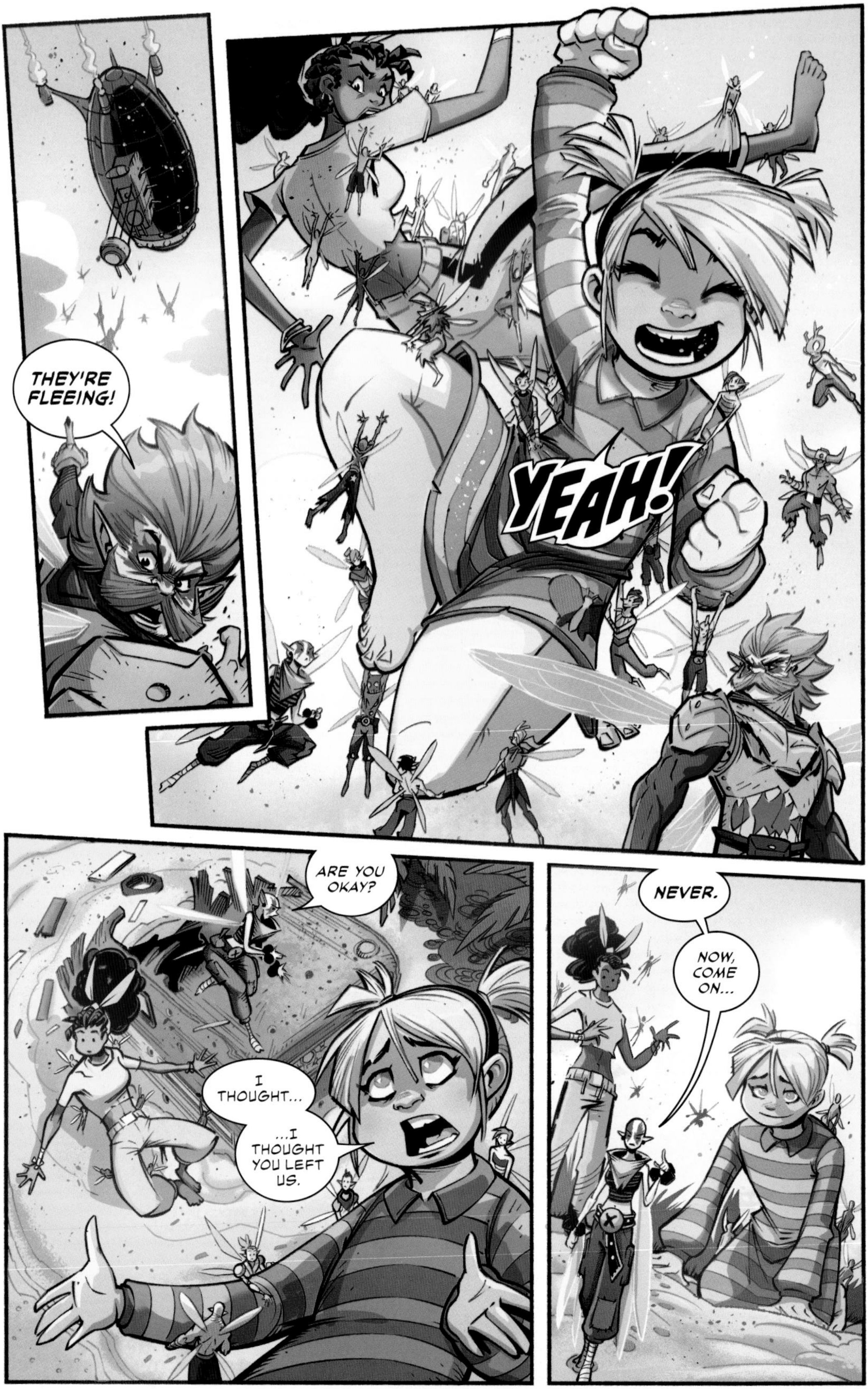

THEY'RE FLEEING!
YEAH!
ARE YOU OKAY?
I THOUGHT...
...I THOUGHT YOU LEFT US.
NEVER.
NOW, COME ON...

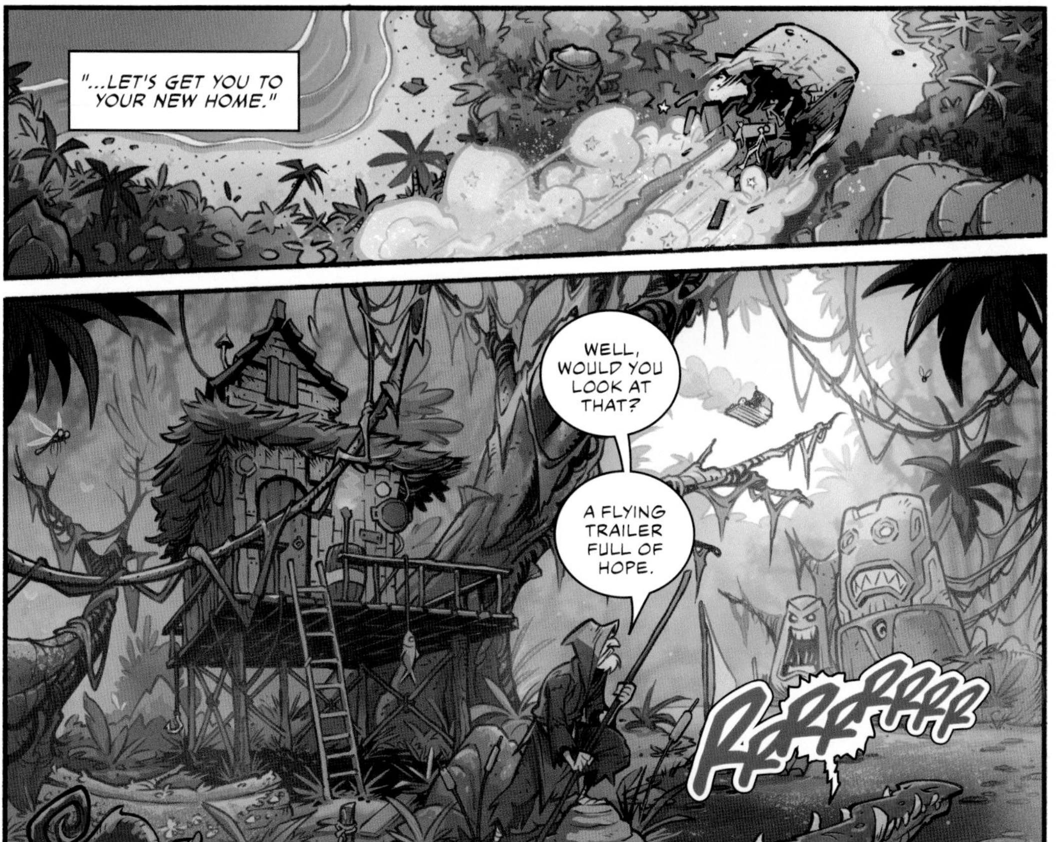
"...LET'S GET YOU TO YOUR NEW HOME."
WELL, WOULD YOU LOOK AT THAT?
A FLYING TRAILER FULL OF HOPE.
PACO ACTUALLY DID IT...
SCRTCH SCRTCH
WE'RE HERE.

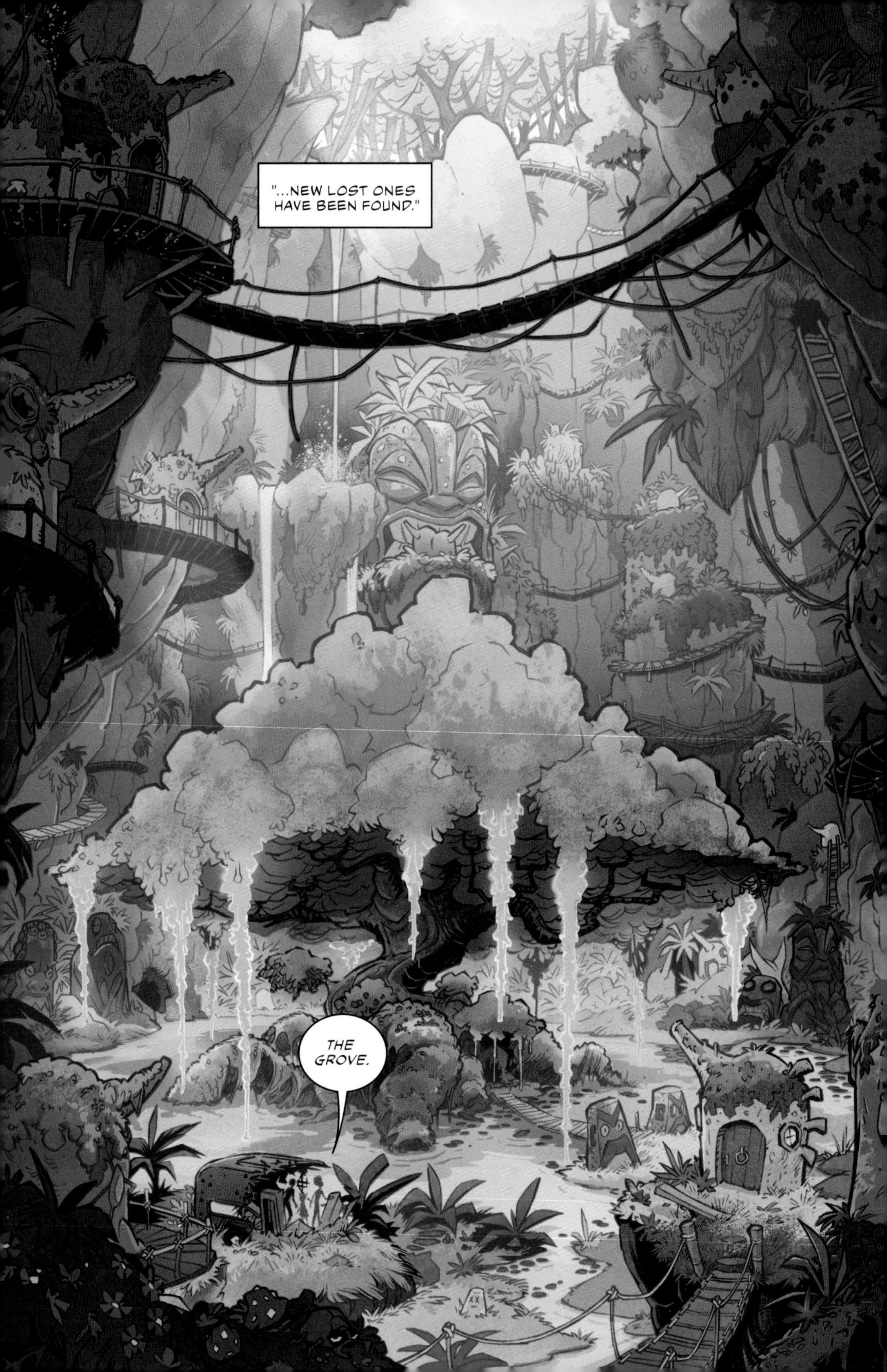
"...NEW LOST ONES HAVE BEEN FOUND."
THE GROVE.

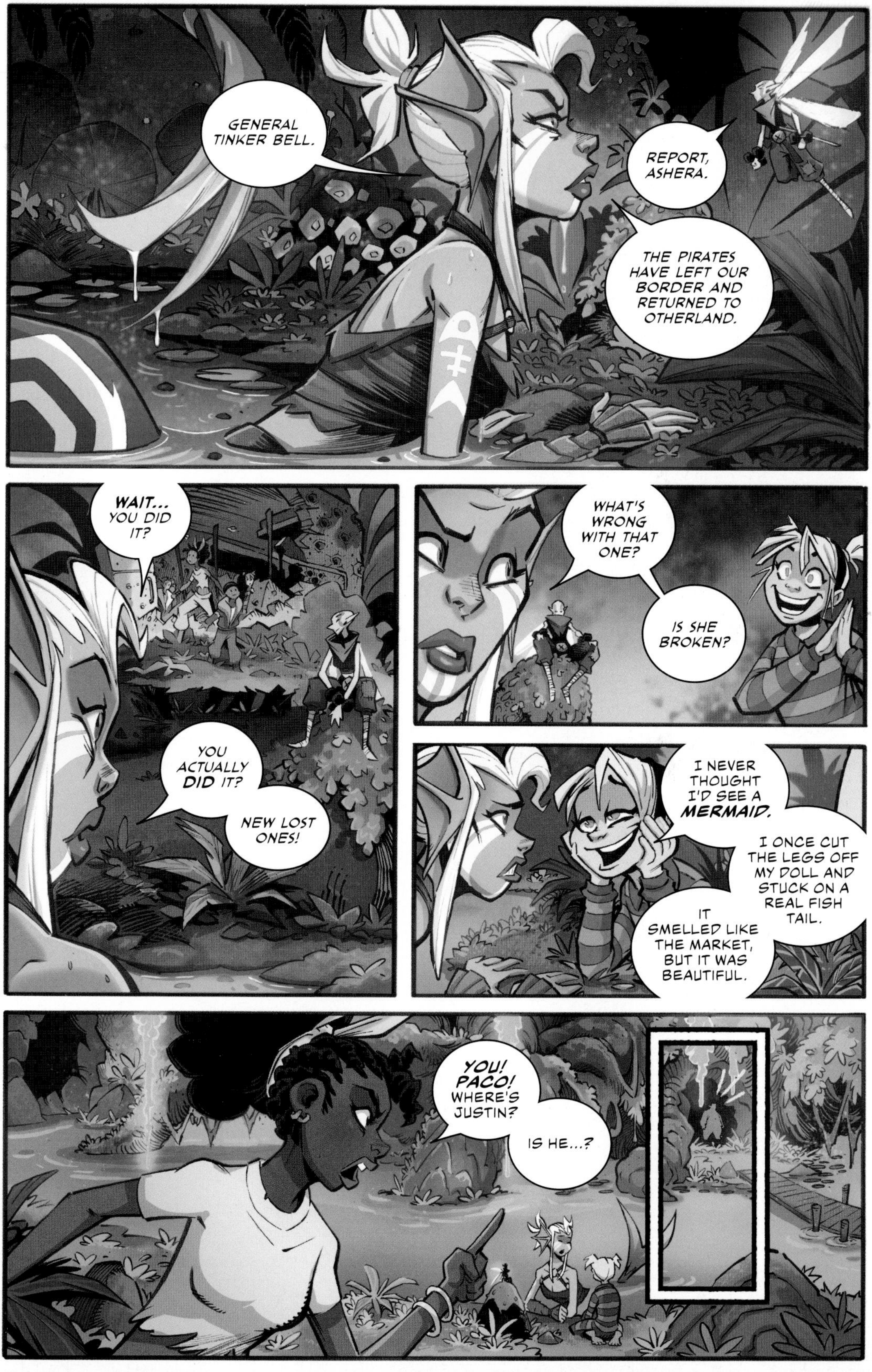
GENERAL TINKER BELL.
REPORT, ASHERA.
THE PIRATES HAVE LEFT OUR BORDER AND RETURNED TO OTHERLAND.
WAIT... YOU DID IT?
YOU ACTUALLY DID IT?
NEW LOST ONES!
WHAT'S WRONG WITH THAT ONE?
IS SHE BROKEN?
I NEVER THOUGHT I'D SEE A MERMAID.
I ONCE CUT THE LEGS OFF MY DOLL AND STUCK ON A REAL FISH TAIL.
IT SMELLED LIKE THE MARKET, BUT IT WAS BEAUTIFUL.
YOU! PACO! WHERE'S JUSTIN?
IS HE...?

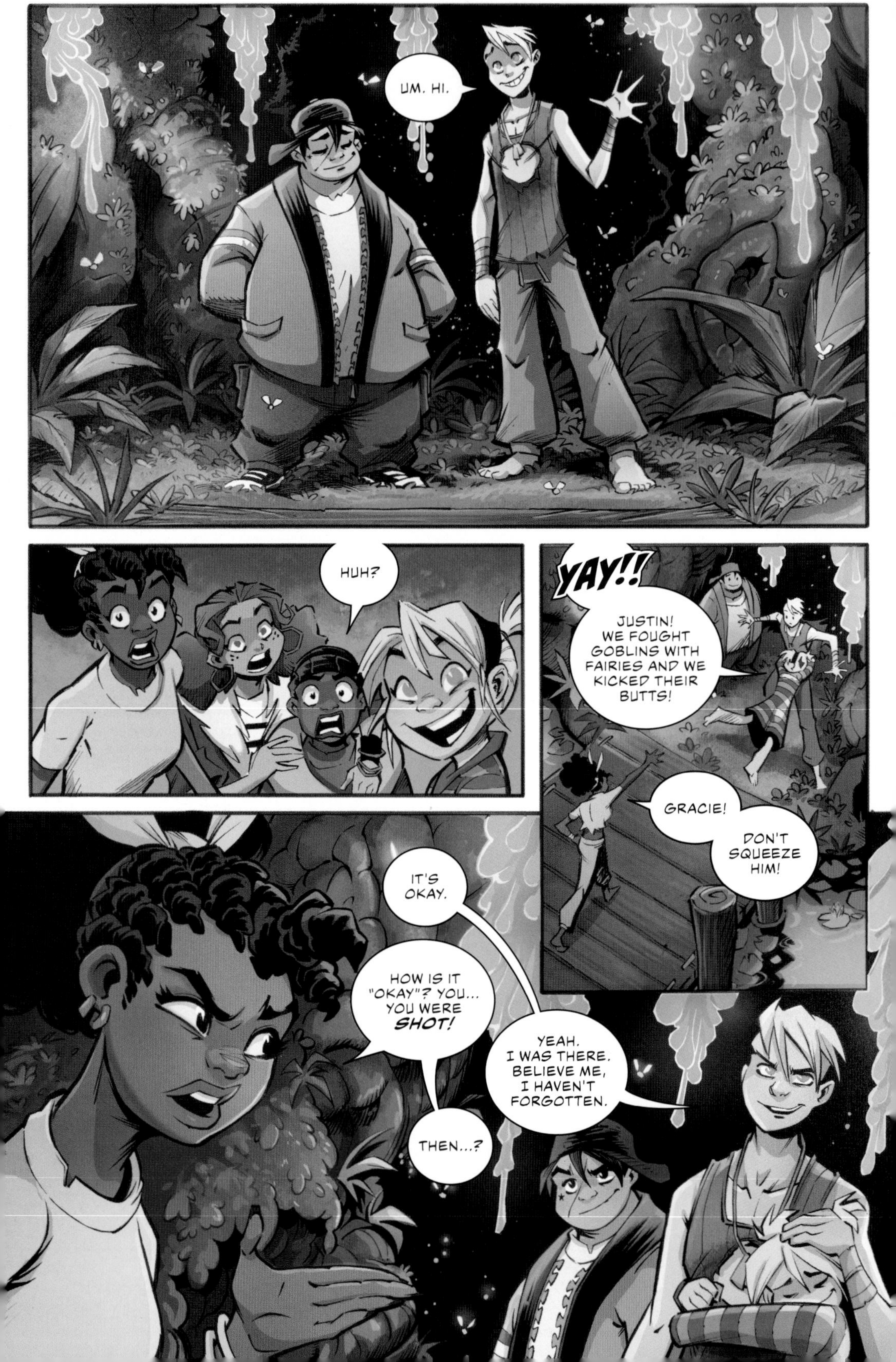
UM. HI.
HUH?
YAY!!
JUSTIN! WE FOUGHT GOBLINS WITH FAIRIES AND WE KICKED THEIR BUTTS!
GRACIE!
DON'T SQUEEZE HIM!
IT'S OKAY.
HOW IS IT "OKAY"? YOU... YOU WERE *SHOT!*
YEAH. I WAS THERE. BELIEVE ME, I HAVEN'T FORGOTTEN.
THEN...?

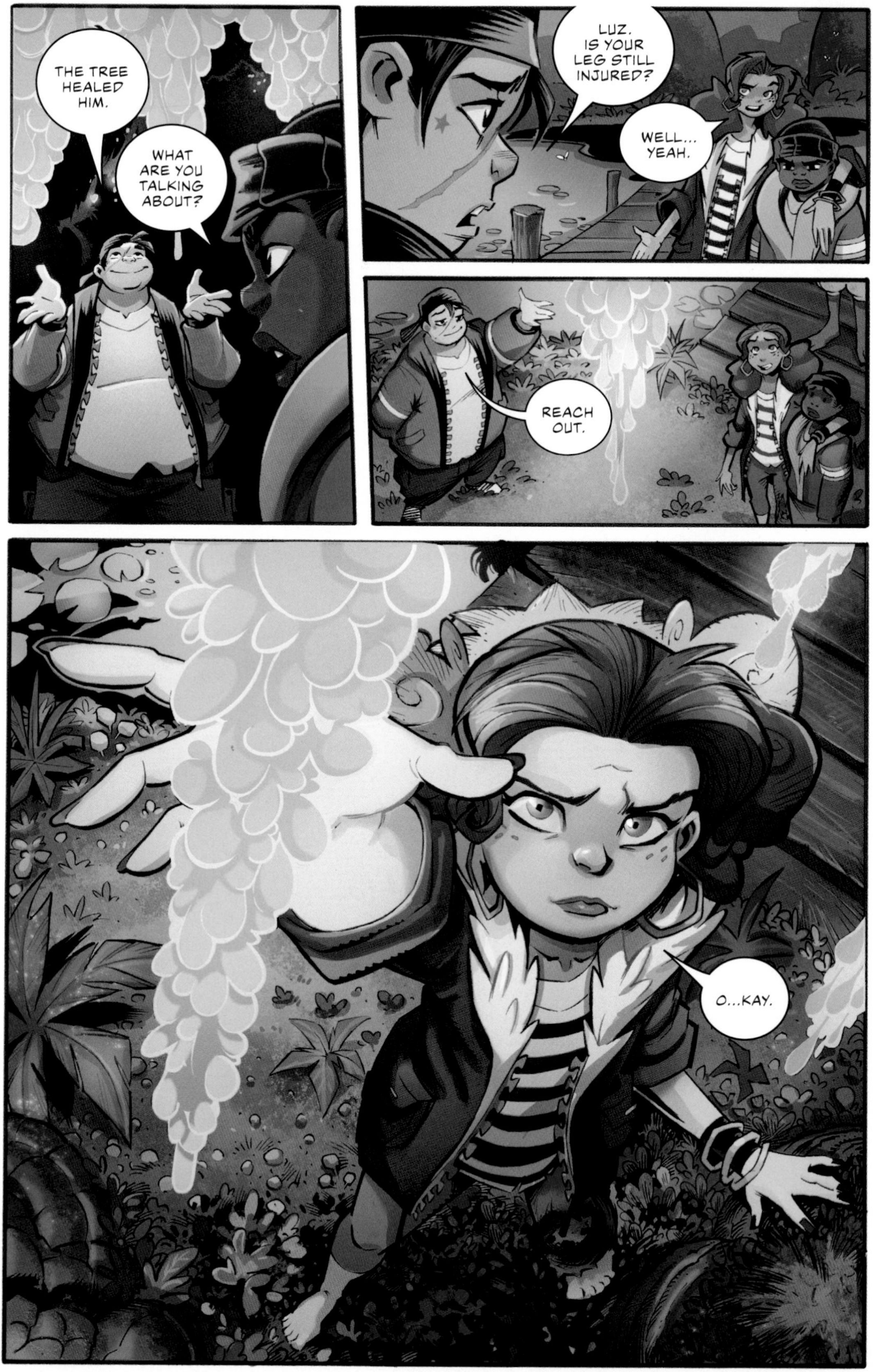
THE TREE HEALED HIM.
WHAT ARE YOU TALKING ABOUT?
LUZ. IS YOUR LEG STILL INJURED?
WELL... YEAH.
REACH OUT.
O...KAY.

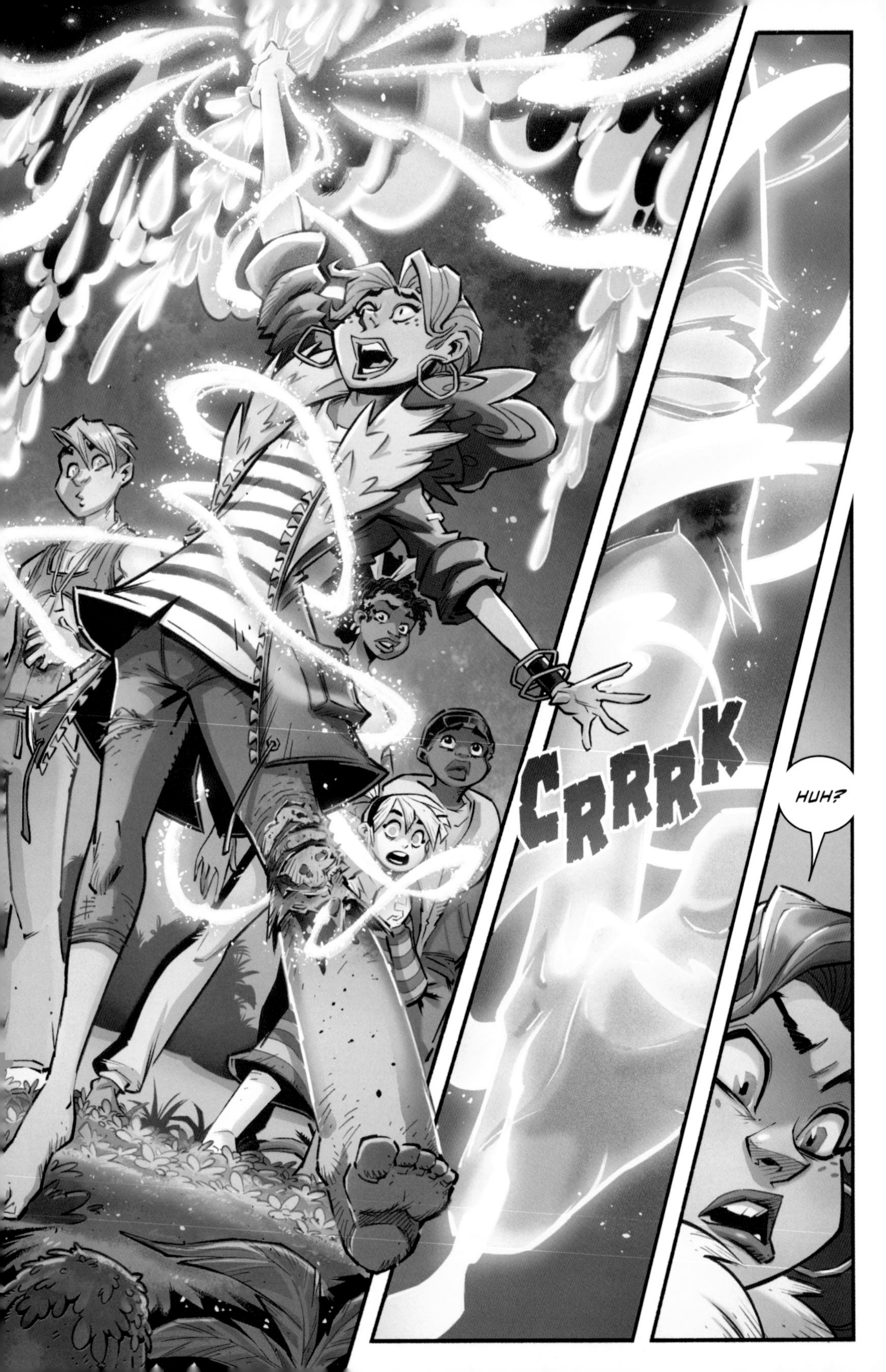
CRRRK
HUH?

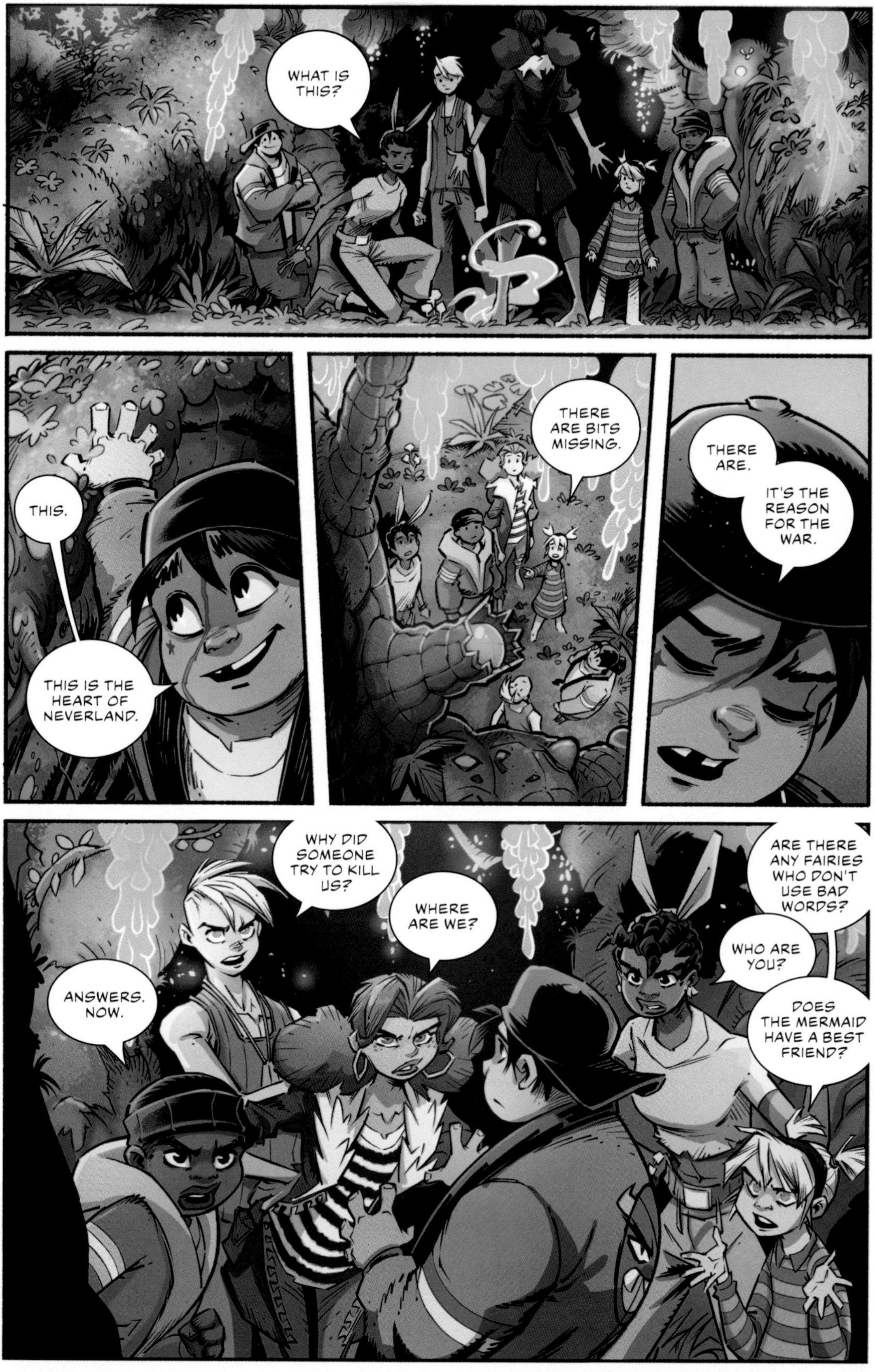
WHAT IS THIS?
THIS.
THIS IS THE HEART OF NEVERLAND.
THERE ARE BITS MISSING.
THERE ARE.
IT'S THE REASON FOR THE WAR.
WHY DID SOMEONE TRY TO KILL US?
WHERE ARE WE?
ARE THERE ANY FAIRIES WHO DON'T USE BAD WORDS?
WHO ARE YOU?
DOES THE MERMAID HAVE A BEST FRIEND?
ANSWERS. NOW.

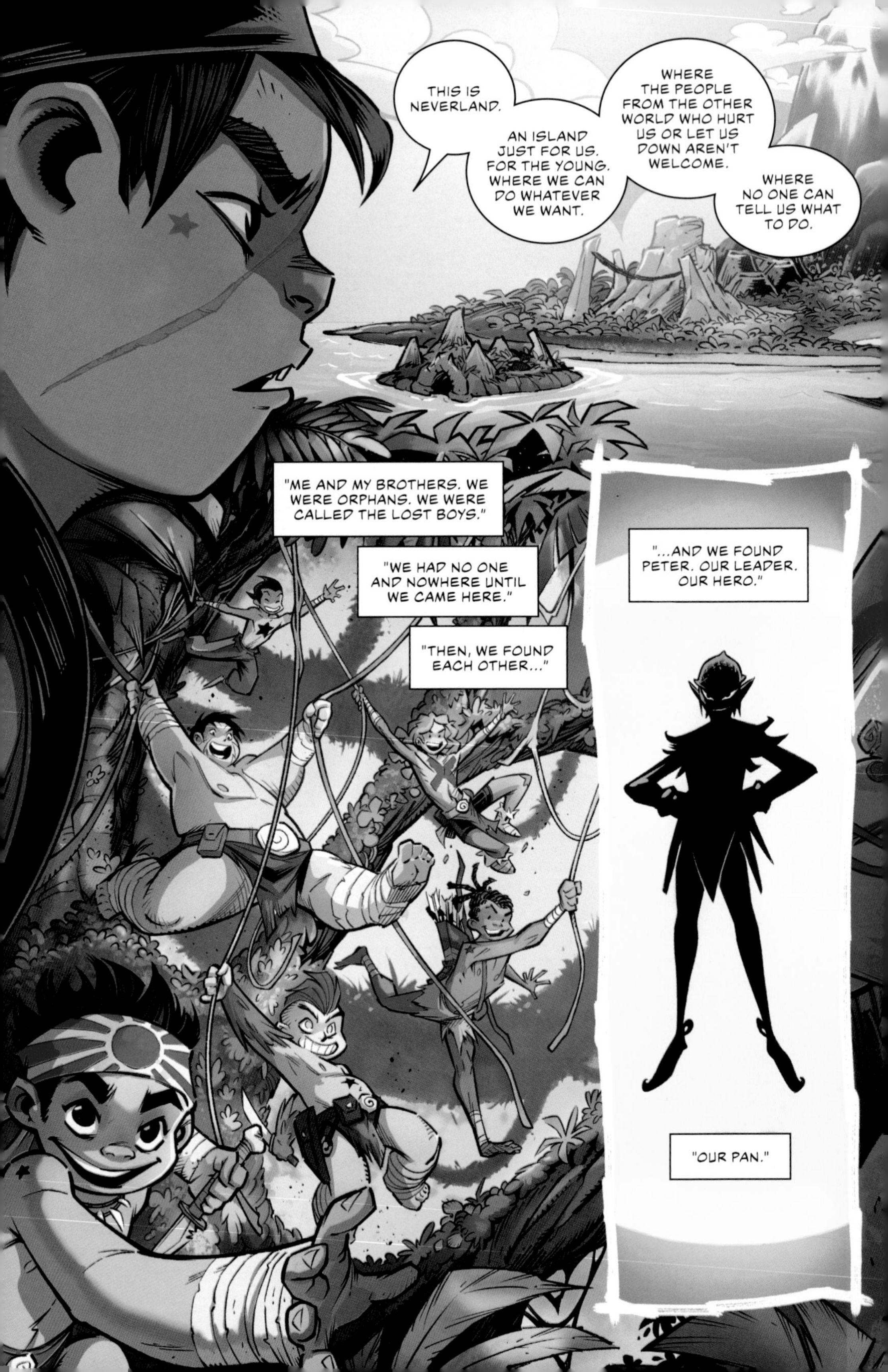
THIS IS NEVERLAND.
AN ISLAND JUST FOR US. FOR THE YOUNG. WHERE WE CAN DO WHATEVER WE WANT.
WHERE THE PEOPLE FROM THE OTHER WORLD WHO HURT US OR LET US DOWN AREN'T WELCOME.
WHERE NO ONE CAN TELL US WHAT TO DO.
"ME AND MY BROTHERS. WE WERE ORPHANS. WE WERE CALLED THE LOST BOYS."
"WE HAD NO ONE AND NOWHERE UNTIL WE CAME HERE."
"THEN, WE FOUND EACH OTHER..."
"...AND WE FOUND PETER. OUR LEADER. OUR HERO."
"OUR PAN."

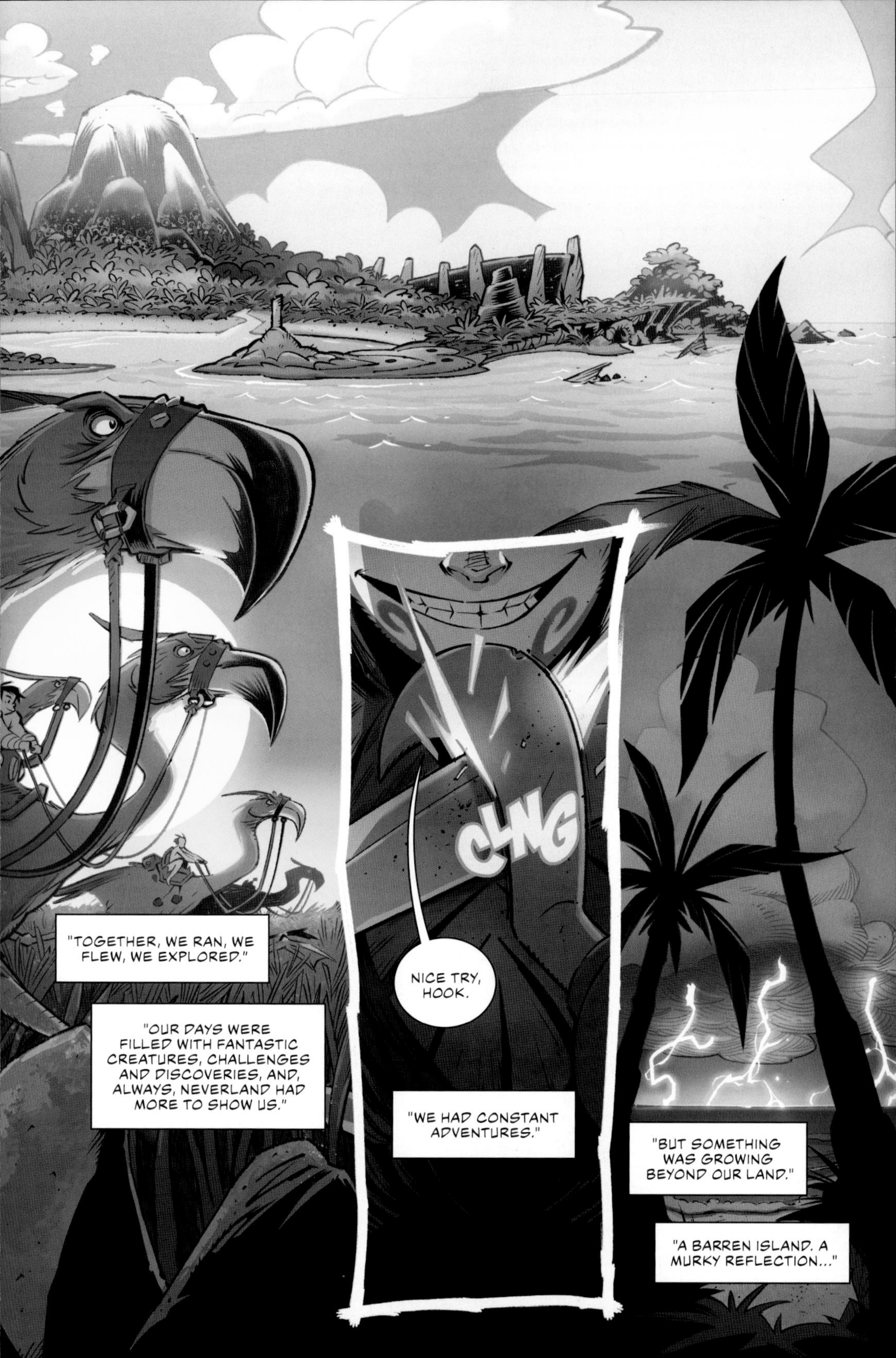
CLING
"TOGETHER, WE RAN, WE FLEW, WE EXPLORED."
"OUR DAYS WERE FILLED WITH FANTASTIC CREATURES, CHALLENGES AND DISCOVERIES, AND, ALWAYS, NEVERLAND HAD MORE TO SHOW US."
NICE TRY, HOOK.
"WE HAD CONSTANT ADVENTURES."
"BUT SOMETHING WAS GROWING BEYOND OUR LAND."
"A BARREN ISLAND. A MURKY REFLECTION..."

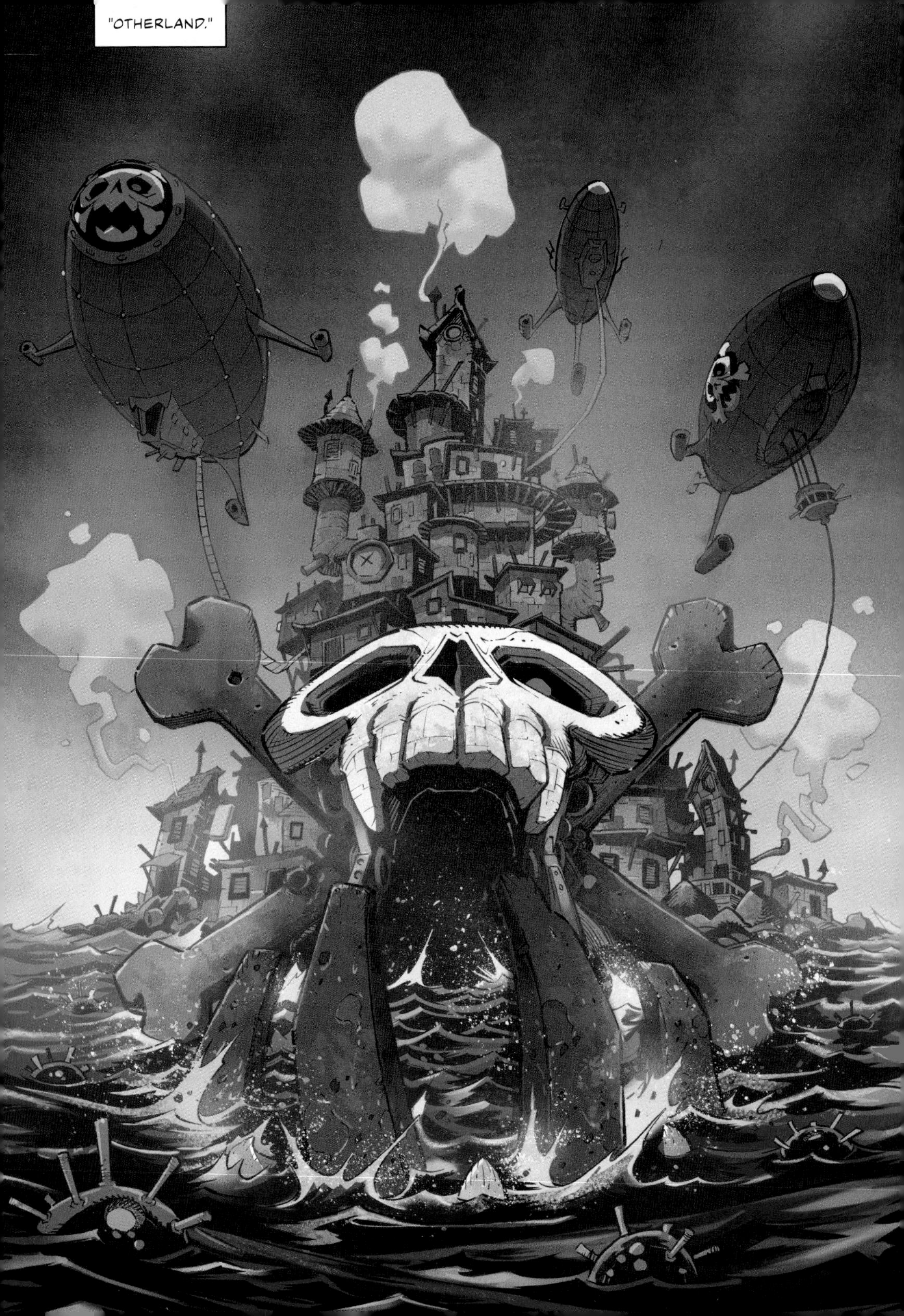
"OTHERLAND."

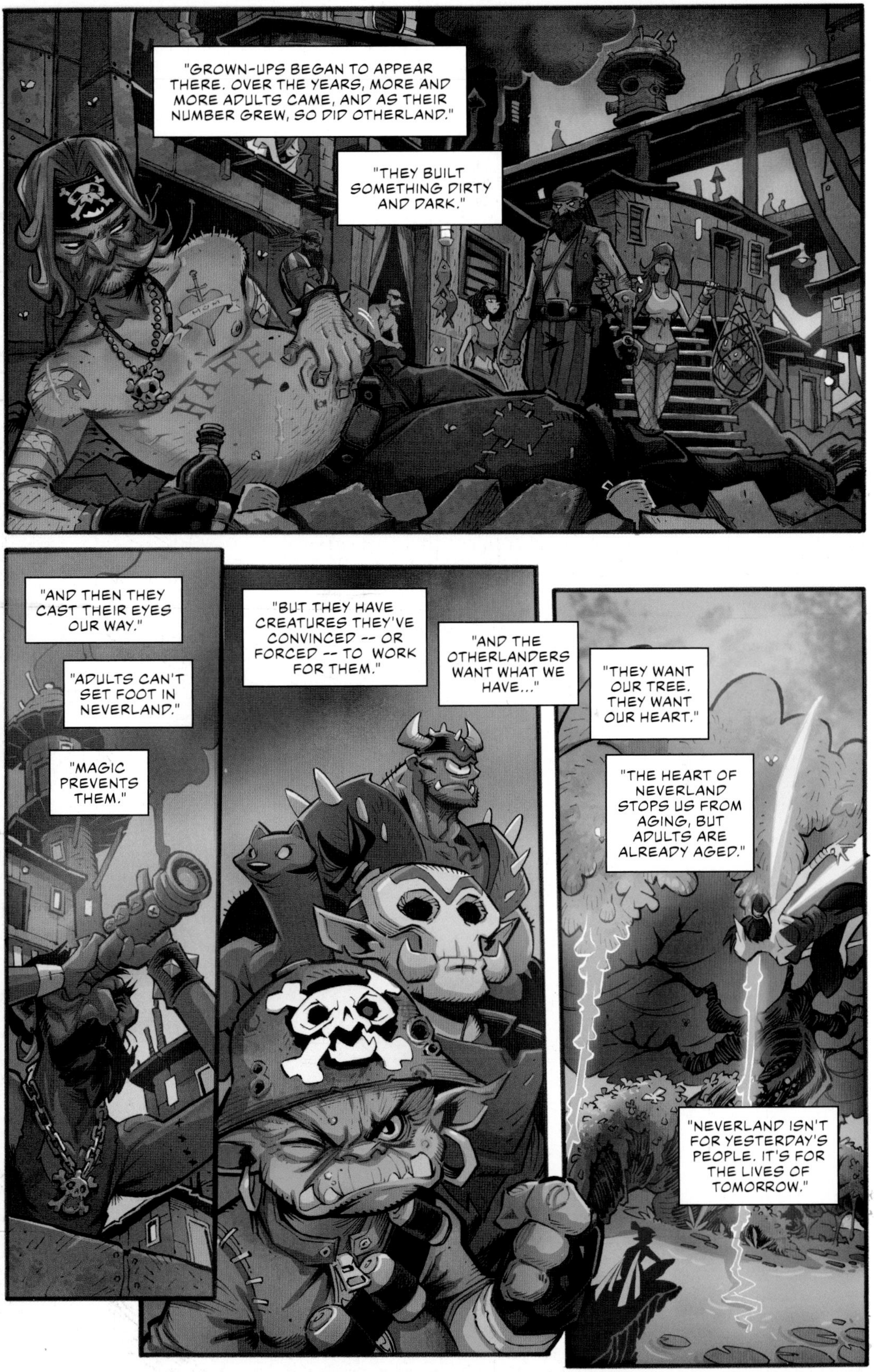
"GROWN-UPS BEGAN TO APPEAR THERE. OVER THE YEARS, MORE AND MORE ADULTS CAME, AND AS THEIR NUMBER GREW, SO DID OTHERLAND."
"THEY BUILT SOMETHING DIRTY AND DARK."
"AND THEN THEY CAST THEIR EYES OUR WAY."
"ADULTS CAN'T SET FOOT IN NEVERLAND."
"MAGIC PREVENTS THEM."
"BUT THEY HAVE CREATURES THEY'VE CONVINCED -- OR FORCED -- TO WORK FOR THEM."
"AND THE OTHERLANDERS WANT WHAT WE HAVE..."
"THEY WANT OUR TREE. THEY WANT OUR HEART."
"THE HEART OF NEVERLAND STOPS US FROM AGING, BUT ADULTS ARE ALREADY AGED."
"NEVERLAND ISN'T FOR YESTERDAY'S PEOPLE. IT'S FOR THE LIVES OF TOMORROW."

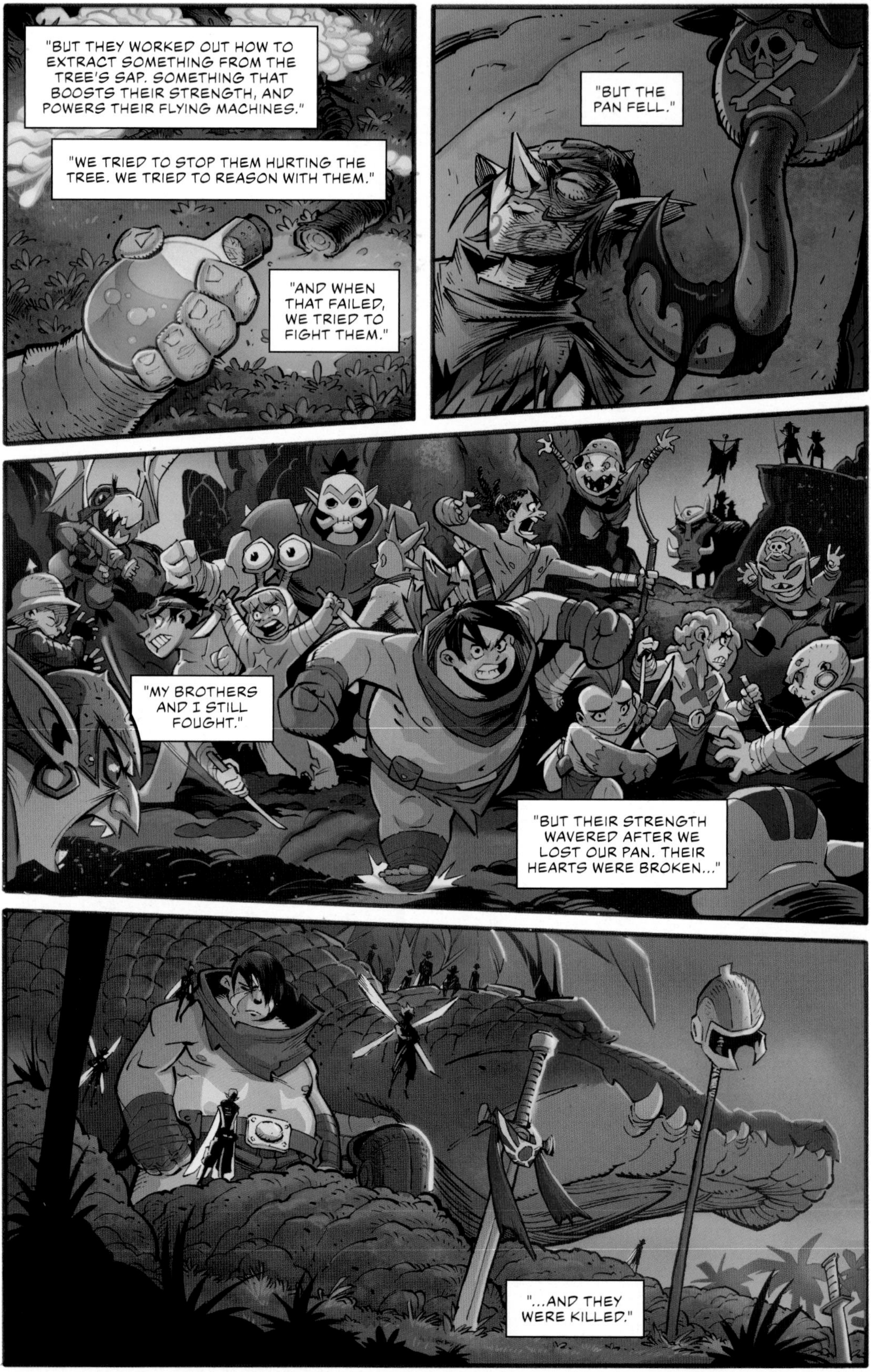
"BUT THEY WORKED OUT HOW TO EXTRACT SOMETHING FROM THE TREE'S SAP. SOMETHING THAT BOOSTS THEIR STRENGTH, AND POWERS THEIR FLYING MACHINES."
"WE TRIED TO STOP THEM HURTING THE TREE. WE TRIED TO REASON WITH THEM."
"AND WHEN THAT FAILED, WE TRIED TO FIGHT THEM."
"BUT THE PAN FELL."
"MY BROTHERS AND I STILL FOUGHT."
"BUT THEIR STRENGTH WAVERED AFTER WE LOST OUR PAN. THEIR HEARTS WERE BROKEN..."
"...AND THEY WERE KILLED."

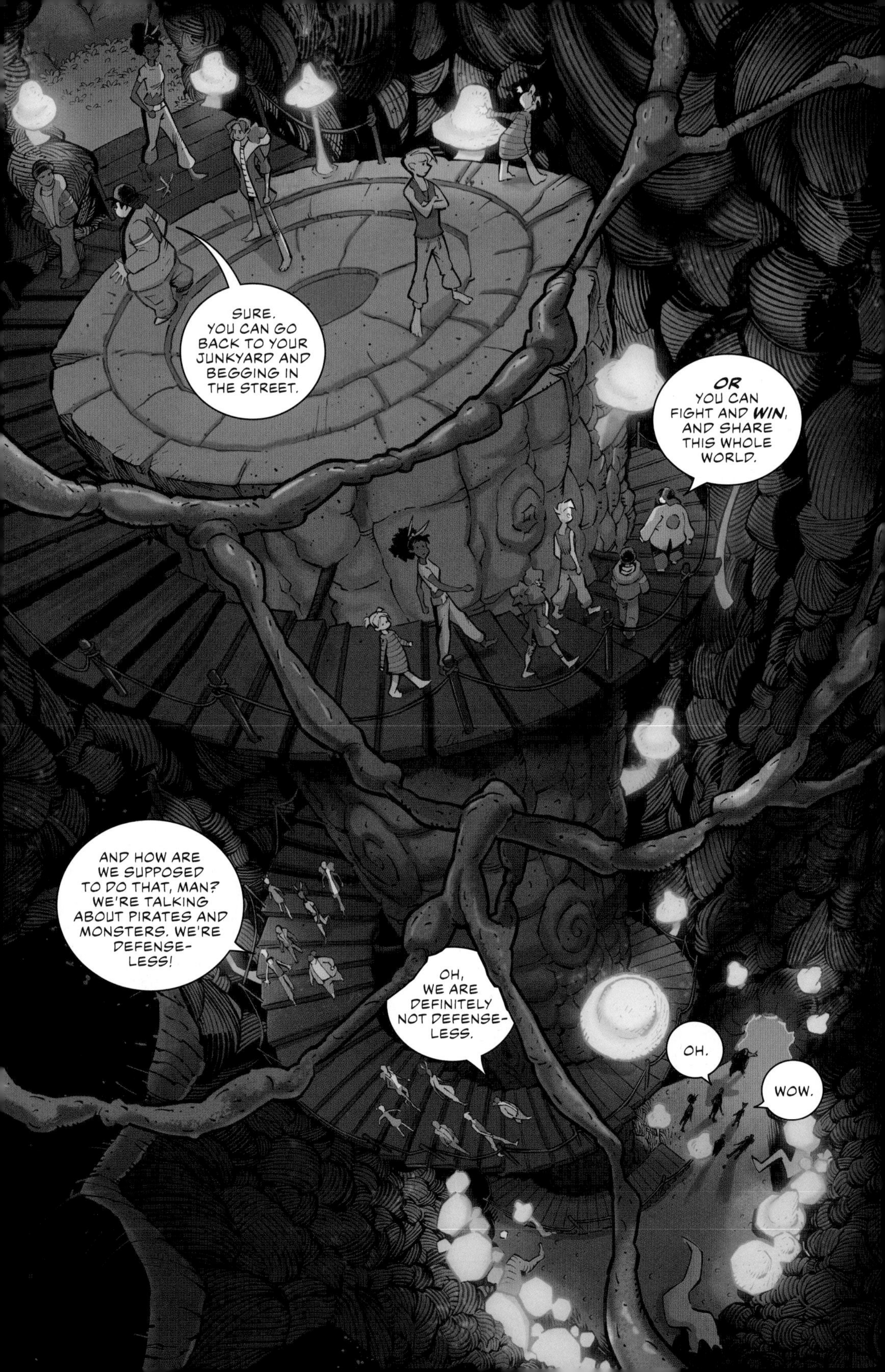
SURE. YOU CAN GO BACK TO YOUR JUNKYARD AND BEGGING IN THE STREET.
OR YOU CAN FIGHT AND WIN, AND SHARE THIS WHOLE WORLD.
AND HOW ARE WE SUPPOSED TO DO THAT, MAN? WE'RE TALKING ABOUT PIRATES AND MONSTERS. WE'RE DEFENSE-LESS!
OH, WE ARE DEFINITELY NOT DEFENSE-LESS.
OH.
WOW.

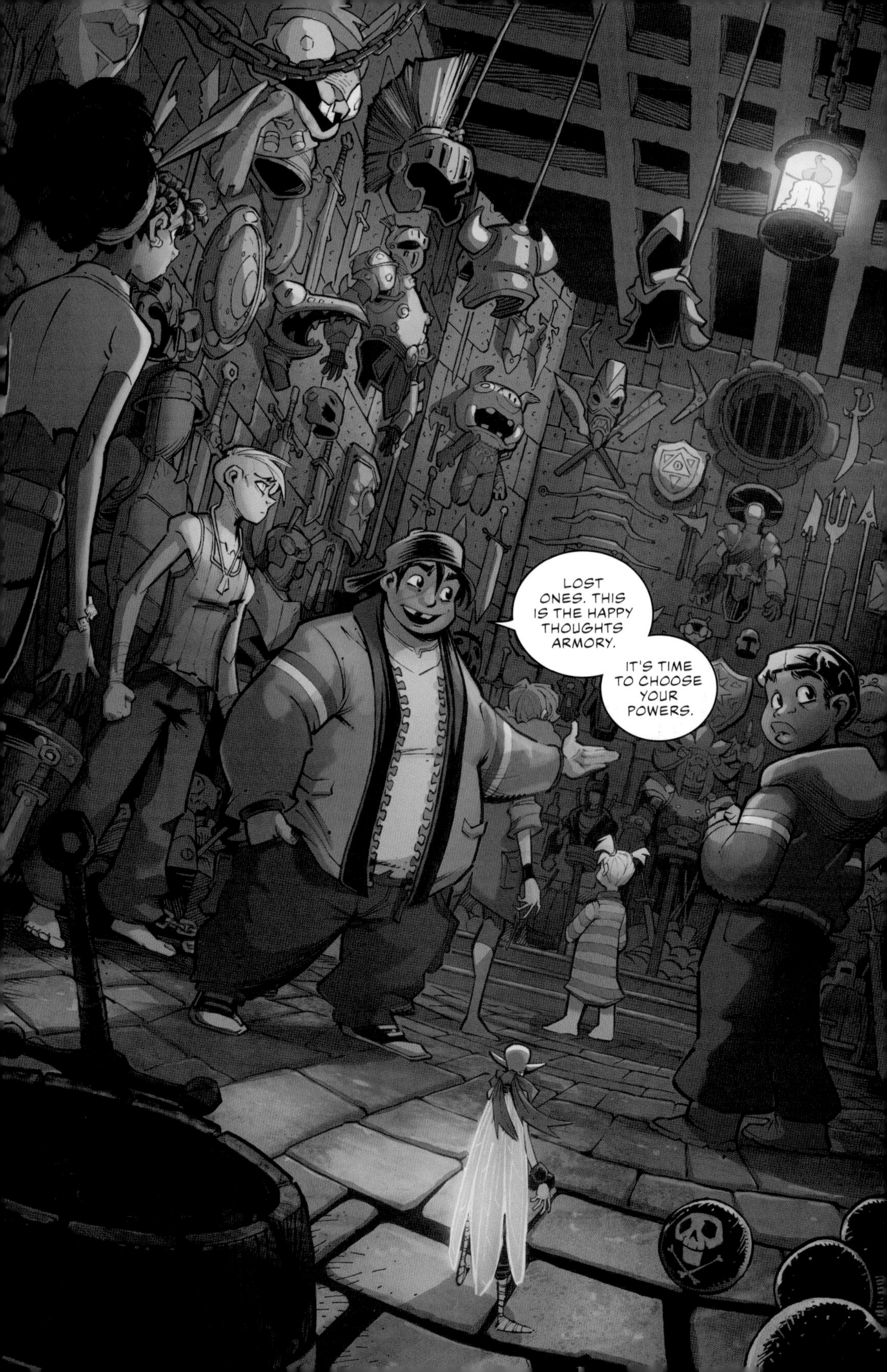
LOST ONES. THIS IS THE HAPPY THOUGHTS ARMORY.
IT'S TIME TO CHOOSE YOUR POWERS.

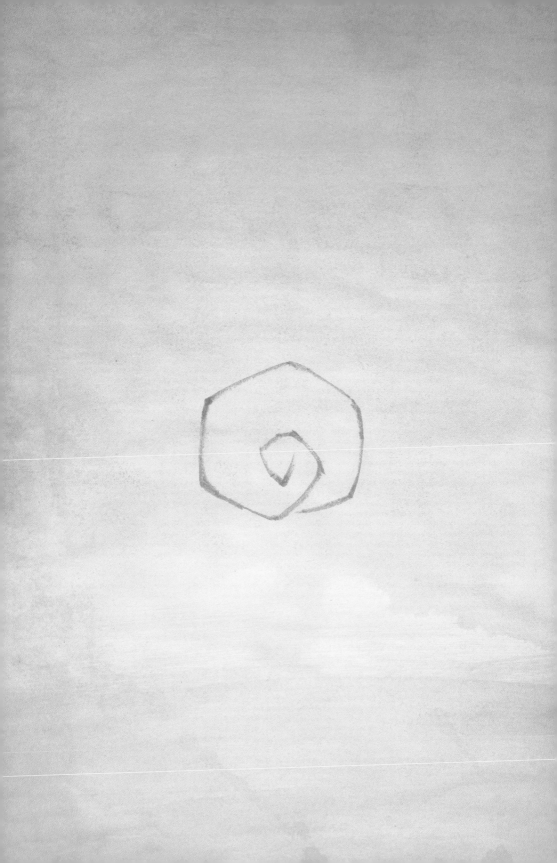

CHAPTER

THREE

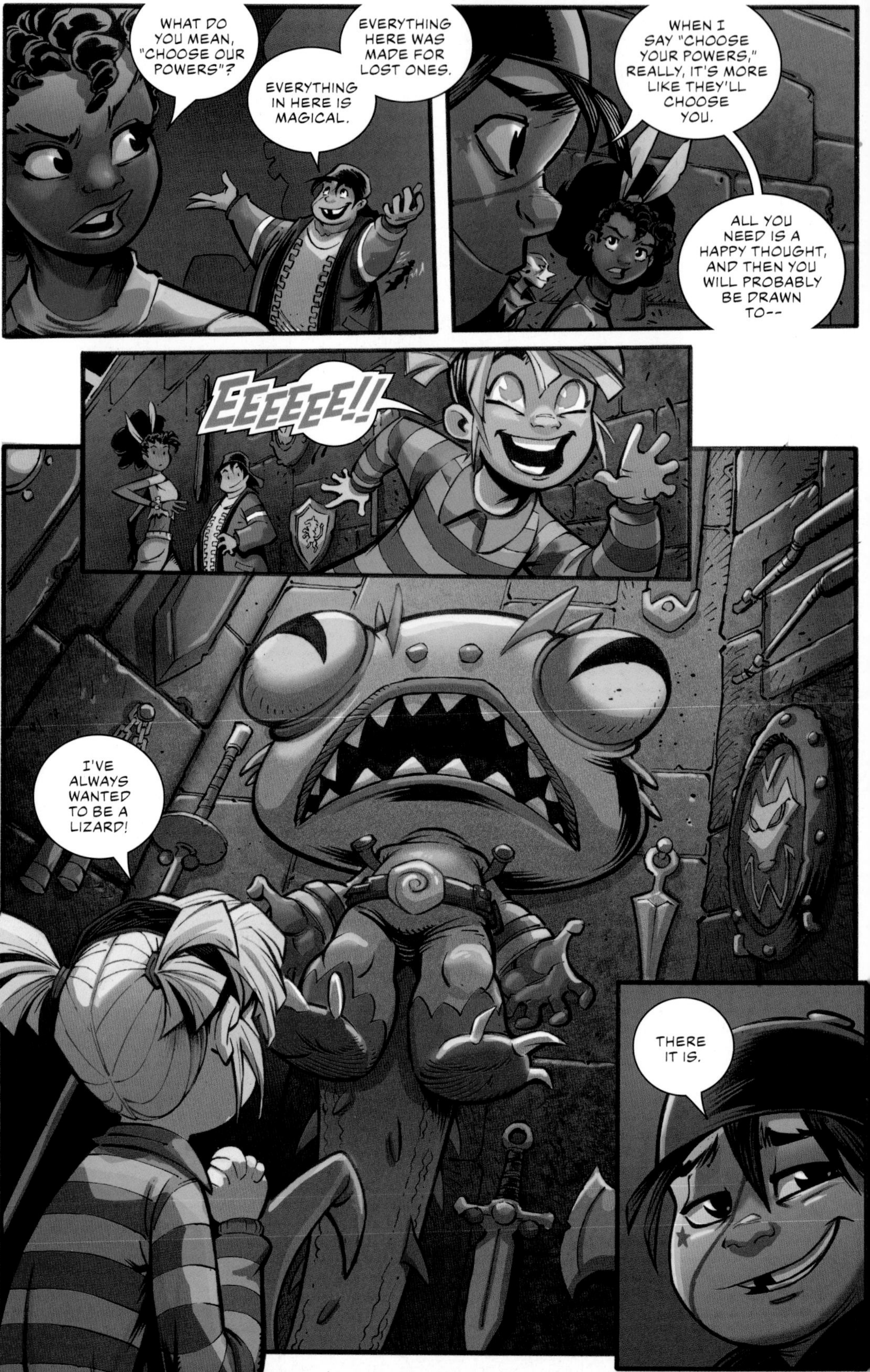
WHAT DO YOU MEAN, "CHOOSE OUR POWERS"?
EVERYTHING HERE WAS MADE FOR LOST ONES.
EVERYTHING IN HERE IS MAGICAL.
WHEN I SAY "CHOOSE YOUR POWERS," REALLY, IT'S MORE LIKE THEY'LL CHOOSE YOU.
ALL YOU NEED IS A HAPPY THOUGHT, AND THEN YOU WILL PROBABLY BE DRAWN TO--
EEEEEE!!
I'VE ALWAYS WANTED TO BE A LIZARD!
THERE IT IS.

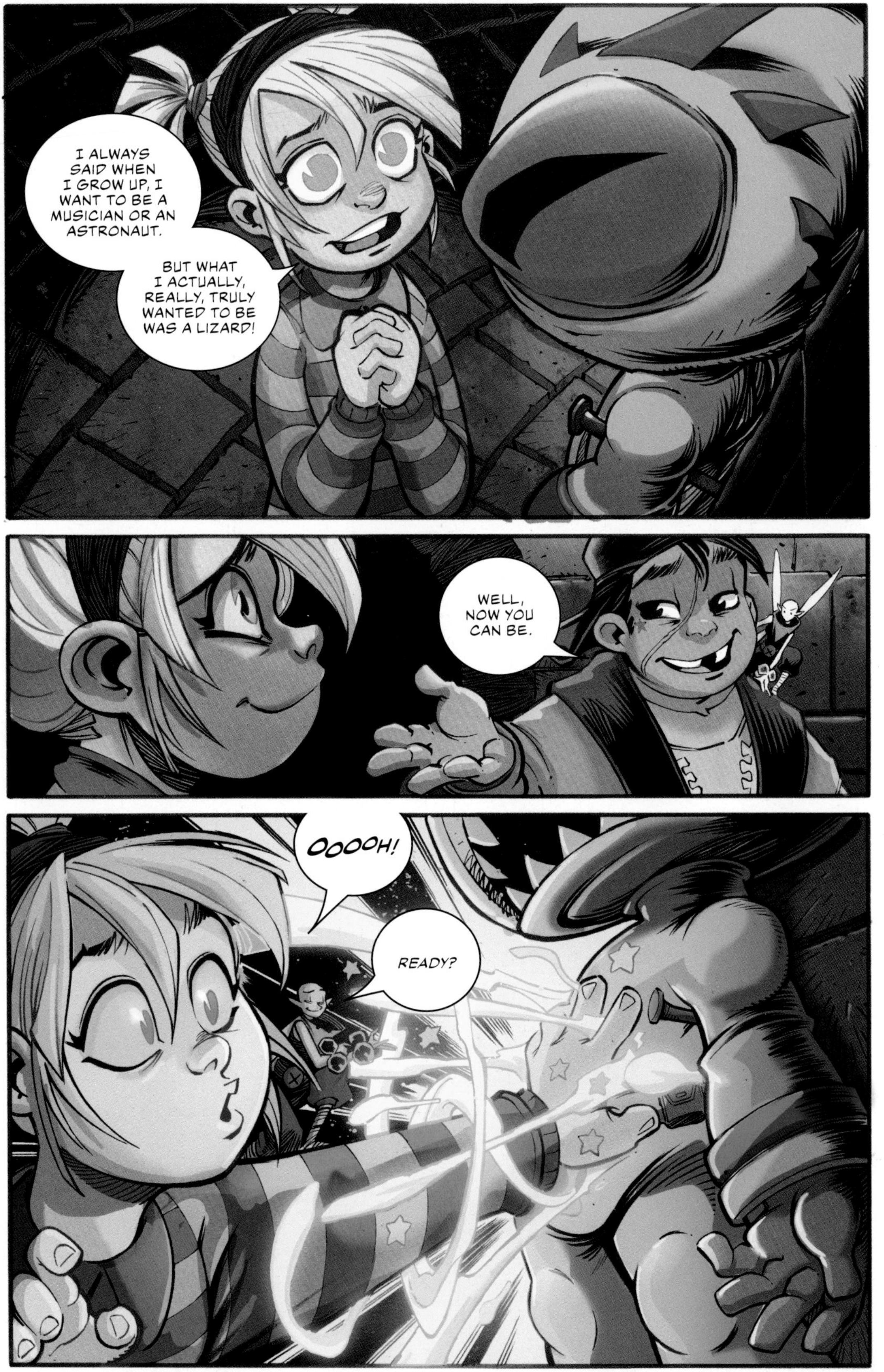

I ALWAYS SAID WHEN I GROW UP, I WANT TO BE A MUSICIAN OR AN ASTRONAUT.
BUT WHAT I ACTUALLY, REALLY, TRULY WANTED TO BE WAS A LIZARD!
WELL, NOW YOU CAN BE.
OOOOH!
READY?

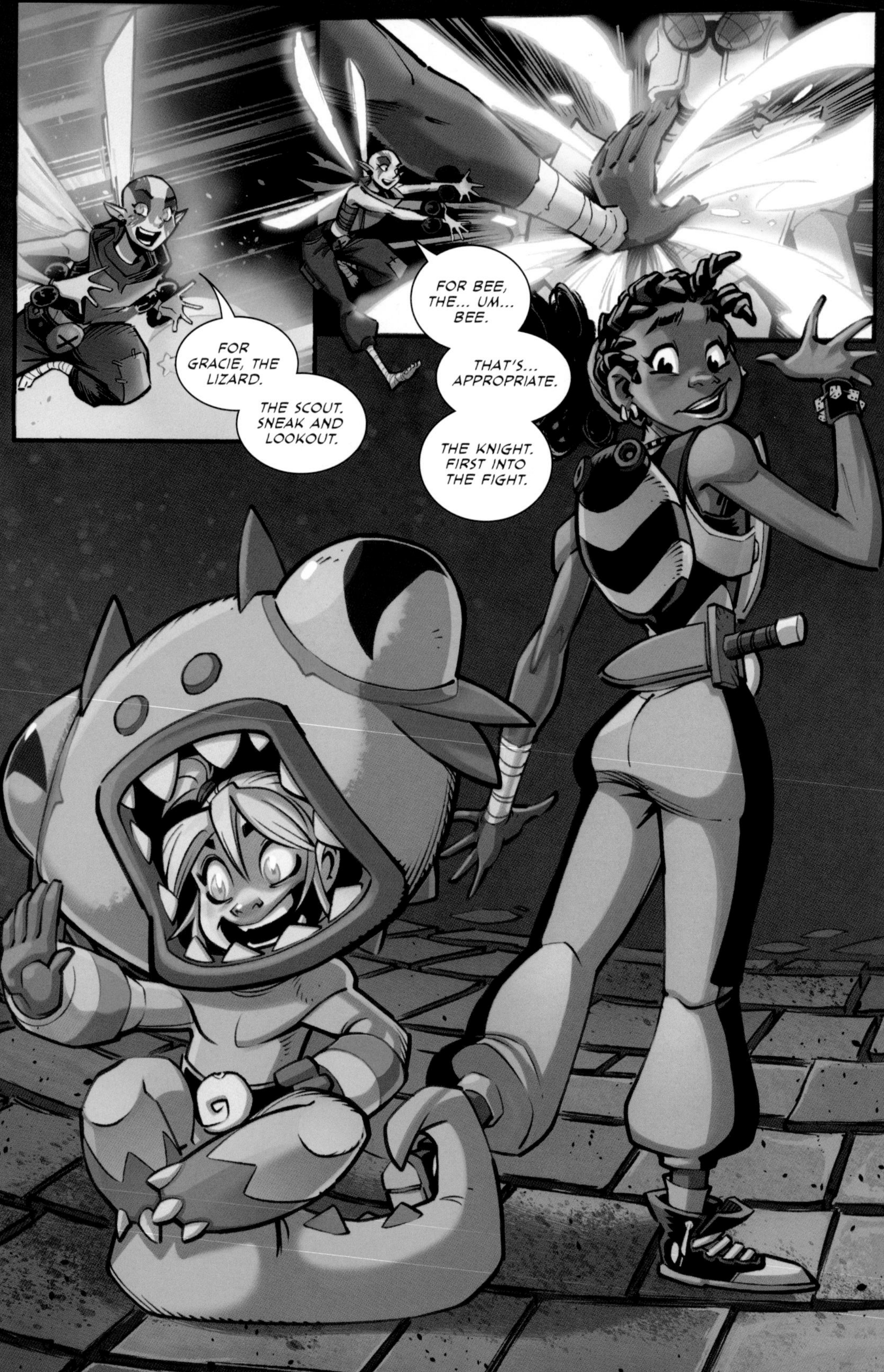
FOR GRACIE, THE LIZARD.
THE SCOUT. SNEAK AND LOOKOUT.
FOR BEE, THE... UM... BEE.
THAT'S... APPROPRIATE.
THE KNIGHT. FIRST INTO THE FIGHT.

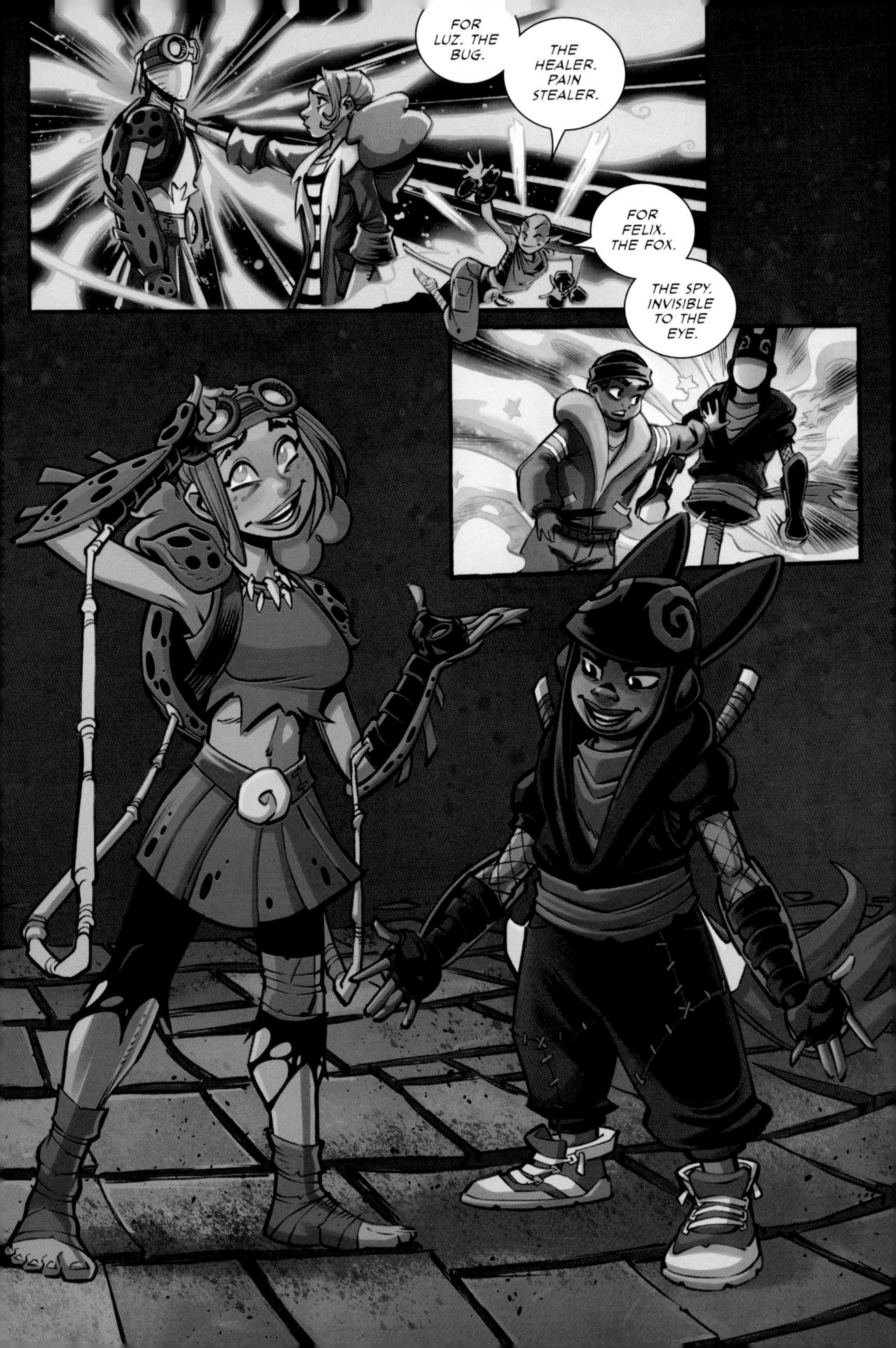
FOR LUZ. THE BUG.
THE HEALER. PAIN STEALER.
FOR FELIX. THE FOX.
THE SPY. INVISIBLE TO THE EYE.

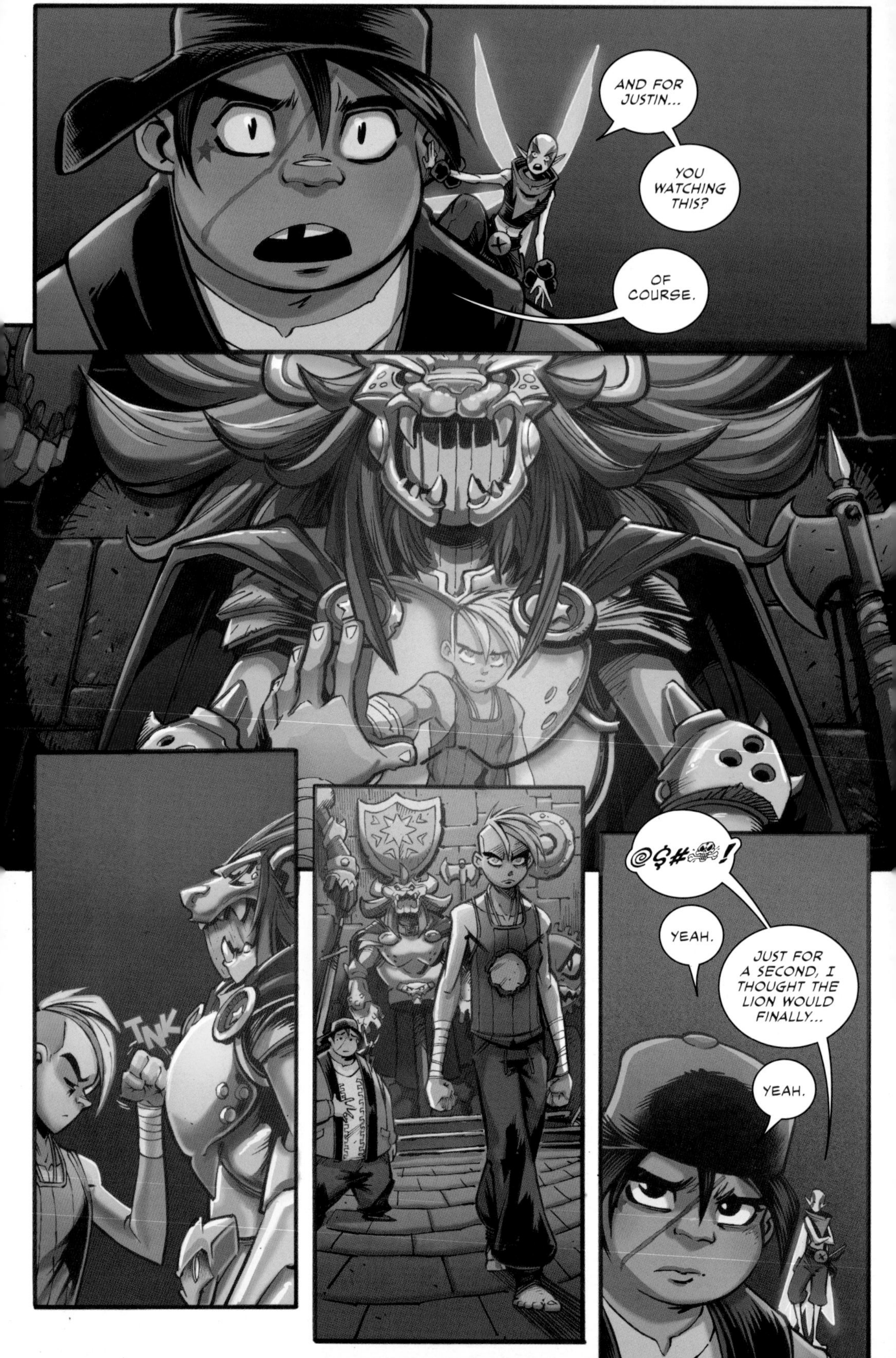
AND FOR JUSTIN...
YOU WATCHING THIS?
OF COURSE.
TNK
@$#☠!
YEAH.
JUST FOR A SECOND, I THOUGHT THE LION WOULD FINALLY...
YEAH.

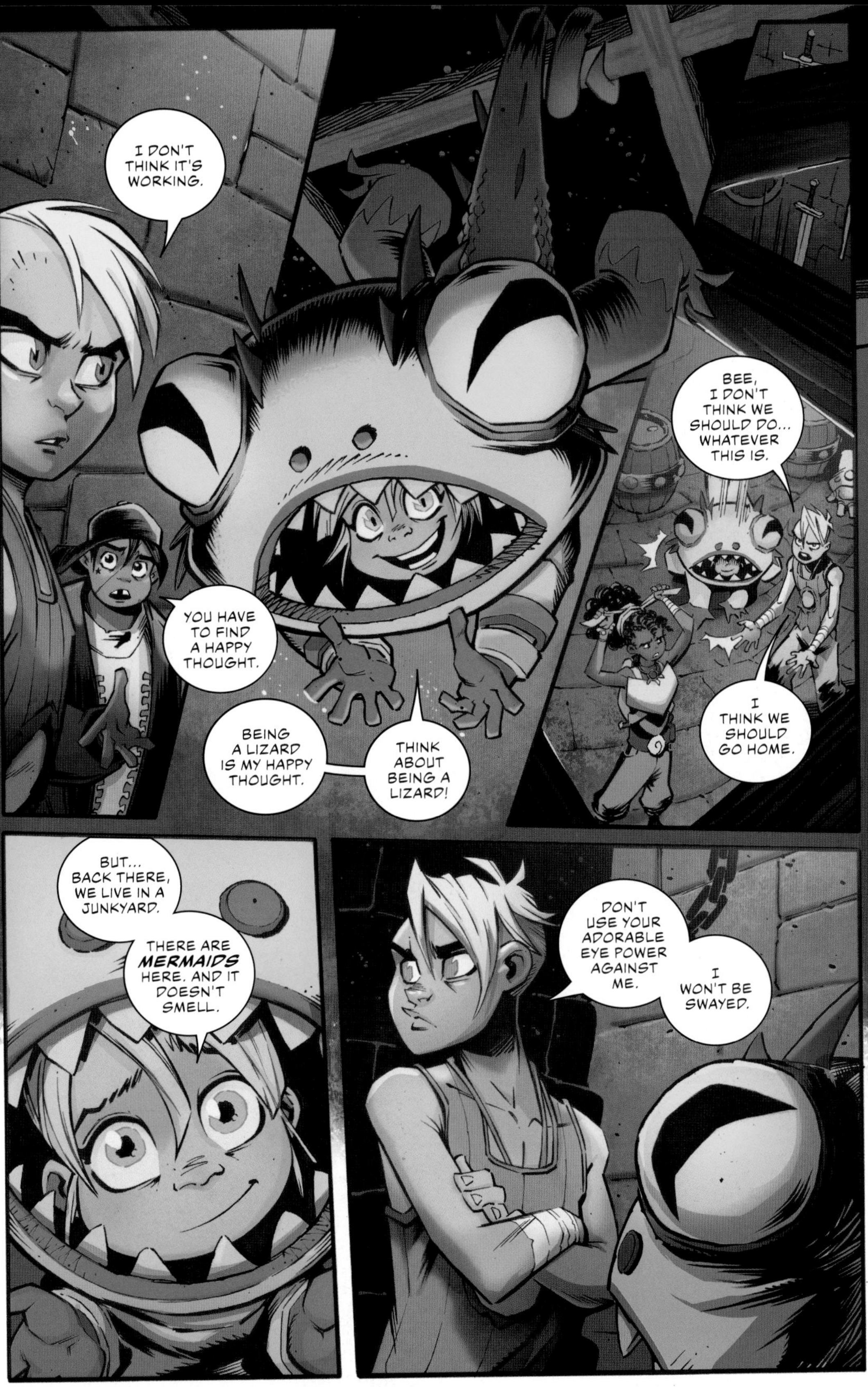
I DON'T THINK IT'S WORKING.
YOU HAVE TO FIND A HAPPY THOUGHT.
THINK ABOUT BEING A LIZARD!
BEING A LIZARD IS MY HAPPY THOUGHT.
BEE, I DON'T THINK WE SHOULD DO... WHATEVER THIS IS.
I THINK WE SHOULD GO HOME.
BUT... BACK THERE, WE LIVE IN A JUNKYARD.
THERE ARE *MERMAIDS* HERE. AND IT DOESN'T SMELL.
DON'T USE YOUR ADORABLE EYE POWER AGAINST ME.
I WON'T BE SWAYED.

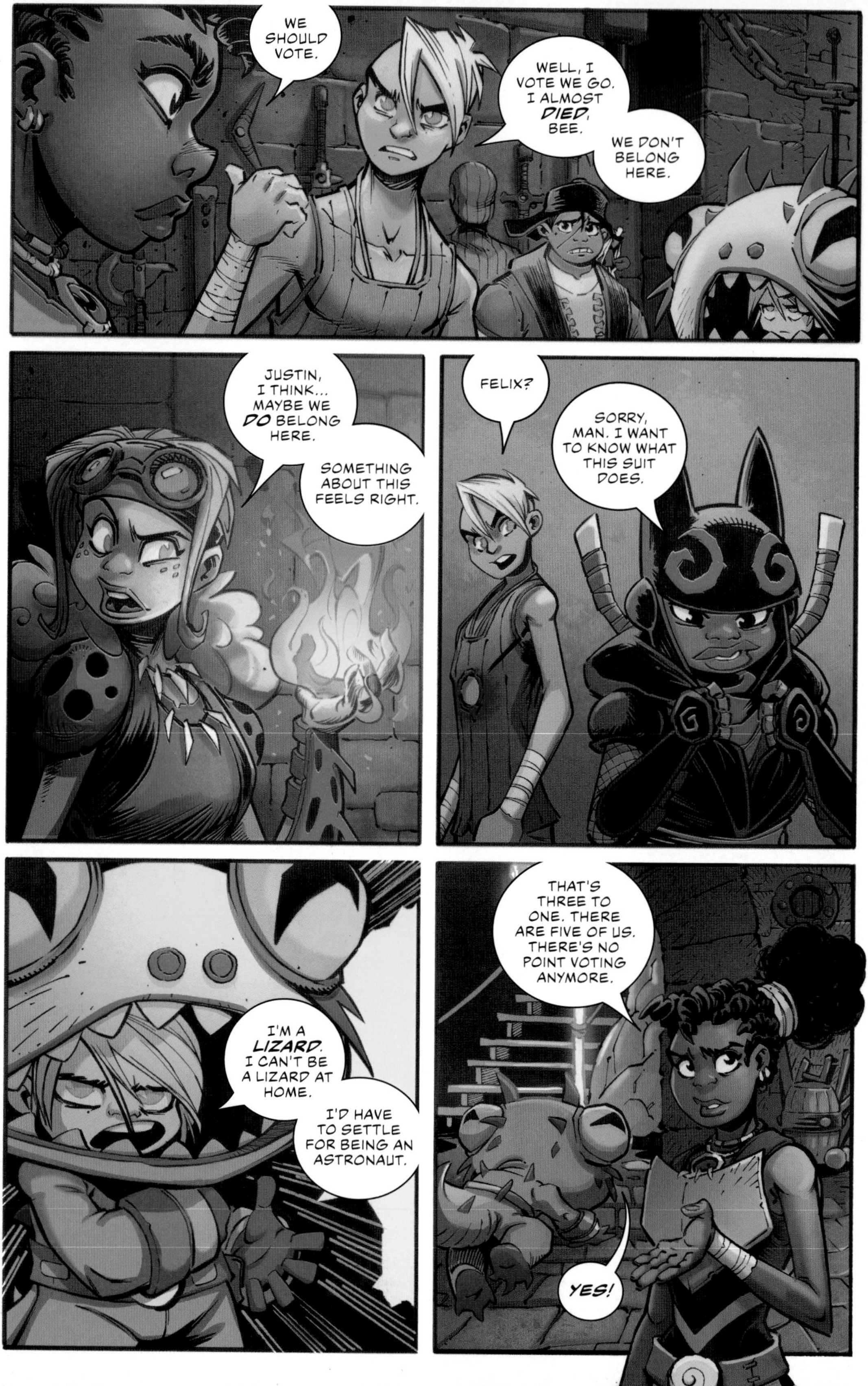
WE SHOULD VOTE.
WELL, I VOTE WE GO. I ALMOST DIED, BEE.
WE DON'T BELONG HERE.
JUSTIN, I THINK... MAYBE WE DO BELONG HERE.
SOMETHING ABOUT THIS FEELS RIGHT.
FELIX?
SORRY, MAN. I WANT TO KNOW WHAT THIS SUIT DOES.
I'M A LIZARD. I CAN'T BE A LIZARD AT HOME.
I'D HAVE TO SETTLE FOR BEING AN ASTRONAUT.
THAT'S THREE TO ONE. THERE ARE FIVE OF US. THERE'S NO POINT VOTING ANYMORE.
YES!

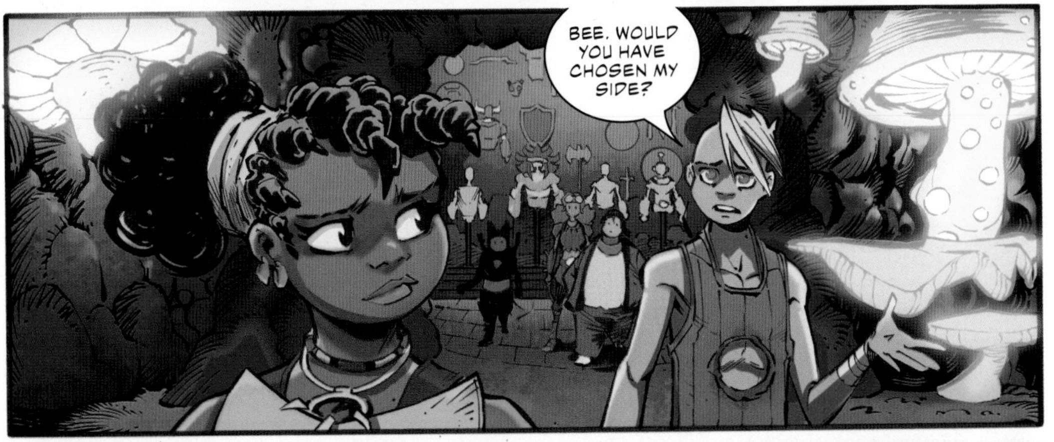
BEE. WOULD YOU HAVE CHOSEN MY SIDE?
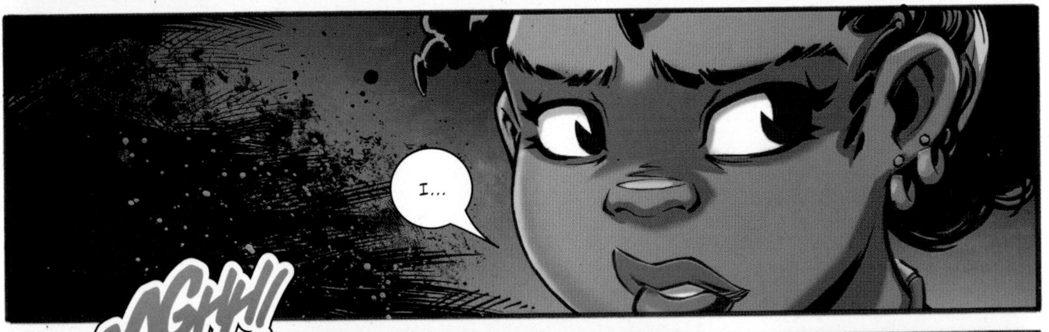
I...
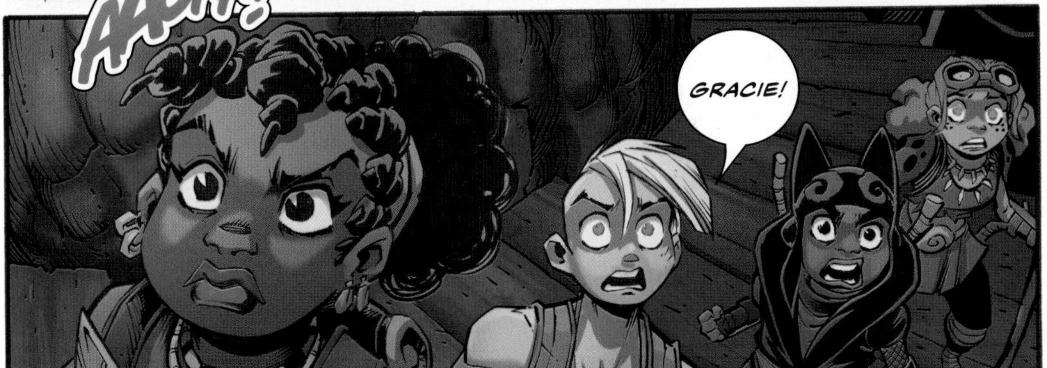
AAGHH!!
GRACIE!
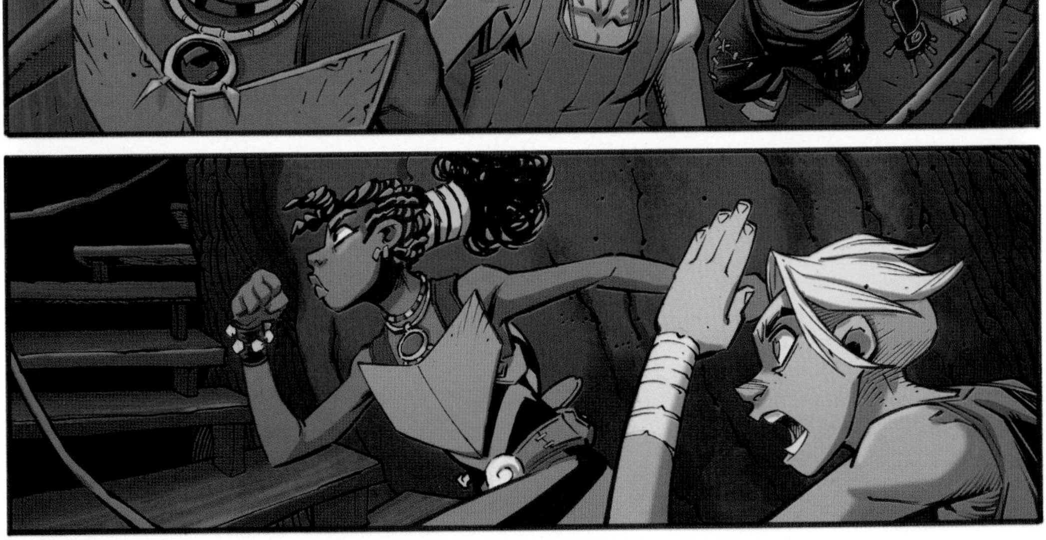

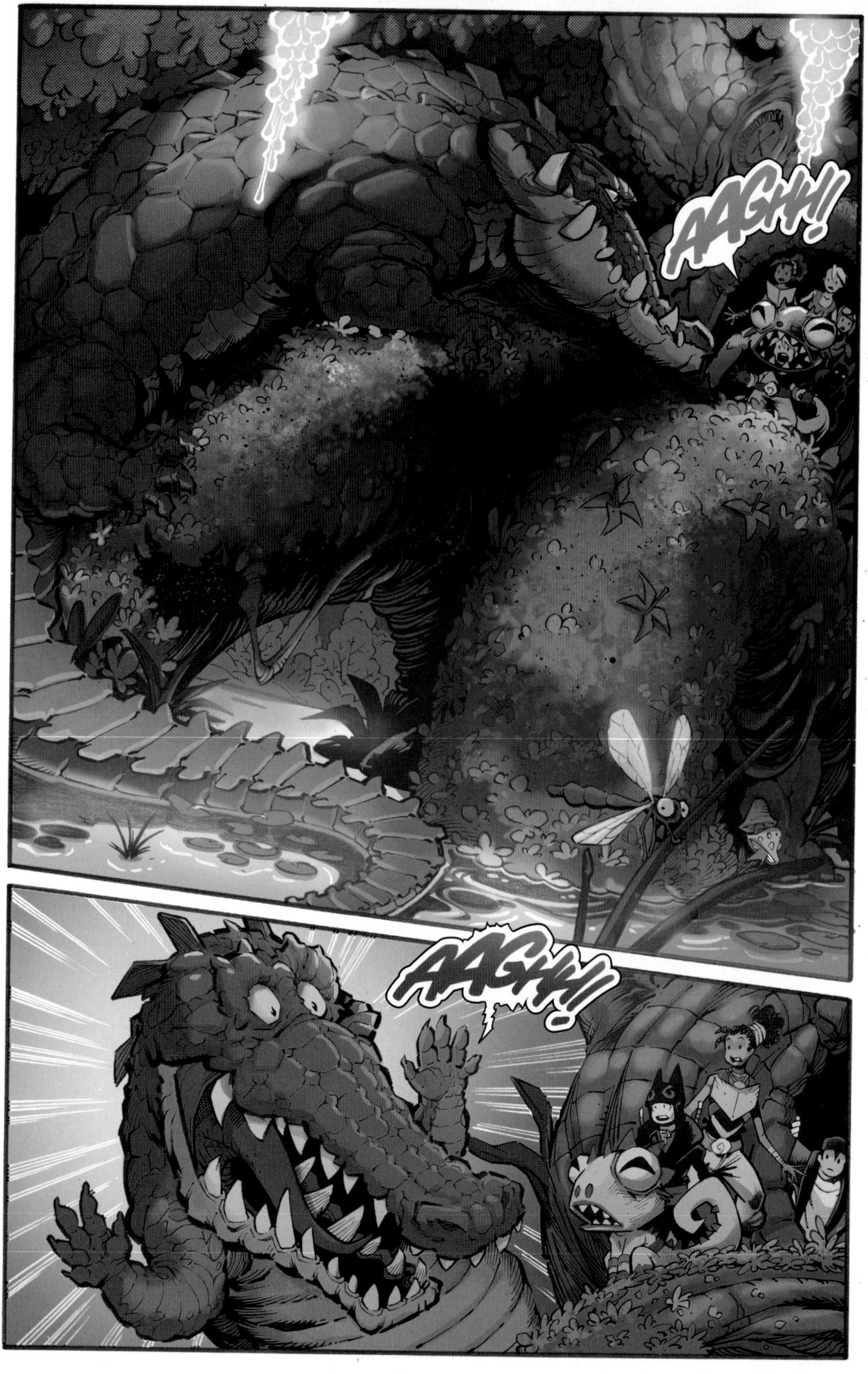
AAGHH!!
AAGHH!!

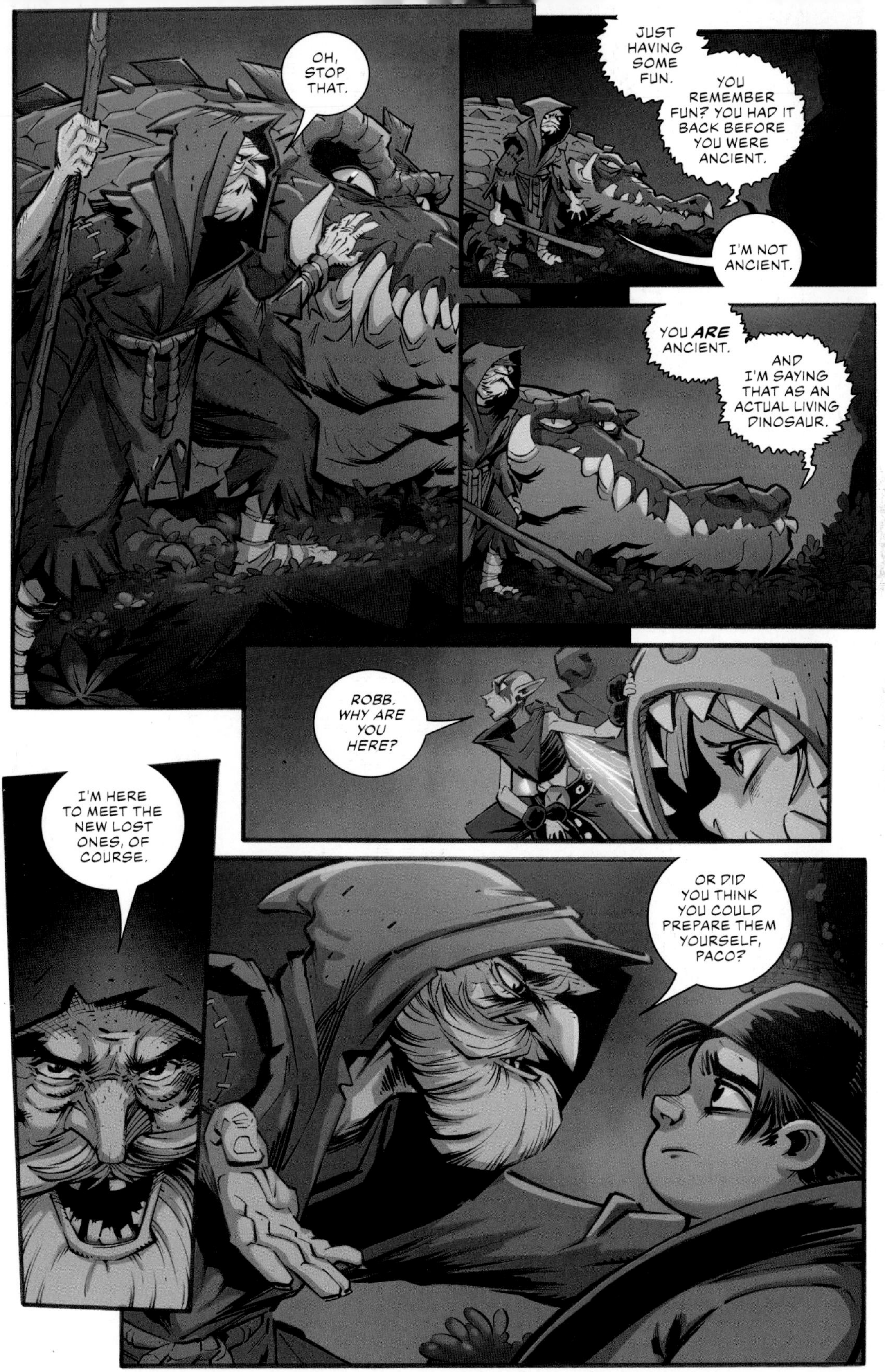
OH, STOP THAT.
JUST HAVING SOME FUN.
YOU REMEMBER FUN? YOU HAD IT BACK BEFORE YOU WERE ANCIENT.
I'M NOT ANCIENT.
YOU **ARE** ANCIENT.
AND I'M SAYING THAT AS AN ACTUAL LIVING DINOSAUR.
ROBB. WHY ARE YOU HERE?
I'M HERE TO MEET THE NEW LOST ONES, OF COURSE.
OR DID YOU THINK YOU COULD PREPARE THEM YOURSELF, PACO?

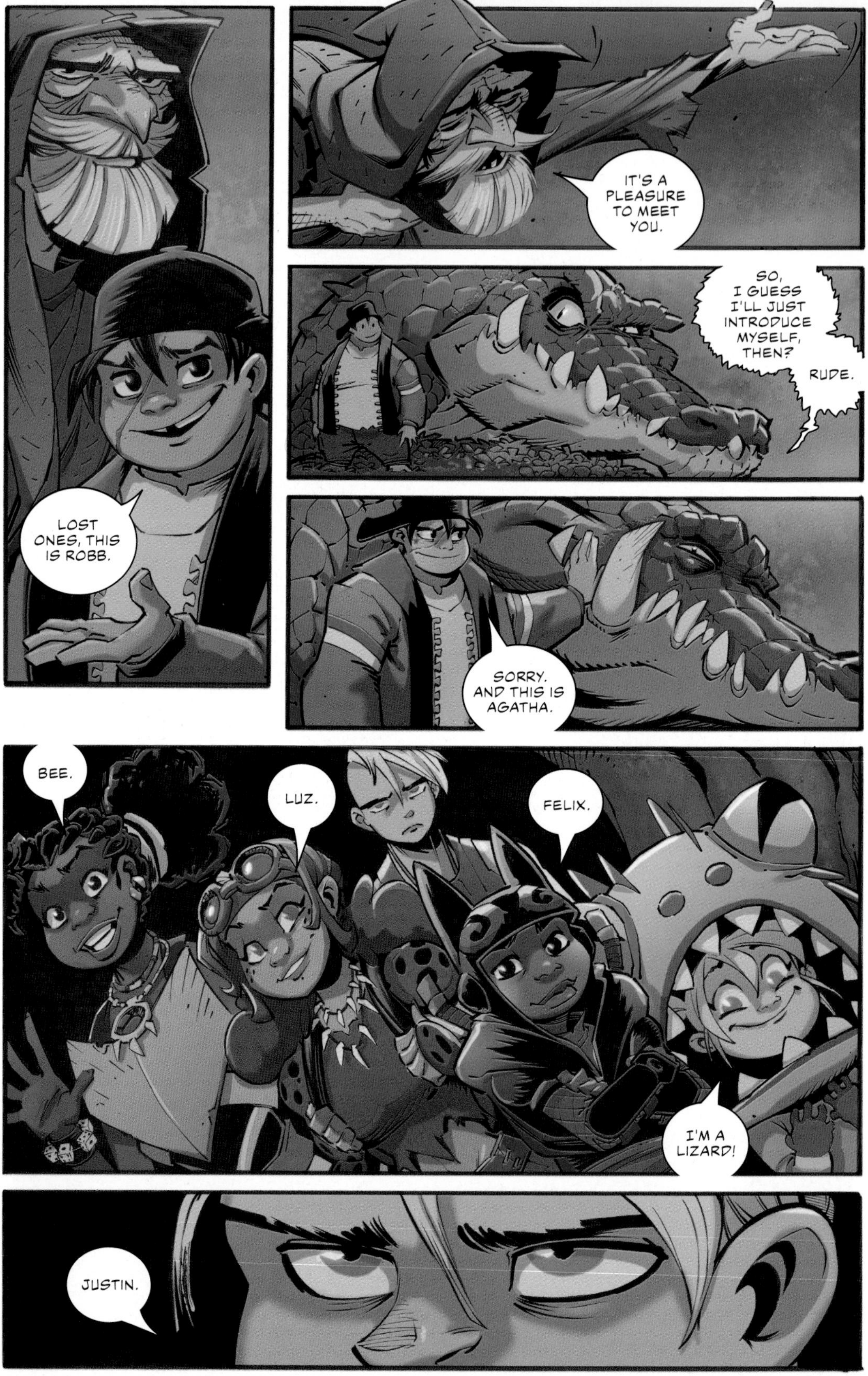
LOST ONES, THIS IS ROBB.
IT'S A PLEASURE TO MEET YOU.
SO, I GUESS I'LL JUST INTRODUCE MYSELF, THEN?
RUDE.
SORRY. AND THIS IS AGATHA.
BEE.
LUZ.
FELIX.
I'M A LIZARD!
JUSTIN.

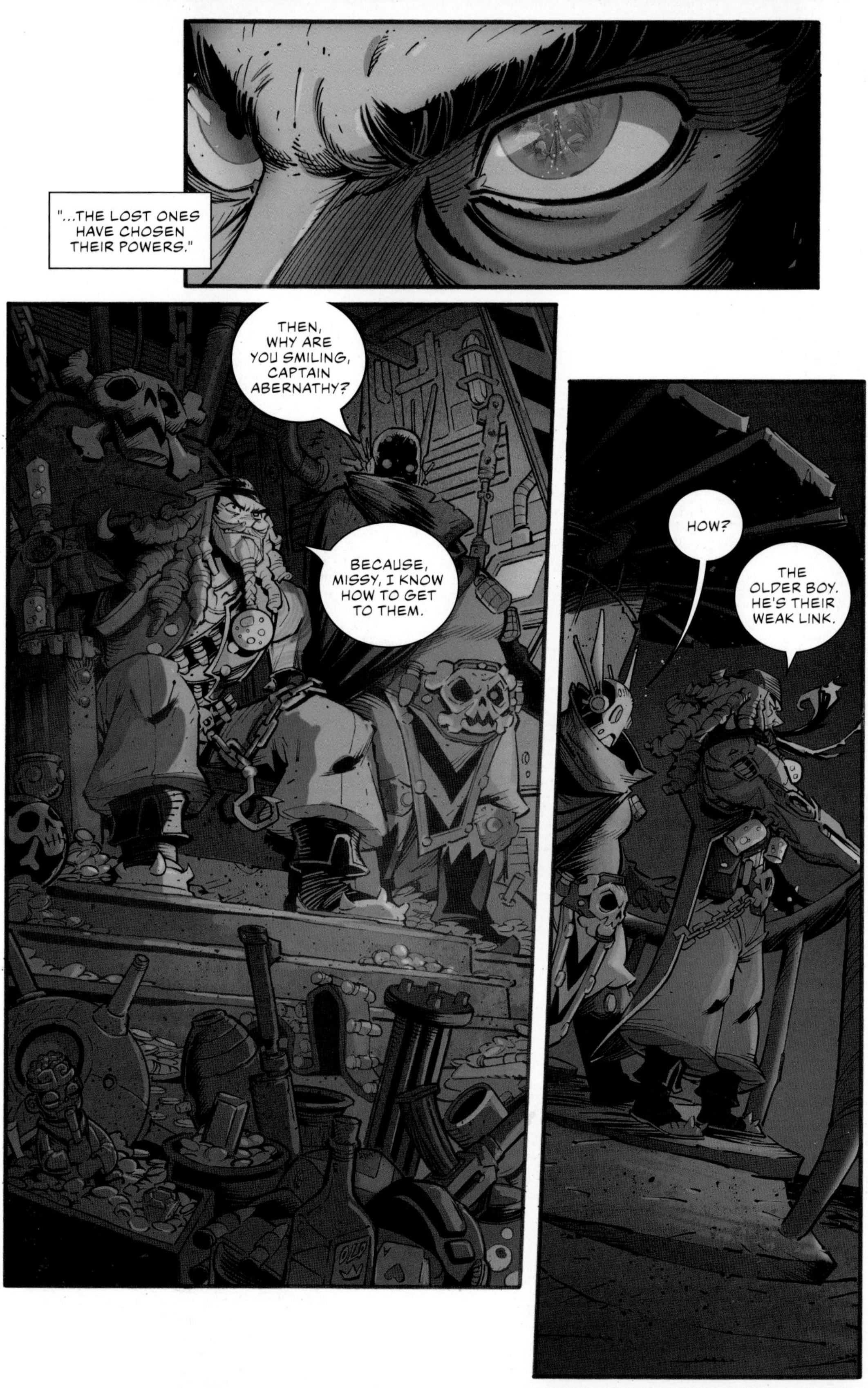
"...THE LOST ONES HAVE CHOSEN THEIR POWERS."
THEN, WHY ARE YOU SMILING, CAPTAIN ABERNATHY?
BECAUSE, MISSY, I KNOW HOW TO GET TO THEM.
HOW?
THE OLDER BOY. HE'S THEIR WEAK LINK.

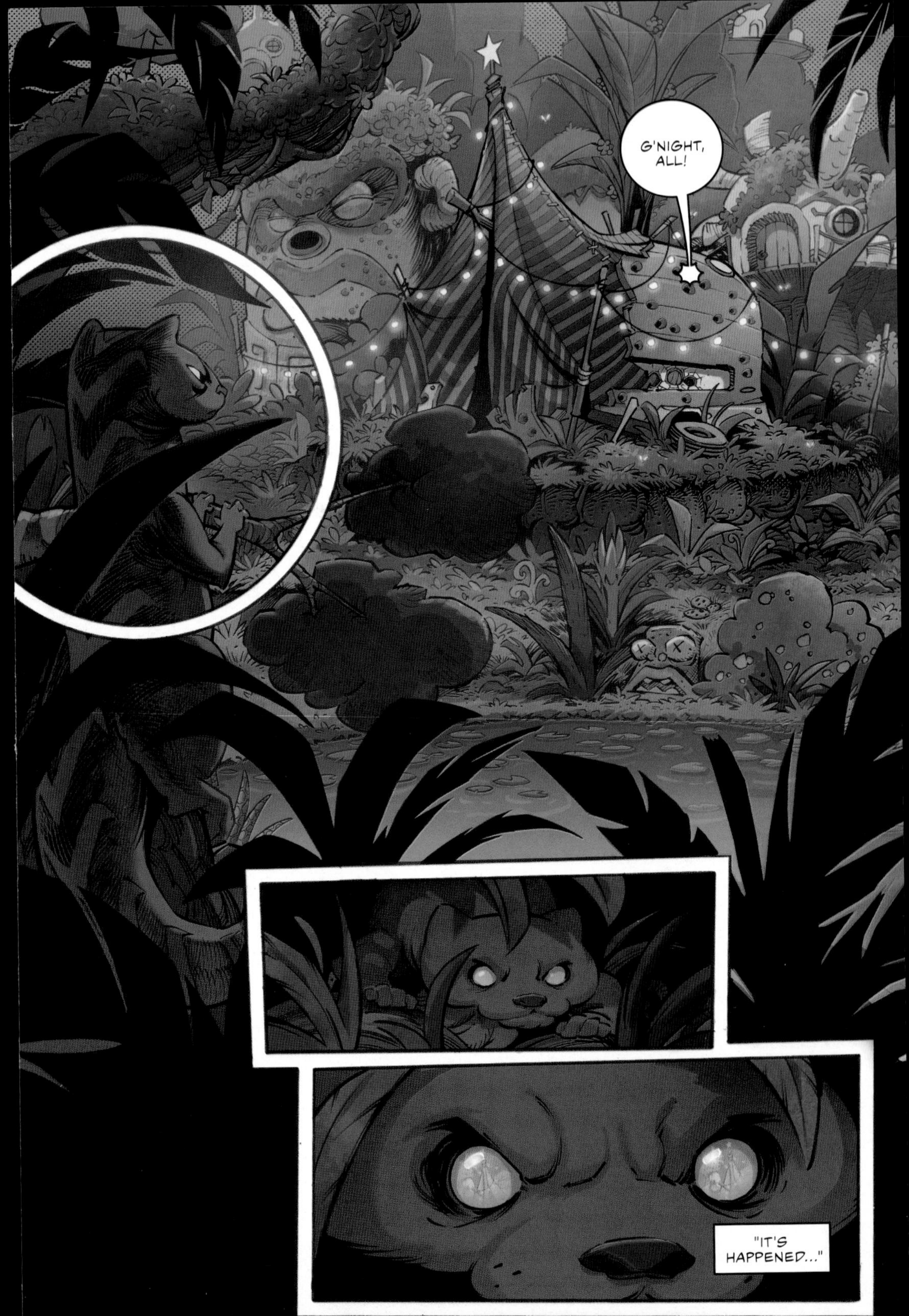
G'NIGHT, ALL!
"IT'S HAPPENED..."

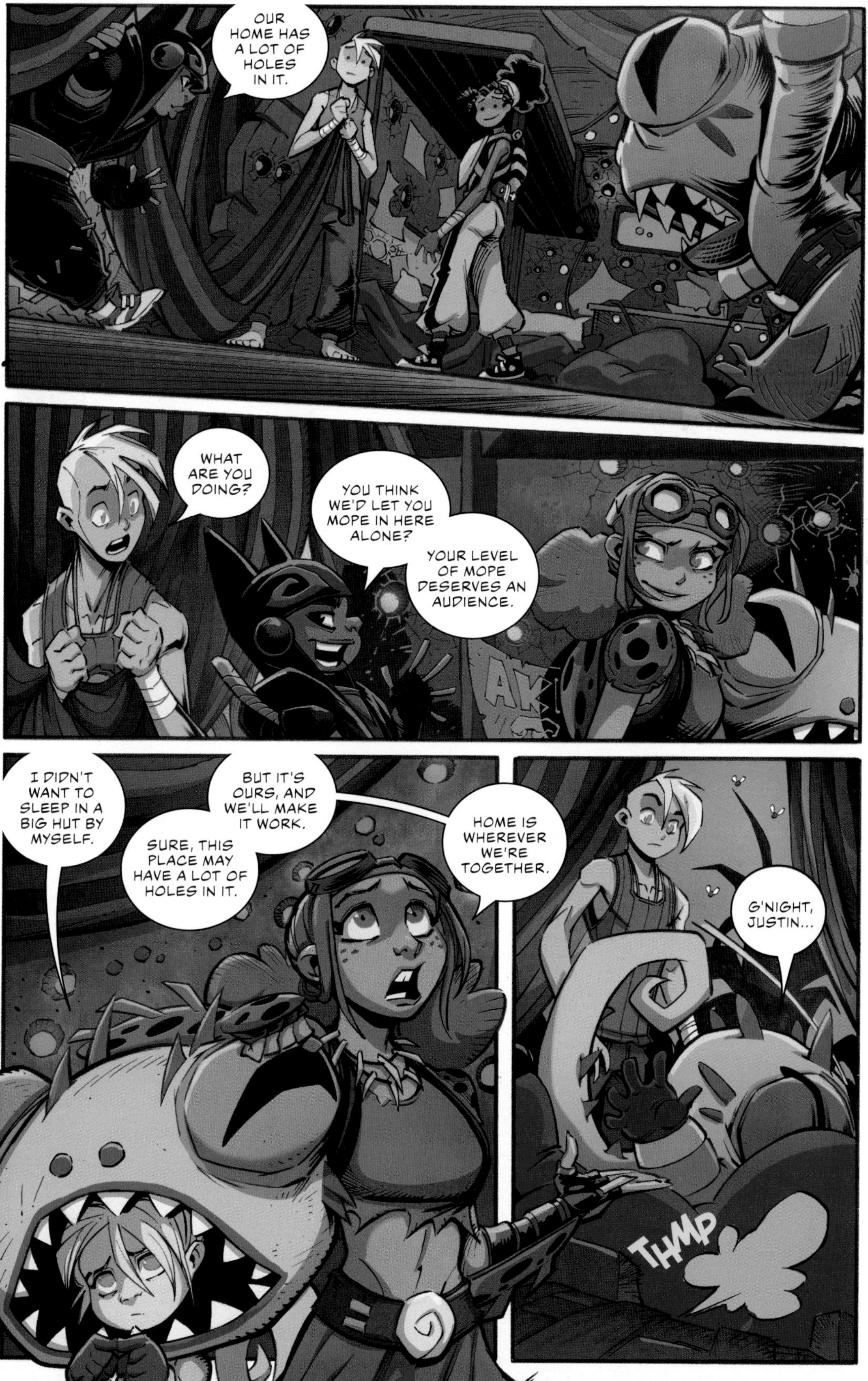
OUR HOME HAS A LOT OF HOLES IN IT.
WHAT ARE YOU DOING?
YOU THINK WE'D LET YOU MOPE IN HERE ALONE?
YOUR LEVEL OF MOPE DESERVES AN AUDIENCE.
I DIDN'T WANT TO SLEEP IN A BIG HUT BY MYSELF.
SURE, THIS PLACE MAY HAVE A LOT OF HOLES IN IT.
BUT IT'S OURS, AND WE'LL MAKE IT WORK.
HOME IS WHEREVER WE'RE TOGETHER.
G'NIGHT, JUSTIN...
THMP

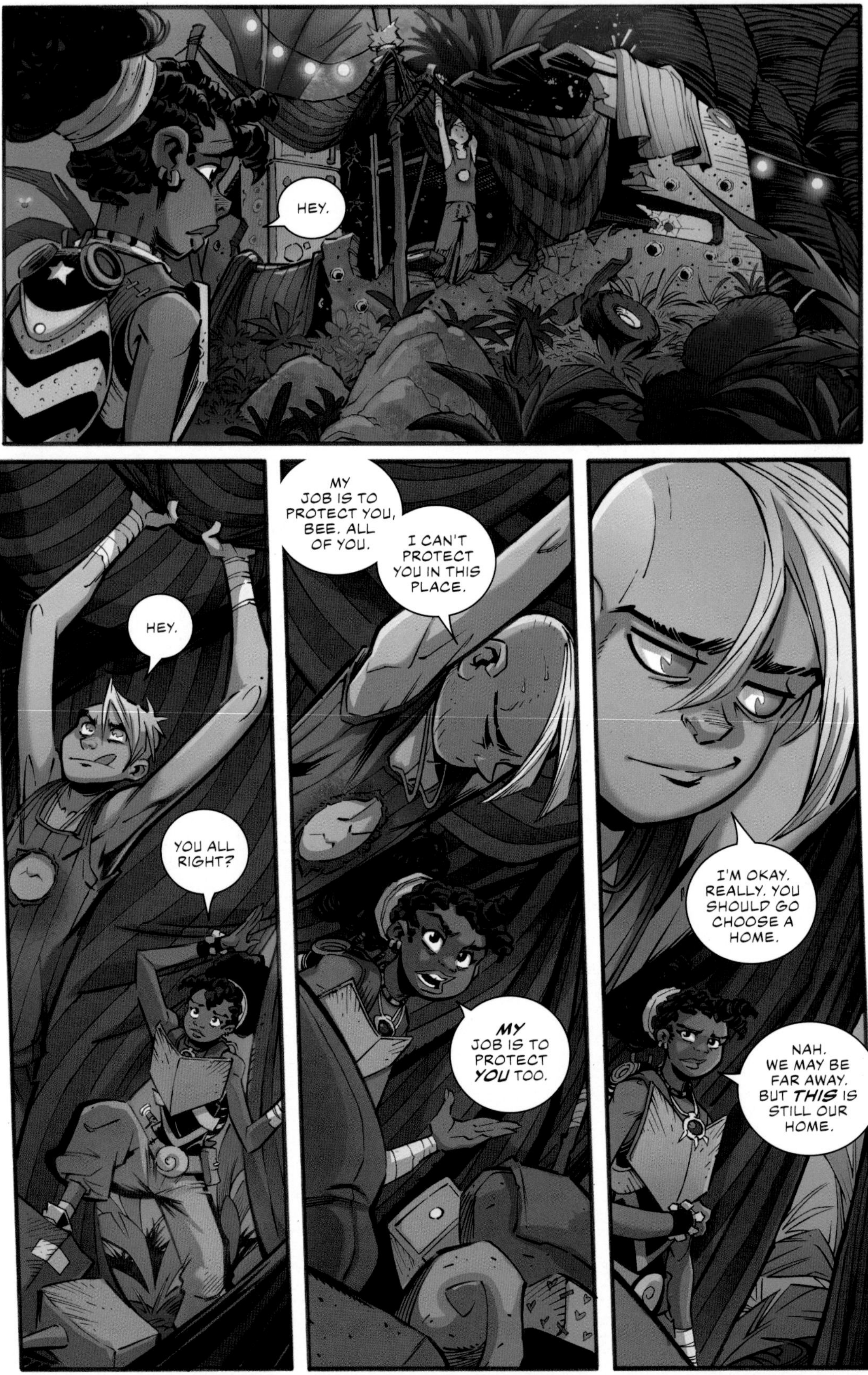
HEY.
HEY.
YOU ALL RIGHT?
MY JOB IS TO PROTECT YOU, BEE. ALL OF YOU.
I CAN'T PROTECT YOU IN THIS PLACE.
MY JOB IS TO PROTECT YOU TOO.
I'M OKAY. REALLY. YOU SHOULD GO CHOOSE A HOME.
NAH. WE MAY BE FAR AWAY. BUT THIS IS STILL OUR HOME.

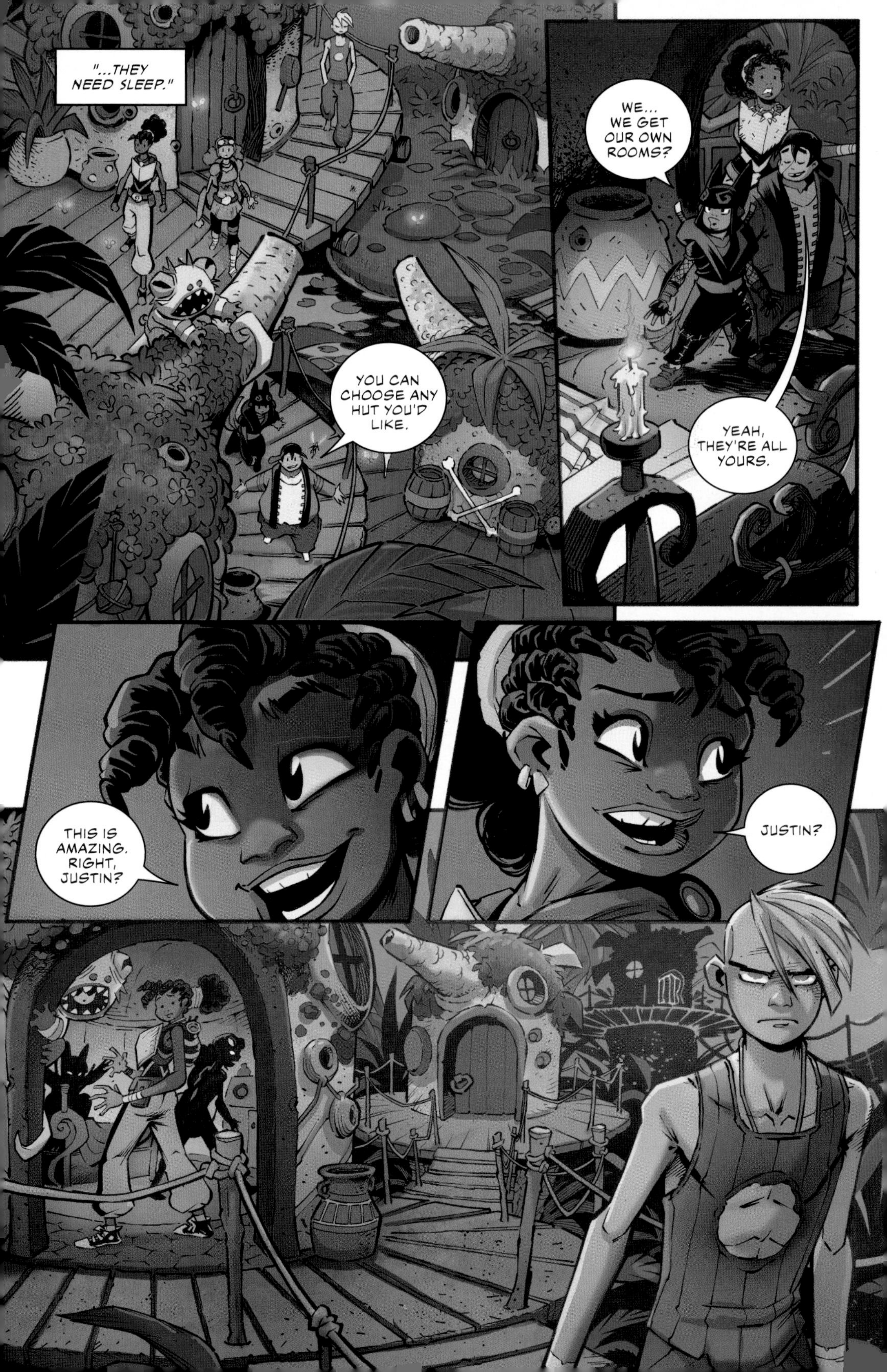
"...THEY NEED SLEEP."
YOU CAN CHOOSE ANY HUT YOU'D LIKE.
WE... WE GET OUR OWN ROOMS?
YEAH, THEY'RE ALL YOURS.
THIS IS AMAZING. RIGHT, JUSTIN?
JUSTIN?

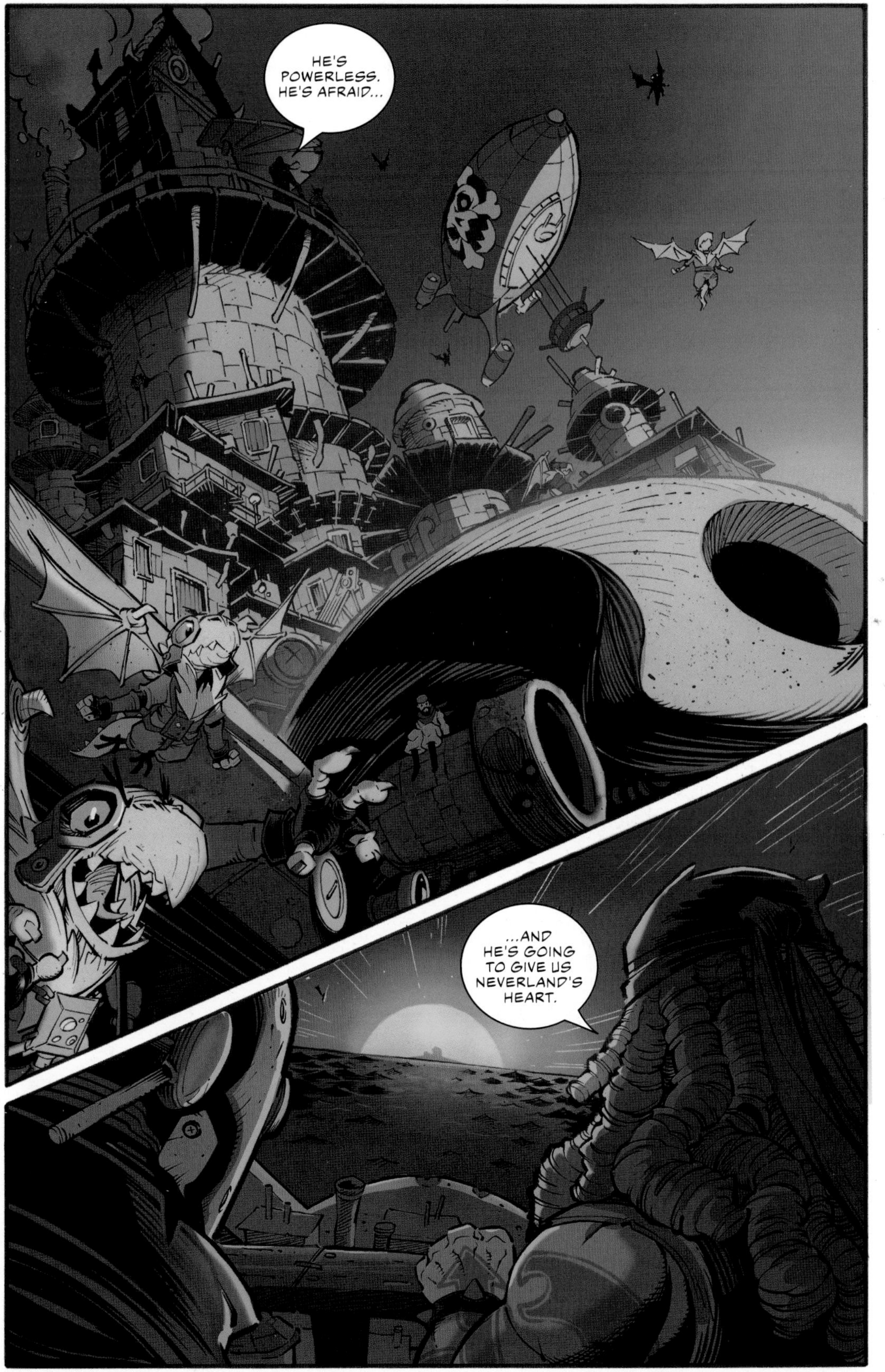
HE'S POWERLESS. HE'S AFRAID...
...AND HE'S GOING TO GIVE US NEVERLAND'S HEART.

CHAPTER
FOUR

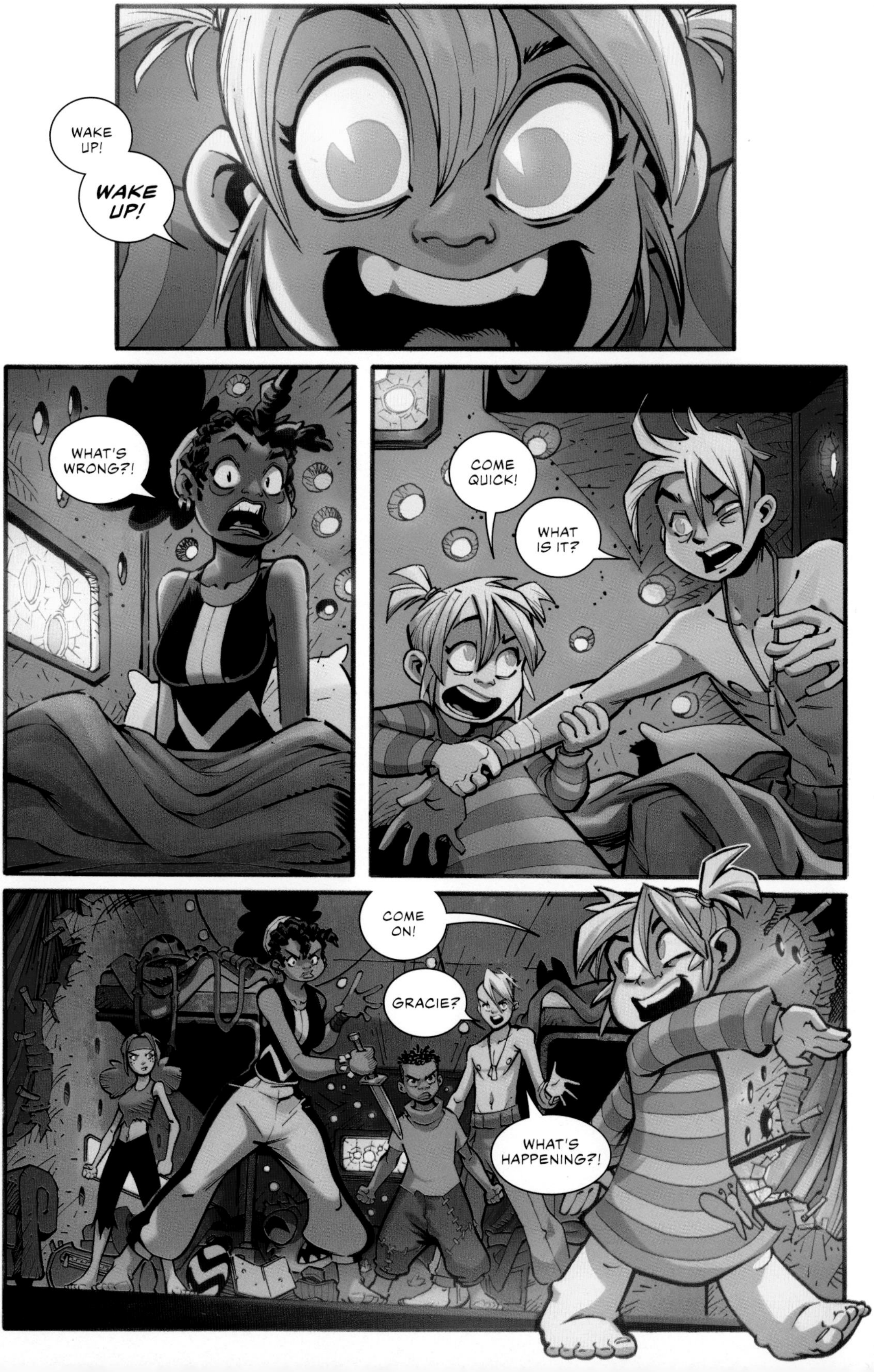
WAKE UP!
WAKE UP!
WHAT'S WRONG?!
COME QUICK!
WHAT IS IT?
COME ON!
GRACIE?
WHAT'S HAPPENING?!

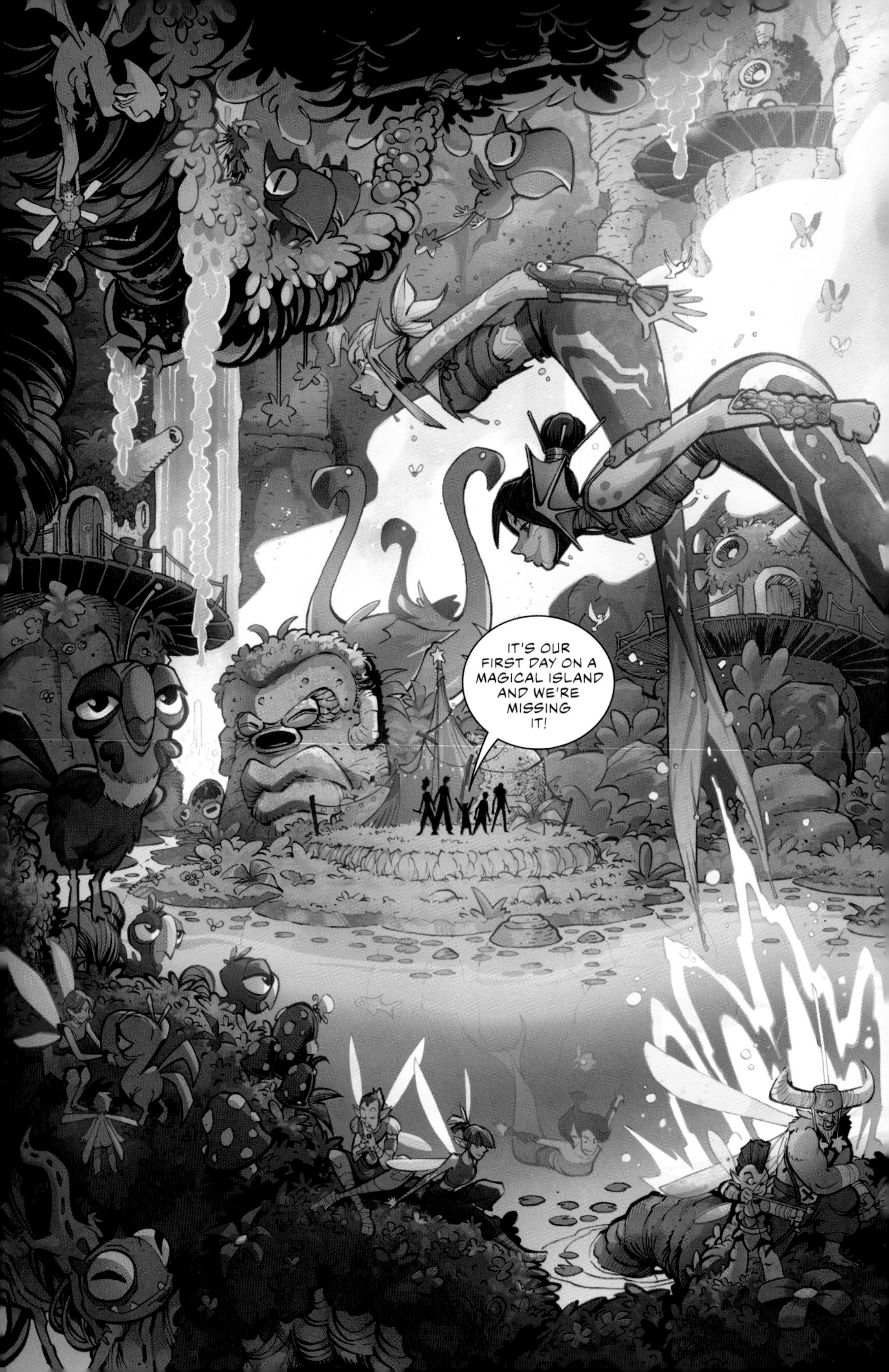
IT'S OUR FIRST DAY ON A MAGICAL ISLAND AND WE'RE MISSING IT!

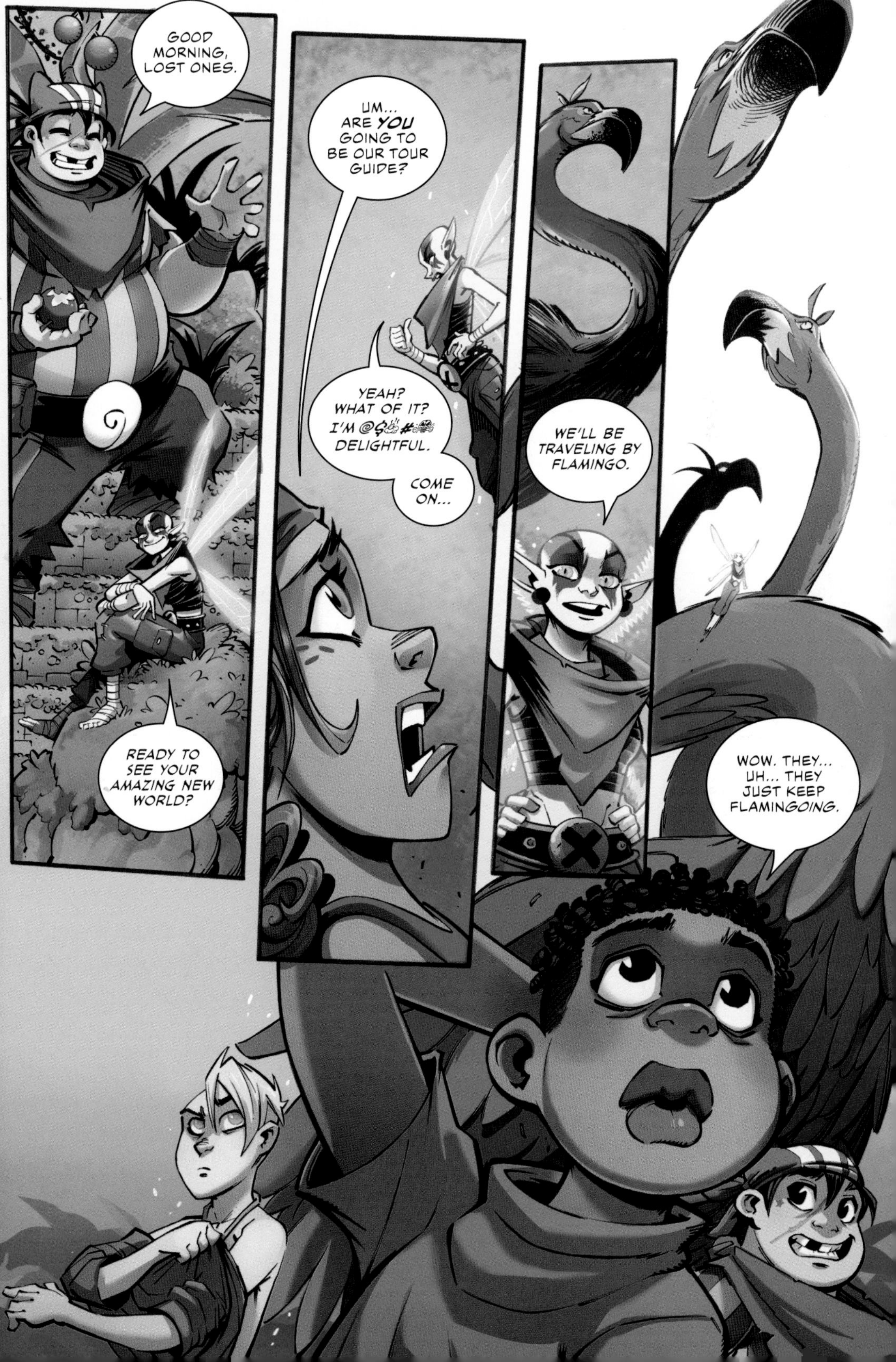
GOOD MORNING, LOST ONES.
READY TO SEE YOUR AMAZING NEW WORLD?
UM... ARE YOU GOING TO BE OUR TOUR GUIDE?
YEAH? WHAT OF IT? I'M @$#* DELIGHTFUL.
COME ON...
WE'LL BE TRAVELING BY FLAMINGO.
WOW. THEY... UH... THEY JUST KEEP FLAMINGOING.

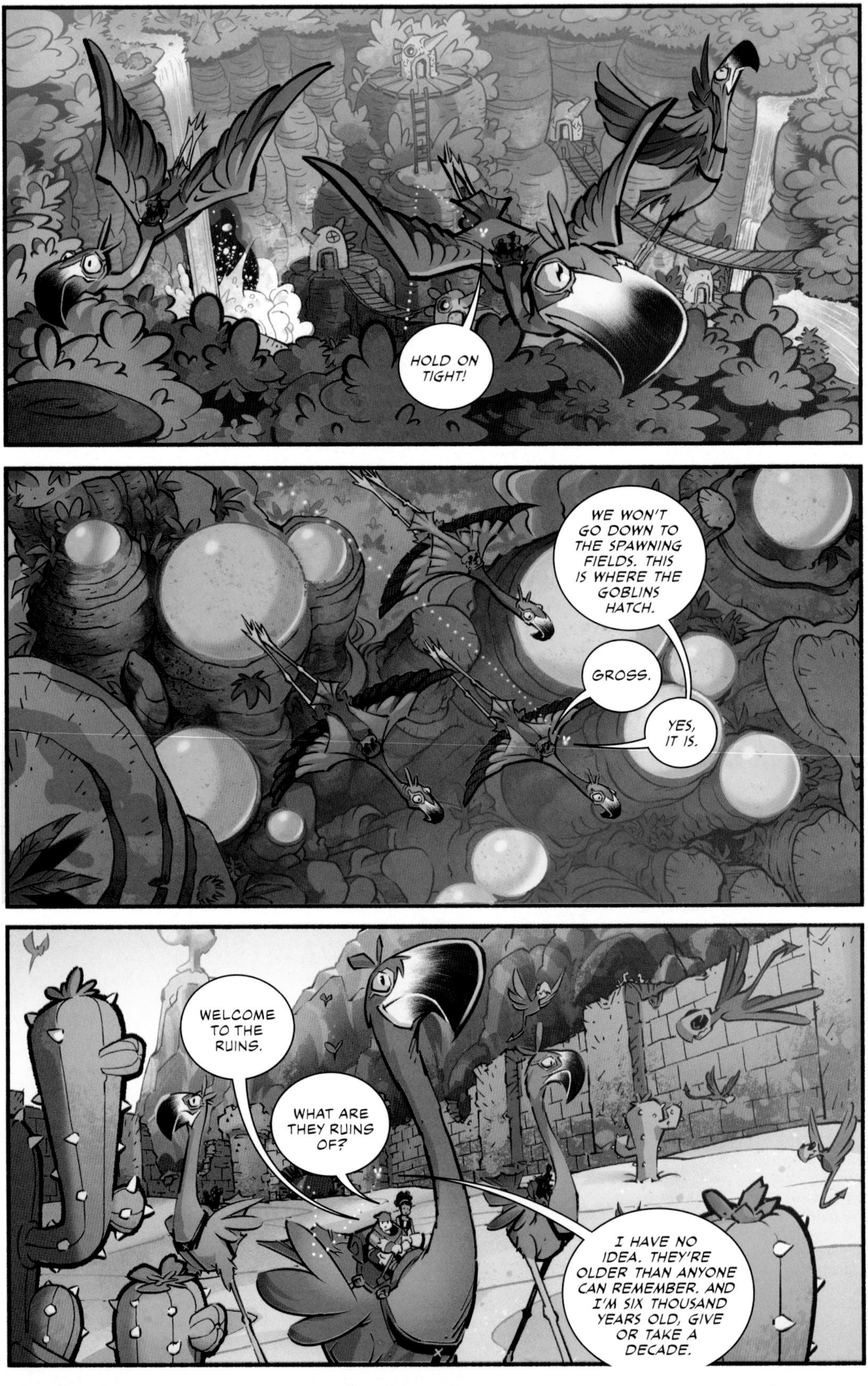
HOLD ON TIGHT!
WE WON'T GO DOWN TO THE SPAWNING FIELDS. THIS IS WHERE THE GOBLINS HATCH.
GROSS.
YES, IT IS.
WELCOME TO THE RUINS.
WHAT ARE THEY RUINS OF?
I HAVE NO IDEA. THEY'RE OLDER THAN ANYONE CAN REMEMBER. AND I'M SIX THOUSAND YEARS OLD, GIVE OR TAKE A DECADE.

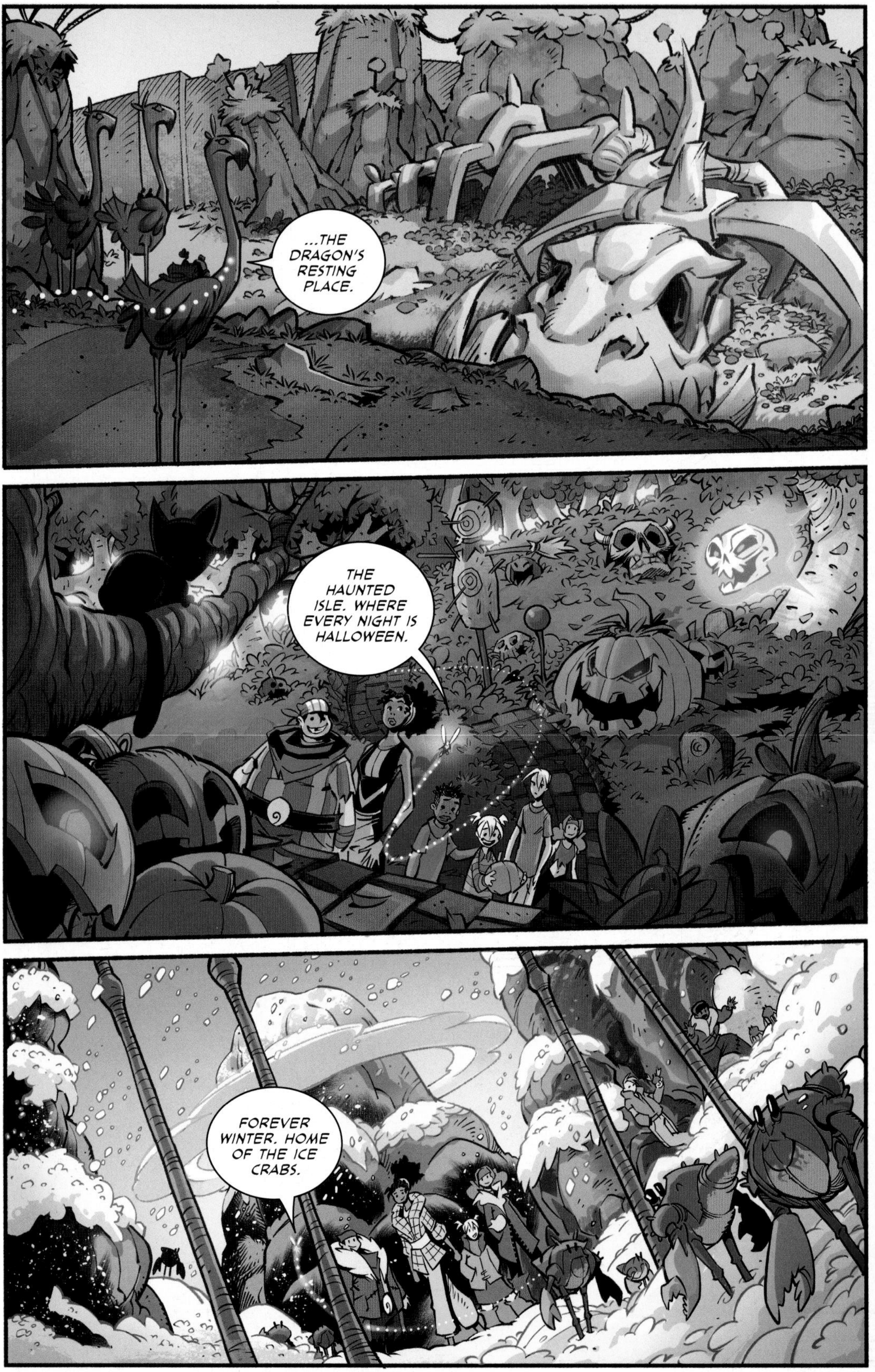
...THE DRAGON'S RESTING PLACE.
THE HAUNTED ISLE. WHERE EVERY NIGHT IS HALLOWEEN.
FOREVER WINTER. HOME OF THE ICE CRABS.

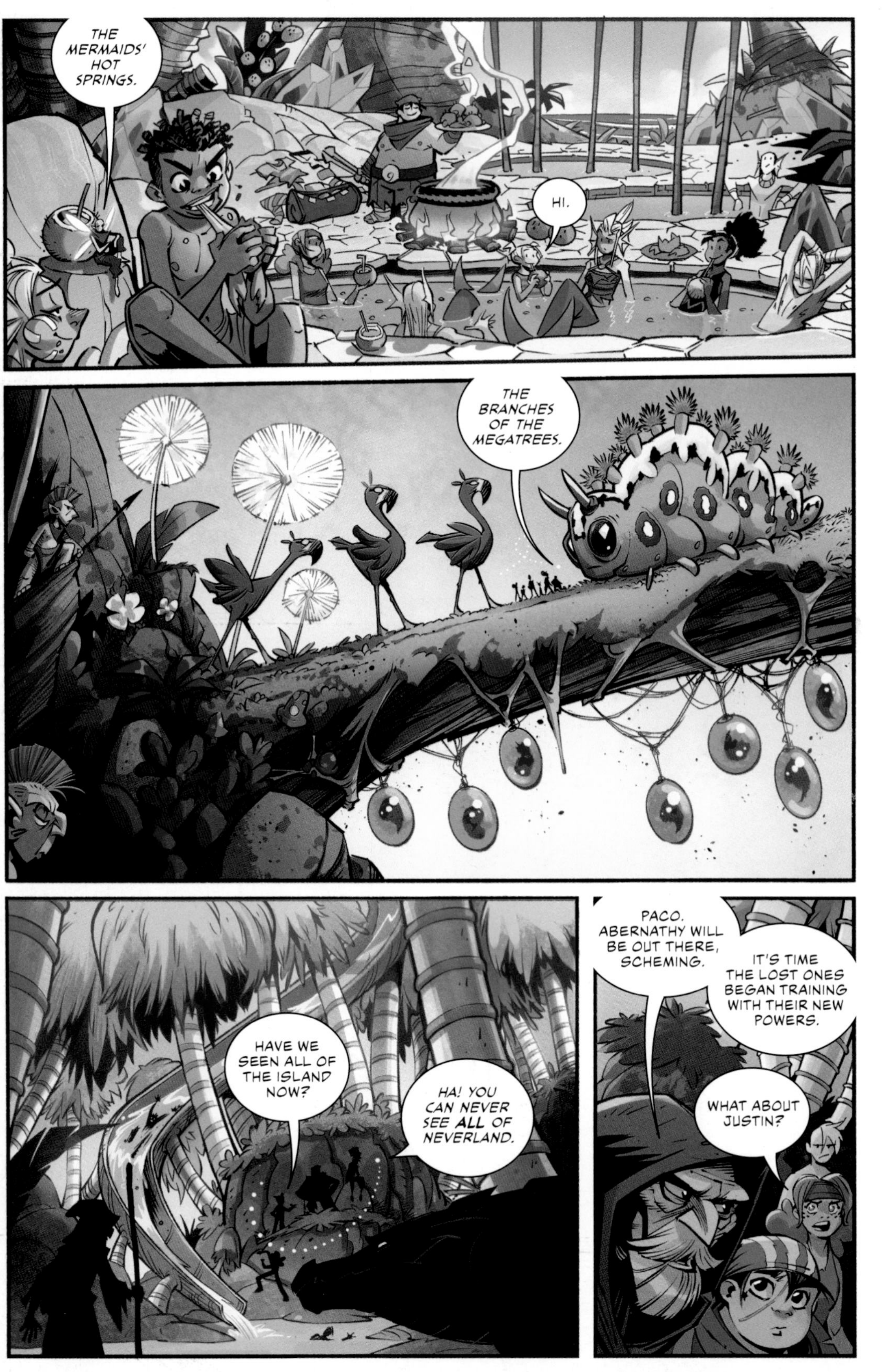
THE MERMAIDS' HOT SPRINGS.
HI.
THE BRANCHES OF THE MEGATREES.
HAVE WE SEEN ALL OF THE ISLAND NOW?
HA! YOU CAN NEVER SEE **ALL** OF NEVERLAND.
PACO. ABERNATHY WILL BE OUT THERE, SCHEMING.
IT'S TIME THE LOST ONES BEGAN TRAINING WITH THEIR NEW POWERS.
WHAT ABOUT JUSTIN?

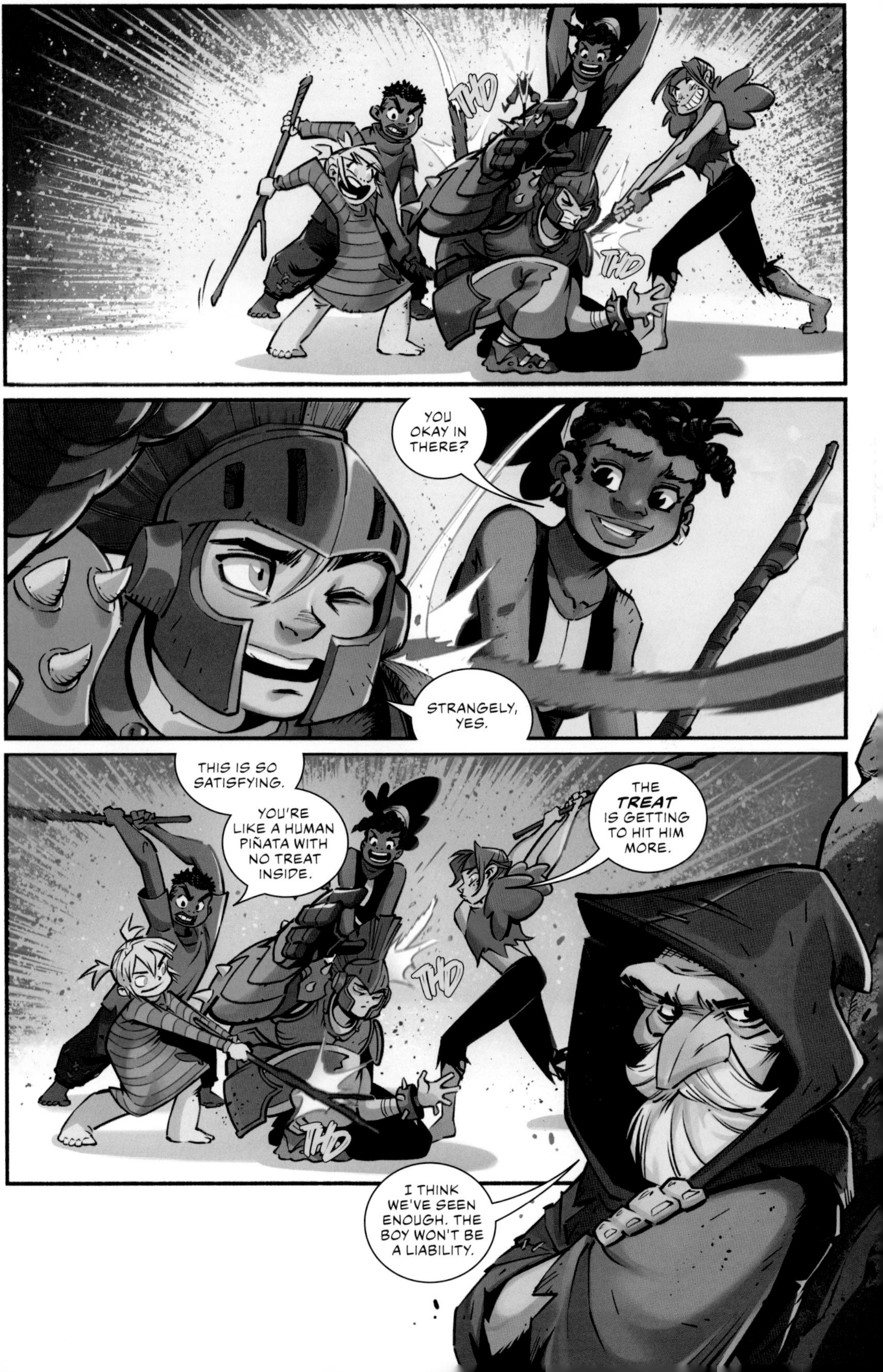
THD
THD
YOU OKAY IN THERE?
STRANGELY, YES.
THIS IS SO SATISFYING.
YOU'RE LIKE A HUMAN PIÑATA WITH NO TREAT INSIDE.
THE TREAT IS GETTING TO HIT HIM MORE.
THD
THD
I THINK WE'VE SEEN ENOUGH. THE BOY WON'T BE A LIABILITY.

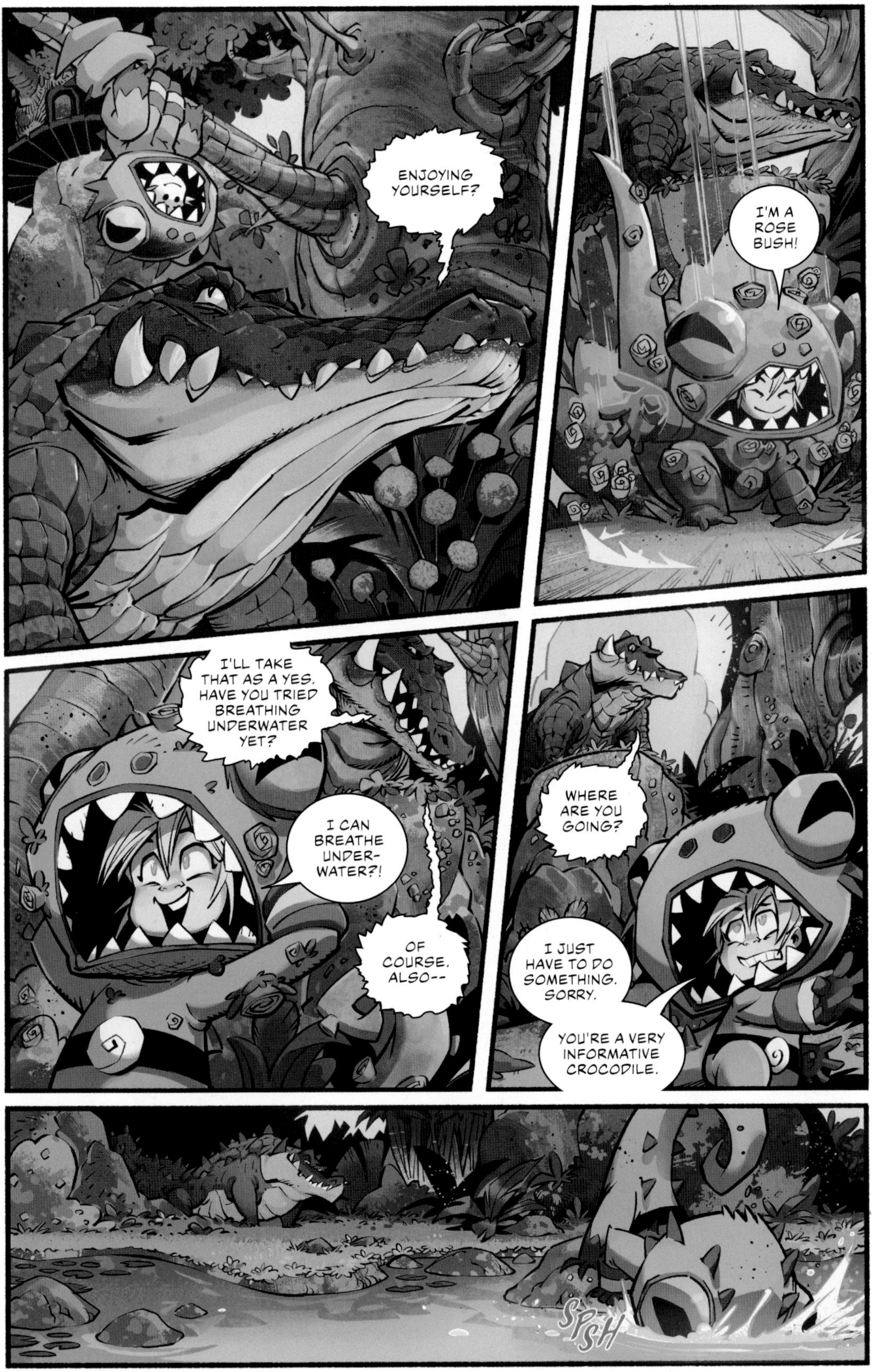
ENJOYING YOURSELF?
I'M A ROSE BUSH!
I'LL TAKE THAT AS A YES. HAVE YOU TRIED BREATHING UNDERWATER YET?
I CAN BREATHE UNDER-WATER?!
OF COURSE. ALSO--
WHERE ARE YOU GOING?
I JUST HAVE TO DO SOMETHING. SORRY.
YOU'RE A VERY INFORMATIVE CROCODILE.
SPSH

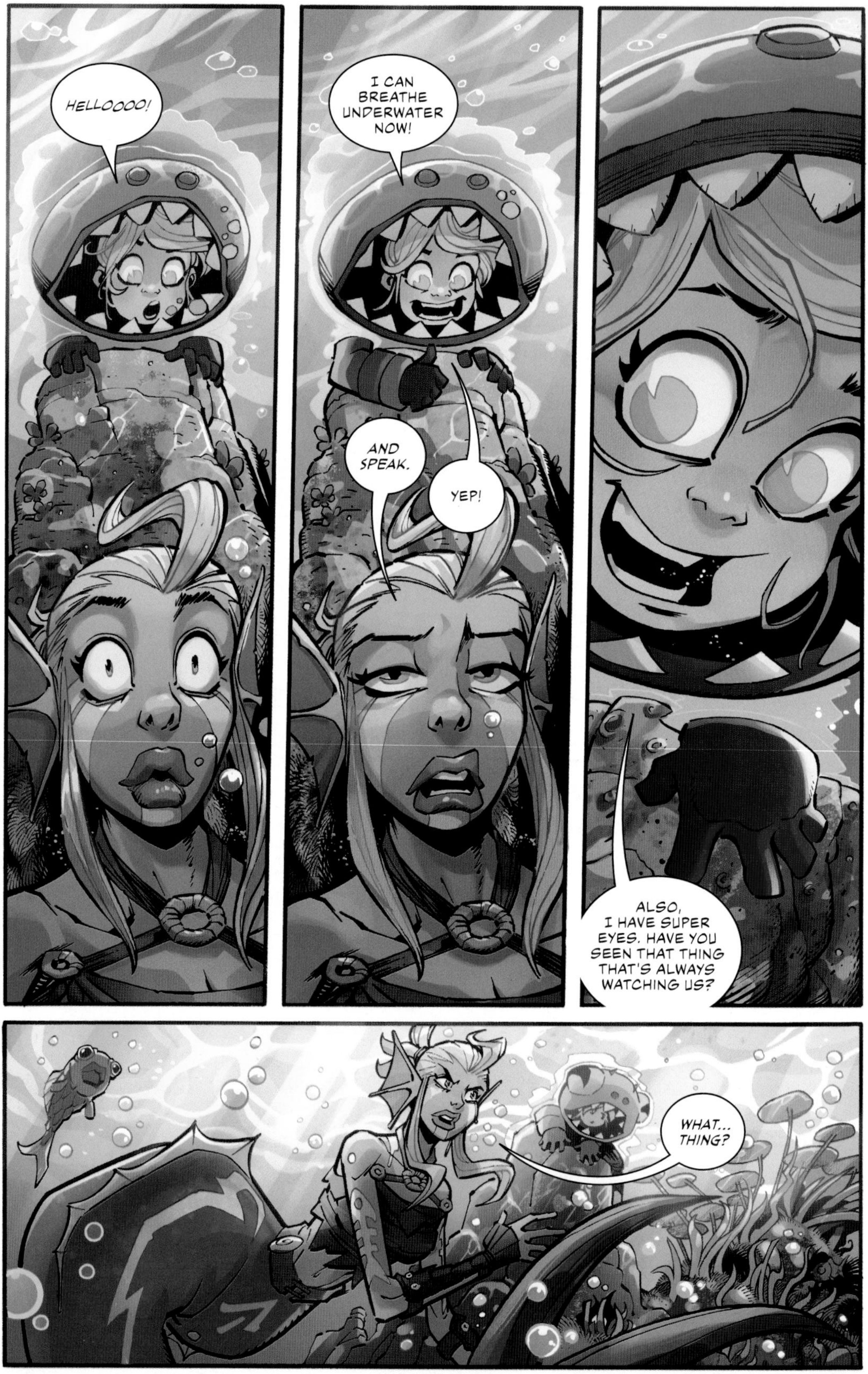
HELLOOOO!
I CAN BREATHE UNDERWATER NOW!
AND SPEAK.
YEP!
ALSO, I HAVE SUPER EYES. HAVE YOU SEEN THAT THING THAT'S ALWAYS WATCHING US?
WHAT... THING?

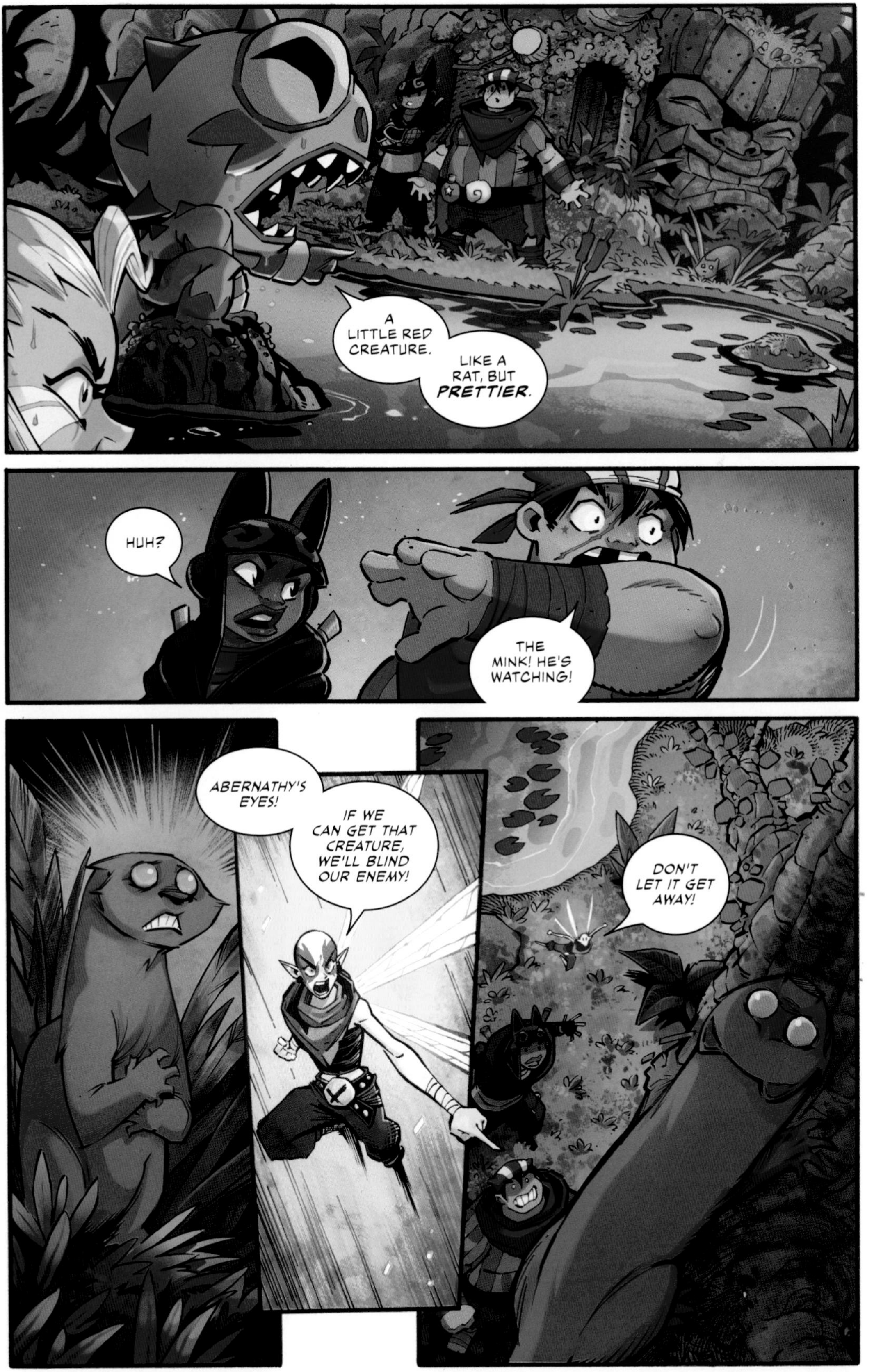
A LITTLE RED CREATURE.
LIKE A RAT, BUT PRETTIER.
HUH?
THE MINK! HE'S WATCHING!
ABERNATHY'S EYES!
IF WE CAN GET THAT CREATURE, WE'LL BLIND OUR ENEMY!
DON'T LET IT GET AWAY!

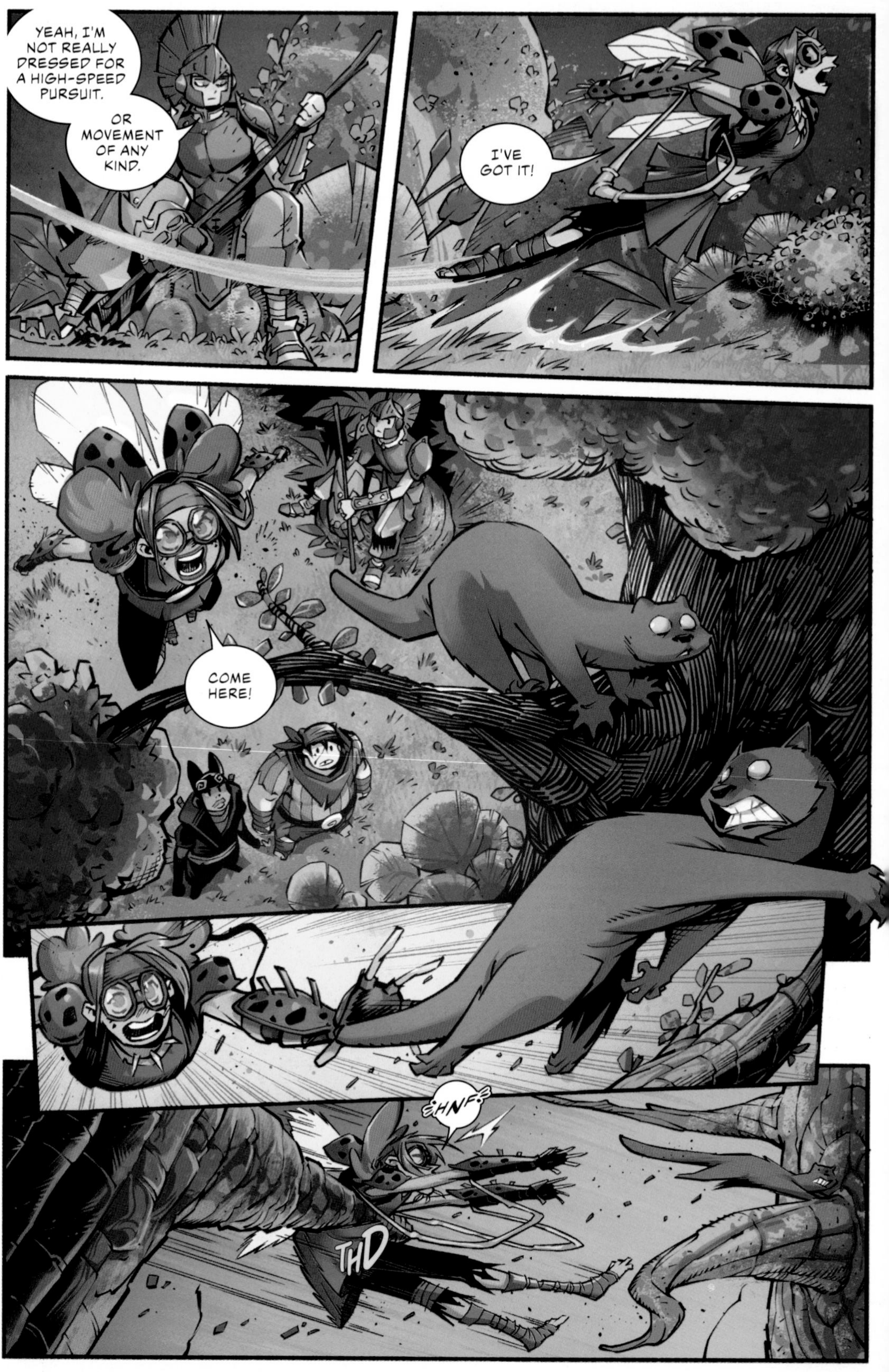
YEAH, I'M NOT REALLY DRESSED FOR A HIGH-SPEED PURSUIT.
OR MOVEMENT OF ANY KIND.
I'VE GOT IT!
COME HERE!
HNF
THD

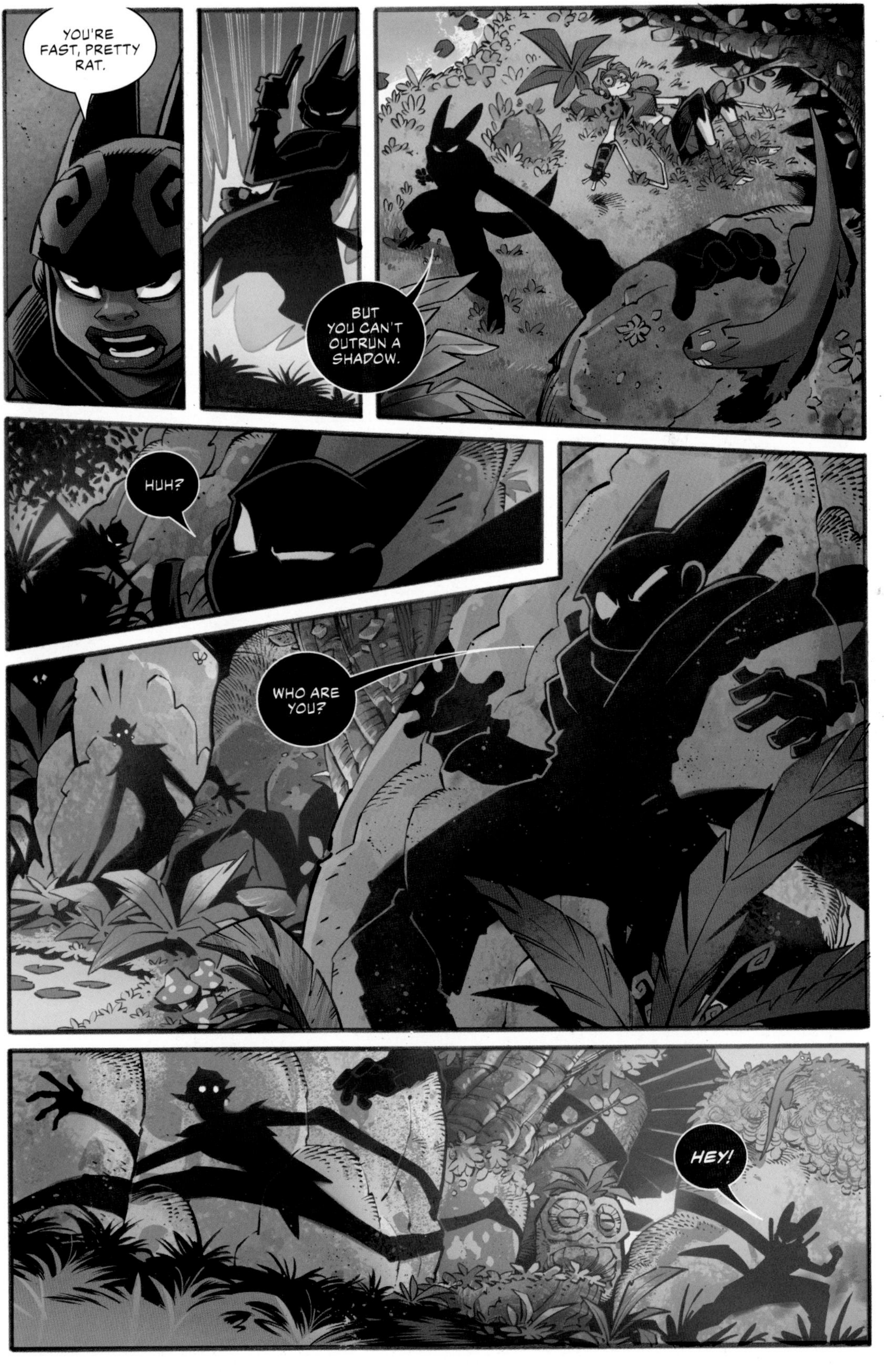
YOU'RE FAST, PRETTY RAT.
BUT YOU CAN'T OUTRUN A SHADOW.
HUH?
WHO ARE YOU?
HEY!

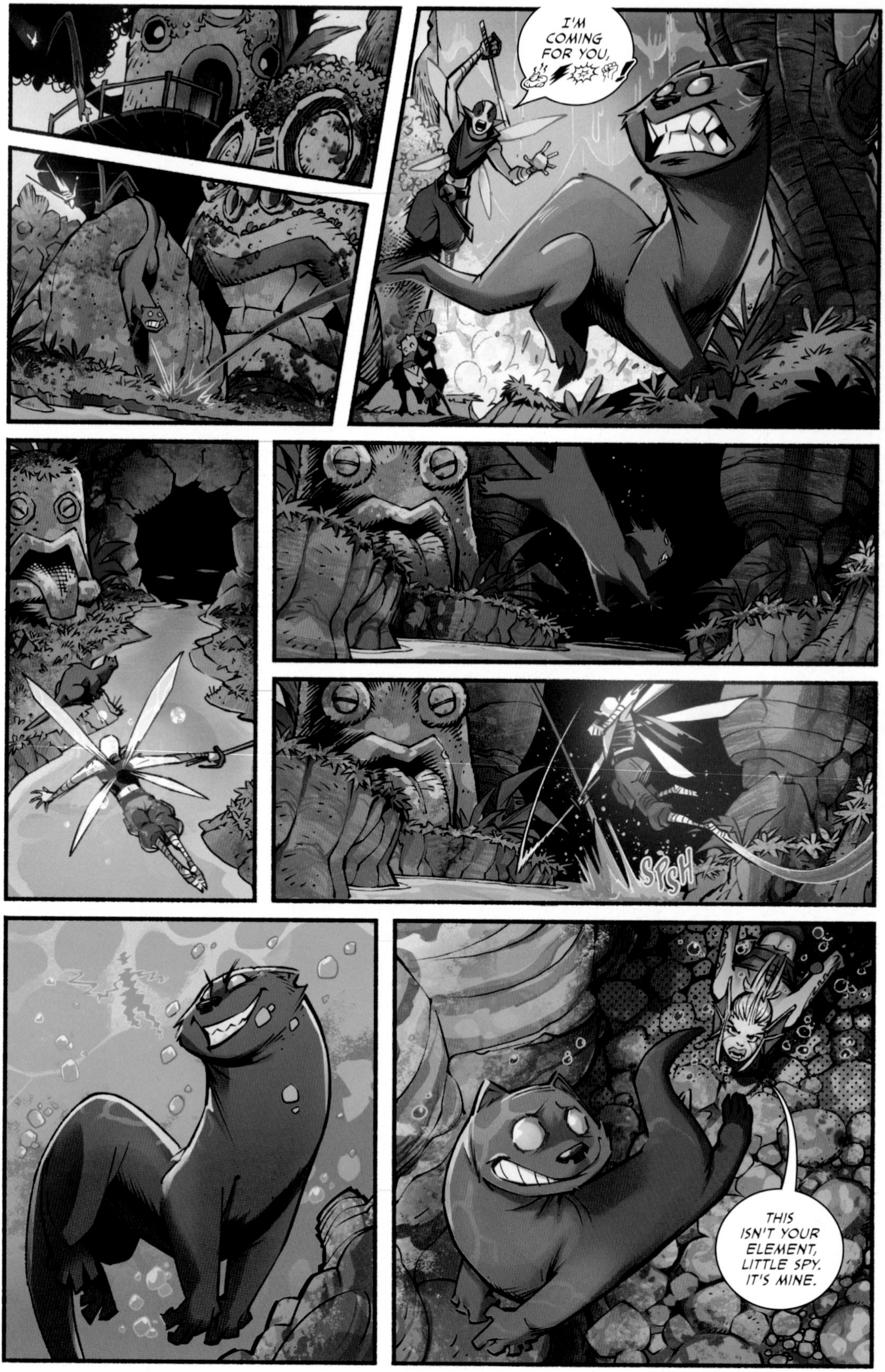
I'M COMING FOR YOU,
SPSH
THIS ISN'T YOUR ELEMENT, LITTLE SPY. IT'S MINE.

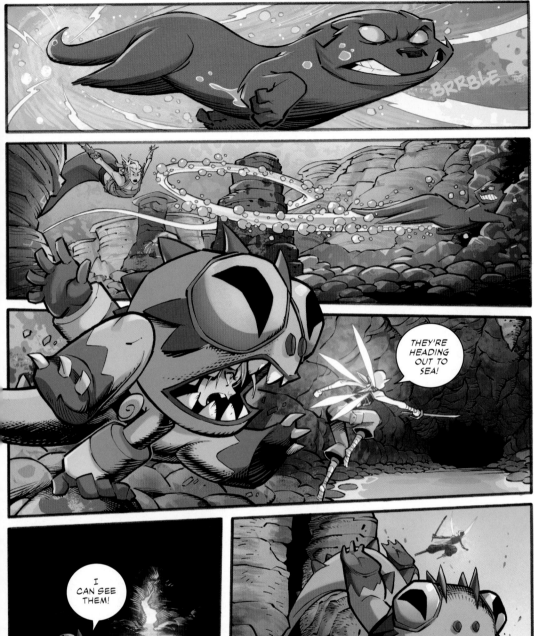

THEY'RE HEADING OUT TO SEA!

I CAN SEE THEM!

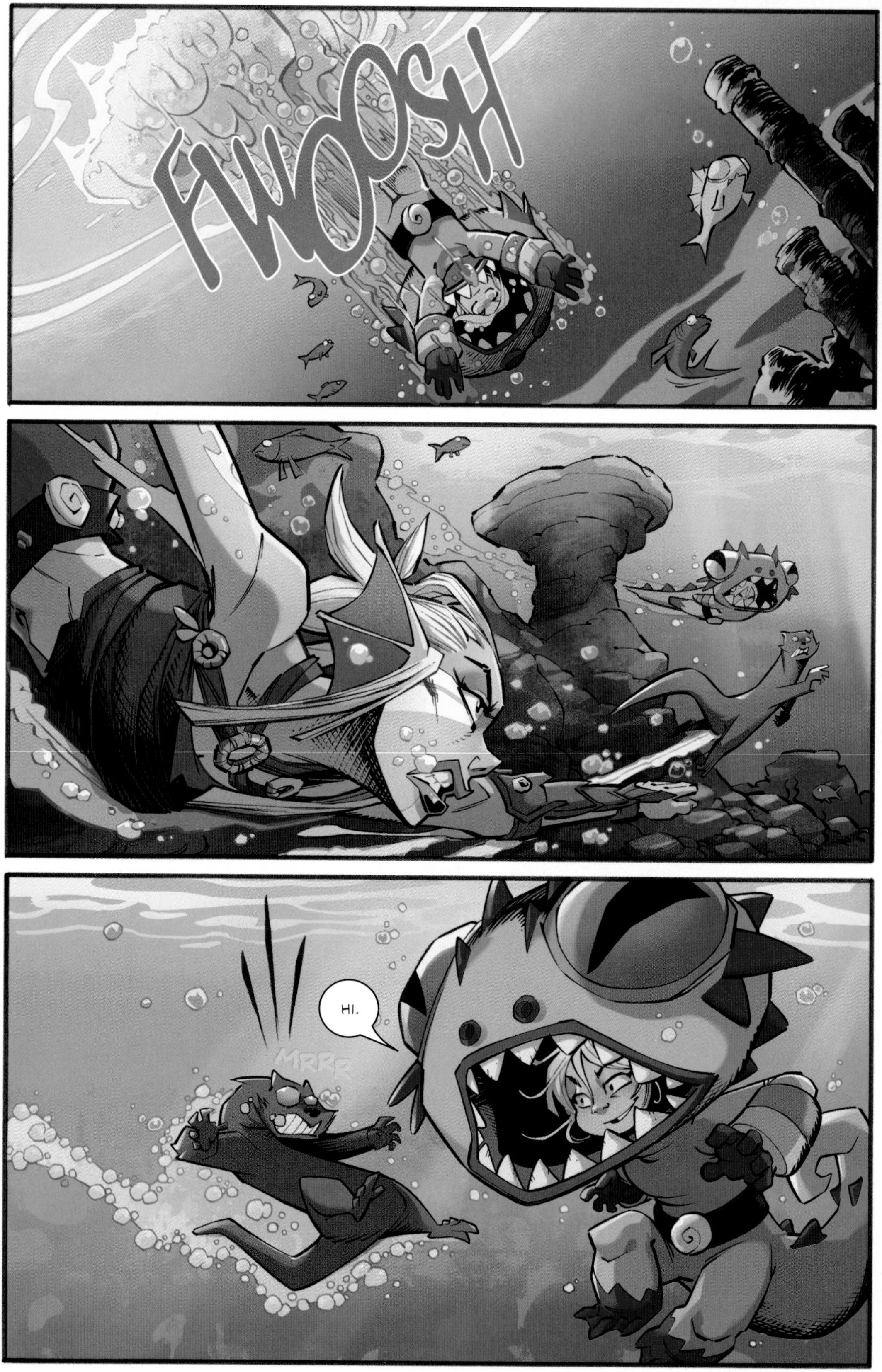
FWOOSH
HI.
MRRR

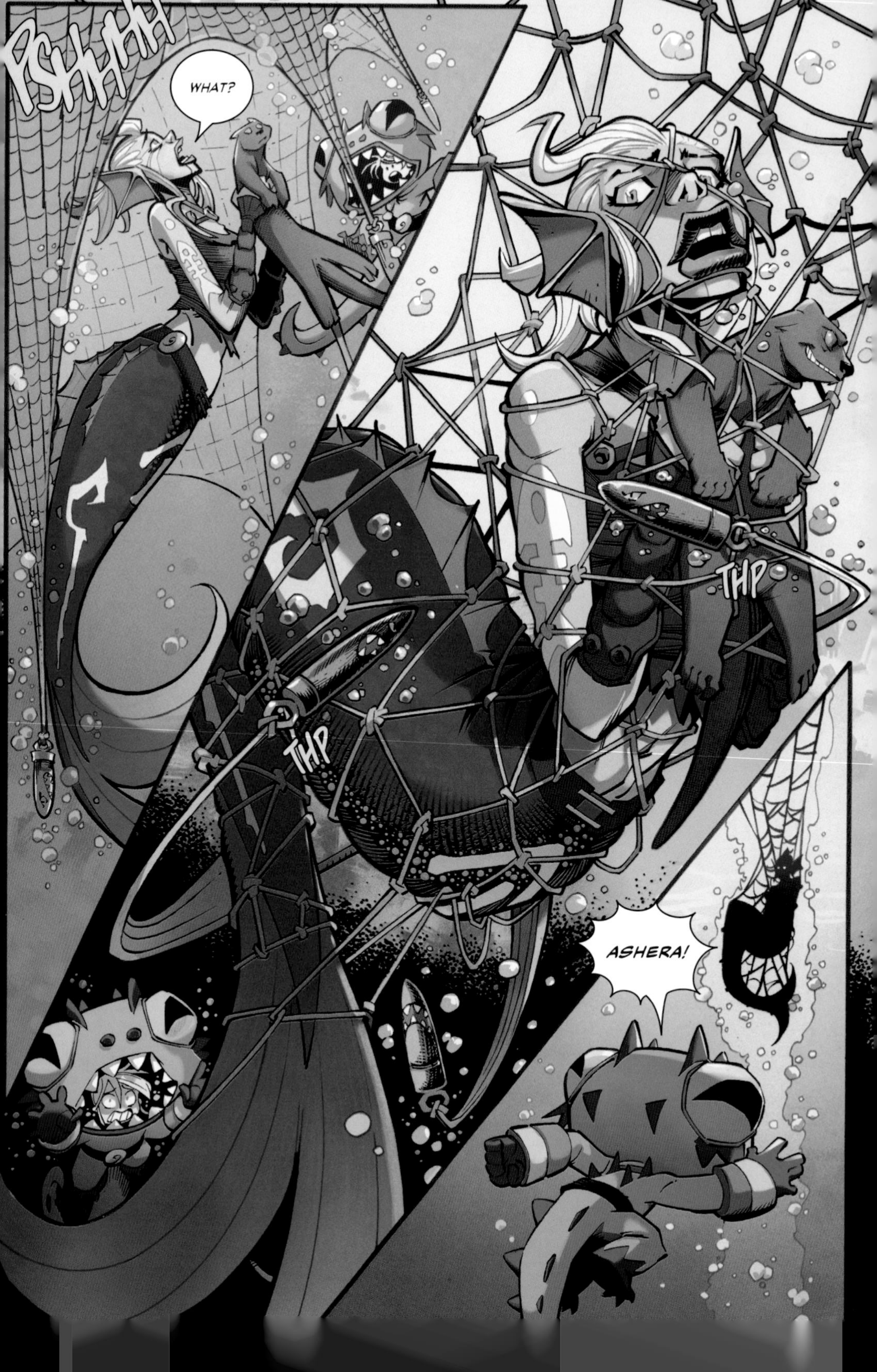
PSHHHH
WHAT?
THP
THP
ASHERA!

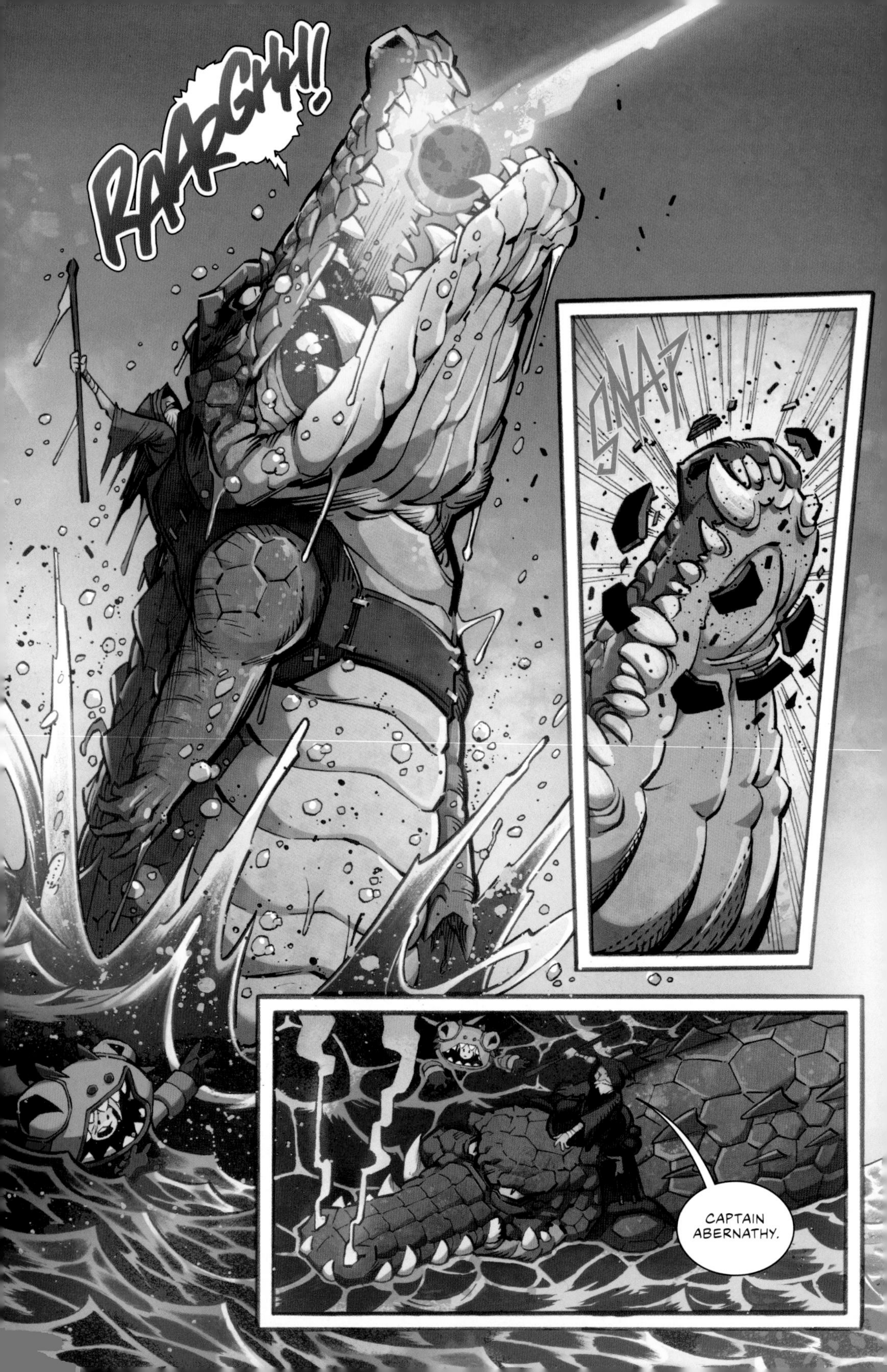
RAARGHH!!
SNAP
CAPTAIN ABERNATHY.

CHAPTER
FIVE

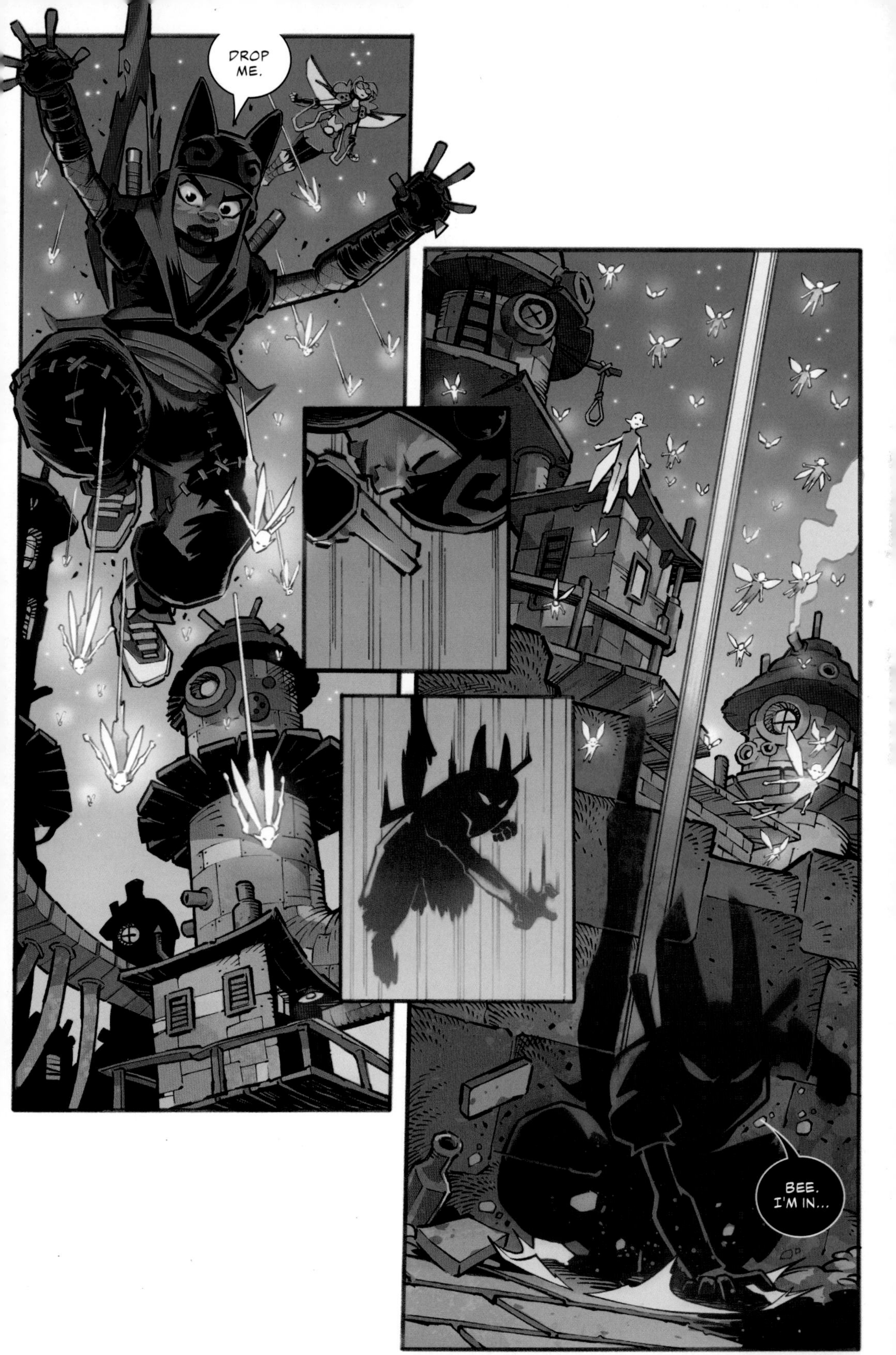
DROP ME.
BEE. I'M IN...

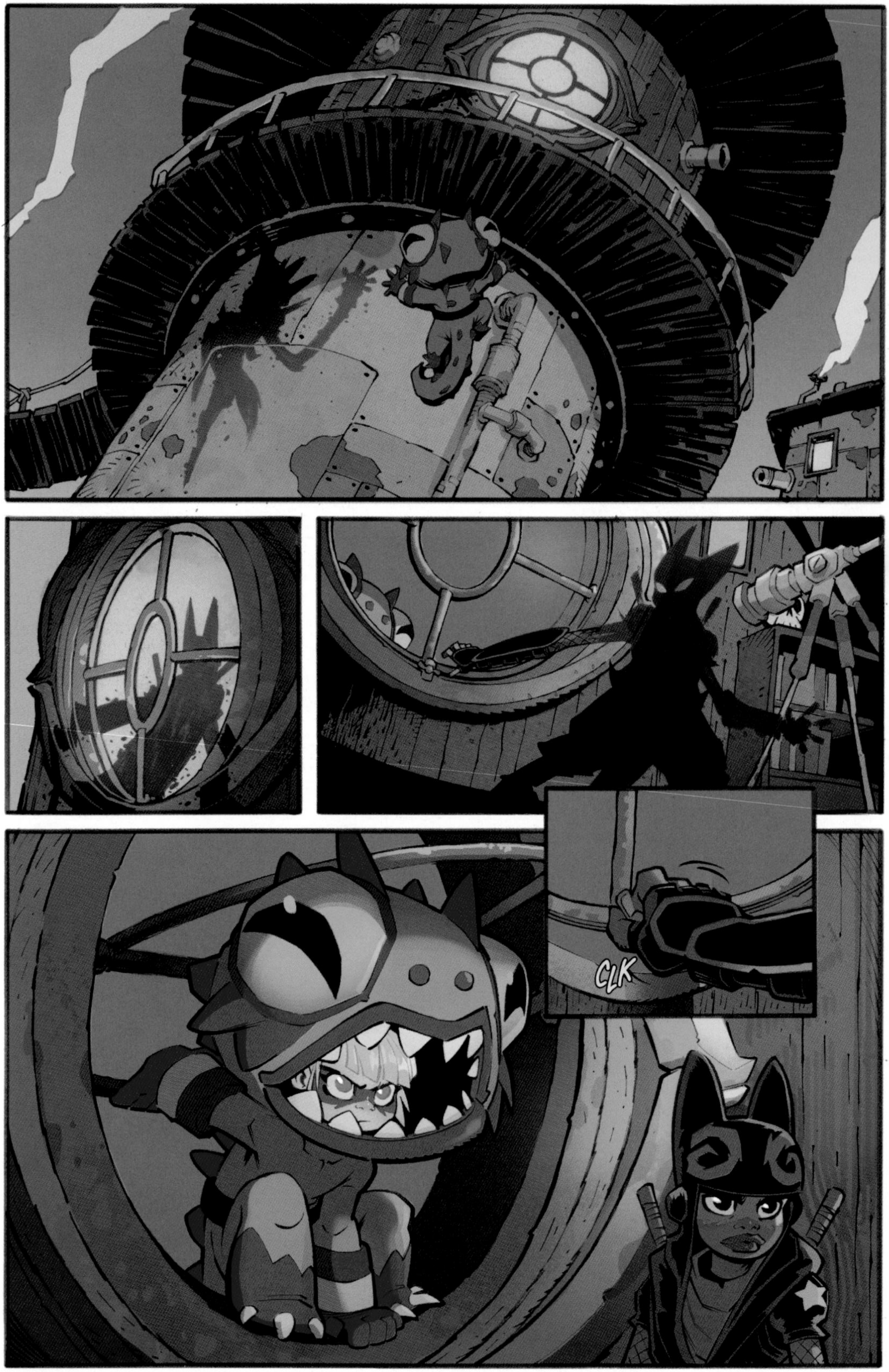
CLK

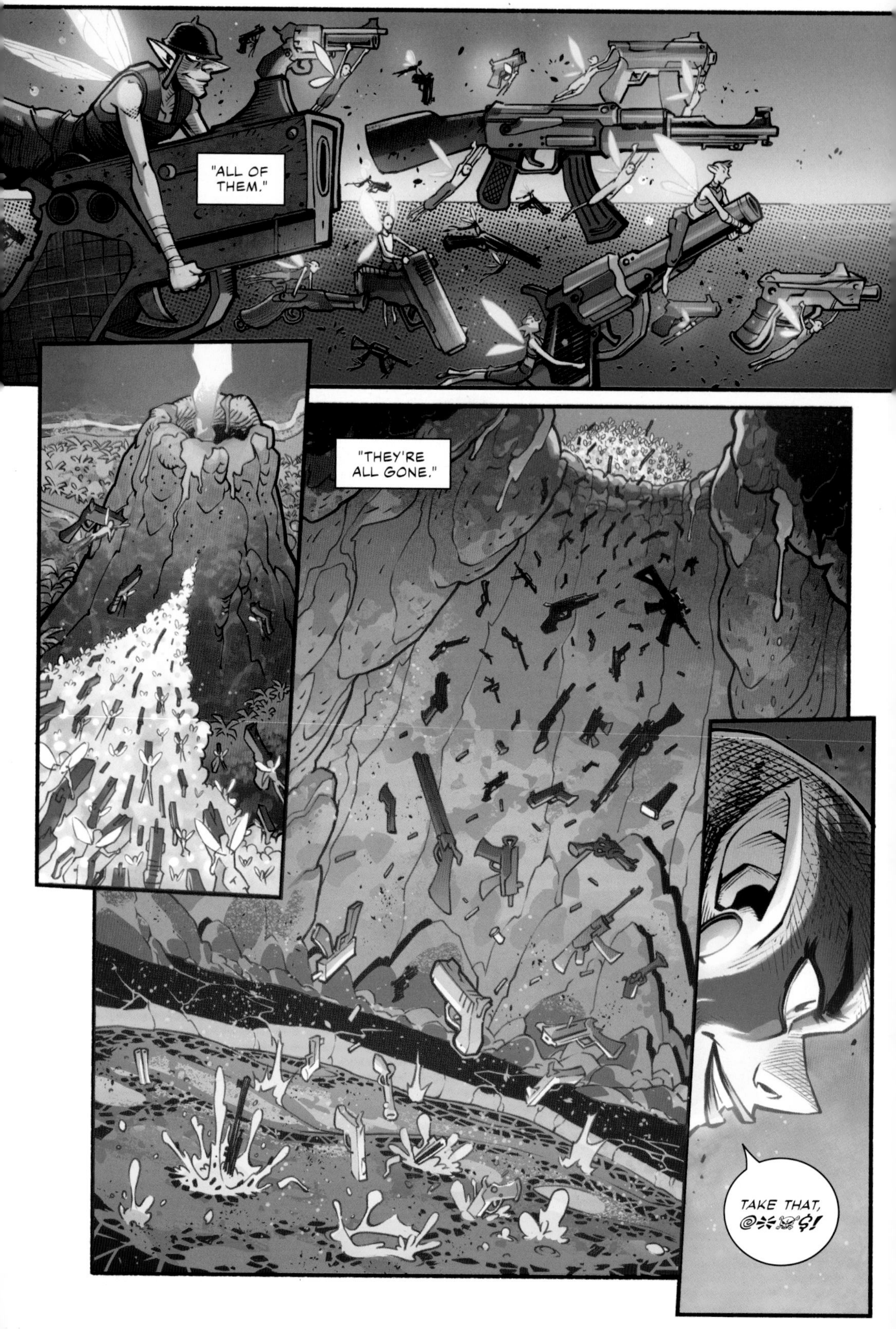
"ALL OF THEM."
"THEY'RE ALL GONE."
TAKE THAT, @*&$!

CHAPTER
SIX

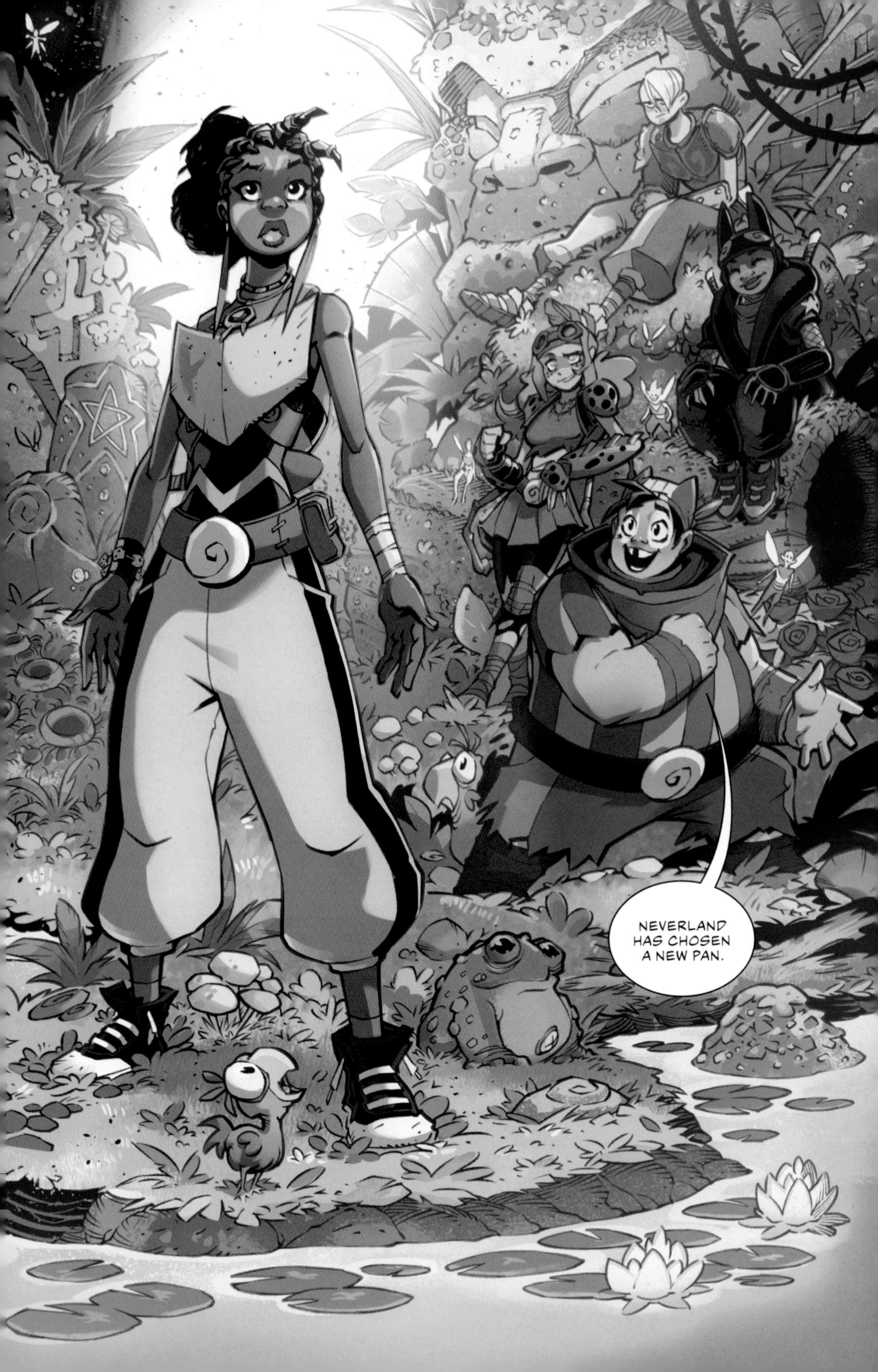
NEVERLAND HAS CHOSEN A NEW PAN.

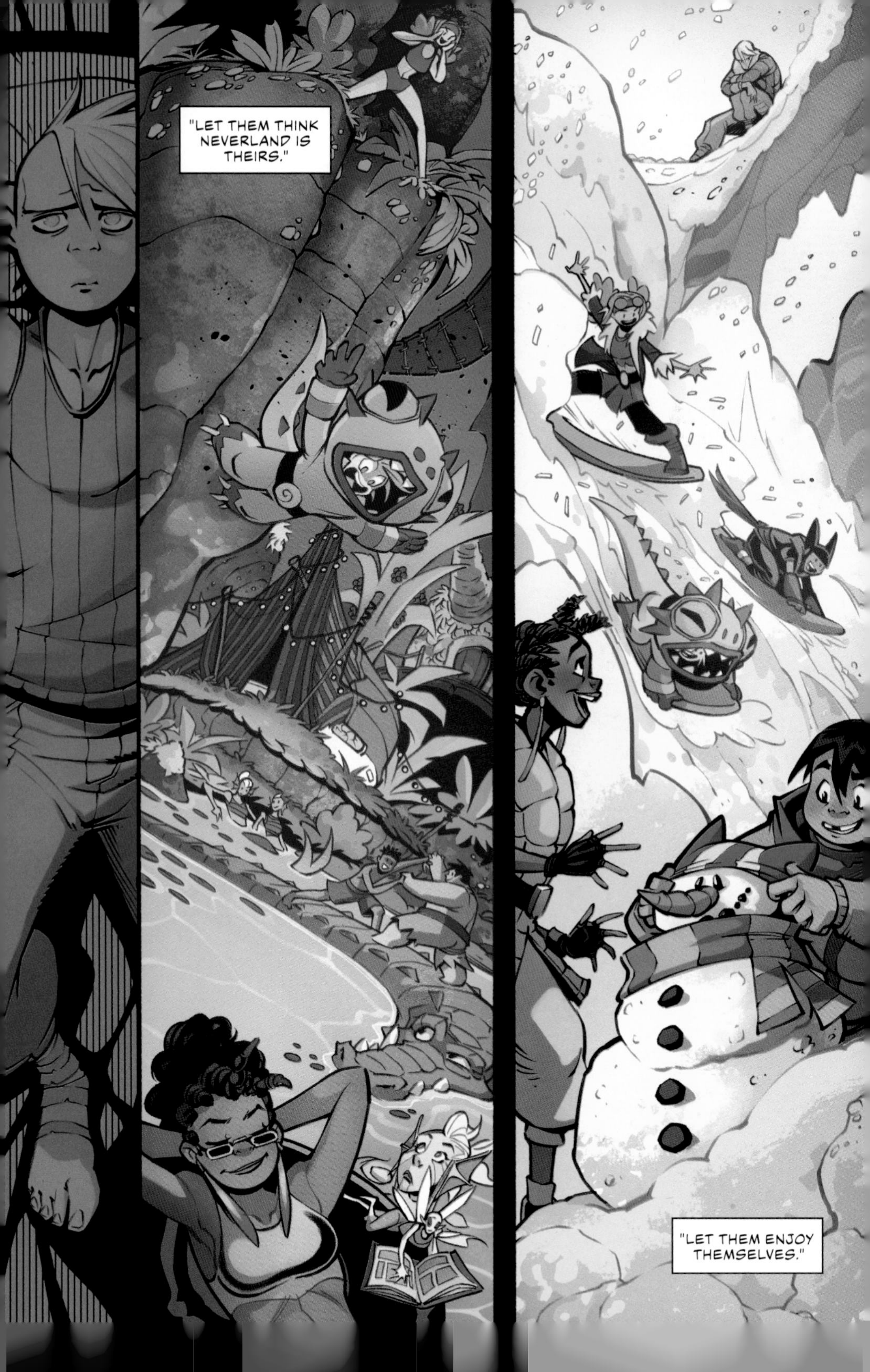
"LET THEM THINK NEVERLAND IS THEIRS."
"LET THEM ENJOY THEMSELVES."

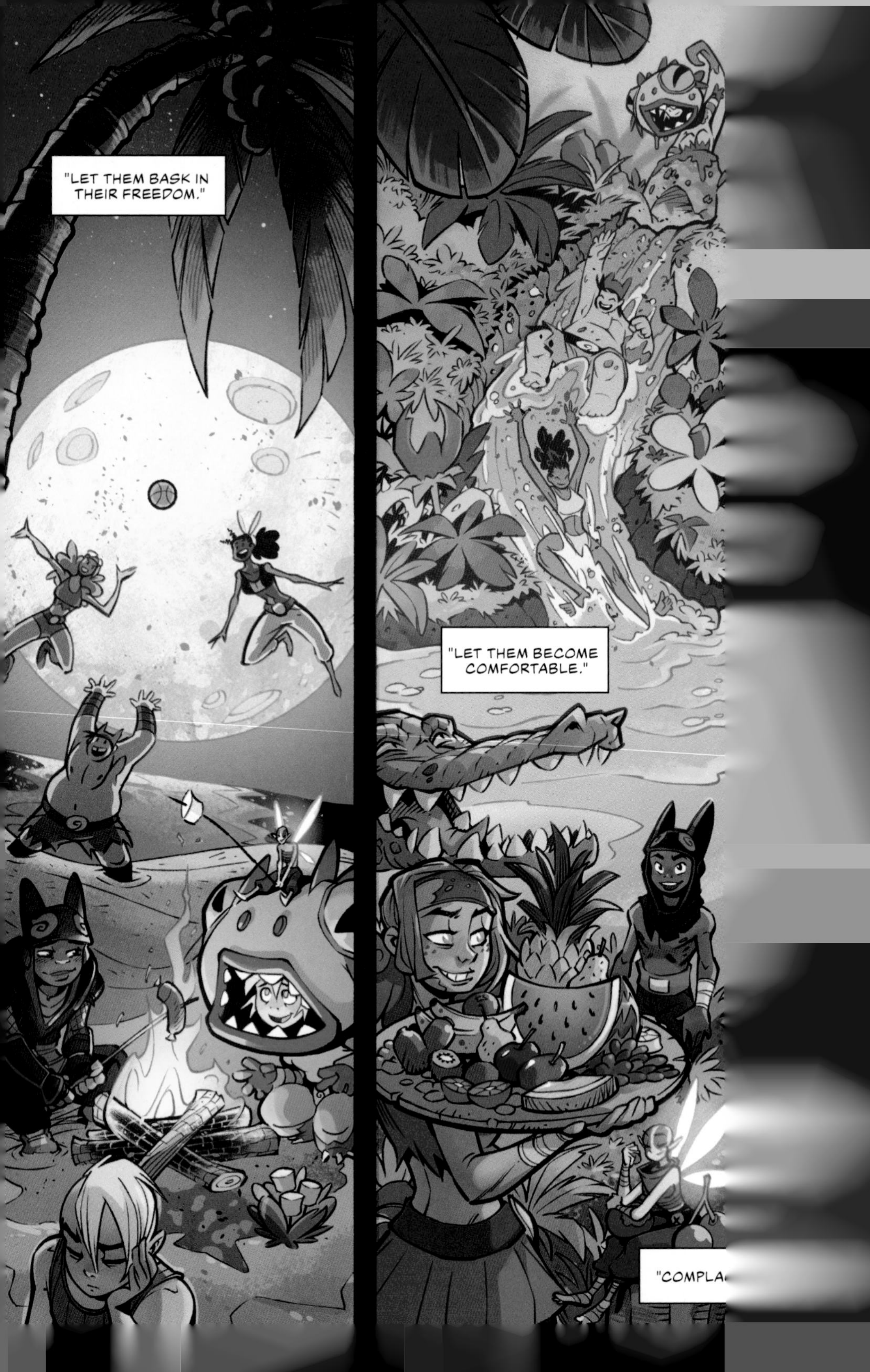
"LET THEM BASK IN THEIR FREEDOM."
"LET THEM BECOME COMFORTABLE."
"COMPLA

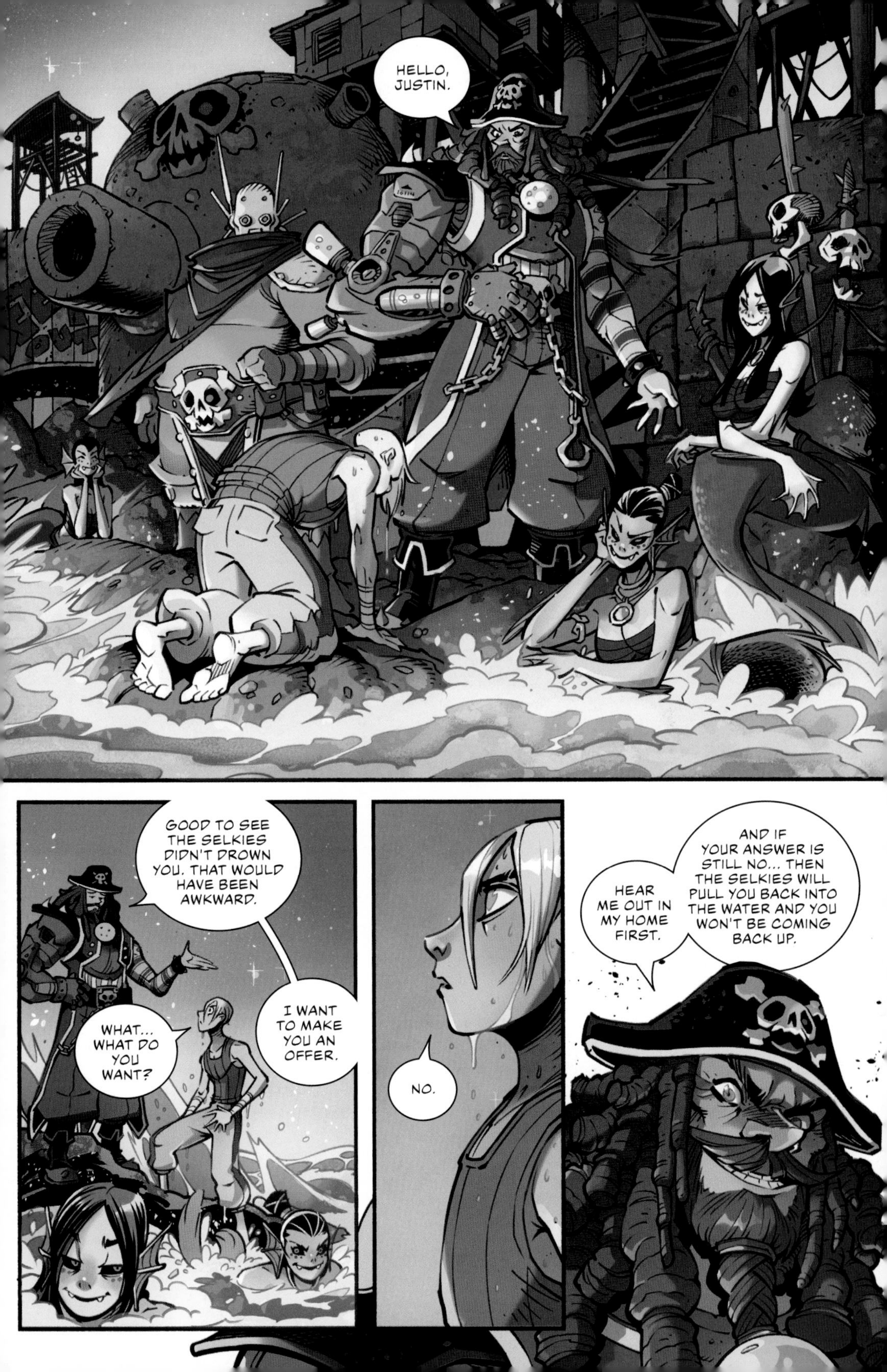
HELLO, JUSTIN.
GOOD TO SEE THE SELKIES DIDN'T DROWN YOU. THAT WOULD HAVE BEEN AWKWARD.
WHAT... WHAT DO YOU WANT?
I WANT TO MAKE YOU AN OFFER.
NO.
HEAR ME OUT IN MY HOME FIRST.
AND IF YOUR ANSWER IS STILL NO... THEN THE SELKIES WILL PULL YOU BACK INTO THE WATER AND YOU WON'T BE COMING BACK UP.

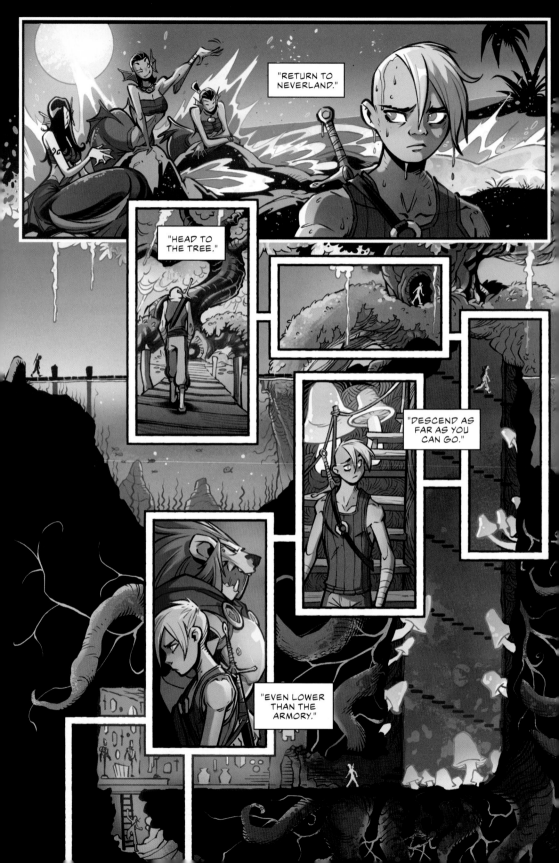

"RETURN TO NEVERLAND."

"HEAD TO THE TREE."

"DESCEND AS FAR AS YOU CAN GO."

"EVEN LOWER THAN THE ARMORY."

"UNTIL YOU REACH THE ARCHIVES."

"THERE, TAKE OUT THE SWORD."

SHA'NNG

"WHERE NEVERLAND'S HISTORY IS HELD IN THE TREE'S ROOTS."

"AND THEN IT'S SIMPLE."

"ONE QUICK STRIKE, AND YOU AND THE OTHERS CAN LEAVE THIS PLACE, JUSTIN."

"ALL THE DANGER OF NEVERLAND WILL BE BEHIND YOU. YOU WILL HAVE DONE A GREAT THING FOR YOUR FRIENDS."

SHNK

I JUST WANT TO GET US HOME.

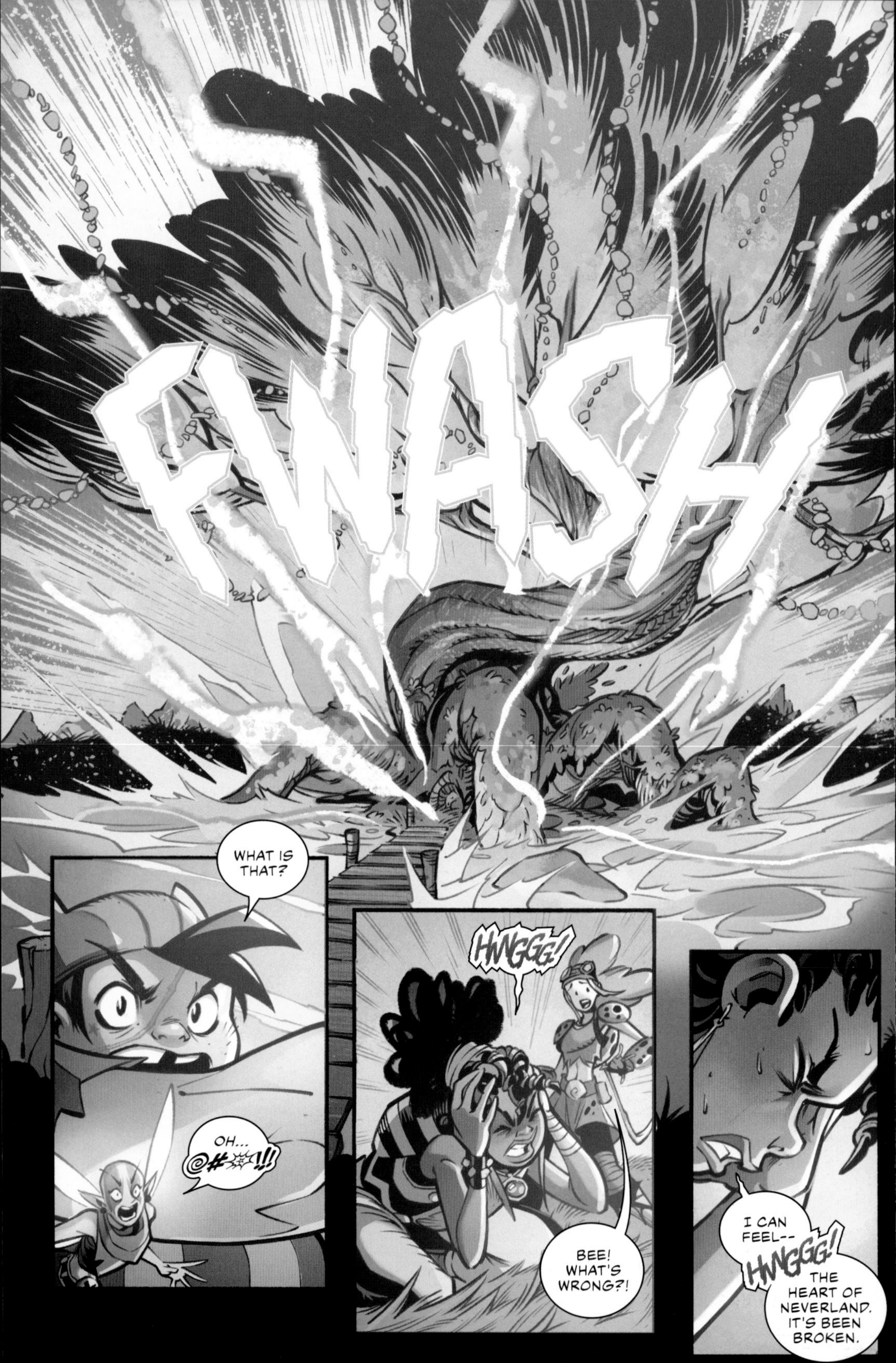
FWASH
WHAT IS THAT?
OH... @#*!!!
HWGGG!
BEE! WHAT'S WRONG?!
I CAN FEEL--
HWGGG!
THE HEART OF NEVERLAND. IT'S BEEN BROKEN.

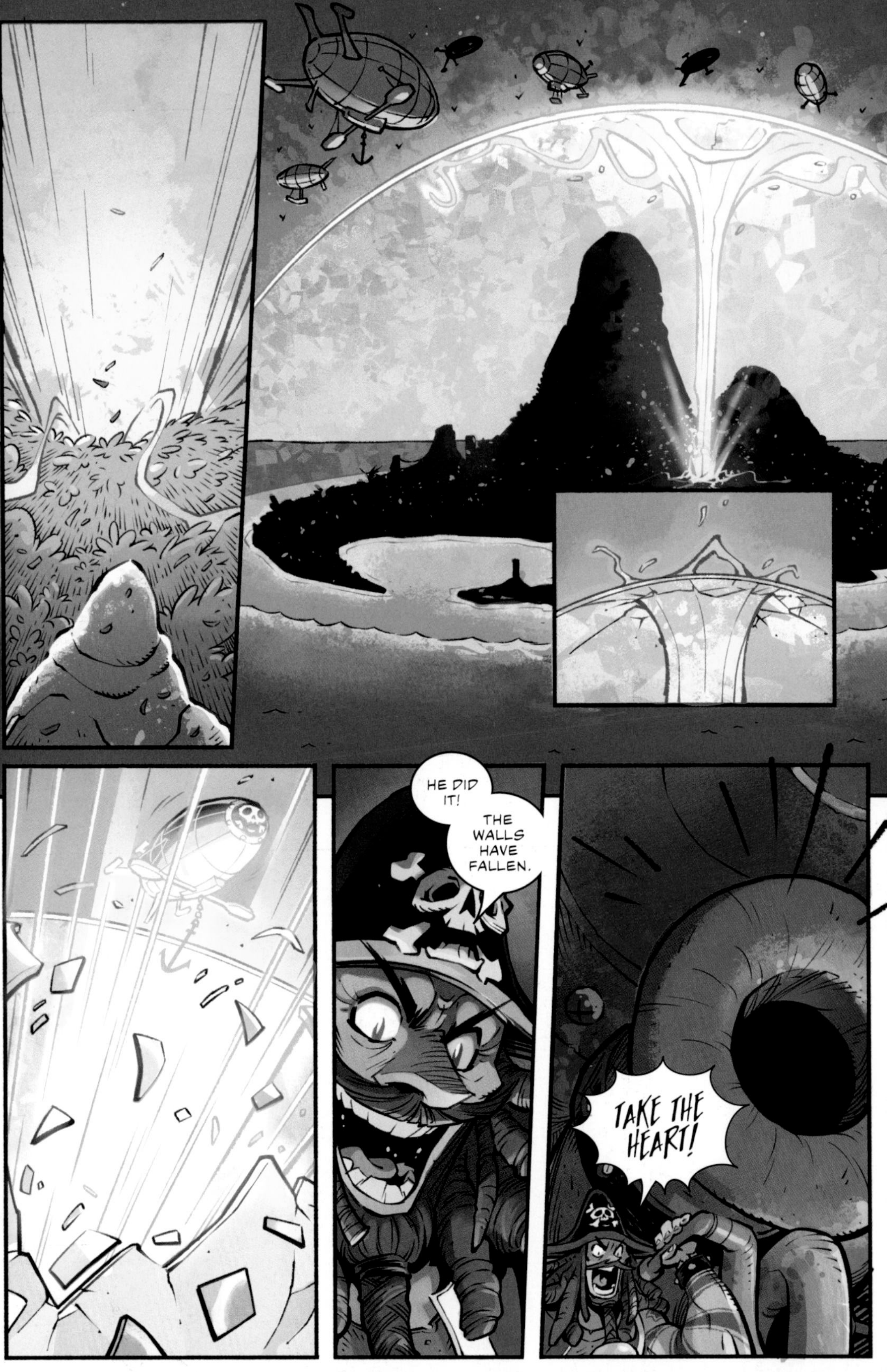
HE DID IT!
THE WALLS HAVE FALLEN.
TAKE THE HEART!

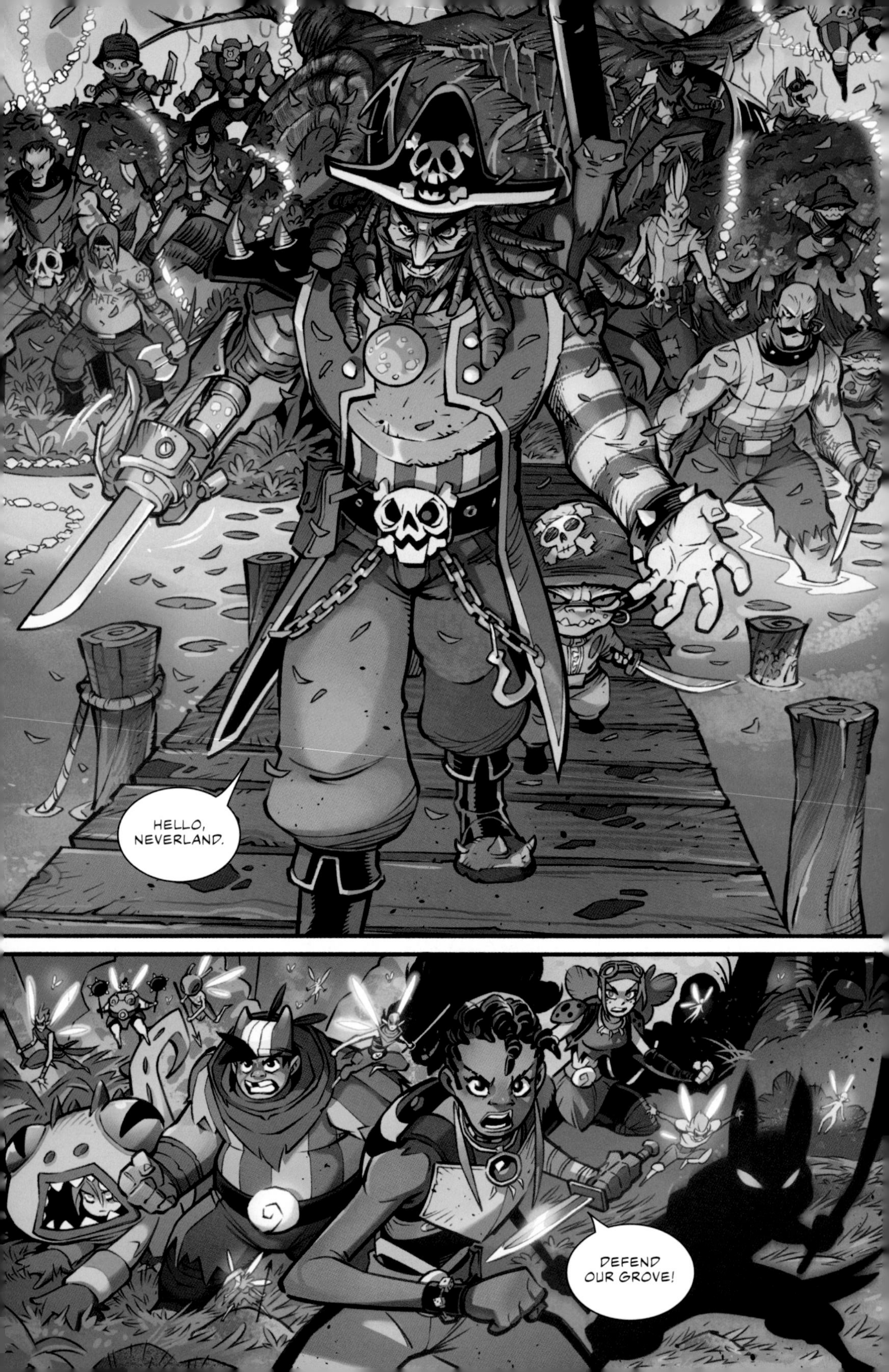
HELLO, NEVERLAND.
DEFEND OUR GROVE!

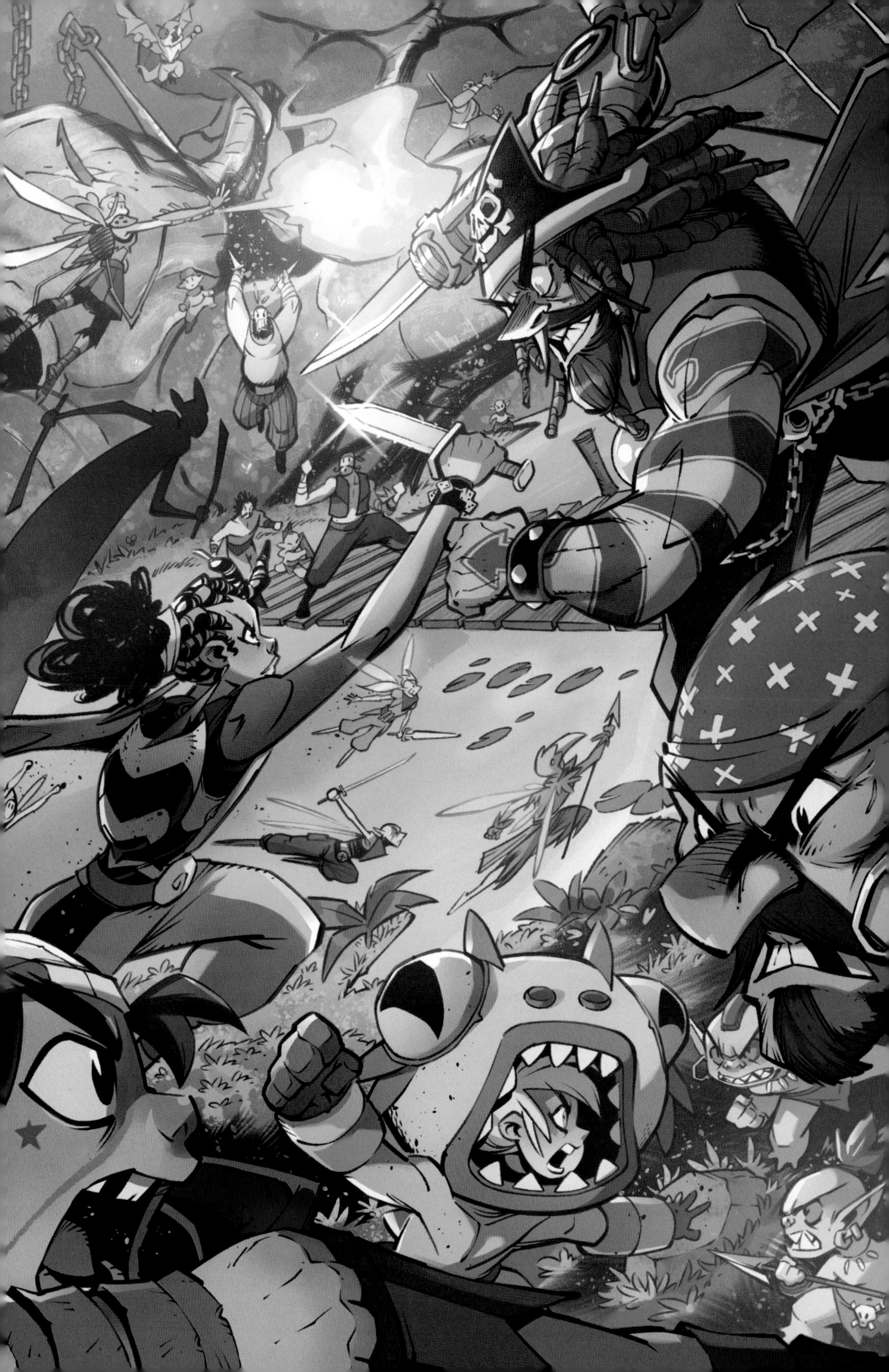

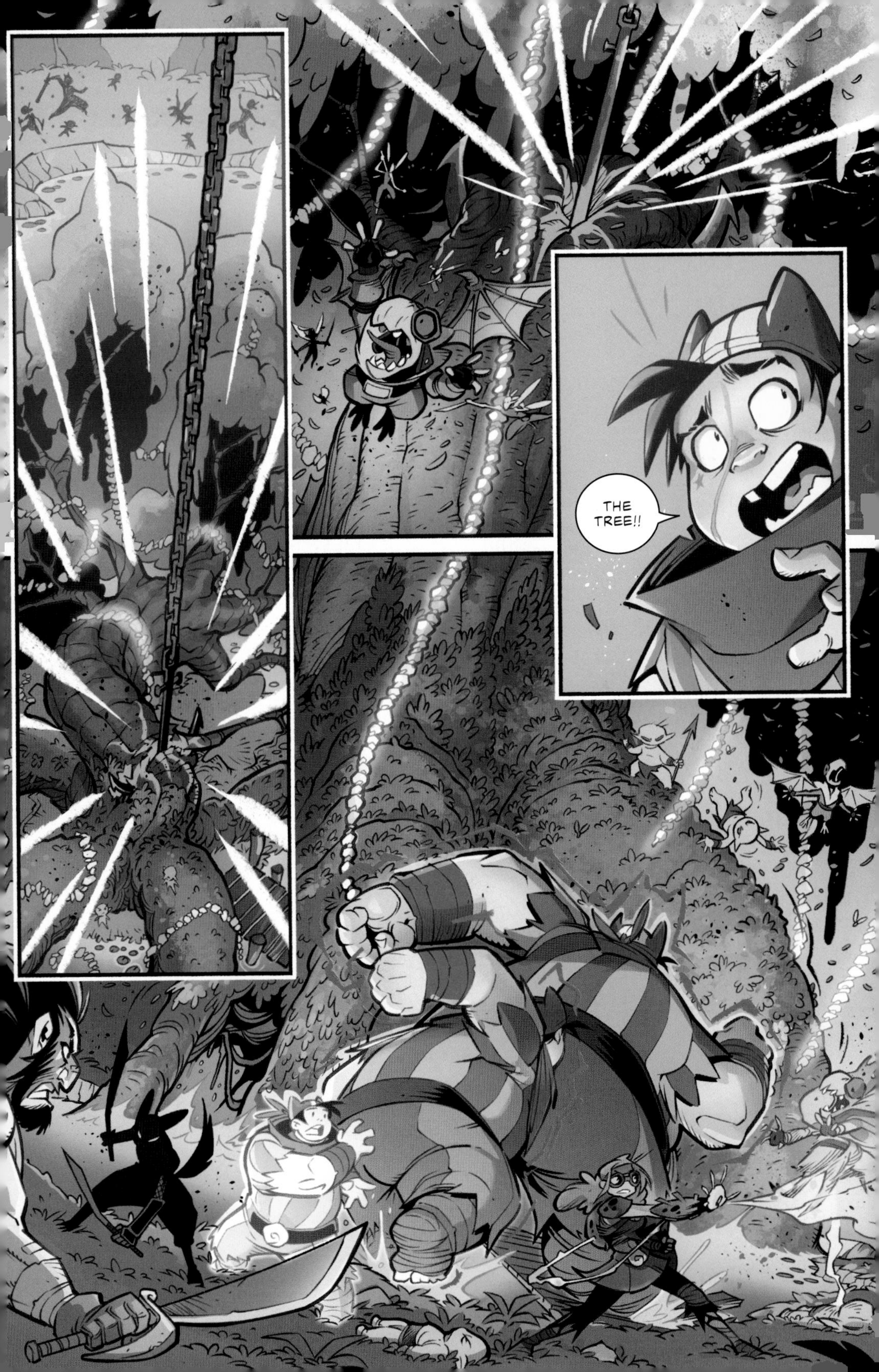
THE TREE!!

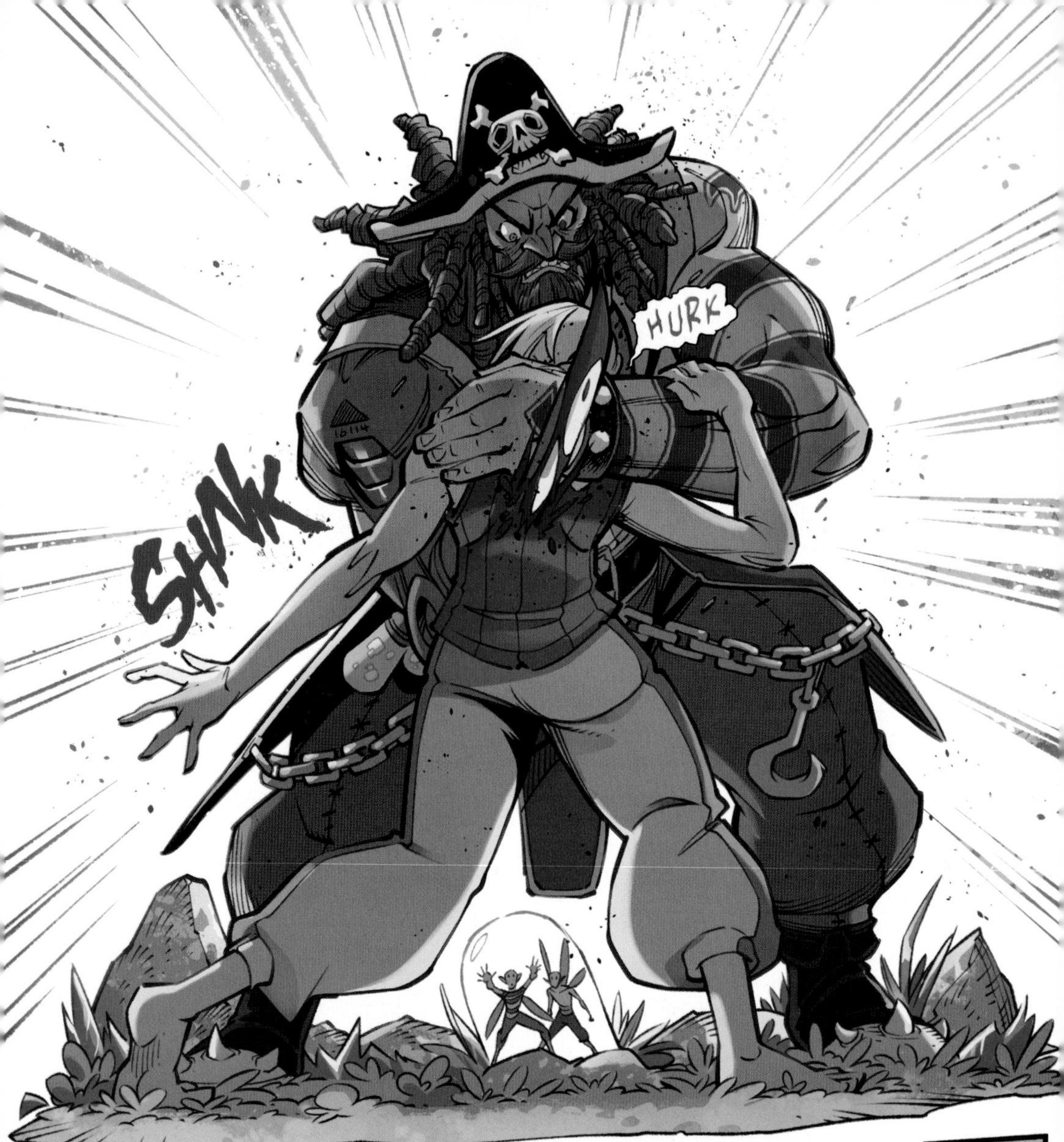
HURK
SHNK

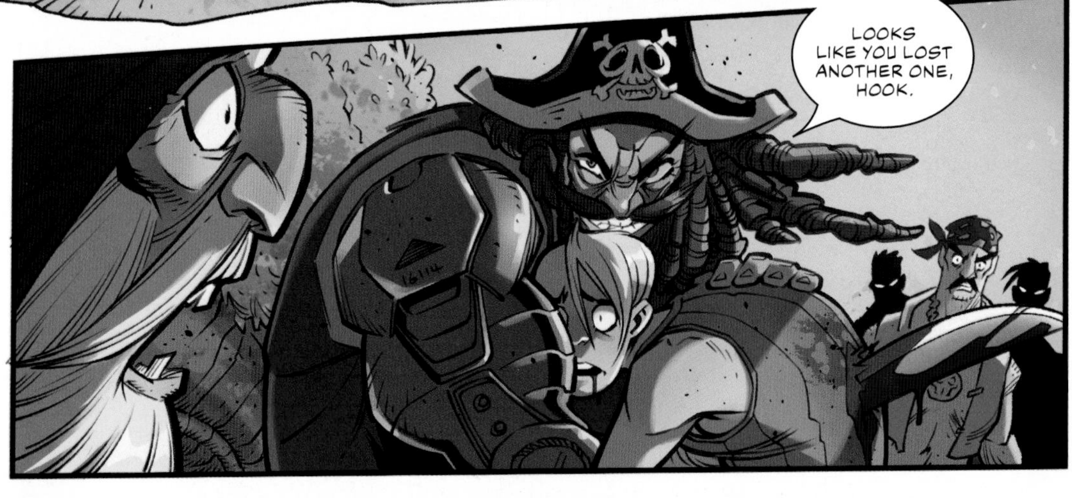
LOOKS LIKE YOU LOST ANOTHER ONE, HOOK.

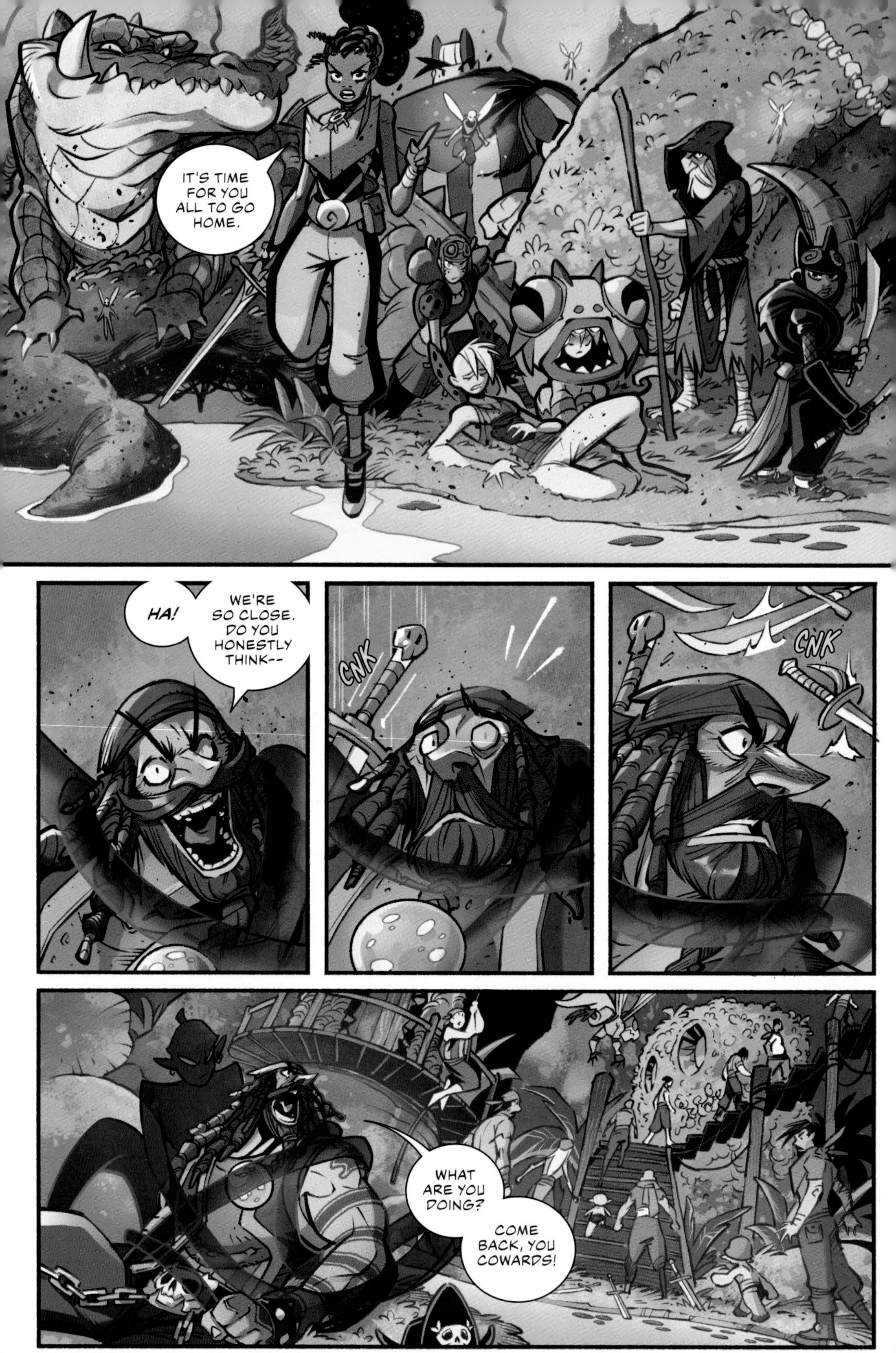
IT'S TIME FOR YOU ALL TO GO HOME.
HA!
WE'RE SO CLOSE. DO YOU HONESTLY THINK--
CNK
CNK
WHAT ARE YOU DOING?
COME BACK, YOU COWARDS!

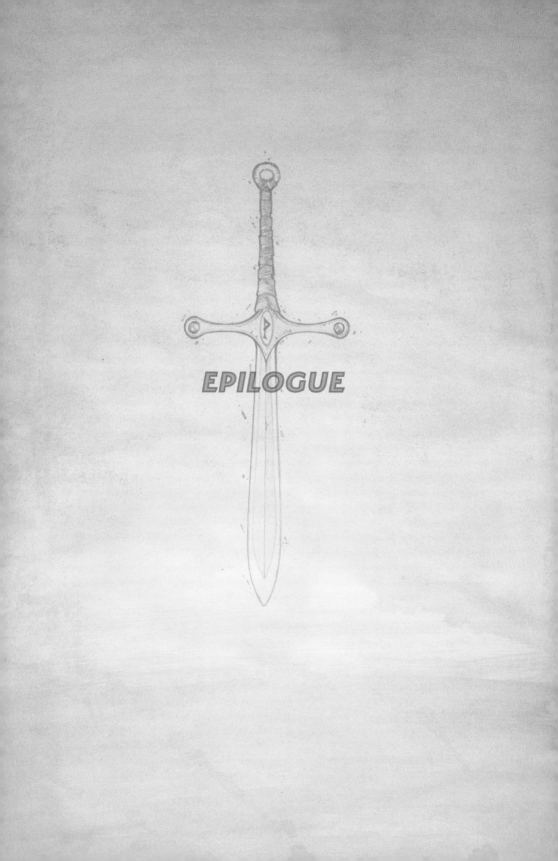

EPILOGUE

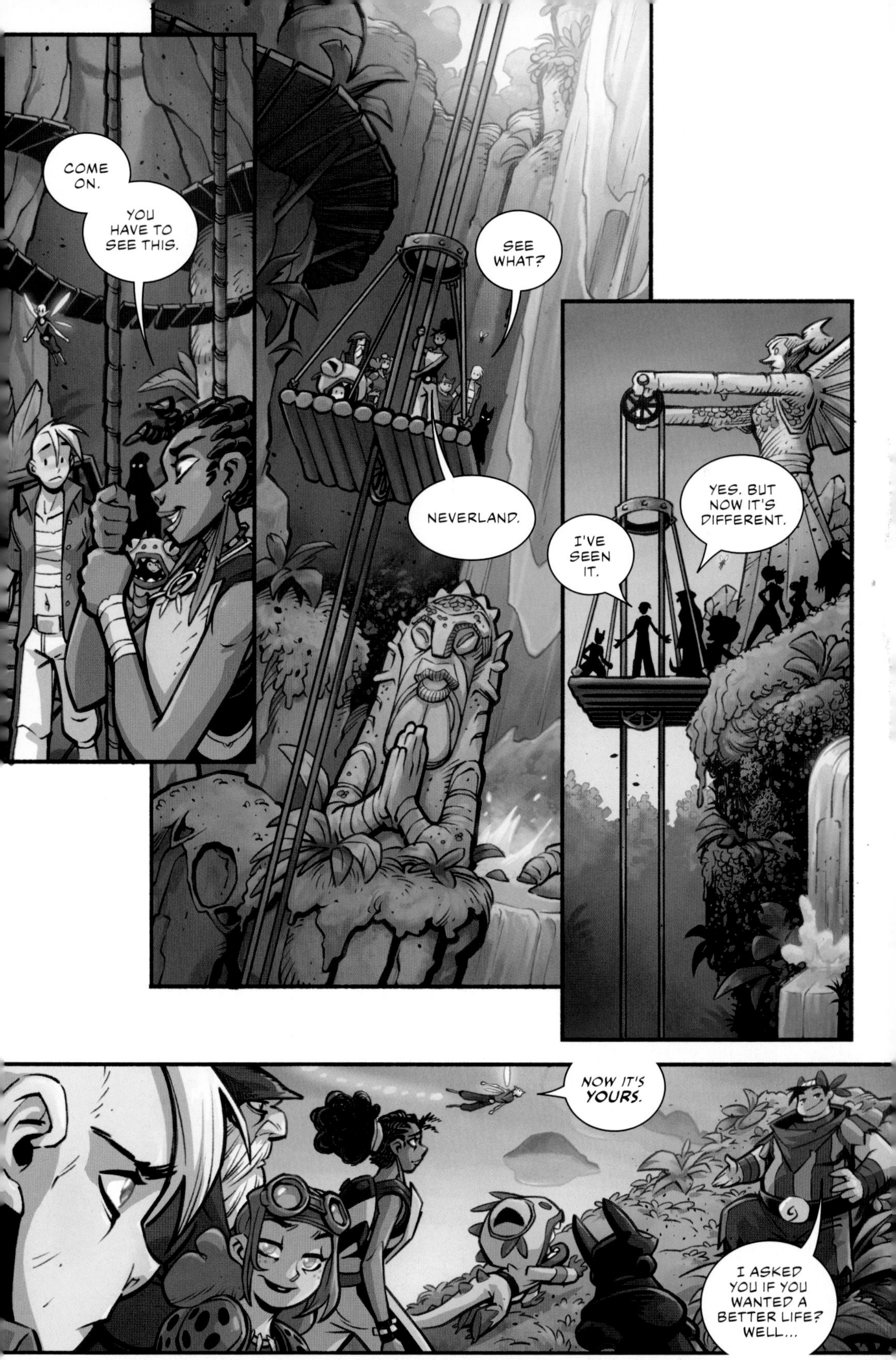
COME ON.
YOU HAVE TO SEE THIS.
SEE WHAT?
NEVERLAND.
I'VE SEEN IT.
YES. BUT NOW IT'S DIFFERENT.
NOW IT'S YOURS.
I ASKED YOU IF YOU WANTED A BETTER LIFE? WELL...

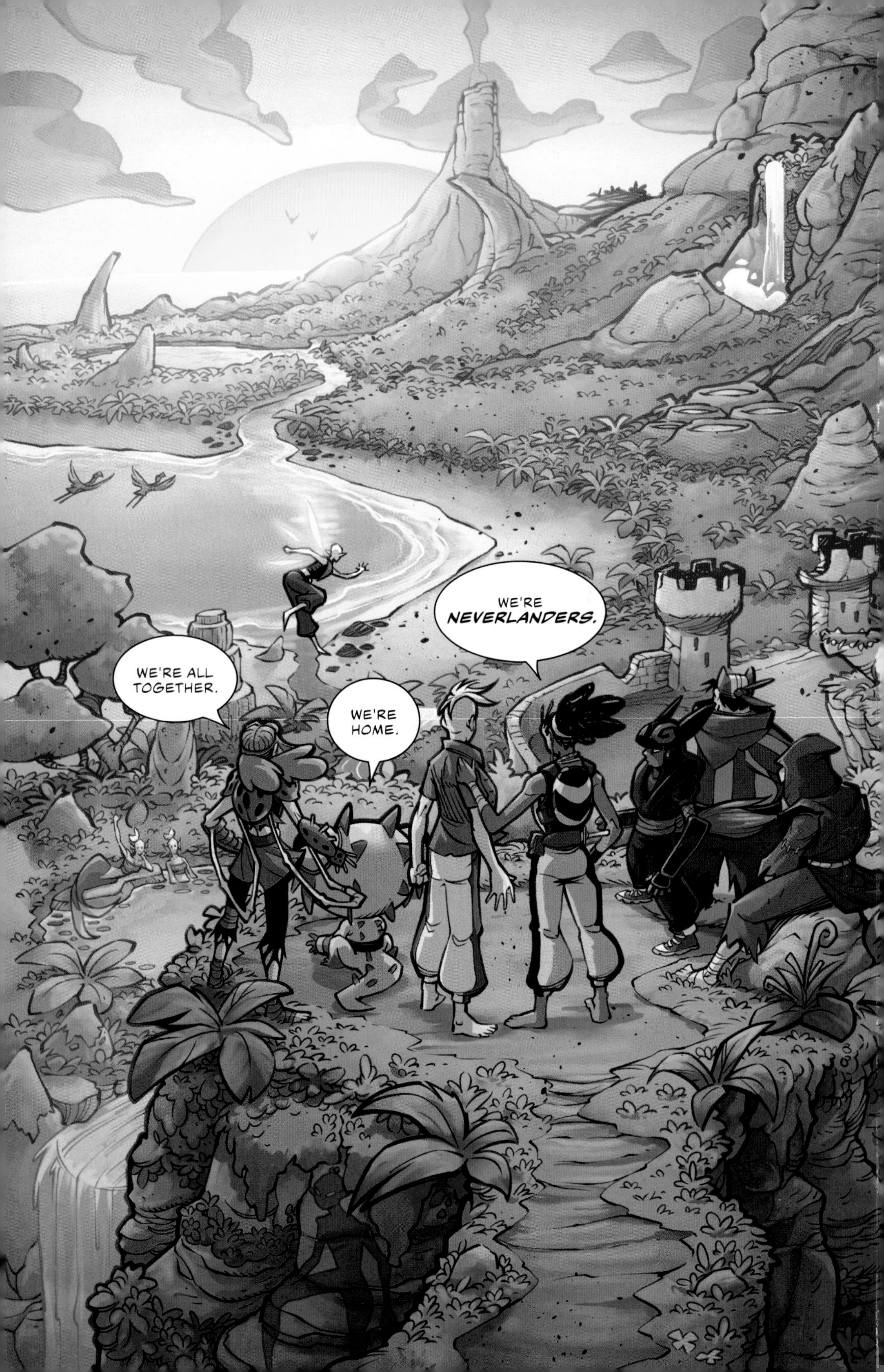

WE'RE ALL TOGETHER.
WE'RE HOME.
WE'RE NEVERLANDERS.